Praise for the novels of JoAnn Ross

THE CALLAHAN BROTHERS TRILOGY

BLUE BAYOU
RIVER ROAD
MAGNOLIA MOON

"The talent for storytelling is obviously embedded deep in Ms. Ross's bones."

—*Romantic Times*, Top Pick

"[I]rresistible. . . . A delicious read with a vast array of zany characters to keep you glued to the pages."

—*Rendezvous*

"The touching love stor[ies] . . . and unforgettable characters create a marvelous read you can't put down."

—*Old Book Barn Gazette*

"Sexual sparks fly. . . . Covering terrain similar to that of Nora Roberts's Irish trilogies, Ross spins a warm romance amid a setting loaded with charm."

—*Publishers Weekly*

OUT OF THE MIST

"The story's robust momentum and lively characters make this a fun, energetic read."

—*Publishers Weekly*

"A great afternoon read. . . . I'm looking forward to the remaining sisters' stories!"

—*Old Book Barn Gazette*

"Ross weaves the search for the missing family treasure and the growing attraction between two creative spirits with aplomb in this charming romance."

—*BookPage*

FAIR HAVEN

"Not only does JoAnn Ross provide her usual impressive blend of tender warmth and fascinating characters, but she also adds a colorful dash of the supernatural."

—*Romantic Times*

"As magical as Ireland itself. . . . A masterpiece of writing from the heart. Storytelling at its all-time best."

—*The Belles and Beaux of Romance*

FAR HARBOR

"A profoundly moving story of intense emotional depth, satisfying on every level. You won't want to leave this family."

—CompuServe Romance Reviews

"A wonderful relationship drama in which JoAnn Ross splendidly describes love the second time around."

—Barnesandnoble.com

HOMEPLACE

"This engrossing story of love's healing power will draw you in from the first. . . . A great read."

—*Old Book Barn Gazette*

"Like cherished silver, *Homeplace* just shines!"

—*Romantic Times*, Barnes and Noble Top Pick

Books by JoAnn Ross

Homeplace
Far Harbor
Fair Haven
Legends Lake
Blue Bayou
River Road
Magnolia Moon
Out of the Mist
Out of the Blue
Out of the Storm*

*Coming soon from POCKET BOOKS

JoAnn Ross

Blue Bayou

POCKET BOOKS
New York London Toronto Sydney

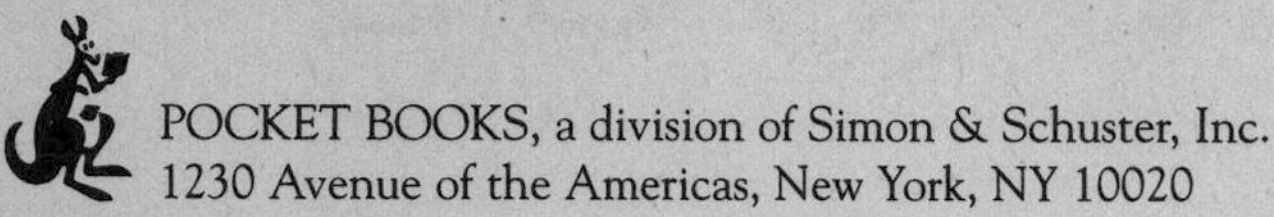
POCKET BOOKS, a division of Simon & Schuster, Inc.
1230 Avenue of the Americas, New York, NY 10020

ISBN: 1-4165-0378-1

This Pocket Books trade paperback edition August 2004

10 9 8 7 6 5 4 3 2 1

Manufactured in the United States of America

For information regarding special discounts for bulk purchases, please contact Simon & Schuster Special Sales at 1-800-456-6798 or business@simonandschuster.com

To Christy Marchand, who took me to Nottaway,
and my guys, Jay and Patrick, with whom I've
passed many a good time,
and last, but never least, Marisa and Parker Ryan Ross,
the lagniappe *in my life.*

Blue Bayou

1

The moon hung full and low and bloodred over the bayou as Jack Callahan sat out on the *gallerie* of the crumbling plantation house, working on a bottle of whiskey that wasn't working on him. It had been a sweltering day, and even at midnight the air, which smelled of damp brick and night-blooming jasmine, dripped with moisture.

The old swing squeaked as he slowly swayed; an alligator glided silently across water the color of burgundy wine, its eyes gleaming in the dark like yellow headlights.

A mist that wasn't quite rain began to fall as he watched the storm gather out over the Gulf and thought back to the night when Beau Soleil had resembled a huge white wedding cake. A night when music floated on the sultry summer air, fairy lights strung through the limbs of the chinaberry trees twinkled like fireflies, and white candles anchored in fake water lilies glowed invitingly on the smooth turquoise surface of the pool water.

White jacketed waiters had circulated with trays of mint juleps and flutes of French champagne while belles in tulle and taffeta danced magnolia-scented nights away. The girls had been mouth-wateringly pretty in airy flowered dresses that showed off their tanned shoulders and long slender legs. And Danielle Dupree had outshone them all.

Danielle. He lifted the bottle to his lips; flames slid down his throat. You'd think, after all these years, he'd be immune to the closest thing Blue Bayou had ever had to a princess. But the memory of that night created a rush of molten heat hotter than any the Jack Daniel's could stoke. He'd known, of course, that he had no business wanting her.

"Never have been any good at taking your own counsel, you," he muttered, slipping back into the Cajun patois he'd spoken growing up among his mother's people.

Celibacy was not an easy virtue at any age. For a testosterone-driven eighteen-year-old kid coming off nine long months banished to a last-chance, hard-time military-styled lockup for delinquents, it was damn near impossible. Especially when the girl in question had recklessly, for that brief, shining time, wanted him, too.

Those crazy days and hot nights were, as his daddy used to say, yesterday's ball score. He might not have ended up on Angola's death row, like Judge Dupree had warned, but he'd definitely gone to hell like so many in Blue Bayou had predicted.

"Gone to hell and lived to remember it."

He was no longer viewed as the devil of Blue Bayou. Even *The Cajun Clarion* had picked up a quote from *The New York Times Book Review* declaring him a new generation's Joseph Wambaugh. Thanks to all those folks in Hollywood, who threw money around like confetti, he now owned the crown jewel of Louisianan antebellum homes. Not that it was much of a jewel at the moment, but he, more than most, knew outward appearances could be deceiving.

During his years as an undercover drug agent, he'd become a chameleon, able to move among the movers and shakers at a Beverly Hills dinner party one night, while the next night would find him working the street scene in Tijuana, then with only a change of clothes and syntax, he'd be hanging out at the beach, listening to surfer songs and making deals and subsequent busts beneath the Huntington Beach pier.

Outwardly his appearance hadn't changed all that much since his undercover days. He still tied his thick black hair in the same ponytail at the nape of his neck and the gold earring served as a daily reminder that trying to outrun your past was an exercise in futility. But even these leftovers from his former life didn't tell the entire story.

A casual observer would never suspect that his mind was a seething cauldron of drug dealers, strung-out hookers chasing their next high, crooked cops, and hard-eyed kids who lost their innocence before their baby teeth.

Scenes flashed through his mind like movie trailers set to fast forward: the wasted body of a Guadalajara whore, her nose still wet from sniffing cocaine; a nine-month-old baby killed in his crib by a drive-by shooting in El Paso; a fourteen-year-old girl in Las Vegas traded by her mother to a biker gang for a weekend's worth of methamphetamine and black tar heroin.

And if those Technicolor memories didn't cause mental black clouds to gather overhead, there was always Jack's personal golden oldie: blood blossoming like a garden of scarlet poppies across the front of a lace-trimmed, white silk nightgown.

Even now, guilt slashed at him like a razor. *Don't get personally involved.* That had been rule one of the job. A rule he'd broken once in his life, with fatal consequences.

The fact that he'd nearly died as well did nothing to soothe his conscience or wash the blood from his hands.

"You didn't have any choice," Jack tried telling himself what the investigators who'd been waiting for him when he'd come out of surgery the next day had told him. He hadn't been in any mood to listen. Not then. Not now. The fact was, he'd screwed up. Big time.

During the years away from Louisiana, Jack had developed the ability to live in the moment, which was handy when your life could come to a sudden, violent end at any time. The covert activities he'd carried out all over the world had been as dangerous as they were secretive, and when they were completed, he shed the more unsavory aspects of his career along with whatever identity he'd taken on, leaving them behind in his dark and murky past.

And then, as always, he moved on.

Some of those who'd worked with him had called him crazy. Others proclaimed him a reckless cowboy. Still others accused him of having a death wish and refused to work with him again.

Jack hadn't much cared what anyone thought. Until he'd held up his former partner's trembling, black-clad widow while she stoically accepted the American flag that had been draped over her husband's mahogany casket.

Back from the dead, he'd turned in his snazzy government badge and his Glock semiautomatic, then walked away from a guaranteed salary, health benefits, and a pension he hadn't believed he'd live long enough to collect, retreating to the isolation of the moss-draped, foggy Louisiana bayou, where he didn't have to worry about being blown away if his Louisiana Cajun accent suddenly came out, blowing his cover story, whatever the hell it was that day.

It was only then that Jack realized he'd been playing at roles for so many years, he'd not only lost his soul, but any sense of who he was.

The first three months, spent in alcohol-sodden oblivion, passed by in a blur. Jack's only vivid memory of those early days after his homecoming was the night he'd hit rock bottom and ended up floating aimlessly through the swamp in his pirogue, stewed to the gills, the barrel of a .38 pressed against the roof of his mouth.

It would have been so damn easy to pull the trigger. *Too* easy, he'd decided, hurling the revolver into the water. The idealistic altar boy who'd confessed his childish digressions every Saturday afternoon at Blue Bayou's Church of the Holy Assumption Jack had been amazed to discover still lurking somewhere deep inside him required penance for adult sins.

Shortly after choosing life over suicide, he'd awakened from a three-day binge, pulled an old legal pad from its long-ago hiding place beneath a floorboard, and begun to write. A week later he'd discovered that while he couldn't exorcise all his old ghosts, he could hold them somewhat at bay by putting them down on paper.

Still working on instinct, when he ran out of clean pages, he went into town, bought an old Smith Corona manual typewriter at a secondhand store—electricity tended to go out a lot in the swamp—and reams of paper. After returning to the camp, he settled down to work, and with words flooding out from too-long-ignored emotional wounds, he wrote like a man possessed.

Things probably would have stopped there if an old friend, who, concerned about his welfare, hadn't ventured out into the swamp to check on him. When he found him sleeping like the dead he'd once longed to be and read the pages piled up on every flat surface, he'd convinced Jack to send them to a New York agent he knew.

Three months later Jack had received the life-altering call offering to buy his first—and decidedly uneven—novel about an alcoholic, burned-out, suicidal DEA agent. Eighteen months after that he'd hit the publishing jackpot when *The Death Dealer* soared to the top of every best-seller list in the country.

Now wealthier than he'd ever dreamed, he spent his days working up a sweat wielding crowbars, claw hammers, and axes, clearing away the kudzu that was threatening to consume the house, tearing apart crumbling foundations, ripping off rotted shingles.

When it grew too dark to work, he passed sleepless nights pounding computer keys, reliving those dark and violent memories that had amazingly also found a huge international audience.

He should have been in tall cotton, but since moving into Beau Soleil's *garconnière*, originally constructed as quarters for the young men of the plantation house, Jack had been haunted by memories which lingered like bits of Spanish moss clinging to a long-dead cypress.

He cursed viciously, then heard an answering whine. Glancing down, he viewed a mutt standing beneath one of the ancient oaks. She was a mess, her frame, long legs, and huge feet and head suggesting that she'd be about the size of a small horse if she hadn't been starved down to skin and bones. Ribs protruded from her sunken sides, her filthy fur was the color of dirty straw, and a nasty wound oozed across her muzzle.

"You and me, we got something in common, *chien femelle*. Two messed-up bayou strays."

She whined again but, seemingly encouraged by him talking to her, started slinking up the steps, her tail between her legs, limpid chocolate brown eyes hopeful.

"Christ, you're a sorry sight. Flea-bitten, too, I'll bet."

She dropped down on her haunches at his feet but was still able to look him in the eye.

"I suppose you want a handout."

She whined. Thumped her tail.

"Somethin' to eat?"

He'd obviously said the secret word. The tail began wagging to beat the band, revealing a remarkably optimistic nature for an animal who'd obviously had a helluva tough time.

"You can crash for the night. But I'm not looking for any long-term relationship here."

She barked. Once, twice, a third time. The expressive tail went into warp wag.

Shaking his head, Jack pushed himself to his feet and crunched across the oyster-shell drive to the *garconnière*, the dog so close on his heels she was nudging the back of his legs.

The contents of his refrigerator were not encouraging. "We've got two six-packs, a half-empty carton of milk I'm not gonna vouch for, and a brick of something green I think used to be cheese."

It was always this way when he was deep in a book. Worse when he was fighting with uncooperative characters as he'd been the past days. He'd forego sleep. Forget to eat, shower, shave. Hell, the entire planet could blow itself to smithereens, but if he was writing, he probably wouldn't notice until he lost power to his laptop.

Despite his warning, the dog's sharp bark suggested she was willing to take her chances.

"Wait a minute." He unearthed a dish from behind the beer, sniffed it, and tried to remember how many days it had been sitting in there.

"You like crawfish jambalaya?"

She barked again. Pranced, her nails clicking on the heart-of-cypress floor.

"Guess that's a yes."

After she'd wolfed the seasoned rice and crawfish down, Jack retrieved a bottle of hydrogen peroxide from the bathroom and cleaned the dog's wound. It had to have stung like the devil, but she sat perfectly still, staring at him with those big brown trusting eyes.

"Don't get used to it. Because tomorrow you and I are takin' a visit to the animal shelter."

The dog taken care of, he took the six-pack over to the old wooden kitchen table that had been handcrafted with trees milled from Beau Soleil's back woods. Those earlier thoughts of Danielle's birthday ball had stirred his balky muse, throwing up a series of *what-ifs* that seemed promising.

What if, he asked himself as he popped the top on one of the bottles, the aging drug kingpin had a daughter? A young woman as distant and unreachable as a star. A woman the alcoholic DEA agent—who was trying to bring her father down—was inexorably drawn to, even knowing it was suicide?

By the time a soft lavender predawn light was shimmering on the horizon, he'd worked his way through the six-pack, and the ceramic crawfish ashtray was piled high with cigarette butts, but the computer screen was filled with new scenes. Jack saved them onto his hard drive, pushed back from the table, staggered into the adjoining room, and crashed on the unmade bed.

As the dog sprawled onto the floor at the foot of the bed with a long satisfied sigh, Jack fell like a stone into sleep.

* * *

Danielle Dupree had always believed in fairy tales. And why not? After all, she'd grown up a princess in a storybook white-pillared plantation home, and even after bayou bad boy Jack Callahan broke her heart, she'd continued to believe in happily-ever-afters.

The only problem with fairy tales, she thought now as she lugged a heavy box of books out to her Volvo station wagon, was they didn't warn impressionable little girls that a few years down that Yellow Brick Road Prince Charming might decide to move into a new castle with a Vassar-educated princess who could better assist his career climb to king, subsequently die in a freak accident, and it'd be back to the ashes for Cinderella.

It had been a month since Lowell's death, yet it still was so strange to think of herself as a widow when she'd expected to be a divorcée.

Dani wasn't certain anyone deserved to have a piano drop on his head. Still, there was some irony in the fact that it happened to be Lowell's fiancée's gleaming white Steinway that had snapped its cable while the deliverymen were attempting to bring it in through the balcony French doors of their fifth-floor apartment.

Dani was, of course, sorry the man she'd married right out of college was dead. After all, he was her son's father. But still, she hadn't experienced any sense of grave personal loss. It certainly hadn't been as devastating as that fateful day nineteen months ago when a reporter from *The Washington Post* had called her and told her to turn on the six o'clock news.

Watching Congressman Lowell Dupree's press conference—held in the Watergate, where apparently he'd leased a cozy little love nest with his brunette barracuda chief of staff—Dani had been stunned to hear her husband tell the world that he was divorcing his wife.

Divorcing her.

Since he was the one who'd been so hot to set up housekeeping with another woman, Dani hadn't understood why he'd dragged their divorce out for eighteen long, contentious months during which time he'd raided their joint bank accounts, held back child support for the flimsiest of grounds that never held up in court, and refused to grant her lawyer access to financial records.

It was only after his death that Dani discovered her husband's high-flying venture into tech and Internet stocks had gone south, leaving him to die deeply in debt.

"Mom, I can't find my Hot Wheels."

"I packed them with your Hogwarts figures in the box with the orange stickers."

Her eight-old-son, Matt, was a die-hard Baltimore Orioles fan, which was why she'd assigned him orange in her moving-box color-coding system. She'd chosen red for herself, since it was supposed to be a power color, and she figured right now she needed all the help she could get.

"I forgot. Thanks, Mom."

"You're very welcome, darling." She drew a line through the box of books on her packing list.

Pleased to have averted a potential crisis, Dani returned to the house to strip the sheets off the king-size bed, which surprisingly hadn't proven at all lonely during the nineteen months she'd been sleeping by herself.

Three hours later the house was emptied, and her son was buckled into the backseat of the wagon with its READ vanity license plate.

"It feels funny not to be going to school," Matt said.

"I know, but you'll be in your new school in just a few days." Dani turned a corner and left the red brick Federal house—along with her former life—behind in the Volvo's rearview mirror. "Today we're going home."

2

The day dawned hot and drenched with humidity. Outside the open window a jay raucously scolded the rising sun, and the distant thrum of an outboard motor echoed from somewhere on the water. When a soft breath fanned against the back of his neck, every nerve in Jack's body went on alert.

There'd been a time when he would have been out of bed like a shot, weapon in hand, adrenaline racing through his veins. Now he forced his mind to calm and thought back to last night.

How much had he drunk? While there had admittedly been mornings in the past when he'd wake up in bed with some strange woman, unable to recall the events that had gotten them there, Jack knew this wasn't one of those times.

He'd been fighting his new book for a week. He remembered telling the construction crew not to interrupt him unless it had to do with blood—and a helluva lot of it—or fire. Then, shutting off the outside world, he'd waded back into battle with his rebellious characters.

He recalled taking a break last night, emerging from the isolation of his writer's cave to check out the work that had been done on the house. Satisfied at the progress, he'd been sitting on the *gallerie* when he'd started thinking about Danielle. Which was always a mistake, though probably inevitable since he was, after all, living in her house.

He remembered the bloodred moon. . . . The flashes of lightning out on the Gulf. . . . The croak of hidden bullfrogs. . . . The dog.

He turned his head, which some fiendish intruder had obviously split in half with a ragged ax while he'd been sleeping, and found himself staring straight into huge, adoring, crusted dark-rimmed eyes.

"I know damn well I didn't invite you up here."

Undeterred by his gritty tone, the mutt stretched her lanky frame. Then licked his face—a long wet slurp.

He wiped the back of his hand over his mouth, which tasted as if he'd sucked up all the mud in the entire Mississippi delta. "Didn't your *maman* ever warn you about climbing into a strange man's bed?"

As her tail thudded against the mattress, Jack wondered how many fleas she'd deposited in his sheets.

He crawled out of bed, allowing himself the indulgence of a few ragged groans that stopped just short of being whimpers. Bracing one hand against the wall, he dragged himself into the bathroom.

He blearily regarded the face in the mirror through eyes as red-veined as a Louisiana road map. He rubbed his hand over the heavy stubble of dark beard. "You should be writin' horror, you. 'Cause you're a dead ringer for *Loup Garou.*" The legendary shapeshifter was the bayou's answer to the Abominable snowman.

Whiskey, beer, and stale nicotine were seeping from his pores. Since it was a tossup which of them smelled worse, he debated dragging the dog into the shower with him, then decided not to bother. She'd get a bath along with her tick-dip at the shelter.

He steamed up the small bathroom, willing the pounding water to beat the poisons out of his aching body and continued to think back on last night. By the time he'd staggered to bed, the drug kingpin's daughter had begun spinning her deadly web for the DEA agent, and he'd unearthed his story's conflict. From here on in, it should be easy sailing.

Too bad he'd probably never finish it. Because odds were he'd be dead by noon.

The crew had already arrived and was at work on the roof of the big house, the drumming of hammers echoing the pounding in his head. Jack let the dog out the screen door, cringing against the squeak of the hinges he'd been meaning to oil for weeks, and watched her sniff around the base of one of the old oaks.

"That's good you're housebroken. It'll make it easier to find you a new family."

After drawing a glass of water from the tap, Jack swallowed three aspirins, then made coffee. He was waiting for what seemed like an interminably long time for the damn water to drip through the dark grounds when a high-pitched barking struck like an ice pick into the most delicate part of his brain.

"Hey, Jack," a male voice called. "Want to call off your mangy guard horse?"

"She's not mine." He pushed open the screen door again and vowed that if he lived another five minutes, he'd find the WD-40 and oil the damn thing.

"Hey, you," he said to the mutt. "Knock it off. Nate's on our side. He's one of the good guys."

She immediately stopped barking. With back fur still bristling, she sat down beside Jack, pressing against his leg.

"Remember when I was building an addition onto Pete Marchand's Tack-in-the-Box store a couple months back?" Nate Callahan, Jack's younger brother and the contractor in charge of Beau Soleil's renovation, asked.

"Yeah, I recall something about that. Why?"

" 'Cause I saw a real nice hand-tooled saddle in the window that'd probably fit your new pal just fine."

"Boy, you're such a comedian I'm surprised no one's given you your own TV show." Jack rubbed his throbbing temples.

"Hangover?"

"Thanks, anyway. But I've already got one of my own."

"Hope it was worth it. So, the dog gotta name?"

"Hell if I know." She wouldn't, if she was depending on him. "She's a stray." Jack leaned a shoulder against the door frame, folded his arms, and braced for bad news. "What's today's problem?"

He'd been warned, before buying Beau Soleil, that restoring the plantation house to its former glory would be a challenge. That had proven an understatement. The truth was, the place was not only a money pit, it was turning out to be one damn thing after another.

The first day he'd discovered he was going to have to replace most of the rotting foundation walls. Things had gone downhill from there.

"No problem. At least not yet. But hell, the day's still young."

Nate held out a foam cup. Jack pried off the lid and appreciatively inhaled the fragrant steam. Risking a scorched tongue, he took a drink of the black chicory-flavored coffee and decided he just may live after all.

"Too bad you're my brother. Otherwise, I could just turn gay and marry you so you could bring me coffee every morning."

"Sorry, even if we weren't related, you're not my type. I've got this personal thing about not locking lips with someone with a heavier beard than mine."

"Picky, picky."

"Though," Nate considered, "it might solve my recent problem with Suzanne."

"Marriage bug bite again?"

"I don' know what's gotten into women lately." Nate whipped off his billed cap and plowed a hand through his sun-streaked hair. "They're fabulous creatures. They smell damn good, too. You know I've always enjoyed everything about them."

"That's no exaggeration." From the moment he'd hit puberty and stumbled across their older brother Finn's stash of *Playboy* magazines, Nate had acquired a genuine appreciation for seemingly the entire female gender. From what Jack had been able to tell, the majority of those females had appreciated him right back.

"Used to be you could hit it off with a woman and the two of you'd pass a good time. Everyone had a little fun, nobody got hurt. Or mad. But no more. Hell, you go out a few times, share a few laughs . . ."

"A few rolls in the hay." Amused, Jack lit a cigarette.

"A gentleman never rolls and tells. But, Christ," Nate continued, "even when both parties agree goin' in to keep things light, the next thing you know, she's askin' whether you like Chrysanthemum or Buttercup better."

Jack shrugged. "Most women like flowers."

"That's what I thought when she first brought it up. But turns out they're not flowers. They're goddamned silverware patterns."

"I'm no expert on the subject, but my guess would be it's best just to go along with whatever the lady likes."

"Easy for you to say. She happens to like Chrysanthemum because it's the same pattern her momma has, is from Tiffany's, and a single damn iced-tea spoon would probably pay my subcontractor bills for a month. But my problem isn't about any damn flatware."

"Just the fact that you know the term *flatware* suggests you're in trouble, little brother."

"My point," Nathan plowed on through gritted teeth, "is that the female pattern is always the same. Have a few dates, share a few kisses, okay, maybe go to bed, and suddenly copies of *Bride* magazine start mysteriously showin' up on the bedside table and you're giving up NASCAR to watch *Sense and Sensibility* on the chick channel."

Jack blew out a surprised cloud of smoke. "You're kidding."

"I wish I were. A guy could die of estrogen overdose watching that movie. Last night it was *Sleepless in Seattle*. And this morning she brought me breakfast in bed."

"Well, that's certainly a hangin' offense. Are we talkin' fresh fruit in dainty crystal bowls and croissants on flowered plates with white doilies? Or a decent manly meal with buckets of grease and cholesterol?"

"This morning it was boudin, cush cush, three fried eggs, and cottage fries."

"Gotta hate a woman who'd fry you up a mess of sausage and eggs." Jack's mouth watered. "Maybe when Suzanne gets tired of cookin' for an unappreciative yahoo, you can send her out here."

"You'd run her off in a day. Besides, it's not the cooking that's my problem, it's the reason a woman who probably grew up not even knowin' the way to the kitchen has gotten all domestic in the first place. Dammit, Jack, I feel like a tournament bass trying to hide out in the shallows, and she's on the bank baitin' the damn hook."

"So, don't bite."

"Easy for you to say," Nate grumbled as they watched the new roof going on. "Good to see you finally coming out of hibernation, even if you look like death warmed over," he said, switching gears. "Does this mean the book's finally starting to go well?"

"Depends on your meaning of *well*."

"I sure don't understand, given all that happened to you, why you'd want to write about murder."

"It's called makin' a living."

"You can't sit at that computer twenty-four hours a day. Ever think about running for sheriff when you get this place all fixed up? Lord knows this parish could use a new one. Jimbo Lott gets more corrupt every year."

"I notice he keeps getting elected."

"Only 'cause nobody runs against him."

"In case you haven't noticed, the reason I came back here is because I'm out of the crime-fighting business."

"Nah. You may be a hot shot novelist now, but you've got our daddy's blood running through your veins. You and Finn always were the most like him, always wantin' to play cops and robbers."

"While you were off dragging lumber in from the swamp."

"Somebody had to build the jail to put the robbers in after you two captured them. I don't believe you can ignore nature, Jack."

"Believe it. I turned in my badge because I finally realized that tilting at windmills just gets you ripped to fuckin' pieces."

"So you're going to spend the rest of your life hiding out here, trying to find redemption by writing your depressing books?"

"Unlike some people who haven't learned how to mind their own business, I don't believe in redemption. And a helluva lot of readers must like depressing, because I sell damn well."

Jack had never been able to figure out why readers the world over would actually pay to share his nightmares, but as his agent and editor kept assuring him, his thinly veiled true crime stories about a divorced, alcoholic narcotics agent who lived on the fringes of society had found a huge audience.

"There's probably an audience for televised executions," Nate said mildly. "But that doesn't necessarily mean the networks should supply it."

"Hell, if they ever figure out a way to get by the government censors, Old Sparky will become a Saturday night blockbuster."

"You know, I'm beginnin' to worry you may just be nearly as cynical as you're trying to convince me you are."

"Not cynical. I'm just a realist. I decided after holding up my dead partner's widow at his gravesite that I'd leave saving the world to people like our older brother."

"You've always had a knack for tellin' stories," Nate allowed. "But ever think 'bout writing more uplifting ones?"

"I just write the world like I see it."

"Well, I sure don't envy you your view."

Jack merely shrugged.

"Speaking of views, the scenery around Blue Bayou's about to get a whole lot prettier."

An intuition Jack had learned to trust, the same one that had saved his life on more than one occasion, had the hair at the back of his neck prickling. As the sun burned off the morning mist, he curled his hand around the cup and waited.

"Danielle's coming back home."

Ignoring the sideways look directed his way, Jack polished off the rest of the cooling coffee and wished to hell it was something stronger.

* * *

Heat shimmered on the empty roadway, a glistening black ribbon that twined its way around laconic waters and through root-laced swamps, unrolling before Dani like a welcome mat. Despite all her problems, the deeper into the bayou she drove, the more her tangled nerves began to unwind. There was something calming about this land that time had forgot. Calming and infinitely reassuring, despite the rumbling from storm clouds gathering on the horizon.

Fields of sugar cane were occasionally broken by an oak tree, or a sleepy strip town, often little more than one house deep, the valuable land being needed more for crops than commerce. Lush green fields were laid out in a near-surgical precision at odds with the personalities of the Cajun farmers who lived there. Here in southern Louisiana the mighty Mississippi hadn't carved valleys as it had upriver. Instead, it had carried rich topsoil washed away from northern states and deposited it across the soggy terrain to create valuable fertile land. Water and bog warred continually, with water winning more battles over the eons.

Pretty Victorian homes stood next door to brightly painted Creole West Indies cottages, which neighbored antebellum plantation homes, many of which were crumbling, reclaimed by time and water. Every so often Dani would pass a sugar mill, whose sweet odor, come winter grinding season, would make the eyes water.

It was a long way from Fairfax, Virginia, to Blue Bayou, Louisiana. An even longer way from the hustle and bustle of the nation's capital to this secret, hidden corner of the world. Dani had missed it without knowing it'd been missed. Trying to keep a demanding life on track, while juggling the roles of congressional wife, student, mother, and librarian, running from a painful past she tried not to think about, had kept her nearly too busy to breathe. Let alone stop and think. Or feel.

Which is why, she thought sadly, she hadn't realized that Lowell had emotionally left their marriage—and her—before they'd returned from their St. Thomas honeymoon.

Matt, who normally passed long drives with his nose in a library book, wasn't saying much about the change of scenery, but whenever Dani would glance in the rearview mirror, she'd see him drinking everything in.

"Some of the kids didn't believe me when I said we were going to be living in a library," he offered from the backseat.

"We're not going to be living *in* the library. We'll be living *above* it."

Dani had been more than a little relieved when an on-line search of the *Cajun Clarion*'s classified pages had revealed an opening for parish librarian. She'd immediately called the number, which turned out to be the mayor's office, and had, in the space of that single phone call, been hired by Nate Callahan, Blue Bayou's newly elected mayor. The pay might not be up to big-city standards, but Dani would have been willing to clean tables and wash dishes in Cajun Cal's Country Café if that's what it took to feed her son.

"Since the library's been closed for the past two months, ever since the former librarian moved to Alexandria to live with her granddaughter, the parish commissioners were so relieved to hear they were going to be able to open it, they threw in the apartment as a *lagniappe*." Which was fortunate, since the salary would have made paying rent difficult.

"*Lagniappe* means 'something extra.' "

"That's exactly what it means." She smiled at him in the mirror. "You're so smart."

His brow furrowed. "What if I was only smart at Fox Run? What if the kids in my new school know more than I do?"

"Your test scores were great, darling." Hadn't she, on the school counselor's advice, allowed him to skip third grade? "You'll do fine here."

"What if they don't like me?"

"Of course they'll like you. And you'll have your cars to break the ice."

"Yeah. I will," he said, seemingly relieved. "Grandpa's really going to live with us, too?"

"Absolutely." Dani refused to consider the prospect of her father rejecting the home she intended to make for them all.

Judge Victor Dupree had always wanted to control everything and everyone around him, which is probably partly why he became a judge in the first place. She'd often thought it was also one of the reasons her mama had run away when Dani had still been in diapers. If there was anything Lowell's untimely death had taught her, it was that life was too short to hold grudges. She and her father had already lost enough years they could have been a family. Her son was going to know who and where he'd come from if it was the last thing Dani did.

And if Daddy doesn't like it, tough.

Thunder rumbled a low warning in the distance. A flash of lightning forked out of darkening clouds, and the wind picked up, rustling the cane stalks.

"Is a hurricane coming?"

"Oh, I'm sure we don't have to worry about that." Dani flipped on the windshield wipers.

"Are you sure? I saw the signs," Matt said over the drumming rain on the station wagon's metal roof. "The evacuation route for when there's a hurricane." Even being more than a year younger than most of his classmates, he was the best reader in his fourth grade. There were times, and this was one of them, that wasn't necessarily a good thing.

"It's just a little afternoon rain, sweetie."

"Too bad." He pressed his nose against the window. "It'd be cool to call Tommy and tell him we were in a hurricane." Tommy had been his neighbor and best friend in Virginia.

"I think I'd prefer we pass on that excitement."

"It'd still be neat."

A siren screamed over the crash of another thunderclap. The flashing lights in the rearview mirror yanked Dani's attention from her dreary thoughts as she glanced down at the speedometer, which revealed that she was going well within the speed limit.

"Are we getting a ticket?"

"I don't think so." She certainly hoped not. The last thing her checkbook needed was a traffic fine and an increase in her insurance premium. She pulled over to the shoulder, breathing a sigh of relief as the red car belonging to the parish fire chief tore past.

Unlike so many of the strip towns which had sprung up to serve the farming and shrimping south Louisiana population, Blue Bayou had been painstakingly designed by a wealthy planter who'd visited Savannah for a wedding and had so admired that city's lush green squares and gracious architecture, he'd returned home and formed a partnership with one of the *gens de couleur libres*—free men of color—an architect who shared his artistic vision.

Together they changed the rustic fishing town named for the blue herons which nested on the banks of the bayou into a planned hamlet which, although the town's name of *Bayou Bleu* had been anglicized over the years, remained an example of the short-lived period of booming antebellum prosperity.

As Dani crossed the old steel bridge leading into town, the gaslights along oak-lined Gramercy Boulevard—which was actually a narrow cobblestone street—flickered on, yellow shimmers through the falling rain, which she was glad to see was letting up as the storm passed on toward New Orleans and Mississippi.

Returning to this hidden corner of Louisiana was like going back in time. Not just to Dani's more recent personal past, but to a romantic era far more distant. It took no imagination at all to hear the clatter of horses' hooves on the cobblestones or the rustle of petticoats skimming the brick sidewalk lined with leafy trees and planters overflowing with color.

Some things had changed since the last time she'd been home, which had been for her father's trial seven long years ago. Lafitte's Landing, the old restaurant, dance hall, and gathering place, was closed; the drugstore where she and her girlfriends would perch on vinyl-seated swivel stools and moon over Johnny Breaux as he'd build hot fudge sundaes was now an Espresso Express, and Arlene's Doll Hospital had become a video rental store.

But Cajun Cal's Country Café still advertised the Friday night fried-fish special; they were still perming hair at Belle's Shear Pleasures, though according to the white script painted on the window, Belle had added pedicures, and the Bijoux Theater still dominated the corner of Maringouin and Heron. They also still had live entertainment on Sunday nights. According to the marquee, this week's singer was billed as *The Chanteuse Acadienne, Christy Marchand*.

Blue Bayou was a pretty, peaceful town where children rode bikes down quiet, tree-canopied streets, where mothers pushed baby carriages, and the residents sat on front galleries beneath lazily circling ceiling fans to sip sweet tea in the afternoons and watch their neighbors.

It was the kind of small rural southern town where Andy Griffith could have been elected sheriff, if Andy had only spoken French. Dani hadn't realized how much she'd missed it until she'd come home.

The lush green town square was flanked on one end by the Church of the Holy Assumption, its twin Gothic spires lancing high into the sky. The silver rain clouds had gathered around the stone towers like pigeons flocking together for the night.

The opposite side of the park was anchored by the majestic

Italianate courthouse, boasting tall stone steps, gracefully arched windows, and lacy cast-iron pilasters. It had served as a hospital during the War Between the States, and if one knew where to look, it was possible to find minie balls still lodged in the woodwork.

A red, white, and blue Acadian flag hung below the U.S. and state flags on a towering pole, and a bronze statue of Captain Jackson Callahan—a local boy who'd risen above his Irish immigrant status by joining the mostly Irish 6th Louisiana Volunteer Infantry known as the Confederate Tigers—graced the lawn.

The soldier who'd begun the war as Private Callahan had fought in virtually every Eastern front battle from the Shenandoah Valley Campaign of 1862 under Stonewall Jackson to the hand-to-hand warfare at Fort Stedman, amazingly returning home in one piece after Lee's surrender at Appomattox Court House in 1865.

The fact that the former ragtag orphan, who'd grown up wild and barefoot in Blue Bayou's Irish swamp, had, by means of battlefield promotions, returned a captain, had been considered by many to be a miracle.

"That's a cool horse," Matt said.

"I always thought so. A lot of people believe that touching his nose before entering the courthouse brings good luck."

"Can we try it?"

"After we get moved into the apartment, we'll come back," Dani promised. Unfortunately, the horse she'd so loved to sit on as a child hadn't worked its lucky magic for her father.

It was in this courthouse that Judge Victor Dupree had sat on the bench for decades, earning a reputation as a hard-line law-and-order advocate whose tendency to throw the book at those convicted in his courtroom had earned him the nickname of Maximum Dupree. It was also in this courthouse he'd been convicted of bribery and perjury and sentenced to seven years in Angola prison.

Dani couldn't resist glancing up at her father's courtroom window. Her heart hitched; tears misted her vision. Blinking to clear her gaze, she reminded herself of the list she'd made while sitting in her kitchen in Fairfax. Her first priorities were to get settled into their new home and enroll Matt in school. Next she'd reopen the library. Then, once those items had been crossed off, she'd tackle the problem with her father.

Fortunately, the storm had passed quickly. Only the occasional drop of rain splattered on the windshield. She turned off the wipers, deciding to take the fact that she wouldn't have to be lugging things into the apartment in a downpour as a portent of more good luck.

The library was two blocks away, on Magnolia Avenue. Dani could have driven there blindfolded. She turned the corner, only to find the street blocked by barricades and the patrol car she'd feared earlier, its emergency lights casting the scene in a surrealistic blur.

This couldn't be happening! She stared in disbelief as she watched the arcs of water spraying from shiny brass nozzles onto the top floor of the three-story redbrick building with the wood and brass Blue Bayou Library sign on the lawn. Men in helmets and heavy yellow jackets dragged heavy hoses, wielded axes, and shouted out orders.

"Wow. Is that our apartment?" Matt asked.

Dani didn't immediately answer. She could barely breathe.

"Wait here," she said. "I'll be right back."

"But, Mom . . ."

"I said, wait here and do not get out of this car," she instructed in the no-nonsense I'm-your-mother-and-you-will-obey-me tone she hardly ever had to use with her normally obedient son. "Do you understand me?"

"Geez, yeah. You don't have to yell."

"I'm sorry." She leaned back and cupped his freckled face between her palms. "I'm sorry I snapped at you."

"Don't worry, Mom." His defensive mood passed, as swiftly as the earlier storm, and he gave her a reassuring smile. "Everything'll be okay."

It was the same thing he'd said the day the moving men had taken his father's things from their house. Her husband had always chosen his career over his family. And in doing so had inadvertently created an intensely strong bond between his wife and son.

"I know, darling." Dani gave him a quick kiss, ruffled his hair, reminded him once again to stay put, then waded into the breach.

3

The fire had drawn a crowd, the spectators watching her dreams go up in smoke with the same fascination they might gather at a train wreck. Dani's feet crunched on the broken glass strewn over the slickly wet pavement like shards of ice. A sooty-faced fireman sat on the wide running board of the fire truck, drinking in hits of oxygen.

"What happened?"

He lifted the mask. "Dunno. Probably a lighting strike." His red-rimmed eyes swept the scene as he stood up and fastened his yellow helmet. "Or electrical." They both looked up at the flames licking from the shattered windows. "That's up to the fire marshal to determine."

Sparks wheeled like orange stars in the darkening sky as he clapped down his face shield and walked away.

Dani's hammering heart sank to her wet sneakers. Just when she didn't think she could feel any worse, she viewed a man wearing the brown uniform and shiny badge of authority swaggering toward her and imagined she heard the warning rattle of a snake's tail over the roar of water. Which was ridiculous. Blue Bayou's sheriff had never been a man to give his adversary any warning.

"Well, if it ain't little Danielle Dupree." His belly strained against the front of his khaki uniform, spilling over his belt. There were dark circles of sweat beneath his arms and red hot sauce stains on his brown tie. He was, Dani thought, the antithesis of Andy Griffith. "Fancy meetin' you here."

The smile beneath his shaggy black mustache held more smirk than warmth. If an alligator could smile, it'd look like exactly like Sheriff Jimbo Lott.

"Sheriff Lott." Voice mild, she resisted rubbing the tension knotted at the back of her neck.

"Any special reason you're at my fire scene?"

The flat-lidded reptilian gaze crawling over her managed to be both sexual and detached at the same time. He'd looked at her the same way years ago, when he'd caught her with Jack out at the Callahans' camp and forced her to get dressed in the glare of his patrol car's spotlight.

When she couldn't quite restrain an involuntary shiver at both the memory and the intimidation in those hooded eyes, his thick lips curved in another sly innuendo of a smile.

"It happens to be my fire scene, as well." Her eyes stung from the smoke. "I was supposed to be moving into that apartment tonight."

"That a fact?" He didn't sound surprised. "Guess that apartment wasn't as bad as some of them shacks out in the swamp, but it sure don't seem much like a place a U.S. congressman's widow would wanna live, either." The flashing lights from the fire trucks shadowed, then highlighted a cruel, self-indulgent face and weak double chins. "Looks like its gonna end up one helluva mess. Lucky you hadn't moved your stuff in yet. Would've been tragic if that fire'd started later tonight, when you and your boy were sleepin'. Y'all would've been lucky to escape alive."

She'd never fainted in her life, but as she imagined Matt trapped in the third floor apartment with those hungry flames and that suffocating, stinging smoke, Dani's head began to spin.

"Yep," he continued as she braced a hand against the side of the fire truck and fought against the swirling vertigo, "too bad you've come all this way, only to have to turn right around and go home."

She drew in a breath that burned. "This *is* my home, Sheriff."

"You've been gone from Blue Bayou for a lotta years, Missy. And it's not like you've got family here, with your daddy locked away up in Angola. Things change, even in these backwaters. Power shifts. Ever hear the old sayin' 'bout folks not bein' able to go home again?"

"Yes." The challenge was a like a cold wet slap in the face. Dani welcomed the anger that steamrollered over her earlier shock. She tossed up her chin. "I've just never believed it."

She was about to cut this unsatisfactory conversation short when someone called her name. Turning around, she saw Nate Callahan leap the black-and-white police barricade. He could not have been more welcome if he'd been wearing a suit of shining armor and riding astride a white stallion.

"Are you okay?" He took both her hands in his, comforting her the way he once had so many years ago, after his brother had broken her heart.

"I'm fine," she lied. "But I should get back to Matt." Another window exploded; shards of glass rained down.

"More'n likely your boy's having himself a high old time," Lott drawled. "Never did meet a kid who didn't get off on fires."

Dani speared the sheriff with a disgusted look, then turned her back on him.

"Why don't you introduce me to your son?" Nate suggested mildly, ignoring Lott as well.

Her throat was raw from smoke and pent-up emotion. As he put a steadying hand around her waist, walking back with her to the wagon, Dani tried not to weep.

What on earth was she going to do now?

The first thing was get hold of herself. This wasn't the end of the world. She'd think of something. After all, hadn't she'd surprised a lot of people, including herself, by not crumbling when Lowell had left her?

She'd picked herself up, turned her part-time library work into a fulfilling career, and had been in the process of building a new life for herself and Matt when that damn piano had changed things yet again.

Dani stiffened her resolve and pasted a reassuring look on her face for her son. This fire was admittedly a setback, but nothing she couldn't overcome. She would not allow herself to think otherwise.

Watching the genuine warmth with which Nate greeted Matt, Dani wasn't surprised he'd grown up to be mayor. He'd always been the boy everyone gravitated to at parties, the one all eyes automatically went to when he was out on a ball field, either tossing spiral passes or diving off third base to steal a home run from an opposing team's batter. By the time he was nominated for senior class president, not a student in the school considered running against him.

All the girls had harbored crushes on him. All but her. Dani only had eyes for his brother, Bad Jack.

"Looks like we've got ourselves more company," Nate observed as a pink Cadillac with mile-long tailfins harkening back to Detroit's glory days pulled up, Elvis's *Blue Suede Shoes* blasting from the radio.

A woman in her sixties, sporting a towering birdnest of orange hair, climbed out of the driver's seat. A cartoon drawing of a fighting crawdad standing on its tail, claws outstretched in a boxer's stance, adorned the front of her purple caftan. Red plastic crawdad earrings flashed with hidden battery-operated lights. Orèlia Vallois was a retired nurse who'd worked in her physician husband's office; Dani could not remember ever seeing her in traditional nurse's white.

"Why, if it isn't pretty little Danielle Dupree, come back home where she belongs," the deep contralto boomed out.

Orèlia had always been one of Dani's favorite people. Warmhearted and outspoken, she'd gone out of her way to treat Judge Dupree's motherless daughter special. She was also one of a handful of people who knew Dani's deepest, darkest secret.

"It's so good to see you," Dani said, grateful for a gift in the midst of disaster.

"It's grand to have you back home again. *Comment c'est?*"

"It's not exactly a banner day."

Behind the rose-tinted lenses of rhinestone-framed cat's-eye glasses, dark eyes, enhanced with a bold streak of purple color that matched the caftan, offered a warm welcome. "*Viens ici, bébé*, an' give Orèlia a hug."

After nearly squeezing the breath out of Dani, Orèlia gave her a quick once-over, then studied Matt, who was observing the gregarious nurse as if she were some sort of wondrous alien from a Saturday morning cartoon. Dani knew he'd never seen anything like Orèlia Vallois in Fairfax County.

"An' this must be your darling *fil*."

"This is Matt." Dani placed a hand atop his head, absently smoothing the cowlick. "Matt, this is Mrs. Vallois."

"Hello, Ma'am" he answered with his best Fox Run manners.

"Aren't you the mos' handsome young man Blue Bayou's seen in a long time." She pinched Matt's cheek. "You have your *maman*'s mouth, Monsieur Matthew."

"I do?" Dani gave him huge points for not squirming.

"*Oui*. You'll break more than a few girls' hearts, you. Why, I bet you already have yourself a special girlfriend."

A flush as bright as the fighting cartoon crawfish rose in his face. He rubbed the darkening red spot where she'd pinched him. "Not really."

"Well, isn't there plenty of time for that? Anyway, it's best to play the field at your age. Besides, now I won't have to worry 'bout female competition while you're living with me."

"Living with you?" He shot Dani a confused look.

"Oh, Orèlia, as much as I appreciate the offer—"

"Now, Danielle, darlin', there's no point in arguing. Besides, I've just been rattlin' around in that big house since my Leon passed on. It'll be good to have some company." She chucked Matt beneath his chin. "Follow me home, and I'll feed this man of yours."

"I really don't want to impose—"

"Stop talking foolishness," the older woman cut her off again. "You need a place to stay and your boy needs food." The gregarious redhead had morphed into the bustling office nurse who'd jabbed more than a few needles into patients' bare butts over a forty-year career. "At least for tonight, then we can talk about your future in the morning, when things are lookin' brighter."

The orange birdnest teetered a bit as she tilted her head and studied Matt. "You look like a chicken-fried-steak man to me. That sound good?"

"I guess so."

"Of course it does. Nobody in this parish makes a better chicken fried steak than Orèlia. We'll get you some dirty rice and buttered snap beans, too."

"Dirty rice?"

"Oh, it's wonderful, darlin'. You'll love it. I can't believe your *maman*'s never cooked it for you."

Deciding this was not the time to try to explain that the only time Lowell had wanted any reminders of his Louisiana constituents, whom he'd always considered beneath him, was when he was hosting his annual Mardi Gras fund-raising party for well-heeled lobbyists and wealthy corporate types, Dani didn't respond to the friendly gibe.

"And some hot-milk cake for dessert," Orèlia decided. "I'll bet you like that good enough."

"I don't know. I've never had it."

"You haven't?" A beringed hand flew to her breast. "*Bon Dieu!* What on earth happened to your *maman* while she was away living with the Americans?"

Knowing that old-time Cajuns considered the rest of the country as something apart from themselves, Dani didn't bother to point out that Blue Bayou was technically as American as Virginia.

Orèlia flicked a measuring gaze over Dani. "Your handsome boy isn't the only one who needs supper. Don't they feed you good in the city, *chère?* You're nothin' but skin and bones. But don't you worry, Orèlia will take care of getting you some curves."

She wagged her hand toward the station wagon. "Now shoo. I'll meet you at the house and flirt with Matty and fix him some supper while you and Nate take care of business."

Events decided, at least in her own mind, she swept back through the crowd like a ship steaming out of harbor to the Caddy.

"The sign says No Parking," Matt pointed out.

"She was probably in such a hurry she didn't notice it." Dani ignored Nate's smothered laugh. They both knew that Orèlia was no fan of rules.

"Are we really going to live with her?" Matt asked.

Dani watched the steam rising from the charred building that was to have been her new home, considered her options, and reluctantly decided that she didn't have all that many.

"Just for a little while," she decided. "Until we can get the apartment repaired."

Fortunately, the lower floors didn't look as if they'd been too badly damaged. She hoped the books would be salvageable.

"When the apartment's fixed up, it'll be better than new," she said optimistically. "I'll start looking for carpenters first thing in the morning."

Already forming her plan to literally rise from the ashes, Dani didn't notice Nate wince.

The dying sun bled red in the water as Jack poled the pirouge up to the dock. The No Name wasn't a place where you could take a pretty girl dancing on Saturday night, or where a family might show up for dinner after Sunday mass.

Neither was it known for its rustic charms, a waterfront tavern where you'd romance a woman over glasses of wine, or where a guy could play a few convivial rounds of pool with pals, listen to some zydeco on the juke, and shoot the bull.

The No Name—the original name had been forgotten after the sign had blown down in a hurricane in the 1940s—was a specialty shop: a bar where you could feed the spiders crawling around in your head and get quickly, ruthlessly, and efficiently drunk enough that you could no longer remember anything about your life. Not even your own name.

And Jack had a shitload of stuff he wanted—needed—to forget.

The thick plank front door had been painted a bright lipstick red by a previous owner, but had faded over the decades to a dirty rust. There were a few muttered complaints from the shadows when he opened the door and let in the bleeding red light. Jack figured the growled curses were probably the most words any of the regulars had managed to string together all day.

The interior was even worse than the outside. It was dark and cheerless, smelling of sawdust and despair. It suited his mood perfectly.

"Give me a double Jack Black, straight up, no water on the side," he said as he slid onto a barstool. There were bowls of sliced lemons, limes, and cherries on the bar and behind it, dark bottles, dim lamps, and dusty bottles of wine.

The bartender, a tall, whippet-lean man with the look of a long-distance runner, which he'd been in high school, splashed the Jack Daniel's into a short glass. "Bad day at Black Rock?"

"You could say that." Jack tossed down the whiskey, enjoying the burn down the length of his throat as it seared its way to his gut and sent smoke upward into his brain.

He shoved the empty glass back toward the bartender, who arched a black brow but refilled it without a word.

Alcèe Bonaparte was in his early thirties, same as Jack. They'd gone to school together, and both their mothers had worked for the Dupree family—Marie Callahan as a housekeeper, Dora Bonaparte as a cook—and they'd grown up together. Despite the fact that Alcèe was African-American and Jack was white, they'd been as close as brothers, with Alcèe playing the role of the good twin, Jack the bad.

Whenever Jack filched beer from the back of the Dixie delivery truck, often as not it was Alcèe who left behind the change to cover the theft.

When Jack got drunk, went on a tear, and bashed in mailboxes with a baseball bat not unlike the Louisville Slugger currently hanging on the wall beneath the bottles, it had been Alcèe who'd convinced him to confess to the judge, who'd sentenced Jack to replacing every one of the vandalized boxes, and working off the cost cutting cane on the Dupree farm.

What the judge never knew, and they sure as hell didn't tell him, was that not only had Alcèe dug the posts for the new mailboxes, he'd passed up a long awaited church trip to the New Orleans cemeteries to labor besides his best friend in the staggering, breath-stealing heat of the cane fields.

With the easy understanding of lifelong friends, neither man spoke. Alcèe continued to pour drinks, washed glasses in the metal sink, and wiped off the bar that was permanently stained, pale white circles left by wet glasses telling the years like the rings of ancient trees.

After ten minutes he disappeared through the swinging doors into the back, returning with a huge po'boy, which he stuck in front of Jack.

"I don't remember ordering that." Unfortunately, Jack could still remember more than he wanted.

"You need somet'ing in your stomach besides whiskey, you. Befo' you go fallin' off that there stool and break your stiff coon-ass neck."

"Don't give me that bayou black boy jive. I happen to know you received a Jesuit education."

Alcèe folded his arms across the front of the gaudy blue-and-white flowered Hawaiian shirt.

"You so smart, you should also know that the Jesuits are Catholicism's kick-butt hardasses. So why don't you eat that sandwich before I have to, in the name of Christian charity, stuff it down your throat."

Jack's curse was short and pungent and bounced right off Alcèe like BBs off a Kevlar vest. Knowing from experience that arguing was useless, he bit into the dripping sandwich and nearly moaned as the flavors of shrimp and sauce piquante exploded on his tongue.

"So," Alcèe asked casually as he took away the empty highball glass and, without being asked, spritzed Coke into a new, taller one filled with ice, "do I owe this visit to the fact that a certain *jolie blonde* is coming back to town?" He tossed some cherries into the Coke and placed the glass down in front of Jack.

"I don't know what you're talking about." Jack took a long swallow, feeling the sugar hit like a firecracker in his head, which he would have preferred muddied.

Alcèe looked inclined to argue when he noticed a grizzled old guy get up from a table in the far corner. He was out from around the bar and as Jack watched, he bent down and talked quietly but intensely to the man who'd opened his mouth to argue, then obviously realized the futility and sagged back down onto the chair. Alcèe sat down at the table and continued to talk to him.

It was common knowledge in Blue Bayou that Alcèe was a former priest who'd temporarily lost his faith and his bearings in a fog of alcoholism. One fateful night on the way back to his New Orleans rectory after a drinking binge in a blues club with an alkie pal, who'd just happened to be a monsignor, he'd driven off the road into the river. He'd survived—just barely—and, after countless dives, had managed to get his passenger out of the car.

Unfortunately, the other man, whose blood later tested at a level nearly three times the legal limit, hadn't been wearing his seat belt. He'd spent a month in a coma and another two years in rehab before being spirited away by the Church to wherever they put their problem clergymen.

Alcèe didn't even try to fight the drunk-driving and reckless-endangerment charges. He dried out and did both his time and his penance while running a prison ministry. When he was released, he left the priesthood and returned home to the bayou. Now the No Name was his parish, the hard-core drunks and strung-out druggies who frequented it, his flock.

Last New Year's Eve he'd gotten himself engaged to a nurse in the maternity ward at St. Mary's hospital, a former beauty queen from Mississippi who was every bit as warmhearted as Alcèe himself was. Jack had agreed to be best man at their wedding next month, something he was looking forward to, even though he felt that in the case of him and Alcèe the title was definitely a misnomer.

The fact was, Jack owed Alcèe Bonaparte big time. He'd been on a fast slide right into hell and might not have lived long enough to see his old friend get married if Alcèe hadn't shown up at the camp that day and convinced him to send his manuscript to a lit grad who'd spent a year in the same seminary Alcèe had attended. The guy had subsequently decided he wasn't cut out for a life of celibacy and had gone on to become a New York literary agent, but he and Alcèe had kept in touch over the years.

The door opened onto a gathering well of darkness. Heads swiveled toward the woman backlit by the neon blue parking-lot light. Even the old drunk seemed to sit up a little straighter as Desiree Champagne glided across the sawdust-covered floor. Her hair was a riot of dark gypsy curls, her eyes the color of wood smoke in autumn.

She was wearing a red silk dress slashed nearly to the navel that hugged her curves like a lover's caress and spindly heels so high Jack marveled that she could walk without breaking both ankles.

When Alcèe started to get up from the table, she waved him off, a diamond the size of Texas flashing like lasers in the smoky light.

"You stay where you are, hon," she said in a throaty voice designed to tug masculine chords. "I can get my own drink." She went around the bar and began mixing a martini. "Hey, Jack." Every male eye in the place was riveted on her as she shook the drink, poured it into a glass, and added a trio of olives. "What are you drinking, darlin'?"

Jack heard Alcèe clear his throat. Ignoring the veiled warning, he answered, "Jack Black."

She poured a shot of whiskey into a glass and held it out to him. *Come and get it,* those flashing dark eyes were saying. *Come and get me.*

After he'd taken the drink, and thanked her for it, she came around the bar, perched on the stool next to him, and crossed her legs, revealing a mouthwatering length of thigh. "It's been a long time." Her lips curved into a sultry seductive smile. Even knowing it was practiced, did not lessen its appeal. "I've missed you."

"I've missed you, too."

It was true enough, Jack decided. He might not have thought about her during the weeks he'd been working on Beau Soleil and slogging away on his book, but a part of him would probably always miss their easy camaraderie dating back to the days when two outsiders found a bit of escape and comfort in each other's arms.

"Did you hear Dani's coming back?" She plucked the olive from the plastic pick with full, glossy lips.

"Nate mentioned it."

"I wonder why."

He shrugged. "I guess 'cause her husband died, so she's coming home."

"The only trouble with that scenario is that *you're* in her home."

He didn't respond, since that thought had been going round and round in his mind ever since Nate had dropped his little bombshell this morning.

The scarlet silk slid off one shoulder when she shrugged. "I guess she'll have to find herself another one."

"No offense, sugar. But I really don't feel much like conversation tonight."

"Fine." She crossed her legs again with a seductive swish of silk. "Then we won't." She sipped the martini, eyeing him over the rim of the glass. "I can't stay long, anyway. Since I think I'm expecting company tonight."

"You don't know?"

"I'm not quite sure." Her fingers stroked the thin stem of the glass in a blatantly erotic way. "Yet."

The gilt-rimmed feminine invitation was lingering in the smoke-filled bar between them. Jack polished off the whiskey and threw a twenty-dollar bill on the bar. "Let's go."

She smiled. "I thought you'd never ask." She blew a kiss toward Alcèe, who was on the black pay phone. Jack knew, from having watched similar discussions over the past months, that he was probably arranging for someone to drive the old guy home.

As he left with Desiree, he waved goodbye to his old friend, who waved back. But there was no mistaking the concern in Alcèe's Bambi-brown eyes.

"Alcèe doesn't approve," Desiree said.

"Once a priest always a priest," Jack muttered as they went out into the steamy night.

"He thinks I'm not good enough for you."

"Alcèe's never been one to judge. Even when he was wearing the collar."

"Perhaps." She thought about that as they made their way across the parking lot, her arm around his waist, his hand on her hip. "I suppose he's used to hookers. Even his old boss forgave Mary Magdalene."

"You're not a hooker."

"Not anymore." She leaned against the shiny red fender of a late model Porsche and looked up at him. "But even if I was, *chère*, you wouldn't be having to pay. Not with our history." She'd been the first girl he'd ever had sex with, and they'd passed some good times in the backseat of his candy-apple red GTO back in high school. She dangled the keys in front of him the same way he supposed Eve had offered that shiny red apple to Adam. "Why don't you drive?"

He hesitated just a moment too long.

"Hey, darlin', if you don't want to, it's no big deal."

He saw the flash of hurt in her eyes. "Sure I want to. It's just that I've got this damn dog."

"A dog?"

"Tied up over by the pirogue."

"I don't believe it." She stared at him as if he'd just told her that he'd returned from a little jaunt to Mars.

"Something wrong with a guy getting himself a dog?"

"Nothing at all." She patted his cheek and with hips swaying, walked over to where he'd left the mutt, who began wildly wagging her tail.

"Oh, she's darling!"

"She's a mess, is what she is."

Desiree bent down to pat the dog, giving Jack an appealing view of her shapely ass. "She just needs a bath. Don't you, darlin'?"

The dog, thrilled to pieces to be noticed, did what Jack figured just about every guy in the No Name would give his left nut to do: She licked the lush swell of Desiree's fragrant breasts.

Desiree laughed merrily, scratched the mutt's ears and, if the wild metronome swing of the dog's tail was any indication, sent her into ecstasy. Desiree kissed the end of the brown nose, then turned back to Jack. "What's her name?" she asked as she returned to the Porsche with the dog.

"I haven't a clue. And I'm not about to give her one 'cause she isn't going to be staying with me."

"Sure, darlin'. That's why you're taking her for boat rides."

"I was gonna take her to the shelter, but got caught up with work and didn't get into town in time to drop her off 'fore it closed."

"Whatever you say." She patted his cheek. "You know, it's good you found her. After all, a dog's supposed to be a man's best friend."

"I'm not in the market for any new friends."

She shook her head. "You can pretend all you want, Jack, but we go back too far for you to be fooling me with that heart-of-stone bullshit." She clicked the remote, standing back as Jack opened her door. "You rescued that dog the same way you rescued me from my son-of-a-bitch stepdaddy back when I was still a girl."

She slid into the driver's seat, turned the key, and brought the powerful engine to roaring life. "Climb on in, darlin'. There's not a lot of room, but your doggie can squeeze in back."

She was speeding out of the lot before Jack had a chance to tell her yet again that the mudball mutt was not *his* dog.

4

Less than twenty minutes after arriving in town, with her son in Orèlia's competent care, Dani was sitting with Nate in a room that had served as the late Dr. Vallois's office. Like the rest of the rooms she'd glanced into coming down the hallway, it reminded her of Aladdin's magic cave.

There was barely enough room to move around in and seemingly less room to breathe. Pretty, delicate little English porcelain boxes shared crowded tabletops with plastic tourist alligators, candles of various shapes, and tacky souvenirs from all over the world.

The cypress-paneled walls were lined with shelves boasting an eclectic collection of books that ranged from worn leather-bound classics to the latest true-crime paperback. It was, she thought, skimming a glance over the spines, a marvelous collection. It was also in desperate need of cataloging.

Dani loved order. Ordinal order, cardinal order, alphabetical order, the world just made more sense when it was logically arranged. Lowell had often accused her of using the Dewey decimal system to organize her underwear. It was an exaggeration. But not by much.

"It's really great to have you back home again, Dani. Motherhood obviously agrees with you."

Nate earned Dani's gratitude for not appearing to notice that she undoubtedly looked like a bedraggled stray cat. She could smell the stench of smoke in her hair and clothes.

"It does. It's the most fulfilling thing I've ever done."

"Since I know you're temporarily strapped for cash, I want to assure you that the parish council will pay your salary even though you probably won't be able to open the library for a while."

"That's very generous."

"Hey, you left your home to come to work here. That fire puttin' a crimp in the timing certainly isn't your fault."

"I appreciate the salary, because, quite honestly, as I told you on the phone, I need it." She absently shifted a carved wooden giraffe across the table next to the matching lion. "But surely it won't take very long to repair the apartment. Since you're a contractor, you must know all the workmen around here. If you'll give me some names, I can start calling around first thing in the morning."

Silence descended, like a stone falling into a deep dark well. "Nate?"

"It might be a problem finding someone to do the work, *chère*. Since nearly every carpenter, painter, electrician, and plumber in the parish is working on Beau Soleil."

"Beau Soleil?"

Dani had assured herself that she'd gotten over the loss of her family home. If the way her mouth had gone dry was any indication, she'd been fooling herself.

"Hell, Dani, I'm sorry. I figured you knew. After all, you signed the sales contract."

"Sales contract?" Needing something to do with her hands, she began straightening the magazines spread across the old mariner's chest in front of her. "Beau Soleil wasn't sold. My father lost it to taxes after he went to prison."

The idea of her father as a common felon was still hard to contemplate and even more difficult to say out loud.

Nate tilted his head and narrowed his eyes, clearly puzzled. "It looked as if he was going to lose it to back taxes. Then he deeded it over to you and Lowell."

"He did what?"

Seeming to read the shock Dani suspected must be written across her face, he poured a glass of tea from a ceramic rooster pitcher Orèlia had brought in when they'd first arrived, and held it out to her.

"I don't understand." She took a sip of the tea and tried to steady her mind, which was spinning like the old Tilt-A-Whirl she used to ride on the midway during the annual Cajun Days festival. "How could Lowell own Beau Soleil without me knowing about it?"

"Beats me." Dani hated the pity she thought she saw in his eyes.

"My guess would be he didn't believe you'd be wild about him sellin' it to the Maggione family."

"The same people my father went to prison for taking bribes from?"

Despite his hard-line legal stands, her father had always been an advocate of legalized gambling. After all, Andre Dupree had won Beau Soleil in a *bourré* game before the War Between the States. Still, Dani would never believe that her father had taken money to cast his parish council vote in favor of a casino run by one of New Orleans's most infamous mobsters.

"That's them. Though, for the record, I never believed your daddy took that bribe."

"Obviously the grand jury that indicted him didn't see it that way," Dani said dryly. It still hurt. Even after all these years. "Why would the Maggione family want Beau Soleil?"

"They figured it'd make a good centerpiece for their casino project."

"Are you telling me that it's been turned into a casino?"

Dani hated imagining the home she'd grown up in filled with roulette tables with clouds of cigarette and cigar smoke staining the ceiling murals. The idea of the discordant jangle of slot machines drowning out the angel fountain in the courtyard was a nightmare.

"No. Before the sale closed, the family got busted by the Justice Department for some money-laundering scheme. Then Papa Joe died, and the family splintered into different factions. By the time they were ready to try to set up shop here, someone else outbid them."

"When was that?"

"Last year."

"Last year?" Grateful she was sitting down, Dani took another, longer drink of tea.

"People around here figured, when your husband showed up with that quit-claim deed you'd signed and put the place on the market, that it must've been part of a property settlement deal the two of you had agreed upon."

"It certainly wasn't anything of the sort. And I never signed a thing."

Dani had suspected Lowell had skimmed the legal boundaries of campaign financing laws. She'd known he was an adulterer and, unfortunately, had possessed all the paternal instincts of a tom cat.

But to discover that he'd stolen her home out from under her was staggering!

"Who bought it?"

Obviously uncomfortable, he frowned down at his hands. "Nate?" She placed a hand on his arm. "Who bought Beau Soleil?"

"Aw, hell, Dani. I hate being the one to tell you this." He hitched in a noticeable breath. "Jack bought it."

"Jack?" The blood drained from her face. Drop by drop.

My Jack? she thought but did not say.

"Yeah." His eyes narrowed. "Are you okay? You've gone dead white."

"I'm fine." That was a lie. She drew in a deep breath that was meant to calm. But didn't. "It's just that . . ." Her voice broke, forcing her to try again. "Well, it's certainly a surprise."

"He's doin' some great work on the restoration." He was studying her carefully. As if, Dani thought, he feared she might shatter into pieces at any moment.

"Isn't that nice?" If she didn't get out of here now, this horrible smile was going to freeze onto her face. "As much as I'd love to hear all about them, I really do need to see how Matt's getting along. It's been a long trip and an eventful day."

"Sure. I really am glad you've come back, Dani. You've been missed."

"I missed you, too." That much, at least, was the truth. Ordering her legs to support her, Dani stood up. "More than I can say. You've no idea how much I appreciate you giving me this job. You saved my life."

"It's you who've saved mine. To tell you the truth, Mrs. Weaver didn't exactly retire. I fired her." He shook his head. "It wasn't that she didn't work damn hard, 'cause she did, but she just didn't have the people skills necessary to run a library."

Dani wasn't particularly surprised Agate Weaver had been fired. The woman who'd been as hard as her name, had stomped around in heavy, sensible shoes, had pulled her hair back into a face-tightening bun, and was constantly shushing anyone who dared speak in the hallowed halls of the library. She was the quintessential stereotypical librarian, the only one Dani had ever actually encountered.

"Well, I'll try to do better."

"A gator on a bad day could do better than that woman. Drove me nuts how she was all the time telling the young readers' groups about me losing that Horatio Hornblower book back in sixth grade. Which wouldn't have been so bad, since at least it showed the kids that we can all screw up, and go on to live productive lives, but she was becomin' more and more difficult to deal with professionally.

"The parish council had a knock-down, drag-out battle with her when she initially refused to have the Harry Potter books in the library because she said they were nothing more than pagan propaganda designed to lead innocent children into witchcraft. I also hated the way she'd decide whether or not to waive late fees depending on how she personally felt about a person, but the last straw was when she decided not to let Haley Villard take any books home because of the cockamamie idea that since the Villards grew peppers, the books might get pepper residue on the pages and blind some other kid who might pick up the dried pepper from the paper, then rub his eyes."

"Well, that's certainly a unique concern." Despite all her problems, Dani was beginning to feel better. Nate had always had that effect on her, which had her wishing, just for a moment, that she could have fallen in love with him instead of his brother.

"How about having dinner tomorrow night? We can catch up."

Was he asking her out on a date? This was definitely not the time to go jumping into the dating pool, especially with a man who'd charmed most of south Louisiana's women between the ages of eight and eighty. Before he was out of his teens.

No, when it came to men and relationships, Nate Callahan, as nice as he was, was definitely out of her league.

"Oh, Nate, I've love to, but I'm going to be so busy, what with this problem with the library, then there's Matt to worry about—"

"Bring him along."

Relief. He wasn't talking about a date. "Can I have a raincheck until I get Dad settled in with us?"

"Sure. The judge can come, too. It'll do him good to get out and around again after all this time away. You know, it's a real nice thing you're doing, movin' him in with you."

"He's my father," she said simply. "I hope the apartment will be finished by the time he's released. You'll have to come visit."

"It'll be great to see him. Jack says he's looking forward to gettin' sprung."

"Jack?"

"Damn. This seems to be my day for screwing up."

"Don't worry about it," she murmured through her hurt. "Obviously it's my day for surprises."

Jack was living in Beau Soleil. Jack had been visiting her father, the same man who'd sentenced the son of his housekeeper to a boot camp for delinquents and forbidden Dani to have anything to do with him after he'd been released.

What on earth did they find to talk about? Did they ever talk about that summer Jack had returned home? And more important, if so, what had her father told him about those months after he'd taken off again?

There was a roaring in her head like the sound of the sea, making it difficult to concentrate. She wrapped her arms around herself and tried to believe the icy air blowing through the wall vents was the reason she was chilled to the bone.

Nate gave her a quick peck on the cheek. "I'll set up a meeting with the fire marshal for tomorrow so we can see what we're going to need to do to get the library up and running again and the apartment fixed."

"I'd appreciate that," she heard herself say.

"I'm spendin' most of my time lately out at Beau Soleil, but how about we shoot for afternoon? About two?"

"That'll be fine. It'll allow me to enroll Matt in his new school in the morning."

Dani managed one final smile and walked him out to his SUV, then returned to the house. She closed the heavy oak and etched-glass door, leaned back against it, shut her eyes, and assured herself that Jack being back in Blue Bayou, even living in her old home, had nothing to do with her.

She told herself that again as she entered the homey kitchen. But when she sat down at the table beside Matt and dutifully expressed delight over the bounty Orèlia had prepared, Dani wondered miserably when she'd become such a liar.

"Don't worry, sugar," Desiree soothed as she ran a hand down Jack's bare chest. "It happens to every guy sooner or later."

"Not to me." Christ. What the hell was the matter with him? He hadn't had that much to drink. Yet. And God knows, Desiree had certainly done her part.

She hadn't bothered with preliminaries. They knew each other too well to need them. As soon as he'd entered her house, she'd pressed herself against him, her nipples diamond hard against his chest, and kissed him with the smooth and clever tongue action she'd always been so good at.

Enjoying the slap of lust, Jack had swept her up and carried her up the Caroline staircase.

The bedroom, which, rather than the stereotypical velvet and gaudy gilt one might think a former New Orleans call girl might favor, was a sea of soothing white. As soon as they entered the room, she'd turned to face him and with her eyes on his, slowly untied the silk sash at the waist of the dress and let it slide down her lush body to where it pooled at her feet on the snowy carpet.

Beneath the robe she'd been wearing a skimpy bra and a matching pair of thong bikini panties so brief Jack had wondered why she even bothered with them. The scarlet lace added another splash of hot color to the cool white decor.

He'd watched, appreciating the view, as she went around, lighting a collection of fragrant beeswax candles.

"I truly have missed you, Jack," she'd murmured once the room was glowing with a warm light.

She'd slipped out of the lace bra, revealing lush, round breasts he knew from their teenage days to be her own.

"Let me show you how much." Engulfing him in a fragrant cloud of the white roses she had specially blended at a shop in New Orleans's French Quarter, she'd run her palm down the front of his jeans, stroking his rock-hard erection.

His entire nervous system had been aroused. Expectant.

"Oh, yes," she'd murmured. Her smiling eyes had echoed the licentious approval in her throaty tone. "This is going to be a very good night."

She'd drawn back the satin comforter and turned on the stereo. But before she could switch it to CD mode, a newsflash broke into the country radio station.

Jack's blood had instantly chilled at the news of a fire at the library where Nate had told him Dani would be living with her son. His erection had deflated like a three-day-old balloon and remained that way, even after he'd learned no one had been in the building when the fire had broken out.

Desiree had certainly done her part to turn things around. Pretending not to notice, she'd unzipped his jeans, pulled them down his legs, then retraced the path with sharp, stinging kisses designed to make any man rock hard.

She'd nibbled at his thighs; blown a warm breath against the front of his white cotton briefs. Then, with a clever practiced touch, she'd released his still-flaccid cock from the placket of the briefs.

They'd fallen onto the bed, rolled around on Egyptian cotton sheets that felt like silk and probably cost as much as Jack's first car. She'd murmured hot sexual suggestions. Things she wanted him to do to her, things she planned to do to him.

But even when her ripe red lips replaced her stroking touch, his mutinous body had refused to cooperate.

"Don't worry about it," she repeated now.

She touched her lips to his, this kiss meant to soothe rather than arouse, then climbed out of bed and walked across the sea of white carpet. Her tousled hair fell halfway down her back; her bare ass was high and firm and appealing. But Jack didn't need to lift the sheet to know that even that seductive sight wasn't working tonight.

She didn't bother closing the bathroom door. When he heard the sound of water running into the tub, Jack dragged his hands down his face. The unpalatable fact was that he was a lost cause and the more she tried, the worse things were going to get.

"Jack, darlin'?"

"Yeah?" He sighed. Glared down at the offending body part, which continued to defy him.

She returned wearing a short white robe that clung in all the right places. "Why don't you get your dog?"

"The dog?" This was the last damn thing he'd been expecting. "Why?"

"Because we're going to give the sweet thing a bubble bath."

Two hours later, with the mutt smelling like a high-class brothel, Jack was sitting in the kitchen, eating his way through a steak Desiree had grilled and ignoring the bits of meat she kept slipping the dog beneath the table.

The mood was relaxed, even comfortable, and as he filled her in on Beau Soleil's progress, and his new book, Jack almost managed to convince himself that tonight's problem had everything to do with overwork and nothing to do with Danielle.

5

She couldn't sleep. Somewhere before dawn, after tossing and turning all night, Dani crawled from her rumpled bed and slipped out of the house. She sat out on the porch, looked out over the still, darkened bayou in the direction of Beau Soleil and wondered if she'd made a mistake coming home to Blue Bayou after all these years.

She'd thought she'd put the past behind her, believed she'd moved beyond the feelings of pain and loss. Oh, granted, every April when she'd write another birthday letter to the daughter who'd never read any of them, she'd sink into a depression that could last the entire month, but she'd always been able to hide it from her husband, her child, and the other librarians she worked with, and eventually it would pass.

But while she'd been lying alone in that single bed in Orèlia's guest room, staring out the window, she'd found herself thinking back to other nights spent looking out another window, hoping against hope that Jack would come and take her away. Bygone scenes had flashed through Dani's mind, forcing her to consider the idea that she may have been fooling herself all these years.

She'd certainly been in deep denial after Jack had disappeared from her life. Despite the fact that the only sex education she'd ever received had been a short vague film about menstruation shown in her seventh grade all-girls gym class, Dani had done enough research on her own at the library to know exactly how unprotected sex could lead to pregnancy. But Jack had been so careful to protect her, always using a condom, she'd never thought it could happen to her.

"Famous last words," she murmured now with a touch of bitter-sweet affection toward that naive and foolish seventeen-year-old girl she'd once been. Even after the condom had broken the last time they'd made love together the night before he'd left town, she'd been quick to assure Jack that it was a safe time of the month for her, even though she'd known otherwise. But surely you couldn't get pregnant from just one slip, and besides, a secret part of herself actually hoped she *would* get pregnant. Then she could move out of her father's house, and she and Jack could get married.

Then she began to throw up, not just in the mornings, but all during the day and evening as well, but having begun to realize that Jack really wasn't coming back, she'd pretended to herself that it would all go away.

One Saturday afternoon, three months to the day after Jack had last made love to her, Dani had taken the bus to New Orleans, where, with a dry mouth and sweaty hands, she'd bought a self-test pregnancy kit at a French Quarter drugstore. Since the instructions had said the test had to be taken in the morning, she'd had to sneak the white paper pharmacy bag into the house, hiding it in the closet behind her shoe rack, as if her father might actually suddenly decide to search her room.

The sad truth had been he would have been more likely to have flown to the moon on gossamer wings than enter her bedroom for any reason. As far as she could tell, most of the time she was invisible to her father, and on those rare occasions when he *would* acknowledge her presence, she seemed more annoyance than daughter.

Time had crawled with nerve-racking slowness while she'd waited for the test results, which, as she'd begun to fear, had proven positive. She'd known she wasn't going to be able to hide her pregnancy forever, but that didn't stop her from being paralyzed by the fear of what would happen when the judge discovered her shameful secret.

Dani had continued to live her lie for another two agonizing weeks, pretending everything was normal, while she felt as if she was dying inside, until finally Marie Callahan, of all people, guessed the truth and dragged her into kindly Dr. Vallois's office, where he'd confirmed what she'd already determined for herself. She was going to have a baby. Jack's baby.

With the clarity of hindsight, Dani realized that Marie must have been as stricken as she herself had been, but the Dupree housekeeper and grandmother of Dani's unborn child had nevertheless literally stood beside her as, with sweating palms and pounding heart, she'd haltingly confessed the truth to an icily cold father.

The night before she'd broken the news of her pregnancy, instead of Jack returning on his own, she'd dreamed that her father would immediately leap to her aid and track Jack down, wherever he was, and insist he married her. He would, of course, belatedly realize exactly how much he loved her, apologize for having caused her so much pain, then, just like her earlier rosy scenario, they'd live happily ever after.

The reality proved far different from the fantasy.

With the same efficiency he'd always demonstrated in his courtroom, Judge Dupree made a series of phone calls and within minutes had found Dani a place to live for the remainder of her pregnancy. Devastated and emotionally overwrought from months of bottling up so much stress, she'd tearfully begged to be allowed to stay at home.

But her father had remained adamant, and two days after her decidedly unwelcome revelation, Marie had driven her to Atlanta and helped her move into a Catholic home for unwed mothers, where the homily at Sunday mass inevitably focused on the biblical story of King Solomon, where the real mother was willing to surrender her child rather than see it cut in two.

A soft shimmering light began to glow on the horizon. Somewhere in the bayou morning birds began to trill, and across the street Chief Petty Officer Daniel Cahouet greeted the new day by standing on his front lawn and playing an off-key rendition of Reveille on his trumpet as he'd been doing every morning since returning home from the Pacific at the end of World War II.

Brushing the tears from her cheeks, Dani stood up and went back into the house to get ready to face what she feared was going to be a very trying day.

"So how bad is the library?" Jack asked as he hammered a piece of crown molding onto the newly plastered wall.

The molding Nate had hand-tooled looked good. Better than good, it had turned out goddamn great. You couldn't tell where the original stuff left off and the new began. It was times like this when Jack allowed himself to feel optimistic about ever restoring the plantation house to its former glory.

"Not as bad as it looked last night." Nate lifted another strip of molding onto a pair of sawhorses. "I couldn't do a full walk-through because the windows were boarded up and a lot of the third floor was blocked off, but from what the fire marshal told me, if we can free up a couple guys from here, and I split my week between the two projects, we could probably get the place livable in a couple months. Less the time it takes for permits."

From his perch atop the sixteen-foot-tall ladder, Jack could see across the bayou where the mist was beginning to rise. His head was clear this morning. Too clear for comfort. It had him remembering things he didn't want to remember. Thinking thoughts he didn't want to think.

"She looks good," Nate volunteered. "A little on the slender side, perhaps, which could just be some female fashion thing. And tired, which is to be expected, after driving down from Virginia. But she still looks damn fine."

Jack drove in another nail. "I don't remember asking how she looked."

"I know. I figured I'd save you the trouble of tryin' to figure out how to slide it into the conversation while pretending you didn't care."

Jack swore, then swung the hammer with more force than necessary, risking denting the millwork. "Her husband was a damn fool."

"It gets worse." The saw screeched as it sliced through the wood, sending sawdust flying. "Turns out she didn't know you'd bought this place."

Jack looked down at him. "You're fuckin' kidding."

"Nope. Hell, she didn't even know they'd owned it all these past years. The guy must've forged her signature on the papers."

"He wasn't just a fool, he was a goddamn son of a bitch."

The force of Jack's voice had the dog, who'd been sprawled in a morning sunbeam, glance up, her expression wary.

Terrific. Now he was scaring dogs. Maybe when he finished up here for the day he could drive into town, drop by the kindergarten, and terrorize little kids.

He climbed down the ladder, reached into an orange bag, and tossed the mutt a Frito. She snatched the corn chip from the air and swallowed it without bothering to chew. Her anxiety sufficiently eased, she sighed, stretched, and settled back to sleep.

"Too bad we didn't know about this before," Jack muttered. "Finn's in D.C. We could have him shoot the bastard."

"Yeah, that's a real good idea. The Mounties might have Dudley Do-Right, but the FBI has Finn Callahan. Not only does our big brother probably not jaywalk, I'd be willin' to bet he doesn't even piss in the shower."

"Good point." Of the three Callahan brothers, Finn was the most like their father. Although only a few years older, he'd also served as their surrogate father after Jake Callahan had been killed in the line of duty.

Nate moved the molding to the miter saw. "Dani's lucky to be rid of the guy even if she does have to keep a lot of plates spinning these days, what with the new job, getting her son settled into a new place, and bringing the judge home from Angola."

"Unfortunately, that isn't the half of it."

"You know something I don't?"

"Other than the fact that fire could have been arson, which could put her and her kid at risk if the arsonist decides to try again?"

"What makes you think it was arson? It's an old building. I made sure the electrical was up to code before I invited her to stay there, but there's always a chance something external, like lightning, sparked that fire."

"Sure, there's a chance," Jack allowed. "But don't you find it a little interesting that the place the judge will be coming home to in a couple weeks just happened to nearly burn to the ground?"

"He's done his time. Why would anyone want to keep him from coming home?"

"If you were the guy who framed him, would you want him livin' in your backyard?"

"You still think he didn't do it?"

"I know he didn't."

"Because he told you."

"Yeah. The judge may be one hard-assed son of a bitch, who's undoubtedly earned his share of enemies during his lifetime, but he's honest to the core. He wouldn't have taken a bribe to save his soul."

"Well, the jury didn't see it that way. And he sure didn't contribute anything to his own defense."

"So I heard." Jack wondered if things might have gone down differently if he'd been living in Blue Bayou seven years ago.

"And now there's another problem?"

"Yeah."

"If you and the judge are thinkin' about playing detective and gettin' involved with the mob to try to prove his innocence, I need to know. As mayor, it's my job to keep the peace."

"Technically that's the sheriff's job."

"Then run for sheriff and we'll have someone who'll do that."

"I told you, I've gotten out of the crime-busting business."

And Jack wasn't one to break a confidence, not even to one of the three people in the world he trusted, his brother Finn and Alcèe being the other two. Unfortunately, the judge had specifically instructed him to keep their conversation to himself.

"Look, I can't talk about why, and it doesn't have anything to do with that old case, but stalling work on that apartment so Danielle will have to stay with Orèlia instead of movin' right into the apartment with the judge would be the best thing you could do for her right now."

"That's not gonna be easy. She's a smart lady; she might accept some initial delays, but I'll need some reason to drag it out."

"Blame me." Jack pounded in two more nails, then jammed the hammer through the leather loop of his tool belt. "Tell her I'm a hard-driving son of a bitch who's holding you to a legally binding schedule and you can't afford any late fees."

"She'd never believe that. You're my brother."

"Trust me. She'll believe the worst."

Nate exhaled a slow, soft whistle. "That won't win you any points, Jack."

"I'm not looking for points." Jack pulled a cigarette from his pocket and jammed it between his lips. "I'm also not looking to get involved in her life. Which, as you pointed out, is already messy enough."

"She's gonna to be furious," Nate warned.

Jack's only response was a negligent shrug, even as the idea of causing Danielle any more pain scraped him raw.

"It must be one helluva secret."

"Yeah." Jack blew out a stream of smoke. "It goddamn is."

He hadn't been quite honest with his brother. The fact was that years fighting the bad guys had made him suspicious of any coincidences. Such as the apartment over the library suddenly catching fire on the very day Danielle Dupree arrived to set up housekeeping for herself, her kid, and her father, Maximum Dupree, who'd certainly sent more than his share of criminals up the river.

But even if Jack's internal radar hadn't gone off the screen when he'd heard about the fire, there was another problem lurking in the wings. One Danielle couldn't be expecting.

He damned the judge for not being up front with her about his health problems from the beginning. Hell, refusing to have any contact with her all these years while he'd been in prison had been unnecessarily cruel, but keeping a secret like this, when who knew how much time they might have together, was even worse.

Oh, he'd claimed he'd been avoiding any contact with her all these years to protect her and her kid from the pain of scandal, but since she'd already suffered enough of that from her lying, cheating husband, Jack suspected it was more a case of the judge's damn stiff pride. And shame. Not only for whatever had landed him in prison, but possibly just perhaps he was feeling guilty about having run his daughter's lover out of town so many years ago.

Jack had already put that in the past. And even if he hadn't, if those prison doctors had gotten the diagnosis right, the judge should be concentrating on forging some sort of paternal relationship with Danielle before it was too late.

Jack had long ago decided that if he'd had a teenage daughter, he damn well wouldn't have wanted her running around with the wild kid he'd been back then. But if the judge had truly cared about what happened to Danielle, he wouldn't have pushed her into marrying that slick politician who, until the breakup of his outwardly perfect marriage and death, had seemed to be on a fast track to the White House.

She'd deserved better than Louisiana congressman Lowell Dupree. And she sure as hell deserved better than him.

6

What do you mean I can't open the library until the work's completed on the apartment?" Dani asked the Blue Bayou fire marshal.

It had been three days since she'd arrived to find her new home in flames. Three very long and frustrating days spent waiting for this man to complete his inspection.

"The third floor is admittedly a mess," she conceded. "But the only thing wrong with the lower floors is some water damage I can take care of myself."

"The other floors appear okay," he allowed. "But the thing is, what you've got yourself here, Miz Dupree, is a hazardous situation. You're gonna have construction crews working with dangerous equipment, carrying ladders around, there'll be hot electrical wires hangin' loose, all sorts of stuff that could endanger innocent citizens."

He chewed on a short, fat unlit cigar and looked around the building, as if picturing the possible chaos. "Nope. Can't risk it."

Since she'd eventually need this frustratingly little man's signature on the final inspection report, Dani managed, just barely, to rein in her building temper.

"It's not as bad as it sounds." He appeared almost sympathetic for the first time since he'd climbed out of his red pickup truck. "Once you get your construction permits, it shouldn't take long to get things fixed up just fine. Better than ever, in fact, since you'll be upgrading the electrical, which should save you from any more unpleasant surprises."

Dani only wished life were that simple. "When will the permits be ready?"

"Oh, I wouldn't know 'bout that." He shrugged and closed his metal clipboard, his work here obviously finished. "You and your contractor—"

"My contractor is Nate Callahan. The *mayor* of Blue Bayou." Surely stressing Nate's position in the town hierarchy might help all those stacks of paperwork she'd had to fill out move through the grindingly slow parish governmental system a bit faster?

"So I heard. Well, anyway, you'll both need to appear at the monthly zoning commission meeting and request a variance if you're planing to live above the library."

"But the apartment's been part of the building for decades."

"Not anymore. It burned up," he reminded her. "Which makes it uninhabitable. A former commission grandfathered the original apartment in, allowing a dwelling in a commercial structure. But as it stands now, you're not zoned residential."

Dani fought the urge to grind her teeth. "Do you expect that to be a problem?"

He shrugged. Adjusted his red-billed cap. "It's not my job to say one way or the other. But, if I were a gambling man, I'd say you should get your permits. Sooner or later."

"When is this meeting?"

"Just had one last week. Settled a little dispute about some private boat docks and allowed Miss Bea's Tea House to serve lunch outside on the building's *gallerie*.

"So"— he chomped on the cigar as he checked a calendar on his clipboard—"that'd put the next one three weeks from yesterday."

"Three weeks?"

"Sorry. It's not—"

"Your job," Dani said dryly.

"No, ma'am. I'm afraid it's not."

Wishing her good luck, he pasted a fluorescent-yellow notice warning that her library was Hazardous and Unsafe for Occupation on the front door, then ambled back to his truck.

"I will get the permits," Dani muttered to herself as she drove to the parish offices in order to attempt to coax the planning and zoning commission secretary into scheduling a special meeting so she wouldn't have to wait another three weeks.

She was on a mission, and although it might be stretching comparisons, she was beginning to understand Scarlett O'Hara's determination when she'd yanked up those turnips.

"She had to save Tara." Thanks to her husband and father, Dani no longer had a huge antebellum plantation house to worry about. "All you have to do is fix up a two-bedroom apartment for your family."

How difficult could that be? This might be the New South, but some things never changed. The ability of a southern woman to survive was as strong in her as it had been in her great-grandmother Lurleen, who'd worked her fingers to bleeding as a dressmaker in order to pay off her husband's gambling debts and save Beau Soleil from those New York Yankee bankers.

Dani refused to complain or whine. She'd win her case before the zoning board. But first, she decided, as she parked in front of Paula's Pralines, she'd pick up a pretty gilt-wrapped box of candy for the zoning commissioner's secretary.

Three days later Dani's vow not to complain had flown out the window.

"I don't understand why the man can't pick up the damn phone," she muttered as she slammed the telephone receiver back in its cradle. "It's not like I'm going to insist he return my home. I just want a carpenter."

After blatantly bribing the secretary with those pralines, two tickets to the Dixie Chicks Baton Rouge concert, and a promise to put the woman's name at the top of the reserve list for the next Jack Callahan novel, Dani had gotten her permits. Which wouldn't do her a bit of good unless she could find someone to do the work.

Oh, Nate had been apologetic. Sympathetic. Even remorseful. But the fact remained that not only was Jack Callahan living in her house, he was standing in the way of her making a new home for her son.

"Perhaps he's all caught up in writing his new book," Orèlia suggested.

"Well, he's got to stop to eat." Dani threw her body onto a chair and snatched a piece of raisin toast from the plate in the center of the table. "Why can't he check his messages, then?"

It stung that Jack was ignoring her. But she'd worn down his defenses that summer. She'd just have to keep trying. After all, the stakes were so much higher this time. Back then she'd only risked her heart. Now the future of her family was at stake.

Dani liked Orèlia a great deal, and enjoyed the older woman's company. And it was, admittedly, a huge help not to have to worry about finding someone to stay with Matt after school while she was fighting her battles with the town bureaucrats and dealing with the million and one moving details. But they needed their own space. Space where Matt could be a normal little boy, free to run through the rooms without worrying about knocking some valued collectible off a table.

The apartment was a good stop-gap measure, until she got her debts paid off, but eventually Dani intended to buy her own home, with a big backyard for a swing set and a tree house.

With a renewed burst of optimism, as she absently centered the napkin holder and salt and pepper shakers, Dani thought that once they were permanently settled, perhaps she'd buy a few plants and take up gardening.

The series of storied terraces surrounding the swimming pool at her former Fairfax house may have won a prestigious national landscape design award and been featured in *Southern Living* magazine, but Dani hadn't been allowed to work in the garden for fear she might disturb the intricately planned design.

As for the lovely furniture that had been in her family for generations, furniture she'd taken from Beau Soleil when she'd married, she'd ending up selling that at a staggering loss to help pay off the enormous attorney bills the divorce had racked up.

Galling was the fact that she'd had to end up paying a major portion of Lowell's lawyer's fees as well as her own.

"*T'en fais pas, chérie,*" Orèlia said when Dani sighed again.

"I'm not worried." She would not allow herself to be. "Just frustrated."

As she rinsed off the empty plate and put it in the dishwasher, Dani wondered, yet again, where the hell Jack was hiding.

The phone was ringing, as it had been for the past two days. The dog quirked an ear that had been torn in some previous fight and looked questioningly up at Jack. When he didn't appear inclined to do anything about it, she lowered her head to her front paws and went back to sleep.

Jack turned off the belt sander he'd been using on the wainscoting and waited for the machine to pick up.

"Jack?"

Her voice, which as hard as he'd tried, he'd never been able to get out of his mind—or, dammit, his dreams—hadn't changed. It was cultured and touched with the soft cadence of the bayou South.

The first three times she'd called, he'd thought he'd detected a bit of nervousness; this time it was definitely irritation lacing those smooth magnolia tones.

"Dammit, Jack, are you there?"

Silence.

He heard a muttered, brief, pungent curse. The receiver on the other end of the line was slammed down. Jack hit the switch on the sander and went back to work.

7

The sky was darkening, the only visible light a band of purple clouds low on the western horizon. Dani had forgotten how quickly night came to the bayou. As she steered the rented boat through the maze-like labyrinth of waterways, fireflies lit up the waning twilight while nutria and muskrats paddled along, furry shadows in waters as dark and murky as Cajun coffee.

Bullfrogs began to croak; cicadas buzzed; blue herons glided among the ancient cypress which stood like silent, moss-bearded sentinels over their watery world.

The boat's light barely cut through the warm mist falling from low-hanging clouds; when the ridged and knobby head of an alligator appeared in the stuttering glow, looking like a wet brown rock amidst the lily pads, Dani's nerves, which were already as tattered as a Confederate soldier's gray uniform, screeched.

"This is nuts."

If she had any sense at all, she'd cut her losses now and return to town. But she'd already come this far, and unless both her internal homing device and the boat's GPS system had gone entirely on the blink, she couldn't be that far from Beau Soleil.

She checked her watch. Despite the way the isolation and deepening shadows had seemed to slow time, she'd been out on the water for less than half an hour.

"Five more minutes," she decided. If she hadn't reached Beau Soleil by then, she'd turn back.

A moment later she came around a corner, and there, right in front of her, was the Greek Revival antebellum mansion. Dani was glad she'd undertaken the nerve-racking trip tonight; as bad as the plantation house appeared, it would have been far worse to first see it again after all these years in the hard, unforgiving glare of southern sunlight.

The double front entrance harkened back to a time when if a suitor happened to catch a glimpse of a girl's ankles, he was duty bound to marry her. In a typically southern blend of practicality and romance, the house had been designed with dual sets of front steps—one for hoop-skirted belles, the other for their gentlemen escorts. The ladies' staircase had crumbled nearly to dust; the other was scarcely better, held up as it was with a complex design of erector-set-style metal braces.

Beau Soleil had survived being set on fire by the British in the War of 1812, cannonballed, then occupied by Yankee soldiers—and their horses—during the War Between the States. It had also stalwartly stood up to numerous hurricanes over its more than two centuries. Seeing the once noble plantation house looking like an aging whore from some seedy south Louisiana brothel made Dani want to weep.

It had belatedly dawned on her, after she'd left town, that her plan to catch Jack unaware could backfire if she came all the way out here only to find the house dark and deserted. But she'd been so frustrated that she'd acted without really thinking things through.

The light in the upstairs windows of the once stately house was an encouraging sign as she eased the boat up to the dock that was still, thankfully, standing. It appeared to be the same dock her father had paid Jack to build the summer of her seventeenth birthday, the summer her carefree, youthful world had spun out of control.

With a long-ago learned skill some distant part of her mind had retained, she tied up the boat behind an old pirogue and then studied the house. Amazingly, most of the centuries-old oak trees had survived time and the ravages of storms; silvery Spanish moss draped over their limbs like discarded feather boas left behind by ghostly belles.

She lifted her gaze to a darkened window on the second floor and envisioned the reckless teenager she'd once been, climbing out that window to meet her lover. Her skin, beneath her white T-shirt, burned with the memory of Jack's dark, work-roughened fingers encircling her waist to lift her down from that last low-hanging limb.

"A smart *fille* like yourself should know better than to sneak up on someone at night in this part of the country," a deep, painfully familiar voice offered from the blackness surrounding her.

Dani yelped. Then hated herself for displaying any weakness. Splaying a palm against her chest to slow her tripping heart, she turned slowly toward the *gallerie*.

He was hidden in the shadows, like a ghost from the past, with only the red flare of a cigarette revealing his location.

"You could have said something. Instead of scaring me to half to death."

"If I figured you and I had anything to say to each other, I would have returned your calls." His voice was even huskier than Dani remembered. Huskier and decidedly uninviting.

"So you did get my messages."

"Yeah. I got 'em." Although night had dropped over the bayou, there was enough light shining from the windows of Beau Soleil for her to see him. He was wearing a gray Ragin' Cajun T-shirt with the sleeves cut off, a pair of jeans worn nearly to the point of indecency and cowboy boots. He was rugged, rangy, and, dammit, still as sexy as hell.

"But you chose to ignore them."

He took a swig from a longneck bottle of Dixie beer. "Yeah."

Well, this was going well. "I happen to know your mother taught you better manners."

"I was never known for my manners. Drove *Maman* nuts."

That was certainly true. He'd been known throughout the bayou as Bad Jack Callahan. A devil in blue jeans with the face of a fallen angel.

"I was sorry when she died."

Unlike so many of the large sprawling Catholic families who made the bayou their home, Dani had no brothers or sisters, nieces or nephews, aunts, uncles, or cousins. After her mother had abandoned them before Dani's second birthday (subsequently dying two years later), there had only been her and her father, and while single fathers may have been a staple on television, her own had left her upbringing to a revolving parade of housekeepers.

And then had come that fateful day when, after the shooting that had tragically claimed her husband's life, Marie Callahan had shown up at the house, her three teenage sons in tow. Marie had quickly stepped into the role of surrogate mother; she'd baked Dani birthday cakes, taken her shopping for her first box of tampons, and soothed her wounded pride when an attack of nerves had her failing her driver's test the first time.

Of course, Marie had also sided with her employer against the two teenagers that bittersweet summer that still, after all these years, lingered in Dani's mind like a dream remembered upon awakening.

When she'd died, too young, of breast cancer, Dani had swallowed her pride and sent Jack a handwritten note of sympathy. He never responded. Nor did he return home for his mother's funeral, something that surprised even his most stalwart detractors, who'd reluctantly admitted that despite his wild devilish ways, Jack Callahan had always been good to his *maman*.

"Yeah. I was damn sorry, too." He sighed heavily as he flicked away the cigarette, which flared in a sparkling orange arc that sizzled, then snuffed out when it hit the water.

After polishing off the beer, he tossed the bottle aside, pushed himself to his feet, and came down the stairs, crunching across the gleaming oyster-shell walk on the loose-hipped, masculine stride that had always reminded Dani of a swamp panther.

Now, as he loomed out of the blackened shadows, his tawny gold predator's eyes gleaming, the resemblance was a bit too close for comfort.

He'd always been outrageously handsome, and the years hadn't changed that. But time had carved away whatever bit of softness he'd kept hidden away deep in his heart. His full sensual lips were drawn into a forbidding line, and a savage slash of cheekbones cut their way across features far more harshly hewn than they'd been when he was younger.

His hair appeared nearly as long as hers and glistened darkly with moisture. It flowed back from his strong forehead and was tied at the nape of his neck in a way that made her think of the pirates who used to escape to Blue Bayou after raiding Spanish merchant ships in the Gulf. Taking in the surprising gold earring he hadn't owned when she'd known him last, Dani decided that all he was missing was the cutlass.

Dangerous was the first word that sprang to mind. Maybe Bad Jack Callahan himself didn't present any danger to her, but the unbidden feelings he'd always been able to stir in her certainly could be.

"You shouldn't have come here, Danielle," he said bluntly.

He'd said those same words to her once before. Warning her off. Dani hadn't listened then, nor could she now.

"You didn't give me any choice, hiding away out here in the swamp like some mad hermit trapper."

He didn't respond to her accusation. Just gave her a long, deep look. Then grazed his knuckles up her cheek. "You're bleeding."

Her skin heated, as if he'd skimmed a candle flame up it. Dani took a cautious step back, lifted her own fingers to the cheek she belatedly realized was stinging and had to remind herself how to breathe.

In.

"It's undoubtedly just a scratch from a tree limb."

Out.

"This isn't the easiest place to get to, with the road gone."

In again.

"Flooding from last season's hurricane wiped out the road," he revealed "Since the place was already crumblin', the parish commissioners didn't see any reason to spend public funds to rebuild a road to make it easier to get to some place no one wanted to go anyway."

"Which, from what I hear, suits you just fine. I suppose you would have been happier if I'd gotten lost coming out here."

"Hell, no, I wouldn't have wanted you to get lost." He blew a frustrated breath between his teeth. "I'm paying to have the road graded, since I've decided it's got to be cheaper than continuing to bring things in by water. If you'd only waited another week, you could have avoided the boat trip."

"I couldn't wait that long."

"Sa c'est fou."

"I've done crazier things."

A rough, humorless sound rumbled out of his broad chest. "I sure as hell won't be arguin' with that, *chérie.*"

Dani was not foolish enough to take the endearment to heart. Hadn't she heard him call his old bluetick hound the very same thing?

"We were both damn crazy that summer," he mused aloud, with something that surprisingly sounded a bit like regret.

Jack was the one who'd deserted *her*. If he'd regretted his behavior, he could have called. Or written. Instead, he'd disappeared off the face of the earth, leaving her to face the consequences of their reckless romance alone.

"I'm not here to talk about that summer."

His eyes, which had seemed to soften a bit with remembered affection, shuttered, like hurricane shutters slammed tight before a storm. "Then why are you here?"

Good question. If it'd been only herself, she would have slept on the street rather than come crawling to Jack for anything. But she had Matt to think of. An innocent little boy who needed a roof over his head.

There was nothing Dani would not do for her son, including winding her way through inky-black bayou waters risking gators and heaven knows how many different kinds of snakes to beg this man for help.

"You seem to have hired every available construction worker from here to Baton Rouge."

"As impossible as it may be for you to fathom, sugar, this place is even worse structurally than it looks. It's a smorgasbord for termites, half the roof blew away in the last storm, the plumbing's flat rusted through, and what the inspector laughingly referred to as an electrical system is a bonfire waiting to happen.

"I could hire every damn construction worker from Lafayette to New Orleans and probably still not have a large enough crew to finish the work in this lifetime."

"Perhaps you ought to just build a new house that won't give you so many problems," she suggested with openly false sweetness.

"And let the bayou reclaim Beau Soleil? Not on your life."

The force in his tone surprised Dani. "I never realized you felt so strongly about it."

He rocked back on his heels as he looked up at the once magnificent house draped in deep purple shadows. For a fleeting second his tawny eyes looked a hundred years old. "Neither did I."

"Well." That unexpected bit of honesty left Dani at a momentary loss for words. She reminded herself of her mission. "I need a carpenter, Jack. And I need him now."

He gave her another of those long unfathomable, brooding looks. Then shrugged again. "I don' know about you, but I skipped lunch today to meet with a pirate who calls himself a septic tank engineer and I'm starvin'.

"There's some chicken in the smoker, and after we take care of that scratch on your face, you can peel the shrimp while I make the roux.

Then we can pass ourselves a good time over some gumbo and jambalaya and see if we can come up with a way for both of us to get what we want."

Determined to settle her business, Dani forced down her concern about getting back to town. Marie Callahan had once told her that the way to a man's heart was through his stomach. At the time, since she'd been sleeping with Marie's son, Dani had known—and kept to herself—the fact that Jack's other hungers had held first priority.

Still, perhaps he might be more amenable to negotiation after a good meal. Even one he'd cooked himself.

"That sounds like a reasonable enough solution."

A waning white moon was rising in the sky as they walked in silence toward the house, the bayou water lapping against the raised narrow pathway. Dani had just about decided that the rumors she'd heard of Jack as a dark and crazy swamp devil, living out here like the fabled *Loup Garou*, were merely gossip, when he suddenly crouched down and plunged his hand into the inky water.

The violent splash sent a flock of ducks who'd been sleeping in the nearby reeds exploding into the sky, firing the night with a dazzling shower of falling stars.

"*Bon Dieu*," he murmured. "I've never seen the ghost fire so bright." He brought up a broad, long-fingered hand that glowed with phosphorescence in the purple velvet dark surrounding them. Sparks seemed to fall back into the water as he stood up again. "You still set this bayou on fire, *mon ange*."

His feral gold eyes drifted down to her lips and lingered wickedly for what seemed like an eternity, as if he were remembering the taste and feel of them.

He moved closer. Too close. But if she tried to back away, she'd risk falling into the water.

"I'm not your angel," she insisted, even as erotic pictures of them rolling around on a moss-stuffed mattress flashed through her mind, making her breasts feel heavy beneath the white T-shirt that had been pristine when she'd begun her long, frustrating day but was now clinging damply to her body.

Although it had to be at least ninety degrees, with a humidity equally high, her nipples pebbled as if she'd dived naked into the Arctic Ocean. She dearly hoped it was dark enough for him not to notice.

It wasn't. "You can lie to me, sugar. You can try to lie to yourself. But your pretty angel's body is saying something else. It remembers, she. The same way mine does."

Dani managed, with herculean effort, to drag her gaze from his, but couldn't resist skimming a look over his broad chest and still-flat stomach, down to where his erection was swelling against the faded placket of his jeans.

"See something you like, *chère?*"

Heat flooded into her face. "You know how it is," she said breezily. "You've seen one, you've seen them all. It is comforting to discover that not everything around Blue Bayou has changed. You still have sex on the mind."

"*Mais* yeah," he countered without an iota of apology. His wicked eyes glittered with predatory intent as they took a blatantly male appraisal from the top of her head down to her sneaker-clad feet. Then just as leisurely roamed back up to her face. "The day I stop reacting to a desirable female is the day I tie some weights around my neck and throw myself in the bayou as gator bait."

Dani was no longer a virginal Catholic girl experiencing sexual desire for the first time. She was a grown woman who, in the years since she'd left home, had overcome a broken heart, married, given birth to a son she adored, and, if it hadn't been for that wayward piano, would have been the first divorcée in Dupree family history.

This bayou bad boy leering at her should not make her stomach flutter and her pulse skip.

It shouldn't.

But, heaven help her, it did.

As they resumed walking toward Beau Soleil, she vowed not to let Jack's still powerful sexual magnetism turn her into some fluttery, vapid southern belle who'd swoon at his feet. Or any other part of his anatomy.

But when he put a casual, damp hand on her hip to steady her as she climbed up the braced stairway to the *gallerie*, Dani feared that if she wasn't very, very careful, she could discover exactly how dangerous supping with Blue Bayou's very own home-grown devil could be.

8

Jack had taken an immediate inventory the minute she'd stepped out of the boat. Five-five, a hundred-ten pounds, blond hair, and although he hadn't been able to see them from the *gallerie*, he knew her eyes were a bluish green hazel with gold flecks. Other than that scratch on her cheek, she had no distinguishing marks or scars. There were probably millions of women in the world who'd fit that physical profile. Yet in none of those women would the physical details have been put together in a more appealing package.

He'd managed to convince himself that just as he'd changed over the years, Dani would have, too. It was true she'd changed. For the better.

There were the expected outer differences: hair that had once flowed to her waist was now woven into a loose braid that fell a bit past her shoulders. Despite the slenderness Nate had reported, her body was more curvaceous than it'd been when he'd last seen her. Touched her. Tasted her.

When they entered the house, the light streaming from the chandelier in the grand entry hall revealed bruise-like shadows beneath her eyes. Long-dormant protective instincts stirred.

Dangerous thinking, that. Bad enough the way those wide, hit-you-in-the-gut expressive eyes still dominated her oval face, bad enough that he could remember, with aching clarity, the taste of her unpainted lips, and God help him, it was fuckin' damn deadly dangerous the way whatever sunshine scent she'd splashed on before leaving town smelled like heaven and drew him like a silver lure.

She'd been forbidden fruit thirteen years ago. Jack was trying to recall all the reasons she still was when he heard a familiar clattering sound.

"Oh, shit. Brace yourself." He managed to jump in front of Dani just as the huge ball of yellow fur came barreling into the hall, tore past him like a running back evading a blocker, stood on its hind legs, braced both huge paws on her shoulders, and began licking her face.

"Well, hello," she greeted the dog, with amazing aplomb for a woman who'd just been attacked by a beast that weighed nearly as much as she did.

He grabbed the leather collar and yanked the stray to the marble floor. The dog wagged its tail and continued dancing around Dani. There was a muddy pawprint the size of Jack's spread hand above her left breast.

"Sorry about that," he muttered. "She tends to be standoffish with strangers."

"So I see." She scratched the enormous head that thrust itself beneath her palm. "I had no idea you had a dog."

"She's not really mine." If he owned a dog, it'd damn well be better trained, like the obedient German shepherds he'd worked with on various drug-smuggling investigations. It sure as hell wouldn't jump up and slobber all over people the minute they walked in the door. "I'm just letting her crash here for a while till I get around to taking her to the shelter in town."

"I see." It was clear she didn't believe him. Which wasn't all that surprising, since he was starting not to believe it himself. "What kind of dog is she?"

"My guess would be a Great Dane-yellow Lab-Buick mix."

Her answering laugh slipped beneath his skin and over his nerve endings like quicksilver. "I always wanted a dog."

"I never knew that."

"There was a lot you didn't know about me," she said mildly. "Why are you locked up inside on such a lovely night, sweetheart?" she asked the dog.

"Because last night she decided to go nine rounds with a skunk, and I don't have enough tomato juice left for a rematch," he answered for the mutt.

"Poor baby." Dani smiled at the dog, who appeared to grin right back. "What's her name?"

"Turnip. Because she just turned up," he elaborated when she quirked a brow.

"Well, it's certainly original."

Her smile faded as her gaze drifted to the mural that covered the walls of the two-story hall, rose to the plaster ceiling medallions he'd repainted, then up the curved sweeping staircase that had shown up in more than one movie.

"That's odd."

"What?"

"I'd always heard that when you come back home as an adult, things are supposed to look smaller, less grand than you remembered them."

"Hard for Beau Soleil not to look grand. Even in the sorry state it's in."

"True." The mural depicted Acadian forced deportation from Nova Scotia and the deportee's subsequent arrival in Louisiana, continuing up the stairs with the story of the star-crossed lovers Evangeline and Gabriel, immortalized by Longfellow. "It's different," she murmured. "But the same."

"I had it cleaned and touched up. It was a bit tricky because in the nineteenth century murals were painted right onto the plaster, which aged as the plaster aged. These days they're done on canvas that's glued to the wall, so the owners can take them with them when they move to a new house."

"Well, isn't that handy." She turned toward him, her expression bland, but the quick, intense flair of passion in her eyes warned that she wasn't as calm as outward appearances might suggest. "I'm going to be honest with you, Jack. I hate the idea of you living in my home."

"Fair enough," he allowed. "But you hatin' it isn't going to change a thing."

"Of all the houses, in all the world, why did you buy this one?"

"Would you have preferred I let the bayou claim it?"

"Of course not."

"How about the mob? Would you have enjoyed coming home to tourists playing blackjack in the summer parlor to a background music of slot machines?"

"You're supposed to be an intelligent man," she said through set teeth. "You should be able to figure out the answer to that yourself."

She moved along the wall, from where the men, women, and children were being herded by British troops onto the ships of exile during *Le Grand Derangement*—The Great Madness—out of Nova Scotia, eventually to the Evangeline oak where the long-suffering, tragic heroine awaited her beloved Gabriel.

"It has such a tragic ending," she murmured, seeming to momentarily put aside her pique. "For a love story."

"Most love stories are tragedies."

"Do you honestly believe that?"

"Sure." He shrugged, wishing he'd kept his big mouth shut. "Look at you and me."

She paled, then quickly recovered. "I didn't come here to talk about us," she repeated, giving him a haughty-princess-to-serf look that didn't exactly have him quaking in his boots. It hadn't worked on him back then, and sure as hell wouldn't now. "And that summer didn't have anything to do with love."

"Maybe not. But it sure was hot." He leaned closer. Skimmed a palm over her shoulder. "And a lot of fun while it lasted."

"Definitive point. It didn't last that long." She batted away his light caress and headed toward the kitchen. "And don't touch me."

"I remember when you liked me touching you." Begged him to, actually, but Jack decided she wouldn't appreciate him reminding her of that.

"That was then. This is now."

"*Oui.* But like you said, some things, they don't change."

"Dammit, Jack—"

This time when she slapped at his touch, he caught hold of her hand. "I still want you, *'tite ange*." God help him, it was the truth. Understanding all too well the dark, drowning sense of inevitability his fictional drug agent felt when he was in the same room with the gorgeous, lethal drug dealer's daughter, Jack drew her closer, until they were touching, thigh to thigh, chest to chest. She was like the Evangeline and Gabriel mural, he considered. Different, but the same. "And you still want me."

"You need a little help with your dialogue." Jack got a perverse kick at the way she lifted her chin. The out-of-reach bayou princess was definitely back. All that was missing was a satin ballgown and sparkly tiara. "The only thing I want from you is a carpenter." She pulled away.

Though it wasn't his first choice, he let her. "And supper," he reminded her.

"Not even that. Just tell me what it'll take to get your cooperation, short of taking my clothes off," she tacked on quickly when his mouth twitched. "Then I'll be on my way."

"You've been livin' in the city too long, you." To please himself, he played with a silky strand of hair that had escaped the braid. "Where people don' know how to take time to enjoy themselves." He wanted his hands on her. His mouth. And that was just for starters. "Things move a little slower here in the swamp."

"Tell me about it. I could have built the damn Taj Mahal in the length of time it took to maneuver my way through the byzantine maze the zoning bureau refers to as policy and procedures to get a permit to get repairs done on the library."

"You could have gone back home." It'd be better—safer—for both of them if she did.

"I did." She tossed up her chin in a way that made Jack want to kiss her silly. "Blue Bayou is my home."

Jack sighed. Skimmed his thumb up her cheekbone. "Let's clean this scratch. Have ourselves a little gumbo. Then we'll talk."

Dani didn't want to stay. For a multitude of reasons. The first being that it hurt, really hurt, to see someone else, even this man she'd once loved, living in the home that had belonged to her family for so many generations. The home she'd always envisioned raising her own babies in.

She also didn't want to stay because Jack made her uneasy. He may be a hotshot writer now, he may have worn a tux when he mingled with Russell Crowe and Jennifer Lopez at the premiere of the movie made from his first book, he may have been interviewed by a breathless Mary Hart on the famed red carpet at the Academy Awards, but beneath the polish he'd picked up since she'd known him—loved him—were those same rough, workingman's hands that had once caused such pleasurable havoc to her body, the flowing black pirate's hair, the unyielding jaw, the lush, sensuous mouth that suggested all sorts of sins and might have appeared feminine had it not been for the contrast of his ruggedly hewn face that had been compared to a young Clint Eastwood. Put it all together and you got a combination more dangerous than mixing TNT and nitroglycerin and setting a match to them. A danger a prudent woman would avoid.

"Sit down on that bar stool and I'll get the medicine kit." His take-charge attitude grated, even as his roughened voice curled through her like dark smoke.

"I'm perfectly capable of taking care of a little scrape by myself."

"You're a guest," he said mildly, as if living in Beau Soleil for a few months made him damn lord of the manor.

Acting as if it were his perfect right to touch her, he put his hands on either side of her waist, lifted her onto a bar stool at a curved granite counter that hadn't been there when she lived in the house. When he left the room, Dani slid off the stool, seriously considered pulling the plug on this fool's effort and escaping back to town. Where it seemed she belonged, since there was no longer any place for her here at Beau Soleil.

"Going somewhere?" he asked casually when he returned with a brown bottle.

"I've decided I'm not hungry after all."

"Then you just watch me eat while we talk about your problem. Meanwhile, let's get this clean."

"Ow!" She drew her head back at the sting when he touched the dampened cotton ball to her cheek.

"Hold still." He caught her chin in the fingers of his left hand and continued to clean the scratch.

"Dammit, you're doing this on purpose."

"Doing what?"

"Using that instead of some nice modern antibiotic cream."

"This happens to be all I've got in the place. Besides, I'm an old-fashioned kind of guy. And I don't remember you being such a whiner."

"I'm not."

"Good. Then why don't you shut that pretty little mouth up and think of something pleasant."

"Such as the sheriff throwing you out of Beau Soleil?"

His damnably sexy lips quirked, just a little, revealing that her barb hadn't stung. "Never happen. Old Jimbo Lott'd have to get off his fat butt first."

"He was at the library fire."

"That's not such a surprise. Mos' everyone likes to see the results of a job well done."

This time it was surprise, rather than pain, that had her pulling away. "Surely you're not suggesting Sheriff Lott set that fire?"

"I'm not saying he did. But I'm not sayin' he didn't, either. The man's definitely got motive and opportunity."

"What motive would he have to burn a library?"

"Maybe he doesn't want you setting up housekeepin' in Blue Bayou. Maybe he doesn't want you makin' some nice cozy place for the judge to come home to."

"I don't understand."

"You don't need to, you." He tossed the cotton ball into a wastebasket and capped the hydrogen peroxide. "All you have to do is just stay at Orèlia's till the judge is sprung. Then go back home to D.C. or Virginia, or wherever you came from."

"I came from here. Washington was never my home. Nor was Virginia. It was only where I had to live because my husband was a member of Congress. *This* is my home," she repeated. And she wasn't going to let Jack or Jimbo Lott or anyone else chase her away.

"Maybe it was once upon a time ago, but as you pointed out, I'm livin' in it now. So, looks like there's nothin' to keep you here in Blue Bayou."

"Only Dupree roots going back generations. Roots I want to pass on to my child."

A guilt she was never very far away from stirred as Dani recalled another child she'd once longed to bring home to Beau Soleil. She took a took a deep breath and decided this was the time to bring up a thought that had been spinning around in her mind ever since Nate first told her that Jack had bought Beau Soleil.

"What if I were to make you an offer? Would you leave?"

He arched a black brow. "You always have been one for surprises, *chère*. Didn't realize you had that much money stashed away."

"I don't," she admitted. "But maybe we could work something out."

"For old time's sake?"

She wouldn't have thought, since he'd been the one to run away, that Jack would want to bring up old times. "Not exactly. But as you pointed out, Beau Soleil needs a lot of work. Surely the renovation must interfere with your writing."

He shrugged and lit a cigarette. "Not that much. I'm pretty much in a zone when I'm working. 'Sides, I sorta like bein' a man of property."

"Why can't you be a man of someone else's property?"

"Because I want Beau Soleil."

"And the great and mighty Jack Callahan gets everything he wants, right?"

His eyes shadowed, just for an instant, then hardened. "Not always." The cigarette dangled from his lips as he skimmed a long, intimate look over her. "But if you were to sweet-talk me real nice, sugar, you and I might just be able to work out some sort of arrangement."

He'd proven himself untrustworthy at eighteen. Dani didn't trust him now. "What kind of arrangement?"

She knew she'd made a mistake asking the question when his eyes glinted and his smile turned from sexually seductive to downright feral. "I could always take it out in trade."

Heat as red as the glowing end of his cigarette shot into her cheeks. "Isn't it strange how time dims memory? I certainly don't remember you being so disgusting."

That was it. If she didn't leave now, she'd give into impulse and start throwing the knives from the nearby oak rack at his head. She'd just have to take her search for workmen a bit farther, to Baton Rouge or New Orleans, perhaps.

"You don't wanna leave now." He caught her by the waist again as she began to march away. "Just when things are beginnin' to get interesting."

"Obviously we have a different definition of interesting." She managed to keep her tone cool even as those long fingers digging into her skin beneath her T-shirt made her feel shaky. Edgy. And, heaven help her, needy.

The only time Lowell had ever touched her was in bed. Then finally, nearly two years ago, he'd stopped touching her all together. She thought that the fact it had been six months before she'd noticed the absence of any sex said a great deal about her marriage.

"The place isn't exactly ready for company. But how about I give you the grand tour? Show you how things are progressin'."

Damn. Trust him to dangle the one bit of bait she found almost impossible to refuse. Dani hesitated, curiosity warring with the primal, survivalist urge to run. She didn't trust him. Didn't like him. Her head knew that. Her heart knew it, as well. But for some unfathomable reason, her body hadn't seemed to get the message. *It* wanted him. It didn't care how obnoxiously arrogant he'd become, or even that he'd stolen her birthright. Her son's birthright. All it wanted—

desperately—was to feel his hands moving over her body, taking that same slow path his dangerously tawny eyes were currently traveling.

She stomped the hot unbidden sexual desire down and reminded her rebellious body that she'd sworn off men after her husband had gone on television and made her the most publicly pitied woman in America. And she'd definitely sworn off *this* particular man after he'd taken off for parts unknown, leaving her to face the worst days of her life alone.

Dani sighed, realizing that although she'd grown up a lot since that summer, the memories still hurt.

Jack waited, giving her time to sort out her feelings. It had to be tough, he allowed, returning home widowed from a bad marriage to find the man who'd taken her virginity, then deserted her without a word, living in her childhood home.

She blew out a breath. Briefly closed her eyes, which had shadowed while he was watching the range of expressions move across her face. Then shrugged. "I suppose it might be interesting to see what changes you've made to my family's home."

His eyes narrowed, but for some reason—a faint leftover shred of southern chivalry, perhaps?—he refrained from reminding her again that it was *his* home now.

9

They began with the English jury paneled library that looked out onto the garden, which had gone to seed. Since flowers were the least of his problems, Jack hadn't worried about that.

"The books are all gone," she murmured, looking up at the built-in shelves that had once held leather-bound first editions.

"The judge put them in storage before his sentencing. Said he didn't want the vultures getting them."

"Well, that's certainly flattering."

"He wasn't talking about you, *chère*. Some of them are a little moldy from bein' in a warehouse in Baton Rouge all these past years he's been away, but I found a place in New Orleans that specializes in restoring old books. Looks like we'll probably be able to salvage most of them."

She stopped running her fingers over the fluted pilasters around the bookcases and looked up at him. "So you now own *them*, too?"

"Yeah." Jack heard the stiff accusation in her voice but refused to apologize. "I'd just come back to town when Earl Jenkins, the guy who owned the warehouse where the judge had stashed the books died, and his kids sold the moving and storage business to some company based in New York City.

"Turns out Earl hadn't bothered collecting any rent, 'cause he figured he owed the judge, who'd gotten his second cousin, Tommy Lee, into an alcohol-treatment program instead of jail after a DUI.

"But the damn Yankee, he didn't care about paying off moral debts, he just wanted the paper one taken care of. The judge had to either come up with the bucks for all those years of back storage, or the books were going to be sold at auction. So he called me."

"Why you?"

"Hell if I know. Maybe he'd read about those Hollywood folks making that movie out of my book and figured I might have enough dough to bail the books out of hock. Maybe he thought that since I owned the house, I might want somethin' to fill the shelves. Or it could be he remembered how I was always sneakin' in here to read them."

What Jack didn't share with Dani was that the judge had eventually turned out to have an entirely different agenda, like wanting the same guy he'd once run out of town, if not on a rail, at least in a candy apple red GTO, to use his—and his FBI brother's—connections in the law-enforcement community to prove that he'd been framed seven years ago. And by whom.

"I never knew you did that."

"That was kinda the point of sneaking. *Maman* was always scared the judge was going to discover me in here and fire her."

There'd been a time, back in his teens, when Jack had thought his *maman* had been overly concerned about losing a job she'd never wanted in the first place. A job she'd been forced to take in order to support her three sons after her husband was killed. It was only later, after the debacle in Colombia—which Jack continued to think of as Callahan's major fuckup—had taken away his own confidence in his ability to do his job, that he'd finally understood how the gunman who'd taken his father's life that day in the Blue Bayou courthouse had not only cost his mother her husband, but robbed her of any sense of security.

Which was why, when the judge had threatened to fire Marie Callahan if her middle son didn't leave Blue Bayou—and Danielle—Jack had thrown some stuff into a duffel bag, headed off across the country to San Diego, and hadn't looked back. Until his world blew up in his face, leaving him nowhere else to go.

"Turns out the judge had known about me reading his books all the time," he revealed. There hadn't been much that old bastard missed. Which was why Jack was surprised he'd let himself get caught up in such an obvious frame.

They continued the tour through the long double parlors which opened up onto a private courtyard designed for steamy hot summers. Then moved on to the formal dining room with the ceiling frescoes which were, like the grand hall mural, being restored. Since it was the largest room in the house, the ballroom was currently being used as an indoor shop, allowing work to continue even on the wettest of days.

As they went upstairs, Jack realized that having been surrounded by construction for so long, he hadn't realized how much he'd actually accomplished. Beau Soleil would be a lifetime project, not just to restore, but to keep up. The funny thing was, he, who'd always sworn to escape Blue Bayou, didn't mind that idea at all.

It was so hard, Dani thought. Seeing all that Jack had done to her home, then having to constantly remind herself it was *his* home now. But even as difficult as she found the rest of his impromptu tour, she was battered by emotions when she walked into her former bedroom.

Once upon a time ago this room had been scented by the potpourri Jack's mother made from Beau Soleil's antique roses. Now the odors of dust and mold assaulted her senses.

"The roof leaked and the moisture went through the attic floor to here," he said as she lifted her gaze to the ceiling, where a brown spot shaped like an amoeba darkened the plaster. "I've got a guy coming in to fix it as soon as I replace the rotted wood on the floor above next week."

"That's good," she murmured absently. She skirted the two sawhorses and went over to the window where an industrious spider had spun a web in the upper-left corner.

"The tree's still there," he said.

"I know." She did not volunteer how, when she'd first arrived, before she'd known he was sitting on the *gallerie*, she'd imagined herself climbing down it. Imagined his hands on her hips, helping her to the ground.

"I had to saw off a limb that kept scrapin' against the window, 'cause I was afraid it'd break the glass."

"I imagine it'd be difficult to find replacement glass this old."

"Not around here. There are one helluva lot of fine old places crumbling away all through the bayou."

But Beau Soleil would not be lost. Thanks to him. Dani tried to be grateful for that.

As she looked around the room, instead of the yellowed wallpaper, crumbling plaster ceiling, and missing baseboards, she saw it as it had once been, when white rosebuds had blossomed on a field of palest green, when creamy molding had run across the top of the wall and a lacy white iron bed, which had belonged to her great-great-grandmother, covered with tea-dyed crocheted lace had dominated the room.

"The bed's out in the carriage house," he said, as if he'd plucked the question right out of her mind.

"It's nice something survived."

"I heard the judge had a lot of the furniture shipped to your house in D.C. after your marriage."

"It was Virginia. He insisted he wanted to close off some rooms since he was the only one living here."

"You gonna have it shipped back?"

"No. I ended up selling it to pay bills."

"What kind of bills?"

"You know." Her shrug didn't come off nearly as negligent as she'd hoped. "The normal day-to-day stuff. Along with lawyer fees from the divorce, and of course there was the funeral."

"Your husband didn't have insurance?"

"Lowell had his legislative insurance, but he'd changed the beneficiary on the policy to his fiancée."

Who'd cut her losses, hadn't bothered to chip in to bury the man she'd stolen from his family, and was currently working for an up-and-coming young congressman from Rhode Island. Dani hoped the politician's pregnant wife kept a closer watch on her husband and her marriage than she had.

"He had some other policies we'd bought together over the years, but he'd cashed them out to cover margin calls on his stocks."

"No offense, but you went off and married yourself one helluva louse."

"I'm afraid you're right. But the furniture wouldn't have fit in the apartment over the library, anyway." A pain she'd thought she put behind her flared, scorching her nerves. When she felt her hands begin to tremble, she shoved them into the back pockets of her shorts.

"Wasn't it Thoreau who said our life is frittered away by details? I should know because I'm a reference librarian and we're supposed to know everything. . . .

"Yes, I'm sure it was Thoreau. He was so before his time, wasn't he? With his *simplify, simplify* message."

Lord, she was on the verge of babbling. Dani never babbled. Not ever. "Those are such inspirational words to live by, aren't they? The world would be ever so much better off if everyone followed his advice."

"Walden Pond might get a little crowded."

Because it hurt, really hurt, to be in this room, where they'd once, during a wonderful, reckless night, made love in that lovely antique iron bed now being stored in the carriage house, Dani flashed him a bright, utterly false smile.

"You're undoubtedly right. But it's Thoreau's idea that's important, isn't it? Not the reality. People don't spend enough time thinking about the impact they have on the world. After all, our environment is so fragile . . .

"Hell." She drew in a ragged breath. When Jack moved toward her, his face showing concern for the crazy lady, Dani backed away and lifted her hands, palms out. "I'm okay. Really. It's just been a long day and the trip out here did a number on my nerves. But I'll be fine. I just need a moment." Thoroughly disgusted with herself, she turned toward the door, seeking to escape with some small shred of dignity intact.

"It got to me, too, *chère*."

His quiet statement had her pausing. She turned back toward him and read the truth in his eyes. "What?" she asked, even as she knew the answer.

"Remembering. You and me, together in here." He tilted his head toward where her bed had once been but didn't take his gaze from hers. "First time I walked into this room I felt as if someone had hit me in the gut with a fist."

He crossed the room to her and leaned close. Too close. "I figured it was just bein' back here again. Told myself that I'd get used to it." Closer still.

"Did you?"

"Not yet. Sometimes, late at night, I come in here, sit on the floor and get a little drunk while I look out at the moon and remember how good you looked—how good you felt—in that pretty white bed."

He braced a hand on the doorframe above her head. "You ever think about that? While you were lying alone in that marriage bed you made, waiting for your husband to come home from his girlfriend and make love to you the way a woman like you should be made love to?"

"No. I didn't," she lied. He couldn't have known. It was only a lucky guess. Ducking beneath his arm, she headed for the back stairs.

"You'll think about it tonight," he predicted.

Dani thought about arguing, but knew that he was right.

As desperately as she wanted to leave, Dani needed carpenters worse. And it seemed the only way she was going to get them was to humor Jack by staying for supper.

"Do you know, I doubt if my father was in this kitchen more than half a dozen times in his life," she murmured, peeling the shrimp while he heated the oil in the old iron skillet for the roux.

Turnip was standing on her hind legs, oversize paws on the counter, licking her muzzle with canine appreciation.

"My uncle started teachin' us boys how to cook about the same time he and my dad taught us to bait our first hook." He yanked the dog down by the collar. "Lie down, you."

Obviously uninjured by his firm tone, Turnip turned around three times, lay down, curled herself into a tight ball, put her head on her back legs, and continued to watch Jack's every move.

He added flour to the oil. The way he whisked the browning mixture with deft, easy strokes suggested he did it often. "It's a Cajun rite of passage, like your first game of *bourré* back from when men had to feed themselves during all those lonely months out at their camps, fishing and trapping."

"Do you still have the camp?" Damn. Bringing up the place where he'd taken her so they could be alone, especially after having been together in the bedroom, was definitely a tactical error.

One Jack thankfully let lie. "The three of us inherited it when *Maman* died. Nate uses it a few times a year, Finn's probably been back twice. I stayed out there when I first came back."

The whisk stilled for a moment. He glanced over at her. "Nate told me you didn't know I'd bought Beau Soleil."

"No." She began peeling a little faster. The pile of shrimp shells grew higher. "That came as a surprise." Her voice was calm, her hands were not.

He turned down the heat. "I'm sorry."

"Sorry that you bought my home? Or sorry that my husband let me think it'd been lost to taxes after my father was sentenced to prison?"

"Helluva thing, your daddy gettin' convicted like that."

"Yes," she said. "It was." She took a sip of the smooth California Chardonnay he'd poured her when they'd first returned to the kitchen.

Jack blew out a breath. "Look, Danielle, we may not be friends, but I'm not exactly your enemy, either."

"Then what, exactly, are you?" Other than the man who'd broken her heart, nearly destroyed her life, then stolen her home.

"I'm the guy who bought Beau Soleil, and if it weren't for me comin' up with a higher bid, your no-good, screw-around husband would have sold her to the Maggione family. You may not like the idea of me living in your fine old Louisiana plantation home, which, may I point out, the Dupree family didn't exactly come into by the sweat of their brow in the first place, since everyone knows old Andre won it on that riverboat by stacking the cards, but the fact is, I *am* living here. And I'm not goin' anywhere anytime soon.

"I'm also not going to apologize for buying her, because she was crumbling back into the bayou from years of neglect, and I'm exactly what she needs to make her beautiful again. But I am sorry that your husband was such a prick."

She hated that he had a point. About everything. "Well, that makes two of us."

"What the hell made you do it? Marry a guy like that?"

"I don't suppose you'd believe I liked the idea of not having to change my last name?"

"Try again. The Dupree name's on mailboxes and tombstones all throughout this parish. It didn't have to be him. Hell, if that was all you were lookin' to do, you probably would've been better off marrying old Arlan down at the Bijoux."

Arlan Dupree, who washed windows and changed the posters at the theater, was in his sixties and slow-witted from being hit in the head during all his years in the boxing ring. Despite having made a living with his fists, he was as gentle as a lamb.

"I suppose, in retrospect, I mostly married Lowell because my father wanted me to."

"That's one helluva piss-poor reason to get married."

"Tell me about it." Dani sighed and began sweeping up the shells as the air in the kitchen grew steamy with spices.

When she'd first met the congressional candidate who'd moved to Louisiana from coastal Texas, his smooth, cultivated Ashley Wilkes charm had proven a balm to the wounded heart she'd been nursing for too long. The fact that Judge Dupree had endorsed both of Lowell's campaigns—the one for the U.S. Congress, and the one for his daughter—had been another plus in his favor.

As distant as her father had been all her life, he'd barely spoken to her since those days of her summer love. She'd been so desperate for his approval, as well as wanting to make up for past sins, that she didn't hesitate accepting Lowell's proposal within weeks after they'd first met. Besides, if she were to be perfectly honest, marrying such a classically handsome, popular man seemed no hardship at the time.

Despite being uncomfortable in the media spotlight that was part and parcel of a tightly contested political campaign, Dani had enjoyed the attention Lowell lavished on her during their whirlwind courtship.

When they married, two weeks before the election, his poll numbers took a huge post-wedding bounce. After all, while the judge might not be the most liked man in the parish, he was highly respected; if the young politician was good enough for Judge Dupree's only daughter, then he was good enough for the voters of south Louisiana. By marrying Danielle, candidate Lowell Dupree rid his campaign of any lingering charges of carpetbagging and went on to win the congressional seat in a landslide.

The night before her wedding, she'd confessed to misgivings. That was when her father told her that Lowell had promised him a federal court appointment—maybe even the Supreme Court *when*, not if, he got to the White House. Both men had been so full of ambitious plans, she thought on a soft sigh. Plans that had nothing to do with her.

"It's hard to explain, but marriage seemed like a good idea at the time. Daddy thought Lowell had a brilliant future, and while being a judge might have made him important down here, looking back on it, I think he liked the prospect of playing on a national stage."

Surprising herself by giving Jack even that much personal insight into her life, Dani wasn't about to tell him that she'd also hoped that marriage would stop her from thinking about him. And those painful, lonely months after he'd left.

"You can't make anyone love you. Not even by trying to live up to expectations and tossin' away your life."

Dani ripped apart another shrimp. "Not that it's any of your business, but I don't consider the years I spent married to Lowell wasted."

"Because of your boy."

"Yes. Because of Matthew."

"He's lucky to have you, Matthew is."

The simple honesty in his deep voice took a little of the wind from her sails. "I'm the lucky one."

She'd never uttered a truer statement. During the nine months of her pregnancy, she'd been concerned, in the secret-most corner of her heart, that perhaps, subconsciously, she was trying to replace the child she'd lost. If that were so, it'd be a terrible burden to place on any infant. But the first time she'd held her son in her arms, she'd loved him with a power that had almost frightened her, it was so strong.

Which was why, even considering how things had turned out, she could never regret having married her husband. Because if she hadn't walked down Beau Soleil's *Gone With the Wind* staircase that fateful day of her wedding, her precious child, the sun around which Dani's entire world revolved, wouldn't exist.

As the conversation shifted to her son, Dani realized they'd slipped into playing roles. For a brief time, it was almost as if they were merely old friends getting together to catch up on life. Which, she supposed, if she had to stay, was better than focusing on the reality of their situation.

She told him about Matt's generosity, his intelligence, his collection of Hot Wheels, and his love of books, which in turn led to Jack's novels, which he seemed surprised to learn she'd actually read.

"I don't know why you'd be surprised. I am, after all, a librarian."

"Bet you don't read every book in the Dewey decimal system."

"No, but if the displays in the front of the bookstores and the library waiting lists are any indication, most of America must be reading yours."

The timer she'd set for the rice dinged. She took the lid off the pot. "Of course I knew, back in high school, that you'd become a famous writer," she allowed, giving him that much, since she knew how hard he'd worked to overcome his father's belief that writing stories was "sissy work."

Having grown up with a larger-than-life father herself, Dani suspected Jack might not have found it all that easy to escape Jake Callahan's broad shadow. She wondered idly if he might still be trying to prove himself to the father he'd lost, then reminded herself that she didn't care.

"You and *Maman* were sure as hell the only people in town who thought so."

"That's because no one else had read your writing."

She'd found the pages out at the camp while he'd been catching fish for their supper and had wept when she'd read the coming-of-age story of a boy whose Confederate father had been killed in the War Between the States by his Yankee uncle.

"*Writing* is a relative term. What I did back then was scribble clichéd, sentimental claptrap."

"I liked it."

"You were easy." He paused in the act of spooning gumbo into bowls. "Hell." He blew out a breath. "I didn't mean it the way it sounded, Danille."

Dani shrugged as she carried the plates of shrimp jambalaya to the table. "I suppose I was, back then." At least where he was concerned. "But I was young. And foolish." And desperately in love.

"And a lousy judge of literature."

She let out a short laugh, relaxing for the first time since she'd pulled the boat up to the dock. "So, what made you turn from historical drama to thrillers?" she asked as they sat down at the table.

"They say write what you know." His tone turned distant as he topped off her wine. "So, want to discuss our carpenter situation?"

Able to recognize when a door had just been slammed in her face, Dani reminded herself of her reason for being here, in this kitchen that was both familiar and new all at the same time and launched into her carefully prepared argument.

10

Thank you for dinner," Dani said later as Jack walked her to the dock where she'd tied up the rental boat. "I can't remember the last time I had gumbo."

"You've been deprived, you."

"So Orèlia keeps telling me. Now that I'm back here, I'm going to have to learn how to cook the food I grew up eating."

She could not have said anything that better reminded him of the vast social chasm that had once separated them. Danielle had lived in luxury, while his widowed mother had slaved away over a hot stove making sure the judge and his pretty daughter never knew hunger.

"Gumbo's not that hard. Jus' a combination of African and Indian recipes, some Spanish seasoning, and my own Cajun culinary genius."

"He said modestly."

"It's not braggin' if it's true."

"Good point. . . . I appreciate you sharing your carpenters."

He'd promised her two men. Which, Nate had already told him, would allow her to open the library in a few days, while still keeping her from moving into the more-damaged upstairs apartment. At least until after the judge's release. "Ready to go?"

She ignored his outstretched hand. "It's very nice of you to offer to take me back to town, but it's not necessary."

"The hell it isn't. In case you've forgotten, the bayou can be a damn dangerous place at any time. But 'specially at night. You could get lost."

"I have a GPS."

"Which isn't gonna be worth squat if some gator decides to flip that little boat of yours and lands you and your fancy tracking device in the water. I'll bet *M'su Cocodrile* would find your sweet little female body one helluva tasty change of pace."

She shivered a bit at that. But held her ground. "It may surprise you to learn that I've grown up, Jack. I'm quite capable of taking care of myself. And my son."

"I've not a doubt in the world that's true. Any man with eyes in his head can tell that you've grown up just fine. Better than fine," he decided, skimming a glance over her. "But I'm still taking you back to Orèlia's."

He flashed her a deliberately provocative grin. "Unless you want to spend the night here."

Because she feared arguing any further would only stir emotions that could lead to others far more dangerous, she threw up her hands. "All right. But I'm only agreeing because we're wasting time arguing."

"We'll take mine," he said, when she started to climb into the rental boat.

"I have to return this to Pete's Marine tonight or it's going to cost me a small fortune."

"Don't worry about it. I'll call Pete and tell him it's my fault, and I'll have one of the guys take it back in the morning."

Dani looked with misgivings at the shallow, narrow boat he intended to take her back to Blue Bayou in. "I would have thought, with all your money, you would have at least bought yourself some fancy bass boat with a big engine."

"Why would I want to dump more gas and oil into the bayou when I've got this?" He ran a hand over the narrow rub rail in a slow sweep that could have been a caress. "My daddy and I built this pirogue the summer before he got killed. She may be old, but she still rides on the dew."

"I've no doubt she does. But *my* boat rides on the water."

He folded his arms. "I never figured you for a coward."

"Good." She tossed her head. "Because I'm not."

"Then prove it."

Blowing out a frustrated breath, she turned on him, hands splayed on her hips. "That's not only a ridiculously juvenile dare, it's an entirely unfounded accusation. If you knew even half of what I've been through, what I've had to help my son get through, you'd never dare suggest such a thing.

"Oh, it's easy enough for you," she said, on a roll now, "coming back to town like some kind of conquering hero, buying respectability—and my home—with all those damn buckets of best-seller money—"

"Dieu." He caught hold of the hand that she'd slapped against his chest. "Don't remember you havin' such a temper."

"I still don't," she shot back. "Usually."

"It's good I provoke you." He uncurled her tightly fisted fingers, one by one. "Shows you have feelings for me."

"Murderous ones." She tugged on her hand. Without overt force, he refused to release it. "Dammit, Jack, if you're going to insist on taking me home, can we just get going?"

"Sure enough, sugar." When he trailed a fingertip over her surprisingly sensitive palm, unwilling desire spiked. Dani ruthlessly squashed it. "You know, you'd probably enjoy the trip better in the daylight," he said. "Are you sure you wouldn't rather stay here tonight?"

"In your dreams."

"Well, you know, I've already tried that. And while it's not bad, in its way, it's nothin' like back when you and I used to get hot and bothered and fuck ourselves blind every chance we got."

She tossed her head. "And to think I used to consider you reasonably sophisticated."

He irritated her further by laughing. "What did you know 'bout sophistication, *chère?* You were just a little girl."

"Apparently you didn't consider me too little to sleep with."

She knew she'd pushed too far when she felt him tense. "Let me give you a hand. Sometimes she's a bit tippy till you get settled in." A razor-sharp warning edged his reasonable tone.

Dani couldn't get a handle on the man. It was obvious he was no longer the bad boy of Blue Bayou. He did, after all, have a respectable occupation, which was not what most people in town had predicted. Despite having bought Beau Soleil, he certainly hadn't surrounded himself with the usual trappings of wealth she might have expected from a best-selling writer whose third book had sold to Hollywood before it was even written.

He was still sinfully sexy, still sultry temptation personified. But there was a quiet strength surrounding him. Plus, although he refused to admit it, a genuine affection toward that big yellow mongrel he'd rescued and named and who so obviously adored him.

Underlying everything else was an edgy, dangerous darkness she couldn't remember having been there before.

She wasn't a coward. But neither was she eager to go back into that dark swamp alone. Assuring herself that all he represented was a ride back to town, Dani gingerly climbed into the pirogue she'd once been so eager to ride in back when they'd race across dark waters to his camp.

For a while neither of them spoke as he poled the boat across the bayou, apparently navigating by instinct and memory. He'd always seemed at home here in the swamp. Which, she supposed, was why he'd chosen to return to Blue Bayou rather than buy a house in some trendy playground of the rich and famous.

"You should be proud of yourself, Jack," she said, finally breaking the silence. "You've done so very well."

"You haven't done half bad either. For a girl who was still a baby when her daddy married her off."

She thought, but wasn't about to say, that having a child alone, without any emotional support or love, tended to make a girl grow up real fast. Unfortunately, that didn't mean that she hadn't jumped from one bad relationship right into another worse one. "I'd graduated from college."

"Hell, that doesn't mean anything. You'd been so sheltered by the judge you didn't know a damn thing about the world. Wasn't a boy in town who'd dare as much as cop a feel with you for fear of the judge puttin' him in the slammer and tossing away the key."

"You weren't afraid."

He laughed, the sound echoing around them. "Hell, I was crazy back then."

"We both were."

"*Mais* yeah. That's sure true enough. But as soon as he found out you'd gotten yourself a taste of sex, the judge put you in a convent."

"I wasn't in any convent. It happens to have been a boarding school in Atlanta."

"Any guys livin' there?"

"Of course not." During the months at the home for unwed mothers, her mail had been censored, telephone calls monitored, and boys had been prohibited from even stepping foot on campus. But that hadn't stopped her from hoping Jack would arrive, like some knight in shining armor to rescue her. "Then after graduation I went to a Catholic women's college."

"Might as well have been convents, then." He took a pack of cigarettes from his shirt pocket, shook one loose, and lit it.

"There may not have been any male students. But I had dates. And sex." All right, that may have been a lie, but Dani excused it as being none of his business.

Jack exhaled a plume of smoke as he battled back the spike of jealousy. "Good for you. *Maman* wrote to me about your wedding."

He didn't reveal that he'd always suspected his mother had waited until after the ceremony for fear he'd try to return home and stop it.

Would he have? *Could* he have? The two questions had bedeviled him for more than a decade. It had also caused him to get drunk on her anniversary for years.

"She said it was like somethin' out of a fairy tale."

"Unfortunately it didn't have the requisite fairy-tale happily-ever-after ending."

"Must have been hard, moving in such powerful circles when you were still just a small-town bayou girl." Jack suspected being rich back home in Blue Bayou, Louisiana, didn't mean squat in the nation's capital.

"I didn't have much time for socializing. I was going to Catholic University in D.C. for my MLS, doing volunteer work, becoming a mother . . ."

Her voice drifted off. She shook herself a little, reminding Jack a bit of how Turnip had tried to shake off last night's skunk stink.

"There seemed to be a dinner or party or reception nearly every night, so I was honestly relieved when Lowell preferred attending most of them—except those hosted by constituent groups from home—with one of his aides or his chief of staff. It made sense, too, in a way, since they weren't really social occasions but political ones."

Jack thought about the photographs he'd seen of the woman her husband had left her for and suspected most women's internal alarms would have triggered at the idea of their husband spending his evenings with a woman whose glossy sophistication bespoke her Main Line Philadelphia heritage.

In contrast, he had to smile when he remembered the day she'd talked him into taking her fishing with him in this very pirogue. In her neatly pressed navy shorts, white designer T-shirt, and a billed cap advertising Bernard's bait shop he'd plunked on her head to protect her face from the sun, she'd looked like a pretty girl on a Louisiana tourist poster. Her feet had been bare, her hair loose, her smile dazzling.

As dusk had settled over the bayou, brightened by the flitting fluorescent green glow of fireflies, he'd taught her how to fry catfish in a beer batter, then they'd eaten them with grilled corn on the cob and shrimp cornbread he'd filched from his mother's kitchen.

After supper they'd sat out on the screened-in porch of his camp and watched the molten sun dip into the water, giving way to a perfumed night lush with promise.

The sex had been different that night. Slower. Sweeter. And infinitely more satisfying. It was only later, as he'd stared up at the canopy of stars while she'd dozed in his arms, Jack had realized, that somehow, when he hadn't been paying close enough attention, he'd fallen head over heels in love with pretty little rich girl Danielle Dupree.

Yesterday's ball score, he reminded himself.

"You were naive, keeping your husband on such a long leash."

She sighed. "If a man needs a leash, the odds of keeping him probably aren't all that high, anyway."

Thinking back on that fateful day when the judge had succeeded in changing both their lives, Jack felt like sighing as well.

"But I've thought about it a lot during these past months," she said. "And I'm actually glad I was never jealous, because then I'd be a different person than I am. I don't want to have to use jealousy to keep my husband faithful.

"I didn't suspect Lowell was committing adultery with Robin because I believed—and still do—that a solid marriage can only be built on a foundation of trust."

"That's probably a more effective theory if both people are deserving of the trust."

"Good point."

"I'd think you would have been an asset with the Louisiana campaign contributors. By marrying you, which pegged him statewide as Judge Victor Dupree's hand-picked son-in-law, the guy overcame his working-class roots." Jack remembered reading that the congressman had been the son of an alcoholic Gulf oil rig worker.

"I suppose I was an asset. Until the scandal." She looked away, out over the still black water. He studied the delicate profile that was etched on every one of his memory cells. "Then it was as if he'd never heard of Daddy."

"He sure took advantage of the judge's problems and bought Beau Soleil at a bargain tax-sale price fast enough."

"I'm trying not to think about that. Because if he wasn't already dead, I'd want to kill him."

"Sounds reasonable."

"It sounds terrible." She shook her head. "I didn't really mean it."

"Didn't you? I'm not sayin' you really would have done murder. But didn't you at least imagine striking back after he humiliated you on television in front of millions of nightly news viewers?"

"All right, I'll admit to a fleeting fantasy involving him driving a flaming Lexus of Death off the Francis Scott Key bridge into the Potomac River filled with politician-eating sharks."

"There's hope for you yet."

Once he'd gotten to know Danielle, Jack had been surprised to discover that what he'd always taken as regal self-assurance, was actually innate shyness and a critical case of the Melanie Wilkes Curse, which seemed to result in certain female children growing up unflaggingly sweet, malleable, self-effacing comforters of the emotionally wounded.

It was, Jack, suspected, a distinctly southern affliction. He'd sure as hell never run across it anywhere else.

"Nate told me you've been going up to the prison."

He heard the question in her voice and chose to dodge it. "From time to time." As the water deepened, he switched on the electric motor and sat down across from her, close enough that their knees were touching.

"I'm surprised. Since my father was the one responsible for you spending that year in the detention work camp."

She didn't know the half of what the judge had done to him. To them both. But Jack wasn't prepared to share the truth. At least not right now. "Hell, he probably saved my life. I was on a pretty slippery slope in those days."

"You weren't nearly as bad as everyone thought you were."

"That was a matter of opinion." When now familiar ghosts rattled their rusty chains, Jack wished for a whiskey. Or better yet . . .

She was definitely curious. Tempted. He saw it in her moon-spangled eyes, in the way her lips parted, ever so slightly as she looked at him.

When a jagged, white-hot bolt of hunger seared through him, Jack fought back the brutal urge to plunder, to crush his mouth down on hers, to tear off her clothes and taste her perfumed skin.

He wanted her bucking beneath him as she'd done that summer out on that moss-filled mattress at the camp, wanted to watch her eyes go blind as he drove her up, then feel her shatter as he filled her, reclaiming what had been stolen from him.

Deciding her taste would definitely be preferable to burning tobacco, he flicked the cigarette away.

"This would be a mistake." Her wide fascinated eyes darkened as they stared at his mouth, belying her soft denial.

"Maybe yes. Maybe no." He slowly leaned forward and felt her shiver when he touched the tip of his tongue to the sexy little indentation between her chin and her bottom lip. "But so what? You've never made a mistake in your life, *chère?*"

"That's the point. I've made too many."

"It's just a kiss, Danielle." He soothed her tense shoulders with his palms. Moved his hands down her arms until his fingers braceleted her slender wrists. Her pulse, beneath his thumbs, skittered. "I won't hurt you."

But he once had. And they both knew it.

"Jack . . ."

Hearing the plea rather than the protest, he took her mouth.

11

Heat, thick and sweet as boiled sugar cane, surged through Dani's veins. Her breath choked up in her lungs as Jack leisurely, thoroughly kissed her.

Somewhere in the bayou, a hound howled at the rising moon. An owl hooted. A jumping fish splashed. But Dani ignored them as the outside world telescoped in, narrowing down to the almost painfully exquisite sensation of Jack's mouth claiming hers.

How could she have forgotten this? How could she have failed to remember how her mind clouded with only the touch of his firm masculine lips on hers? How could she have forgotten *him?*

The truth, she admitted, for the first time in more than a decade as he tilted his head, changing the angle, deepening the kiss, degree by breath-stealing degree, was that she hadn't.

In nine years of marriage she'd never had an orgasm with her husband. She'd never trembled at his touch, never wanted him to rip her clothes off and bury himself deep inside her with a force that would make her scream.

Lowell had certainly never made her scream.

The thought of how her husband might have reacted if she actually screamed during lovemaking caused a little gurgle of laughter against Jack's mouth.

"I must be losin' my touch if this is makin' you laugh."

"That's not it. A thought just crossed my mind."

"Why don't you think later?"

Before she could answer, his mouth was on hers again, sending her swirling back into the mists.

This kiss was harder. Hotter. Deeper. Dani moaned beneath the pressure of his mouth as it fed on hers. Her heart thundered in her ears as he dragged that ravenous mouth down her throat, teeth raking against her heated skin.

When he released his hold on her wrists, and cupped her breasts, she arched against his hand and feared they could both end up in the water when the pirogue rocked.

"I knew it." His deep voice was rife with satisfaction. The pressure lessened, as his mouth cruised up to nibble on her earlobe.

"What?"

"That you'd taste good." He teased her nipples into aroused, aching points. "Feel good." A small, needy sound escaped from between her ravished lips as anticipation wound like a tightened spring. "That some things never change." Proving that he still knew his way around women's clothing, he unfastened the back of her bra with a single deft motion, freeing her breasts to his touch.

"It's only chemistry." She moaned as his kneading caress grew increasingly rough and caused a low, throbbing ache that seemed to vibrate all the way into her bones.

"Don't knock chemistry." His touch gentled again; but the feel of his fingers trailing slowly down her torso was no less seductive as they left a weakening trail of sparks on her flesh beneath the cotton T-shirt. "It's what turns dinosaurs into gasoline, carbon into diamonds, and hops into beer."

He palmed her, the heel of his hand pressing against the placket of her shorts, sending time spinning backward, tempting her nearly beyond reason. When she felt those same wickedly clever fingers that had unhooked her bra move to the button at her waistband, Dani drew back.

"As much as I appreciate the science lesson, Professor Callahan, if it's all the same to you, I'd just as soon not tip the boat over." Even as she struggled for some semblance of composure, the ragged need in her voice gave her away.

"We'd have to be a helluva lot more sedate than I intend to be with you, that's for sure," he agreed easily. "Anytime you want a refresher course, just whistle."

Dani knocked away his hand when he moved to refasten her bra, wanting—needing—to do it herself and gain some control over the situation. "You really can be horrendously insufferable."

He flashed her a wicked, cocky smile. "It's one of my many charms."

"Insufferable," she muttered, folding her arms across breasts that could still feel the erotic touch of his hands as the pirogue drifted back into the reeds.

Jack stood up and began using the pole again, pushing against the mud to navigate. They could have been the only two people in the world as they continued through the inky black darkness, the boat's yellow headlight cutting a swathe through the rising fog on the way back to Blue Bayou.

The scent that had blossomed from Dani's pearly white skin lingered in Jack's mind as he returned to Beau Soleil. He'd said good night to her at her car, which she'd left in Pete's Marine's parking lot.

She was right about having changed. She was no longer that nubile teenage princess who could crook her little finger and bring every male in the parish to his knees. Every male but him, he'd once vowed.

Before that fateful summer, Jack had prided himself on his ability to avoid her silken snares. He'd initially considered Danielle Dupree a pampered, spoiled girl who flirted, flattered, and charmed as only a pretty southern belle could. It was only when he'd discovered that beneath the polished veneer was a very vulnerable, very lonely young woman, he'd fallen. Hard.

After tying the pirogue to the dock, he spent a long time sitting on the *gallerie*, staring out over the inky water. And remembering.

At seventeen Jack had believed himself to be the toughest guy in the bayou, and there'd been few who'd argue his self-appraisal. He'd been hell on wheels, driving his *maman* crazy, bringing her to frustrated tears more than once, but there had been so goddamn much anger driving him, he couldn't stop. Not even for her.

Not even when his older brother Finn had come home from college and broken his nose after he'd been caught siphoning gas from Judge Victor Dupree's caddy.

Whenever Jack viewed his life, which he tried like hell not to do all that often, it seemed to be divided into chapters.

The first consisted of those years when his dad had been alive and his mother had done whatever mothers did to create a warm and comfortable home.

Then had come the flash point, that sweltering summer day a wild-eyed, pissed-off swamp dweller had burst into the courtroom determined to kill Judge Dupree for signing the restraining order aimed at keeping an abusive husband from continuing to beat his soon-to-be ex-wife black and blue. Jack's father, Blue Bayou's sheriff, had been on the stand, testifying in a DUI case. When he saw the revolver, he did what came naturally. He dived onto the judge, pushed him down, and got himself mortally wounded in the process.

Jake Callahan hadn't been wearing a bulletproof vest. It was too hot, and besides, Blue Bayou was a peaceful place. A good place to raise a family, his dad had always told his *maman*, who'd smile and agree. Of course, she'd agreed with just about everything her husband said. And he'd agreed with her right back.

They'd been, even after two decades of marriage, flat out crazy about each other, which had embarrassed the hell out of Jack on more than one occasion.

Like the night before the shooting, when they'd slow danced a lot closer than parents were supposed to at his father's surprise fortieth birthday party. The night his father had eaten smoked boudin and chicken, laughed with his many friends, and kissed his wife as they'd danced to a sad Cajun song about love gone wrong.

Fourteen hours later Jake Callahan was lying in his middle son's arms, blood spurting out of a wound in his broad chest, turning the black-and-white marble floor into something like a Jackson Pollock painting.

Jack had come to the courthouse with the po'boy his mother had fixed for his father's lunch. He'd arrived just in time to catch the action. But hadn't been able to do a damn thing to save his father's life.

And had never quite forgiven himself for that failure.

"Fuck." He rubbed his forehead. Squeezed his eyes shut and welcomed the swirling white dots that replaced the scene that was frozen, like a fly in amber, in his mind.

Chapter Two consisted of those years when he no longer gave a shit about anything. Or anyone. Least of all himself.

The judge, perhaps out of a feeling of guilt, obligation, or kindness, Jack had never figured out which, hired the widow Callahan on as Beau Soleil's housekeeper. While Jack began his downward slide into delinquency. He ditched school, drank too much, smoked too much—pot and Marlboros—and if trouble was anywhere within a three-parish radius, he'd find it.

When he was seventeen he stole Sheriff Jimbo Lott's cruiser to go drinking and racing the backroads with a trio of badass buddies who probably hadn't had a working brain between them. There'd been a new moon. The night was pitch, the fog was rising off the water, and Jack had been plowed when he spun around a corner too fast and went sailing into the bayou.

They'd all gotten out with only a few cuts and bruises. It had taken a salvage team from nearby Lafourche parish to pull the wrecked cruiser out of the mire.

And the judge finally lost patience with his housekeeper's son.

Since the parish was too small to have a juvenile court system, Judge Dupree claimed jurisdiction. Justice may have been blindfolded, but she was swift.

The judge made a few phone calls, and within an hour Jack had been interviewed by an intake case worker, referred to the D.A, who'd immediately pressed charges, landing Jack before the bench, where the judge sentenced him in less time than it had taken him to hotwire that patrol car and he was sitting, handcuffed, behind the grill in the back of a DPS cruiser headed to the Juvenile Detention boot camp before the sun had risen.

At the time he'd been too drunk to be fully aware of the events of that night, but later, when he sobered up and remembered the stone-cold hatred in Sheriff Jimbo Lott's eyes glaring at him across the courtroom, Jack realized that the judge could well have saved his life.

By lights out that first night, Jack had also come to the conclusion that compared to most of the other delinquents in the camp, he was a wet-behind-the-ears baby when it came to hard crime. He stopped swaggering and actually listened to the Scared Straight lectures given by the Angola lifers who were bussed to the youth camp each month.

It didn't take long to figure out that as much as he might hate his life, a future behind prison bars was no future at all.

He made goals. The first was to get out of this place alive. Understanding that education was his way out of Blue Bayou, his second was to graduate on time from high school, join the navy, spend some time seeing the big wide world outside the swamp, then let Uncle Sam pay for college.

His third goal was somehow, someday, to make his mother proud of him.

For twelve excruciatingly long weeks he wasn't allowed any interaction with the outside world. Even phone calls were off limits.

When Marie Callahan finally arrived with Nate at the camp for her first visit, Jack would have had to have been blind not to see the hurt in her moist green eyes. She never laid a guilt trip on him. She didn't have to because always hovering unspoken between them was the shame Jack would have caused his father if Jake Callahan had still been alive.

He did his time, building up his body with intense physical training and building his mind in the library, where he read every book in the place. Twice. On the day before his eighteenth birthday, Jack walked out of the camp gates a free man.

A party had been in full swing when he arrived at Beau Soleil. Surrounded by a gaggle of adoring boys, Danielle could have been Scarlett O'Hara at the barbecue at Twelve Oaks.

He was headed to the kitchen when she spotted him.

"Jack! You're home!" Before he could escape, she'd run around the end of the sparkling blue pool and taken hold of his hand. "Come dance with me."

Wanting to save the bus fare, he'd hitched his way home, leaving him hot, dusty, and sweaty. He figured he fit into this scene about as well as a skunk at a garden party.

"I don't think that's such a good idea."

"Oh, pooh, don't be a spoilsport." Her remarkable eyes danced, her moist, too-tempting cherry pink lips coaxed. "It's my seventeenth birthday and I refuse to take no for an answer."

He couldn't help laughing at her persistence. She's always been a sweet, pretty little girl, who'd, his brothers had ragged him, obviously idolized him as she followed him around Beau Soleil like a little blond puppy. Then, when she turned fourteen and began being battered by female hormones, she turned as dogged as one of his daddy's old tracking hounds.

There'd been no escaping her. If he was working in her daddy's fields, she'd show up with a thermos of icy sweet tea that tasted, beneath the sweltering summer sun, like ambrosia. If he was lying beneath his car, cussing up a blue storm while fixing yet another damn oil leak, the enticing scent of flowers would waft into the garage over the smell of grease and there she'd be, pretending to be in desperate need of a screwdriver for some alleged household chore.

And Jack had definitely learned to stay away from the swimming pool, where she'd lie in wait, a wild child in a skimpy bikini she didn't begin to fill out, too young to know what kind of danger she could be courting.

He'd done everything he could at the time to convince Danielle that he wasn't interested, even while he tried not to break her innocent heart. Finally, after attempts to hide from her had failed and reasoning only fell on deaf ears, he'd had no choice but to tell her straight out that he already had a real woman, someone who knew how to please a man, a woman who didn't have to sneak out of the house to be with him and leave his bed before dawn because it was a school day.

She'd surprised him with her remarkably calm reaction, but it was obvious from the pain in her expressive eyes that she was crushed. Before he could try to smooth things over, he'd gotten drunk, stolen Jimbo Lott's cruiser, and ended up in juvie camp.

Danielle hadn't visited him. Her father certainly wouldn't ever have permitted that and neither would Jack. But not a week went by that he didn't receive a letter from her, telling him all about the goings on at Beau Soliel and at school, how his *maman* was, and his brothers. The tone was always light and chatty, in no way revealing either her crush or his curt treatment of her.

"Please, Jack?" she'd wheedled prettily that fateful night. "Surely you're not going to cause me crushing humiliation by rejecting me while the entire parish is watching?"

No. He may have been known around these parts as Bad Jack Callahan, but even he wasn't that cruel.

"Just one dance," he'd said. "Then I've gotta go tell *maman* I'm home."

"She'll be so thrilled. She wasn't expecting you until tomorrow." There was honest warmth in her smile.

"They needed my cot, so they sprang me a day early."

"I'm glad." She went up on her toes and twined her slender white arms around his neck. Her young firm breasts softened against his chest.

As he'd drunk in the scents of shampoo and lingering sunshine and everything that was sweet and lovely and innocent and female, Jack had smelled the snare the same way a wild animal could sense a trap buried in the swamp.

He'd reminded himself of his plan to escape this small town, warned himself that the southern belle who felt too damn good in his arms represented a helluva lot more trouble than he'd already managed to get involved with over his admittedly rocky eighteen years. Then hadn't listened to a word.

"*Dieu*, when you're right, you're right," he muttered now.

There were still times when he thought back on it and was amazed at the risks they'd taken. Crazy. That's what they'd both been that summer.

He wasn't going to think about Chapter Three, Jack decided. Those days returned to haunt him enough while he was sleeping; there was no point in reliving them when he was awake.

And now, here he was at Chapter Four. Right back where he'd started.

Same house.

Same girl.

"Proving," he said to Turnip, who burst out of the door the moment he opened it and began sniffing the night air as if searching out skunk, "that fate has one goddamn screwed-up sense of humor."

12

True to his word and more trustworthy than when he'd promised to meet her out at his daddy's camp and had never shown up, Jack arrived at the library the next day while Dani was going through the ruins, sorting out anything that was salvageable. If her heart lifted a little as she watched him climb out of the truck and walk toward her on that lazy, loose-limbed stride, she told herself that it was only because of the two carpenters he'd brought with him.

As they'd walked through the apartment, which still smelled of smoke and looked as if a horde of vandals had sacked it, both men demonstrated a reassuring knowledge of the work needed to be done to make the apartment livable.

"Won't be long before it'll be better than new," the younger man, Derek McCarthy, assured her. "And you and your boy can settle in."

"Could you give me a ballpark figure how long that might be?"

"Probably a month," John Reneaux, the older of the two men said as his gray eyes swept the scene. "Maybe two."

"That long?"

"We'll work fast," Derek promised. "And you'll be able to open your library up a lot sooner than that."

Which was, Dani thought, trying to look on the bright side as they went right to work, better than nothing. She watched Derek moving with catlike agility and confidence along the top of a rafter, and thought about how much difference a day could make. What a difference Jack had made.

"Thank you," she said after she'd walked him back to the truck, which, she noted with veiled amusement, boasted a bumper sticker proclaiming him to be *Coonass and Proud.* "I honestly do appreciate your generosity."

"It's no big deal." He rubbed his thumb up her cheek.

The light caress sent her pulse skittering.

Across the street Ernie Egan was sitting out on the bench in front of his barbershop, smoking his pipe between haircuts as he'd done for as long as Dani could remember.

Max Pitre was sitting beside him and from the way Ernie was jabbing his pipe in Max's direction, Dani guessed they were arguing about something. As they'd done for as long as she could remember.

Mrs. Mercier was arranging plump chickens, pork chops, and various sausages in the chilled display cases in the front window of the Acadian Butcher Shop while her husband unfurled the cheery striped green-and-white awning.

Arlan was changing movie posters at the Bijoux, and in the little park across the street a dark-haired woman was teaching her little girl, who appeared to be about a year old, how to toss bread to the ducks floating on the bayou water.

All around her, life seemed to be continuing on as normal. But for Dani, the world stopped spinning.

Jack combed her hair behind her ear.

A familiar thrill danced up her spine.

His lips quirked, but his gaze grew thoughtful as he looked down into her face. Unwilling desire percolated. Dani could feel it, bubbling up from some deep well of emotion inside her. Everything took on a slow-motion feel as he lowered his head.

A mistake, she warned herself. But did not, could not, move.

He brushed a quick, friendly kiss atop the crown of her head. "See you around, *chère*."

Caught off guard yet again, Dani blew out a surprised, frustrated breath, then shook her head to clear the fog as he drove away.

"What did you expect?" She rubbed at her cheek, which felt unreasonably hot, and was chagrined at the soot that came off on her fingers. "You undoubtedly look like a ragpicker."

And a far, far cry from the way she'd looked that night of her birthday party, when he'd finally granted her the wish she'd been wishing on the first star of the night for five years, ever since his mother had come to work at Beau Soleil.

The birthday night he'd held her in his arms. That moon-spangled, magical night when she'd been poised on the brink of womanhood, dancing with the man she firmly believed she was destined to spend the rest of her life with.

"You don't want to get involved with him," she warned herself firmly. After all, if his brother, Nate, was in another league, Jack was in an entirely different universe. As his truck turned the corner, she vowed to keep reminding herself of that fact.

"Dani?"

When she recognized the woman calling from the park, she laughed, welcoming the distraction. "Marisa? Is that you?"

Marisa Parker had been her best friend all through school. As little girls, they'd shared Barbies; in high school they'd exchanged confidences about boys and crushes. Then Dani had been sent to Atlanta for most of her senior year, Marisa's father, an oil engineer, had gotten transferred to Saudi Arabia, and they'd lost track of each other.

Dani hadn't realized how much she'd missed her friend until she watched her running across the street, pushing the stroller in front of her.

"I can't believe it!" Like the two teenagers they'd both once been, they hugged each other and rocked back and forth. "I heard you were coming home, but you didn't call—"

"I didn't know *you'd* come back," Dani said.

"Dennis teaches sixth-grade math at Assumption."

"Dennis? Are you talking about Dennis McGee?" He'd driven Marisa crazy; they'd fought nearly nonstop from the fifth grade on.

"Yep." Marisa flashed a gold band. "We got married three years ago. Tammy's our first." She pressed a hand against her flat stomach. "And Tyler or Kelli is on the way."

"How wonderful." Dani looked down at the baby, who was looking up at her, studying her with solemn blue eyes, and felt a prick in her heart. "Hello, Tammy. Aren't you a pretty girl?"

The baby's copper-penny-red brow puckered and she looked ready to cry. "She's at that stranger-danger age," Marisa said, plucking her daughter from the stroller and bracing her on her hip.

"She's precious," Dani said. "I'd heard you were living in New York." Dani bent down and picked up the stuffed dalmatian the baby dropped. When she held it out to her, Tammy continued to regard her suspiciously but snatched it away.

"I was. Living in SoHo and working on Madison Avenue cranking out advertising art."

"Did you like advertising?" All through high school Marisa had talked about going to Paris, having wild hedonistic affairs with crazed painters, and becoming a famous artist.

"It was okay." She shrugged. "Art's art, right? Even if it's telling the world about a new panty hose."

"Absolutely," Dani agreed loyally, secretly wondering how many kinds of panty hose the world really needed. Tammy looked Dani straight in the eye, then threw the dalmatian again.

"Hell, who am I kidding? I was miserable. Then, since my dad retired here, and Mom went back to teaching music at Assumption, I came to visit for the holidays. I went to the Christmas pageant, and to make a long story short, Dennis was there, we bumped into each other over the punch bowl at the cast party, and I was blindsided by a chemical brainbath that just about knocked me off my feet. I went home with him that night." She dimpled merrily. "And never left."

"I'm so happy for you."

"I'm happy for me, too," Marisa said as Dani bent down and retrieved the dog yet again. She glanced over at the building. "I hear you're going to reopen the library."

"That's my plan."

"I'm so glad. As bad as Mrs. Weaver was when we were growing up, she'd become an absolute terror in her old age."

"So I heard. I'm really looking forward to it; I have some ideas I wanted to try in Fairfax, but since I wasn't branch manager, and the last hired, I was pretty much relegated to reference work."

"And now you're in charge. Must be a nice feeling."

"It is nice to have the freedom to be innovative. Of course I'm also in charge of date stamping and reshelving. And if I hate my boss, I have only myself to blame."

They shared a laugh, and for a moment it felt like old times.

"I'm really sorry about all you've gone through," Marisa said. A shadow crossed her face. "I wanted to call. Or write, but your number was unlisted."

"Matt and I are surviving. I wouldn't wish the past two years on my worst enemy, but there have been some advantages. I've gotten tougher and I've definitely gained a better sense of who I am and what I want from life. And I actually speak my mind."

"Hallelujah, this calls for a celebration. I always wondered if you were going to spend your entire life playing the role of the quintessential Goody Two-shoes southern girl."

If the accusation had come from anyone else, Dani might have been offended, even if she was reluctantly coming to the conclusion it was true.

"Not always," she countered, thinking of Jack.

"That's right, you did have your little rebellion that summer before your senior year. I can't say I blame you. If I wasn't a happily married woman, I might have had an attack of rampant lust while I was working on Beau Soleil."

"You worked on Beau Soleil?"

"Yeah. I've gotten into painting again. I got my master's in art restoration and have landed a few jobs working on murals. I'm also teaching art classes two days a week at Assumption and an adult class at the community center on Wednesday nights."

"So it was you who touched up the mural?"

"It surely was. What did you think?"

"I think it's wonderful. And a much better showcase for your work than panty hose."

"Well, it was certainly a challenge. But fun. And thanks to Jack giving me the chance, I've picked up a few more jobs in Baton Rouge and New Orleans." When Tammy reached her arm back to send the dalmatian flying yet again, Marisa deftly plucked it from her daughter's pudgy hand. Which set off an ear-piercing scream.

"It's past her nap-time. I'm afraid she inherited my temper, which Mom says is payback for all the trouble I gave her." She plunked the wailing baby into the stroller. "We'll have to have lunch soon, reminisce about old times, and catch up. I'm dying to know what's going on between you and Bad Jack."

"Absolutely nothing."

"Yeah, it looked like nothing." She fanned her face as Tammy slapped her pudgy hands onto the stroller tray. "I got hot and bothered just watching the two of you."

"You're pregnant. Rampant hormones go with the territory."

"Well, that's certainly true enough." She hugged Dani again. "I'll call as soon as you get settled into your new job and we'll set a date for lunch. I can't wait to tell you about Luanne Jackson's supposed affair with some married state senator."

Luanne Jackson had been two years ahead of them in school, with curves that would put Kim Basinger to shame, a mass of long dark hair, and smoky eyes that offered sensual favors. She'd left Blue Bayou right after high school for New Orleans, where rumor had her changing her name to Desiree Champagne as soon as she'd stepped off the Greyhound bus. The stories went that she'd worked for a few years as one of the Big Easy's highest paid call girls before marrying Jimmy Ray Boone, a wealthy south Louisiana car dealer. Since Boone had been a big contributor to Lowell's campaigns over the years, Dani had occasionally hosted the couple at fund-raising parties and had always felt uncomfortable around his wife.

It hadn't been because of the prostitute thing; not being one to judge others, Dani figured that was between Luanne and her husband. No, this had been something entirely different. It had been almost, Dani had considered on more than one occasion, as if Luanne had some reason to resent her. Once, a few years ago, after another of those strangely strained dinners, Dani had wondered if the other woman might be having an affair with Lowell, but then he'd gone on television proclaiming his love for his chief of staff, and she'd immediately put the question out of her mind.

After Jimmy Ray had died—making love, the stories went—Luanne had surprised everyone by returning home and building a huge home on the outskirts of town. She may be, with the possible exception of Jack, the wealthiest person in the parish, but it appeared the widow was still Blue Bayou's Scarlet Woman.

As she watched her former best friend cross the street and load Tammy and her stroller into the minivan, Dani experienced a low tug of something that felt like envy.

She didn't begrudge Marisa her happiness. But it did strike Dani that her friend was living the life she'd once thought *she* would be living. Marisa had always been the one with the career plans, while all Dani had ever wanted was a husband and a houseful of children.

Reminding herself that she was no longer the lovesick teenager who'd once dreamed of making an idyllic life with Jack, the girl who'd envisioned having make-believe tea parties with daughters in pink tutus and attending Little League games for sons who'd wrestle in the backyard and put frogs in their sisters' sock drawers, Dani shook off the uncharacteristic self-pity, put aside her gilded, unrealistic romantic fantasies, and returned to work.

13

Like a child before the first day of school, Dani had a hard time sleeping the night before the library opened. She told herself she had nothing to be nervous about. After all, she was well prepared. The new books she'd ordered had arrived, been unboxed, cataloged, and were sitting on the special *New Release* shelves Derek had built for her, waiting for residents of Blue Bayou to take them home.

She'd had additional lighting installed to brighten up the interior and had covered the bulletin board that had held an outdated jumble of memos and notices dating back years with a bright, eye-catching sunshine yellow burlap and had tacked up glossy covers of suggested novels for the upcoming summer vacation season. She also posted notices announcing the formation of a book discussion group, a weekly children's story hour, and a reading competition for the middle school children, the weekly prize being free passes she'd cajoled Delbert Dejune, owner of the Bijoux Theater, into donating.

She'd spent the day before the opening cleaning until the windows sparkled like crystal and the old-fashioned oak catalogue cases, which Derek and John had moved from the storage room for her, gleamed with a lemon-oil sheen. As much as Dani appreciated her computer, which had every book in the library catalogued and was connected to other libraries throughout the state, she suspected that here, where time moved a little more slowly, some patrons might prefer the old-fashioned cards. As she secretly did.

The little pieces of paper were cut and ready for note taking, short yellow pencils sharpened. She'd designated the children's reading center by painting a corner of the room a welcoming sunshine yellow and had found a rug woven in crayon colors at an antique store in Houma.

A woman on a mission with a limited budget, she'd talked the owner into cutting the price by half, then throwing in a sturdy pine table for another five dollars. Derek had cut the legs down for her, making the table, which she'd painted a bright crawfish red, the perfect height for little readers.

Knowing when a valuable resource had dropped into her lap, she recruited Marisa to add her talents to the project, and by the night before the reopening, a parade of beloved book characters danced across the yellow wall.

At precisely ten o'clock on the morning of her first day on the job, she unlocked the door, a welcoming smile on her face, ready to greet the first patron. When five minutes passed, then ten, then ten more, she began to worry that perhaps the people of Blue Bayou had gotten so accustomed to not having a library, they'd just decided they could do without one.

Then, at ten twenty-eight, Marisa walked in the door with a half dozen other women she introduced as mothers of children in Tammy's playgroup.

"We're in desperate need of escapism," she announced. After asserting that the reopening of the library had saved their collective sanity, they made a beeline for the romance novels Dani had finally finished cataloging late last night.

From then on it was as if the floodgates had opened. Dani wondered if there was anyone in town who hadn't had a sudden need to check out a book. She knew that a great many of the people came out of curiosity but didn't care. So long as they came.

Finally, after lunchtime—which she'd skipped in order to find a book on boat building for Wilbur Rogers and another about dog training for Annie Jessup, whose fiancé, Jimmy Doyle, had surprised her with a cocker spaniel puppy for her birthday—the crowd cleared out, leaving Dani to catch her breath.

As soon as she solved this one last problem, she could duck into her office and eat the sandwich she'd brought with her.

"It's a red book," the woman repeated impatiently.

"A red book," Dani agreed with a smile that had begun to fade after five minutes. "About sex."

"Not sex," the woman corrected. Her silk dress, diamond earrings, and matching brooch were definitely overkill for a weekday. "Fantasies."

"Fantasies of a sexual nature," Dani clarified. Right now her own fantasies were centered more around a Big Mac and fries.

"Do you have a problem with that?" The woman's eyes frosted.

"Of course not." Dani wished she was wearing her *I Read Banned Books* pin.

Did she look like a stereotypical prude librarian who kept any books with a remotely sexual content hidden away beneath the counter? The kind she'd seen while watching *Citizen Kane* with Orèlia the other night on the classics movie channel—that bun-wearing, pursed-lip glaring dragon lady who ruthlessly guarded the gates of knowledge from perceived infidels?

The idea was too depressing to contemplate.

"I was just trying to narrow things down," she said mildly. "There are quite a lot of titles on fantasies."

"This one has a red cover."

"Red. Right." Dani decided that if she ever had the opportunity to build a library from scratch, she'd cross-catalogue all the books by color, since that's how so many people seemed to remember them.

The woman glanced around, combed a self-conscious hand through her sleek, expertly streaked blond hair, then leaned across the desk and whispered a single word.

Without so much as blinking an eye, Dani nodded and searched the computer database for *whips*.

Success! She plucked a stubby yellow pencil from its clothespin can holder Matt had made her for Mother's Day last year in Cub Scouts and wrote *Whips and Kisses*, along with the catalogue number onto a piece of paper.

"It's on the second floor. I can show you."

"That's all right. I can find it." As if uncomfortable having shared even that possible glimpse into her private life, the patron snatched the paper from Dani's hand and headed off toward the elevators, four-hundred-dollar high heels click-clacking on the pine floor.

"You're welcome," Dani murmured.

Since the Blue Bayou library was a great deal smaller than the Fairfax County branch she was accustomed to, Dani was exceedingly grateful for the inter-library loan system. She was filling out ILL requests when the door opened and in Jack strolled, looking outrageously sexy in jeans, a black T-shirt, and those wedge-heeled cowboy boots that gave even more of a swagger to his walk.

"Anyone ever tell you that you look too damn sexy to be a librarian?"

"Perhaps you should join the twenty-first century," she said sweetly. "Things have changed. Why, I can't remember the last time I wore my hair in a bun."

He tilted his head and studied her. "Wouldn't make any difference if you did. Any male with blood still stirring in his veins would just fantasize taking out the pins and running his fingers through it."

When a too vivid, long-ago memory of him arranging her waist-length hair over her bare breasts flashed through her mind, Dani began straightening the reservation requests, tapping the edges together. A good many of them were for Jack's latest.

"Tell me you're not here to take your carpenters back."

He briefly glanced up at the hammering coming from the third floor as if he'd forgotten that the men were working up there. "No. Actually, I came to check out the librarian."

"You really ought to find a collaborator to help write your dialogue. Because that pickup line probably goes back to a time when books were carved in stone."

"Next time I'll do better." He toyed with the ends of her hair. "What I really need is to get myself a library card."

"A library card?" Dani knocked his hand away. Jack had always been one to touch easily and often. Having grown up in a house where casual affection was an unknown, alien thing, with the exception of her child, Dani was not.

"This is a library, isn't it?"

"Of course it is."

He tucked his thumbs in his pockets, the gesture drawing her attention to the front of those outlaw black jeans that intimately cupped his sex. "Then I guess I've come to the right place."

She forced her gaze back to his face, which wasn't all that much of a help due to the devilish, knowing look in his eyes. "Why do you want a library card?"

" 'Cause I agree with Groucho Marx. 'Outside of a dog, a book's a man's best friend. Inside of a dog, it's too dark to read.' "

She absolutely refused to smile. Letting her guard down for even a minute with this man was just too dangerous. "Don't you have a book of your own to write? Or some paint to scrape?"

"The book's in the mulling stage. My heroine is temperamental." His smile was slow and rakishly seductive. "Like most beautiful females I know."

He made himself comfortable on the edge of her desk. "As for the paint, it'll be there tomorrow. Maybe I'll even check out a book on solvents." He trailed a lazy finger down the back of her hand and set her nerves to humming. "See if I can find somethin' to replace elbow grease."

"I'll need a photo ID." The trick, Dani told herself firmly, was to keep everything businesslike.

His lips quirked a bit, as if he privately thought she was being a bit petty demanding identification, which she admittedly was, but stood up again and whipped his driver's license out of the back pocket of his jeans, which, when he handed it to her, Dani took as yet more proof that life wasn't fair. Wasn't there some law against taking a terrific picture at the DMV?

She typed the information into the computer, then printed out the card.

"Just remember," she warned as she handed it to him. "I know where you live. Plus I can look up lots of ways to get back at people who don't return library books."

"Sounds kinky."

As if on cue, the blond chose that moment to return with her red *Whips and Kisses* and two other thick books of erotica.

"Go ahead." Jack moved out of her way. "I'm going to be a while."

"If you're sure." She gazed up at him as if she were a chocoholic and he'd been dipped in Hershey's syrup, causing Dani to wonder if that particular scenario was in any of those sex books she was checking out.

He flashed her an all-too-appealing smile, appearing worlds different from the grim-faced man on the jacket photo of his books. "My *maman* taught me to always let pretty ladies go first."

It was all Dani could do not to roll her eyes as the patron squeezed in front of him. The sexuality she radiated was turning the artificially cooled air in the library so steamy Dani could barely breathe.

Jack glanced over the woman's shoulder, then lifted his eyebrows at the titles as Dani date-stamped the books.

After slanting him one last-ditch come-hither look, the woman left the library.

"I'd sure as hell love to have myself a little glimpse into her fantasy life," he mused.

"If you leave right now, you can probably catch up with her." How fast could a woman walk in those ridiculous ice-pick heels anyway? "I've no doubt she'd be delighted to share a few of the more kinky ones with you."

"*Non*," he decided. "She's pretty enough. But not my type."

Dani would not demean herself by asking what his type was these days.

He placed both hands on her desk and leaned toward her. "Wanna know what kind of lady I like?"

He was close. Too close. "Not particularly."

Needing space, Dani swept up a stack of books from the return bin and headed off to reshelve them.

"Too bad. Because me, I'm gonna tell you." He took the books from her.

"What do you think you're doing?"

"Makin' up for an oversight."

"What oversight is that?" She shelved the book on animal husbandry he handed her and moved on to the next row.

"I never carried your books to school like a proper boyfriend."

"It was summer. There wasn't any school." She slipped a how-to book on building your own deck between one on construction materials and another on roofing. "Besides, you were hardly a proper boyfriend."

"That's true enough." His chuckle was warm and wicked. "Nothing proper about me. Which I seem to recall was just the way you liked it."

He handed her another book and followed her around the corner. "You ever do it in the stacks, *chère?*"

"Of course not."

"Me neither." Dani suspected the smile he flashed was undoubtedly much like the one Lucifer had pulled out to convince all those heavenly angels into joining him in hell. "It'll give us something to look forward to."

"I wouldn't hold your breath." Though she'd go to her grave before admitting it, his sexual arrogance fit him as well as those snug black jeans.

"You're a tough nut to crack. Good thing for both of us I've always enjoyed a challenge."

He took the last two books from her hands, tossed them onto the rolling cart nearby, then shifted her so that her back was against the book-filled shelves.

Dani drew in a sharp breath. “Don’t.”

“Don’t what?”

“Whatever it is you think you’re going to do.” Her voice hitched. “This is a public library, Jack.”

“And I’m the public.” He moved in, pressing his body against hers. His fully aroused body. “You’re trembling.”

The husky note in his voice felt like a caress. “I am not,” she lied.

“You don’ have to worry, Danielle. I’m not gonna hurt you.”

“I’m a librarian.” Her pulse quickened and her bones began to melt as he lowered his head and brushed his lips against hers.

He nibbled on her bottom lip and drew a shudder from deep inside her. “A very tasty one.”

“We can’t do this,” she complained, her body belying her protest as it molded compliantly against his. It took every ounce of restraint she possessed not to start rubbing against him.

“Don’t look now, but we’re doin’ it pretty damn well. So far.”

“That’s my point.” She managed to get her hands between them before she did something that would land her on the front page of the *Clarion*. And perhaps even on Jimbo Lott’s police blotter. “We’ve already gone too far.” She pushed against his chest. “Are you trying to get me fired?”

She felt him tense. Then back away. “Not today.” He was looking at her not with lust, but an odd, unreadable sort of curiosity that had her more nervous than the sex thing. “Thank you.”

“For what?” She scrambled to tuck her blouse back into her skirt before someone came looking for her.

He kissed her fingers, which seemed to have established a direct connection to other, more vital body parts. The bad-boy grin returned. “For giving me a new fantasy to contemplate while I’m getting all hot and sweaty pounding nails this afternoon.”

Danielle knew she was in deep, deep trouble when the thought of Jack Callahan all hot and sweaty was almost enough to make her go running after him.

14

The day of Dani's trip to Angola prison dawned dark and rainy. Not a very propitious sign, she thought as she watched the water streaking down the kitchen window. She knew Matt was picking up on her nervousness. His eyes followed her, concern easily readable in them.

"Don't worry, sweetie, it's going to be okay." She ruffled his hair. "Better than okay. It's going to be great." She wondered which of them she was encouraging, her son or herself.

"Do you think he'll like me?"

"I *know* he'll *love* you. How could he not? He's your grandfather. And you're a very special boy."

There was a knock at the front door. A moment later Orèlia entered the kitchen with Jack. "Look what the cat dragged in," she said with robust cheer.

"Morning," he greeted them.

Dani's nerves were already tangled enough. She didn't need Jack making them worse. "What are you doing here?"

"It's lovely to see you, too, *chère*." He skimmed a look over her. "Don't you look pretty as a speckled pup. You remind me of Audrey Hepburn in that movie. You know, the one about eatin' breakfast in a jewelry store."

Having no clue what the appropriate attire to wear to a prison might be, she'd changed clothes three times before finally settling on the simple sleeveless black dress. She'd twisted her hair into a smooth French roll she hoped would withstand today's humidity.

It was foolish to be dressing up for her father, but although she'd assured herself that she'd grown up, that she no longer yearned for his approval, Dani had also decided there was nothing wrong with looking her best when he saw her for the first time in more than seven years.

"A jewelry store's a funny place to eat breakfast," Matt said.

"Perhaps. But it's a very nice movie nonetheless." Dani snatched up his cereal bowl and headed toward the dishwasher.

"Mom, I'm not finished yet."

"Oh." She felt Jack's amused look as she plunked it back down in front of him. "Sorry."

"You must be Matt," Jack said. "I'm Jack Callahan."

Matt eyed Jack's hair and earring. "You're not a pirate, are you?"

" 'Fraid not."

"I didn't think so," he said a little wistfully. "But mom told me about the pirates who used to live here, so I thought just maybe a few might still be around."

"None that I know of," Jack answered. "Except for a couple subcontractors I've been dealing with lately," he added on afterthought. "And I'm not real certain, but I suppose, since my *maman*'s people have lived here just about forever, there's a chance I might have a pirate lurking somewhere in my family tree."

"That'd be cool."

"I guess it would, at that." Jack grinned. "I'm an old friend of your *maman*."

"From when she lived here?"

"Sure thing. We went to school together."

"Mom said she went to the same school I'm going to. Holy Assumption."

"That's the one. So, what's your favorite class?"

"Reading."

"Hey, mine was, too. Looks like we got somethin' in common, you and me."

"Did you like made-up stories?" Matt asked. "Or real ones?"

"Both. They each have their appeal."

"I like made-up ones," Matt said. "Sometimes I think up stories, but I've never written any down."

"You should." Jack tugged the Orioles cap lower over Matt's eyes. "An imagination is a great thing. You wouldn't want to waste it. . . . What else do you like to do? I liked recess a lot."

"Me, too."

"Is the baseball diamond still there?" Jack asked.

"Yeah. But I don't play baseball."

"Guess you're a hoops man." Jack rubbed his jaw and studied Matt. "Or maybe football. You look like a running back to me. I'll bet you can slip through the line like greased lightning."

"Not really. I don't play because nobody picks me for their team."

"I didn't know that." Dani was surprised. He'd always been one of the more popular boys at Fox Run. "It's probably because you're the new boy in class," she said consolingly.

"That's not it. They don't pick me because I don't know how to play."

Oh, Lord. She didn't need this. Not now. Not with a possible confrontation with her father looming and Jack seeming to take up most of the cozy kitchen.

"I wish you'd said something before now. But don't worry, we'll get a book and learn together."

"It's okay, Mom," he assured her quickly, looking as if he wished he hadn't brought the subject up. "The guys let me keep score, 'cause I'm real good with numbers and have all the rules memorized. Besides, you can't learn to play baseball from a book."

"Of course you can," the librarian in her rose to the occasion. "You can learn to do anything from a book."

"Your *maman*'s right," Jack said. "Books are powerful tools. But sometimes it's easier to learn things by doin' them. Me, I'm no Barry Bonds, but I used to play with my brothers, one who was good enough to get himself a scholarship playing third base at Tulane. How 'bout I give you a few pointers?"

"Really?"

When the wild hope in his eyes lit up enough to banish all the clouds from here to Mississippi, Dani enjoyed seeing her son so excited. She was also disturbed that Jack was the cause.

"Sure. It'll be fun. Maybe we can talk your *maman* into shagging fly balls."

"That'd be way cool. Did you used to play with her? When you were in school together?"

"*Mais* yeah." Dani heard the choked laughter in his voice and didn't dare look at him. "Your *maman* and me, we played some mighty fine games once upon a time ago."

Matt looked up at Dani, as if seeking confirmation. When she didn't immediately respond, his gaze shifted out the screen door. "Mom, look." He pointed toward the lawn where a six-foot-long alligator lay, seeking warmth from a narrow ray of sun that had broken through the dark pewter clouds. "The alligator's back."

"Bet you never saw any gators at your old house," Jack guessed.

Dani admired the subtle way he'd managed to point out a benefit to their move, a positive counterpoint to balance her son's less-than-positive playground problems.

"The most we ever had in Fairfax was squirrels."

"Squirrels are okay. But a gator's somethin' special. When I was a boy, just 'bout your age, we had one who lived at our house. My daddy tried like heck to get it to move on down the road. But *M'su Cocodrile*, which is another name we Cajuns sometimes call our gators, he liked it right where he was. So Daddy had to figure out some other way to deal with him."

"Did he shoot it?"

"Nah. That wouldn't have been fair. Since the gator was jus' lying there soaking up the sunshine, minding his own business. *Mon Dieu*, he'd stay out there all day, so long his shiny black skin would turn all gray and ashy lookin'."

"So what did he do?" Matt asked. "Your dad, not *M'su Cocodrile*."

"He tamed him."

"No way."

"Way. My hand to God." Jack lifted his right hand. "Now, it's not easy, trainin' gators, but my daddy, he was a patient man. The first thing he did was get down on his belly, flat out on the ground, so he was lyin' eyeball to eyeball with *M'su Cocodrile*."

"Really?"

"Absolutely. And then they had themselves a staring contest, that ole gator and my daddy."

Matt's eyes had widened to huge blue saucers. Dani tried to remember the last time she'd seen him so engaged in anything, and came up blank.

"Who won?"

"My daddy, of course. Wasn't a man nor beast in the state could stare him down. And I know, having tried it a time or two myself."

"Did *M'su Cocodrile* go away after he lost the staring contest?"

"*Non*. Oh, he wasn't happy about bein' bested that way, he. So he up and slapped his tail onto the water so hard—*wham!*"—Jack slammed his palm onto the table and made Matt jump—"water went sprayin' so high in the air, the weather guy on KXKC over in New Iberia reported that it was rainin' *crevi* over three parishes. That's a little teeny crawfish," he explained.

Clearly skeptical, Matt rubbed his nose. "Crawfish were coming down from the sky?"

"They sure were. Oh, it was somethin' to behold, let me tell you. But *M'su Cocodrile*, even as mad as he was to be bested by a man, still wasn't about to leave, because he liked our front yard so much. But we didn't have to worry any longer."

"Why not?"

"Because, you see, my daddy had already proven who the better man—or gator—was. So they came to an understandin', my daddy and *M'su Cocodrile*, that they'd just leave each other to his own business. Later my daddy taught him to bellow."

"I seem to recall alligators knowing how to do that without any special training," Dani interjected dryly.

The story was all lies, of course. But it was certainly entertaining her son.

"Sure enough they do," Jack agreed without missing a beat. "But I'll bet you never heard of one who'd do it on command."

He turned back to Matt. "All my daddy had to do was whistle." He pursed his lips and let out an earsplitting sound that had the alligator out on the lawn lifting his wide, corrugated head. "And *M'su Cocodrile*'d come from wherever he was in the swamp and pull himself up onto our lawn.

"Then he'd arch his back, which was as wide as this table, just like this"—he demonstrated again—"and let out a huge roar people could hear all the way across Blue Bayou, even down to the Gulf, where shrimpers would say that roar was the spookiest thing they ever did hear."

"He roared? Like a lion?"

"Not exactly. More like if you were to cross a lion with a locomotive. This was a roar that warned folks that they'd better not make the mistake of foolin' around with *M'su Cocodrile*. That sound shimmied itself right up your backbone and down again, rattlin' all your bones.

"Why, the family who lived down the road a ways swore that gator just roared their house right off its foundation."

"Wow." Matt let out a huge breath. "That's amazing."

"I thought so, too." Jack winked at Dani. "I sure did like that old reptile. He was an ugly fella, but likable, in his own way. Every day, round noontime, he'd come up to the boat dock, beggin' handouts. Got so my *maman* would make an extra po'boy just for him."

"I never heard of an alligator eating sandwiches."

"Oh, they're not choosy. They'll eat most anything you toss their way."

"What happened to him?"

Jack rubbed his jaw. "I don't know. One day he just up and went away. When I got a little older and learned about girls, how pretty they are and how good they smell, I sorta figured he met up with a lady gator and decided to set up housekeeping in *her* bayou."

"Alligators don't smell good."

"They do to other gators." The grin he flashed earned one back in return from Matt. Story finished, he turned to Dani. "You ready?"

"For what?"

"To drive on up to Angola and pick up the judge."

"I was intending to do that myself."

"Well, now, I can see why you might want a little privacy the first time you see your daddy after all these years, but the thing is, I sorta promised the judge I'd be the one to come fetch him."

"I see." An entirely different type of jealousy than the one caused by the erotica-reading blonde stirred. "I was planning to surprise him."

"Oh, you'll be doin' that, sure enough. Even with me doing the driving."

"Won't it be a little crowded in your truck?"

"Would be, if I'd brought it. But I've got the GTO today."

"Do you really have a GTO?" Matt breathed the name of the car with awe. Dani knew that in her son's personal hierarchy, this outranked even a pirate.

"Sure do. Three deuces, a four-speed, and a three-eighty-nine. That big ol' engine can suck birds from the sky. Have to be careful whenever I drive past mamas taking their newborns for walks, so I won't accidentally suck their little babies right out of their carriages."

"Mr. Callahan has always been fond of exaggeration," Dani informed her son.

"Why don't you call me Jack," he suggested to Matt. "Since Mr. Callahan sounds awful formal for friends. And to tell the truth, I haven't sucked any babies up, but like I said, that's because I'm real careful whenever I drive by 'em.

"My aunt Marielle found the car out in her barn over in New Iberia after her husband passed on and gave it to me way back when I was in high school. It needed the rust ground off it and a new paint job, but the minute I lifted that old tarp and saw what Uncle Leon had been hidin' under there all those years, I thought I'd died and gone to heaven."

"Wow." Matt exhaled a long breath, enthralled by the thought of such a wondrous event. "You were really lucky."

"Yeah. I've had to store it for a lot of years, since I was sorta moving around the world, but the first thing I did when I got back here was get her detailed and lookin' as fine as ever. So you like cars, huh?"

"Yessir!"

"I doubt if there's a Hot Wheels car my son doesn't own," Dani said.

"Mom doesn't understand it's a guy thing," Matt explained to Jack.

The remark was so out of character, Dani could only stare at him.

"Your mom's a terrific lady, but what can you expect from someone who drives a station wagon?"

"That car just happens to be the safest vehicle on the road," Dani informed him. She'd studied all the crash tests before buying it five years ago to ensure Matt's security.

"Probably is. But it's still a chick car. A mom chick car," he tacked on.

She folded her arms. "Perhaps that's because I *am* a mother. Who wants to keep my child safe. It also happens to be a grown-up car. Unlike some others."

"The GTO sure isn't for grown-ups," Jack agreed easily. "That's what's fun about it." He grinned at Matt again. "There's a car show in Baton Rouge next month. Wanna go check out the new concept cars?"

"Wow! Can I, Mom?"

"*May* I. And we'll see."

"You can come, too," Jack offered magnanimously. "Maybe find yourself a nice new minivan."

"Thank you." Her answering smile was sweetly false. "I'm quite happy with the vehicle I have."

"Please may I go, Mom?" Matt asked again on something perilously close to a whine.

"I said, we'll see."

"Give your mom some space, Matt," Jack suggested. Then he winked, guy to guy. "I'll work on her on the way to the prison."

Dani folded her arms, preparing to stand her ground. "I still don't need you to drive me—"

"I think it's a grand idea," Orèlia entered the argument. "You wouldn't want to risk making a wrong turn along the way, gettin' lost in the storm, and keeping your papa waiting."

Dani refrained from pointing out that since her father had, by his own choice, by ignoring all her letters and phone calls and refusing to let her visit the prison, waited seven long years to see her and his only grandson, a few minutes one way or the other wasn't going to make that much difference.

But it would. The idea of her father being in prison was horrible enough. The mental image of him walking out with no one there to meet him was unthinkable.

Jack was standing there, leaning against the refrigerator door, legs crossed, hands in his pockets, appearing deceptively easygoing. But the steely look in his eyes assured Dani that she didn't stand a chance to win this one.

Knowing when she was licked, she relented on a huff of breath. "All right. It appears I don't have any choice."

"Oh, you always have a choice, *chère*," he responded easily. "And this is a good one you're makin'."

She kissed Matt, said goodbye to Orèlia, who'd watched the little drama being played out in her kitchen with undisguised interest, then made a dash through the rain to the car, which he'd painted the same candy apple red it had been that summer.

"You really didn't have any right to do this," she muttered when they were both in the car.

"Far be it from me to start a day out by arguing with a pretty woman, but you're wrong. I told you, sugar, I made a promise."

"I don't know why *that* should bother you. Since you've certainly broken promises before."

"Be careful what buttons you push, Danielle." He twisted the key in the ignition. "Because sometimes a person can get into trouble when they don't know what they're talking about."

The engine came alive with a mighty roar that vibrated through her bones, reminding Dani of those reckless drag races that could have gotten him killed, even though he'd always won. "I know what happened," she countered. As soon as she'd shared the innermost secret of her heart—that she loved him—he'd taken off.

He shot her a look. "You're dead wrong."

The easygoing man who'd offered to teach her son how to play baseball, who'd invited him to a car show, and concocted that ridiculous tall tale about Sheriff Callahan taming an alligator was gone. In his place was a rough, dangerous man who looked every bit the devil people had once claimed him to be.

Not having any idea what to say to this intimidating stranger, Dani held her tongue on the drive out of town.

Perhaps it was because the rain streaming down the window and the dark, lowered sky heightened the intimacy of their situation, perhaps it was because he'd been thinking of her continually these days as his heroine took on more and more of Dani's traits.

Perhaps it was because whenever he did finally fall into bed after a long day of working on the house and an equally long night of writing, his dreams were filled with her.

Or it could be, Jack considered, because she was back in the same car where they'd passed so many hot summer nights. More than likely it was all of the above, but the woman was driving him crazy.

The scent blooming from her skin was like green meadows after a summer rain, reminding him all too vividly of the day they'd gotten drenched going out to his camp in the pirogue. They hadn't bothered to dry off. He'd dragged her to his bed as soon as they'd gotten in the cabin door, and they'd rolled around on the moss stuffed mattress, ripping at each other's clothes, her soft white hands as desperate as his, her mouth as hungry, her slender body as fluid as water, as soft as silk, as hot as hellfire.

He wondered if she'd taste the same.

Wondered if she'd still make those sexy little noises when he took her breasts into his mouth and sucked so hard he could feel her tightening around him.

Wondered if she'd still scream when she came?

"I don't understand why you're doing this," Dani said, breaking the silence.

"I told you, I promised the judge."

"I wasn't talking about driving to the prison. I'm referring to the way you've been treating me. It was obvious you didn't want to see me when I first came home. You wouldn't return my calls, you made me come all the way out into the swamp at night to track you down at Beau Soleil, and when I did, you said the same thing you told me that summer, that I should stay away from you."

"You probably should."

"Then why did you show up at the library and talk about carrying my books? Why did you go out of your way to be nice to Matt? Was all that talk about baseball and cars just a way to sleep with me?"

"*Bon Dieu*, I'd never use a boy to get sex from his *maman*." Since it grated that she'd actually believe he was capable of something that low, he decided if she was going to think the worst, he might as well help her out. He twisted his mouth into a mocking leer of a smile. Then winked. "I can handle that all on my own."

"You're doing it again." Jack liked the heat in her voice. Liked that he could still get beneath her skin and tap the passion he knew flowed there.

"Doin' what?" he asked, knowing exactly what she was talking about.

"Swinging back and forth between treating me like you'd just as soon I pack Matt in the car and drive back to Virginia, then acting as if you want me in your bed—"

"Oh, there's no acting goin' on there. I definitely want you in my bed. Or *your* bed. Or the backseat, like in the good old days, and on top of your tidy little library desk.

"The truth of the matter is that I want you just about every place and every way there is to do it, sugar. And a few that haven't been invented yet."

"That's just sex."

"Hell yes, it's sex. And it'd be damn good. The best you've ever had."

"When you get around to using that library card, Jack, you might want to check out a dictionary."

"Why?"

"So you can look up your picture under *arrogance*."

"It's not braggin' if it's true," he repeated what he'd said when she'd complimented him on his gumbo.

Jack gave her points for trying, but he wasn't buying that cool act. Her hair was already escaping the neat French roll, little tendrils of it trailing down her cheek. She could pull her lips into as tight a line as she wanted, but any man still alive below the waist could see that full, luscious mouth had been created to satisfy male fantasies.

In her little black dress and pearls she could have been on her way to some uptown lady's tea. But Jack could see beneath the almost prim exterior to the woman who, ever since she'd landed back in town, had him thinking too damn much about dark rooms, hot nights, and tangled sheets.

He reached across the space between them and caressed her leg.

"We didn't have all that much in common back then." He slipped a finger beneath the short hem of her skirt, traced a slow, figure eight on the silky skin at the back of her knee, and was rewarded by her sharp intake of breath.

"Jack—"

"The princess and the jailbird," he murmured, ignoring her intended protest. Not quite sure which of them he was tormenting more, he kept his eyes on the rain-slick road while moving his hand higher. "But we were sure damn good at driving each other crazy."

She didn't even attempt to answer that. Her breath turned choppy as his fingers skimmed up the inside of her thigh to play with the elastic band at the leg of her French-cut panties. He had the hard-on of his life and heaven was just a few inches away.

"Dammit, Jack, would you just knock it off?"

It was like turning off a lightbulb. One minute she'd been lifting her hips, like a fluffy marmalade *'tite chatte* begging to be petted. The next she was jerking away as if he'd replaced his finger with a red-hot poker.

Which, Jack thought with grim amusement as he returned his hand to the steering wheel, was damn close to what he wanted to do.

She massaged her temples. "I don't know what gets into me whenever I'm with you."

"Same thing gets into me, sugar. Lust, pure and simple."

"It's not simple." She leaned her head against the back of her seat and pressed her fingers against her eyelids. "Nothing about you has ever been simple."

"Me?" He lifted a hand to his chest. "I've always been an open book."

It was, admittedly, a lie. But Jack had gotten so used to lying, it sure wasn't going to keep him up at night worrying about it.

"The kind of book that comes in a brown paper wrapper."

She shot him a bleak, confused look that if his groin wasn't throbbing so damn hard would have probably strummed any lingering chords of conscience he might have buried somewhere deep inside himself.

"How do you do it? Five minutes with you and I'm seventeen years old again."

He shrugged. "You're not a teenager anymore, Danielle. You're a woman. A beautiful, desirable woman with a strong sex drive. You should be celebrating, you. Instead of fretting that pretty head over somethin' that's as natural as breathing."

"For you, perhaps."

"*Mais* yeah." Just as he'd refused to deny it the other night, he would not now.

"I'm not made that way."

"Coulda fooled me." As often happened in this lowland country, the rain ceased as quickly as it had begun. When the sun broke blindingly through a break in the clouds, he pulled a pair of sunglasses from his shirt pocket and shoved them onto his face. "Another couple minutes with my hand up your skirt, and you would have been jumping right into my lap."

"That was a mistake." She pretended a sudden interest in the stands of cypress outside the GTO's passenger window. "One that won't be happening again."

"You go ahead and tell yourself that if it makes you feel better. But I remember having to wear a shirt all that long hot summer because your fingernails kept stripping skin off my back. And don't think I've forgotten how you went off like a Mardi Gras firecracker the first time I put my mouth between your legs. And—"

"I get the point," she cut him off. "But for your information, I was only that way with—"

She slammed her mouth shut, but it was too late.

"With me." Hell, perverse as he was, Jack was even enjoying the way she was glaring at him.

"Arrogant," she muttered.

"And good," he reminded her. "The best you've ever had, I believe you were going to say."

She arched a blond brow. "Now you're a mind reader?"

"*Non*. I don't have to. Not when your pretty face and curvy little body is saying, 'I want to fuck Jack Callahan.' "

"I've never used that word in my life."

"Don't have to say it to do it, angel."

She cursed. It wasn't the *F* word. But it was damn close. Jack grinned.

"Good as I was, I've gotten a whole lot better. Jus' you wait and see."

"Why don't I take your word for it, and we'll leave it at that," she suggested on a huff that did appealing things to her breasts.

Of course, everything about Danielle Dupree was proving appealing. Which, if he had any sense, would scare the shit out of him. But oddly enough, as successful as he'd become these past years, for the first time in a very long while Jack was enjoying himself immensely. Enjoying her.

15

If it weren't for the seriousness of her mission, if they were only out for a Sunday drive, Dani would have appreciated the stunning scenery. Towering oak trees draped in silver Spanish moss lined the road, pecan trees stood in straight rows in rolling fields and towered over houses in small yards. The azaleas were in bloom, dazzling the eye with riots of color.

"You know," she murmured as the scenery flashed by the passenger window, "you won't be able to keep your promise to meet my father at the prison if you end up getting us both killed."

He slanted her a sideways look. "Wanna know one major difference between men and women?"

"Not particularly. But I've no doubt you're going to tell me."

"A man can actually quietly enjoy a car ride from the passenger seat."

"And women don't necessarily feel the need to drive faster than the speed of sound."

"This car, she wasn't meant to go slow." As if to prove his point, he stepped on the gas causing the car to shoot forward as if shot out of a cannon. "I remember a time when you liked to go fast."

"I was seventeen. There should be a general amnesty for any stupid, reckless things people do in their teens."

"You're not gonna get any argument from me on that, sugar."

Although he was still breaking the speed limit, he eased up on the gas. Just a little. Silence settled over them, broken only by the sound of Steve Riley and the Mamou Playboys doing the *Creole Stomp* on the radio.

"How much farther?"

Dani had been to the prison once, when a friend's parents had taken both girls to the rodeo put on by the inmates every Sunday in October. But that had been a very long time ago, and needless to say, she'd never had a reason to return. Until now.

"About fifteen more minutes."

Another milepost blurred by. Jack muttered a rough French word Dani didn't recognize, but didn't need a translator to know it was a curse.

"What's wrong?"

He blew out a breath. "Look, I made a promise to the judge."

"I know. To pick him up today."

"There's more." He shook his head. His smile was rife with a grim humor she couldn't decipher. "Who would have thought I'd have any conscience left, me?" he murmured, more, Dani thought, to himself, than to her.

At a loss, she wished she could see his eyes and realized, as she never had before, how much Jack kept hidden.

He'd always been so outrageously outspoken, seeming to enjoy scandalizing people by ignoring the polite and complex rules of southern society, that if you didn't look carefully, as she was doing now, you'd never notice how much he actually held back.

"I've been trying like hell to keep my word, but this isn't fair to you," he was saying when she shook off the sudden insight, deciding to think about it later. "If the judge ends up living with you—"

"He will be living with me." Dani would not allow herself to think otherwise.

"Then you have the right to know he's not well."

Icy fingers twisted at her stomach. Dani stared hard at a trio of Lycra-clad cyclists who were framed in the window for an instant as she and Jack sped past. "Exactly *how* not well? What's wrong with him?"

"In a nutshell? He says he's dying."

She shifted in her seat, turning not just her head, but her entire body—which throbbed as if it had been hammered with a two-by-four—toward him.

"I don't believe that." It couldn't be true. Surely her father would have broken down and written to her about that?

"Hell, Danielle, I'm sorry." His expression echoed his words. "I tried to talk him into at least lettin' the prison doctors get in touch with you, but, well"—he shrugged—"you know how mule-headed he can be."

"He doesn't want anything to do with me," she said flatly. "Even when he's dying." Of all the things her father had done to hurt her over the years, this was the worst.

"He didn't want to burden you."

"Burden me?" Dani's voice cracked. "He's my father, dammit!" She looked out the window again, the rolling green hills blurred by a veil of unshed tears. "We're supposed to be a family."

"I figure he feels he let you down when he broke the law."

"I refuse to believe he broke the law. But even if he had, he would only have done it to save his home. The same way Annabel Dupree did when the Yankee army marched upon Beau Soleil."

The former New Orleans socialite had killed every chicken on the place and roasted them for the invading Northern troops to keep them from looting and burning the plantation home.

Desperate times called for desperate measures. Dani had grown up on grand tales of the various sacrifices that had been made by her ancestors to keep the house in the family for generations.

"The judge always set some pretty high standards. As hard as he was on others, he was even harder on himself. Which, I suppose, is why he refused that plea bargain people say the D.A. practically got down on his knees beggin' him to accept."

"My father, unfortunately, can be incredibly rigid."

He certainly hadn't given into her tears when she'd begged to be allowed to continue dating Jack. He'd called him a delinquent, and perhaps he had been. But these days people would see an angry boy who'd been emotionally wounded that horrific day he'd held his dying father in his arms. The day Jake Callahan had given his own life to save Dani's father.

Fate, Dani thought on a soft, sad sigh, often seemed like a web, all the people and events being complexly connected, destined, no matter how they might struggle against its silken threads, to meet at the center.

Nor had he relented when she'd wanted to stay in Blue Bayou during her pregnancy. Or that memorable day, a week before her daughter had been born, when she'd used her single weekly allotted telephone call, pleading to be allowed to keep her child.

"You say he's dying. What's the diagnosis?"

"Congestive heart disease."

Hope instantly fluttered delicate wings in Dani's heart. "That's not necessarily fatal. Has he gotten a second opinion? A third? Or is the only medical care he's had the past seven years a prison doctor?"

"Hell, I don't know. It was like pulling teeth to get him to tell me as much as he did."

"Which was?"

"Apparently he signed up to be part of some medical test group five years ago after his first heart attack."

"First?"

"He's had two, that I know of. The second one got him kicked out of the test group, since instead of gettin' better, he's worse than he was."

"Which means for five years his heart problems were getting worse because he wasn't getting appropriate treatment?"

"That's how those tests work. You can't go combining regimes or no one would ever know which drug was working and which wasn't."

That earlier valiant hope took a nosedive. Dani managed to pull it up again.

"Surely there's something that can be done. Bypasses, transplants, shunts, that roto-rooter procedure I saw on some television news magazine, new drugs, defibrillators, all sorts of things."

"Like I said, I don't know the details. But I do know it was his choice to take part in the study. Nobody held a gun to his head."

"Why would he do such a thing?"

"Beats me. But knowing the judge, I'd guess he was trying to give back to society. Maybe make amends for what he did."

"Even if he did those crimes, which I'll never believe he did, that's what going to prison is supposed to be about. You do your time, pay your debt, and resume your life."

Damn the man! How could he be so egocentric? Didn't he realize he wasn't the only person affected by such a life-and-death decision? He might not want to acknowledge them, but he had a family. A daughter and a grandson he should have been thinking about.

She'd just begun the climb out of despair into irritation rising quickly to a healthy, cleansing temper when the prison came into view. If Jack's GTO was like a time machine back to the 1960s neither of them had ever personally known, this was like going back a hundred and fifty years.

Formerly a plantation farmed by slaves who'd been forcefully uprooted from their homeland in Angola, Africa, the Angola State Penitentiary was the largest—and one of the toughest—in the United States. Bordered by the levee of the Mississippi River on three sides, the eighteen thousand acres were now tended by a convict workforce.

When two straight lines of prisoners carrying hoes and shovels marched along the levee into the cotton fields, guarded by armed men on horseback, the harsh reality of her father's life these past years hit home.

Her stomach, which had been tied up in knots, lurched. "Could you please pull over?"

He didn't hesitate. Then got out of the car and waited calmly at the side of the road while she threw up.

"I'm sorry." The tears she'd been fighting broke free, trailing down her cheeks. She dashed at them with the back of her hands. "It's just that I'm beginning to feel like those balloon clowns they used to sell at Cajun Days. Every time I think I'm managing to stand on my feet, I get knocked down again."

He took out a square white handkerchief and silently handed it to her.

"Thanks." Dani blew her nose. "I didn't realize there was anyone anywhere in the world who still used these things."

"I'm an old-fashioned kinda guy," he said mildly as he retrieved a stick of gum from his shirt pocket.

Nervous about today, Dani hadn't slept well last night, and the sugar from the Juicy Fruit hit like a jolt in her bloodstream.

"And you may feel like one of those balloons, sugar, but the important thing is, you keep gettin' back up again."

She sniffled. "It's not that I have much of a choice. A single mother can't afford the luxury of a nervous breakdown."

"Maybe you just need someone to take a bit of the burden off your shoulders for a while."

He skimmed his palms over the shoulders in question. Then, as if it were the most natural thing in the world to do, drew her into his arms.

"Why, what a dandy idea." As if it were the most natural thing in the world for her to do, she rested her head against his shoulder. Just for a moment, Dani assured herself. "So, are you going to call my fairy godmother, or should I?"

He chuckled, but when he tipped her face up with a finger beneath her chin, lifting her gaze to his, his warm eyes were more serious than she'd ever seen them.

"You're spinning a helluva lot of plates right now. What with trying to get the apartment livable again after the fire, a new job, settling your boy in a new school, taking your father in."

"I'm handling things."

"Sure you are."

Jack liked the little sparks of temper and resolve he kept witnessing. The Danielle he'd known back then had been frustratingly acquiescent. In fact, the only time he'd ever seen her go after something was when she'd wanted him. And then it had been damn the torpedoes, full speed ahead.

Jack had long ago come to the conclusion that there was nothing more powerful than a teenage girl determined to snare herself a boyfriend.

"You're handling everything damn well, from what I can tell," he said. "But all of us could use a little help now and then. So how 'bout you let me be in charge of makin' you feel good?"

"I suppose feeling good would involve sex?"

"That's one of the most fun ways."

She looked up at him through moisture-brightened eyes. "Jack. Write this down. I am not going to have sex with you."

"Sure you are." He lifted her knuckles and grazed them with his smiling lips. "But me, I'm a patient man. Meanwhile, we'd better get movin'. Before one of those guards with the rifle in his lap decides to check out what we're doing here hangin' out on the side of this road."

"I hate thinking of my father working on a prison gang," she said when they were headed toward the prison.

"Then don't. Because he never so much as lifted a hoe."

"Because of his illness?"

"That might've had something to do with it. If he'd been in the general population. Which he wasn't."

"He wasn't?"

"Dani, the guy's a judge," he reminded her. "A hardliner who spent most of his adult life sending people to prison. *This* prison. Do you think the warden's actually going to risk having him spend his days and nights with grudge-carrying felons who are more than likely armed with some lethal homemade weapon?"

Dani had thought of that, early on. Then forced it out of her mind, when her father refused to have any contact with her and the worry became too difficult to handle. Heaven knows Lowell had been no help. He'd refused to even speak about his former mentor, the man who'd gotten him elected.

Nor had he done a single thing to attempt to get his father-in-law's sentence commuted or win a pardon for the man everyone, including the sentencing judge, acknowledged had, despite how people may have felt about him personally, been a pillar of integrity.

"He's been in solitary confinement for seven years?"

"Pretty much. But the past year they've let him volunteer in the hospice program, which I think has been good for him."

Dani drew in a deep, shaky breath. "I hate this."

"You could've stayed home."

"Not coming out here. I hate all this."

She waved a hand, taking in the fields, the workers bent over their hoes like some painting of slaves in the 1800s, the guards on their horses, the swamps on the fourth side of the penitentiary, the high fences, towers, the compound of buildings they were approaching.

"I hate thinking of my father wasting so many years behind bars with common criminals."

"Nothing common about the judge," Jack agreed.

Dani was grateful that he didn't point out, as he could have, that her father may not be common, but what he'd been convicted of, no matter the reason, had indeed been a criminal act.

And while she wasn't about to admit it, she was also grateful that she wasn't going to have to face her father for the first time after all these years alone.

As it turned out, things didn't go as badly as Dani had feared. They went worse.

To begin with, her father looked nothing like the larger-than-life figure she remembered. Despite Jack having warned her he was gravely ill, the first sight of him came as a terrible shock.

His formerly thick black hair was now a wispy bit of white, his complexion, beneath its prison pallor, the sickly hue of library paste. The white suit he'd always worn with the confident panache of Tom Wolfe strained at the seams.

"I thought he'd be thinner," she murmured.

"I checked with a doc in town about heart disease," Jack surprised her by revealing. "She said that when the heart isn't pumping right, fluids tend to build up, making a person look heavier, even when he isn't eating very much."

Rather than marching through the prison gate on his former robust stride, her father's stooped shuffle nearly broke Dani's heart.

"You gonna be all right?" Jack asked quietly when she sucked in a harsh painful breath.

He was leaning against the red fender of the car, arms folded over his chest.

"Yes." Dani set her face into a fixed half smile. She would not allow her horror to show.

Her father lifted a hand, as if to greet Jack. Then, as he viewed Dani standing beside him, his face darkened. "What are you doing here, Danielle?"

"Hello to you, too, Daddy." She kissed his cheek and steeled herself against the coldness that was even more painful than she remembered. "I came to bring you home."

"Don't have a home anymore." He shot a look toward Jack, whose expression remained inscrutable. "Callahan's livin' in it now."

"So I recently discovered."

His eyes, which were still as bright and avid as an eagle's, bored into hers. "You saying that husband of yours never told you he picked it up for back taxes?"

"No. I'd been under the impression that we'd lost it years ago."

He looked at Jack, who nodded. "Well," the judge decided on a shrug, "guess it doesn't matter all that much. What's done is done. Might as well get this show on the road."

Dani climbed into the backseat, leaving the passenger seat for her father, who did not seem inclined to speak as they headed back to Blue Bayou. A strained silence filled the car.

"Matt's really looking forward to meeting his grandfather," she volunteered after they'd gone about ten miles.

"I told you to tell the boy I was dead."

"The *boy's* name is Matthew and since I don't lie to my child, that wasn't an option."

"Better he think his grandfather dead than find out he's a jailbird."

"Matt knows you made a mistake you were punished for."

"So you told him his grandfather was put in time-out for seven years?"

"Something like that," she said evenly as Jack shot her an encouraging look in the rearview mirror. Not wanting to get into an argument that might make her father angry and cause him to have a heart attack before she could even get him home, Dani took a deep breath and tried again.

"Matt's a very special boy, Daddy. He's warm-hearted and extremely tolerant. He's always the first to make friends with the new children in his class. And he reads way above his grade level."

"So did you. Didn't you win the reading certificate every year?"

"I never realized you were aware of that."

"Just because I didn't come to the school awards assemblies didn't mean I didn't know what was going on. After all, who do you think wrote the checks to pay for those fancy frames Mrs. Callahan kept buying?"

Dani's spirits took a little dive at the idea that the only reason her achievements stuck in her father's mind was that they'd cost him money. For not the first time, she also realized how fortunate she'd been to have Marie Callahan as a surrogate mother during those turbulent teen years.

"Jack says you volunteered in the hospice program."

"Jack talks too much." The judge glowered Jack's way.

Jack shrugged, obviously unwounded.

Reminding herself that part of her reason for returning home had been to try to establish a sense of family for her son, Dani refused to allow her father's negative attitude to ruin their long-awaited reunion. "I hadn't realized they had hospice programs in prison."

"Eighty-five percent of the inmates in Angola are going to die in there. You think they all get shived in the shower? Most die of old age. Like they say inside, life's a bitch, then you die."

"What a lovely thought." Perhaps the prisoners ought to start printing it onto the license plates.

Dani wondered why she was even trying. She'd never been able to get through to the man. What on earth had made her think time would have changed the chasm between them that had often seemed as wide and deep as the Grand Canyon?

"I hope you're not going to talk this way to Matt."

"Should've told the boy I was dead."

Dani exchanged another glance with Jack in the mirror, hating the pity she viewed in his eyes.

"His name is Matthew," she repeated firmly. "Whether you like it or not, Daddy, we've come back home to Blue Bayou and you're going to live with us and get to know your only grandson, because if you really *are* terminally ill, the least you can do is make the most of your time.

"So, you may as well just get used to the idea and quit being so damn negative because I refuse to let Matt feel as shut out of your life as I always did."

He turned around and looked at her with blatant surprise. "When did you get that smart mouth?"

"When I discovered that nobody was giving out plaques to good, acquiescent southern girls."

He shot a look at Jack. "I suppose you've got something to do with this."

"Not me." Jack shrugged. "Though personally, I think it suits her."

"Figures you'd be all for her sassing her daddy. You also didn't have any right to go tellin' her about my heart condition."

"And have you keel over one morning and have her not at least know enough about your medical history to tell the EMTs? Besides, she's your daughter. She obviously, for some reason I sure as hell can't fathom, loves you. And she's damn well entitled to know the truth."

"Would you two stop talking about me as if I weren't in the car," Dani complained. "I'm horribly sorry you're ill, Daddy, and I don't want to unduly upset you, but if something bothers me, I'm going to speak my mind and you're both just going to have to damn well deal with it."

Her father folded his arms, glared out the window, and cursed beneath his breath. Dani met Jack's gaze in the mirror again. When he winked, she managed a faint, reluctant smile in return.

16

Jack kept telling himself that he shouldn't care that the judge was acting like a first-class prick to his daughter. After all, Danielle was a grown woman, capable of making her own choices. Her father might have wanted her to marry Lowell Dupree, but from what he'd heard, no one had held a shotgun on her, or dragged her kicking and screaming down the aisle.

No one had asked her to come back to Blue Bayou, either, and he knew the judge sure as hell hadn't invited her out to Angola today. It was obvious the old man wasn't turning cartwheels about her coming back home.

Hell, truth be told, Jack didn't want her here in Blue Bayou. He didn't want her, with her big hazel eyes and sweet lips and sexy little female body messing with his mind, making him think of things and times he'd done his best to forget.

He didn't want her *here*. But, *mon Dieu*, he sure as hell wanted *her*. It was just sex, Jack assured himself. That's all it was. That's all he'd let it be.

A woman like Danielle Dupree would take too much out of a man. Hell, he was already being sucked into emotional quicksand. When he'd found himself having to curl his fingers tighter around the steering wheel, to keep from punching the judge in his frighteningly puffy gray face for having made her look on the verge of crying again, Jack knew he was getting in even deeper.

Worse yet was the increasingly strong desire to take her back to Beau Soleil and make love to her in that once pretty room where they'd spent so many stolen nights, and promise to protect her.

Now that, Jack thought, was a fucking damn dangerous thought.

He'd stopped believing he could protect anyone that day in a Colombian warehouse when because of him, a helluva lot of people had died and a good woman had been widowed.

"What on earth?" Dani stared in disbelief at her son. His darling freckled face was bruised and battered, his bottom lip was swollen, his eye—surrounded by ugly purplish blue flesh—was nearly swollen shut, and his knuckles were bleeding.

"I didn't have any choice, Mom. I had to fight."

"There's always another choice besides fighting. You never fought at your old school."

"I didn't have to back there."

"I don't understand. Assumption is a Catholic school."

"Not all kids at Catholic schools are altar boys," Jack pointed out, reminding Dani that he certainly hadn't been.

"So, did you manage to get some licks in?" he asked Matt.

"Yeah." His split lip curved into a cocky grin. Dani didn't know whether to laugh or cry when her son's masculine pride revealed a bit of the man he would someday become.

"Good for you." Jack ruffled his hair.

"If you don't mind," Dani said, her voice frost, "I'd just as soon my son not believe problems are solved with his fists."

"Spoken just like a damn female," the judge scoffed. He shot a considering look down at the filthy boy Dani had dressed in his best T-shirt and jeans this morning for the meeting with his grandfather. "Sometimes men have to make a stand."

Matt nodded. "Like Gary Cooper did in *High Noon*. When he had to face down the bad guys." Dani decided that was the last time she'd let him stay up on a school night to watch old movies with her on the Western Channel.

"Precisely. Just don't go making a habit of it or you'll end up in trouble." The judge held out a blue-veined hand. "I'm your grandfather."

"Yessir, I know." Matt stuck his filthy hand into the judge's larger one. "That's what I was . . ." He slammed his mouth shut.

The judge arched a frosty brow. "So you were fighting about me, were you?" He may be ill, but there was definitely nothing wrong with his mind.

"Yessir." Dani was a bit surprised when Matt didn't appear all that intimidated by a man who'd been known to cause hardened criminals to quake in their shoes. "Some of the kids on the bus said you were a jailbird."

"They were right."

"I'm reading a book about this kid who got sent to this camp for bad boys for stealing sneakers. But he didn't really steal them, he was just in the wrong place at the wrong time when they fell on his head because of the curse put on his family by a one-legged gypsy after his great-great-grandfather stole a pig. So, it was really just a mistake." He sucked in a deep, noisy breath. "Just like Mom said you got sent to prison by mistake."

"It was a mistake of my own making. And I paid the price."

"Whenever I make mistakes Mom says she still loves me. Even when she has to punish me. So, you don't have to worry, Grandpa, because she'll still love you, too."

Dani wondered if it was moisture or a trick of the overhead light that made her father's eyes shine.

"I need some fresh air," he said gruffly. "That fool car was too damn stuffy." He shuffled out, leaning heavily on his cane.

"Well, that was interesting," Dani murmured.

"It's okay, Mom. Grandpa probably just has to adjust. Like me at school." Matt's forehead furrowed. "Mrs. Deveraux, the bus driver, said she was going to tell the principal about the fight. So, I guess you'll be getting a call to come to the school for a conference."

Dani sighed. It would be just one more in a recent long list of first-time experiences. "I suppose so."

Then, because she was feeling guilty for having put her child in a situation where he was forced to defend his grandfather with his fists, she smoothed the hair Jack had ruffled.

"Why don't you go upstairs and take a bath. Then I'll put some antibacterial cream on your knuckles, and we'll discuss alternative problem-solving methods."

"Okay. But I really didn't have any choice, Mom."

She watched him go up the stairs. "I can't believe he actually got in a fistfight," she murmured.

"He wouldn't be the first kid to have to stand up to bullies," Jack said mildly. "Won't be the last."

Dani rubbed her temples where the headache she'd had all day was escalating to jackhammer proportions. "He's just a baby."

"He's eight years old. That's no baby. You can't keep him in bubble wrap. It's no good for him."

"Excuse me." She folded her arms. Her voice and her gaze frosted over. "I should have realized you were an expert on child-rearing. Having so many children of your own." Even as she'd tossed that sarcastic comment at him, her conscience twinged and a familiar ache spread across her chest.

Instead of appearing offended, his deep, answering laugh rumbled through her. "*Mon dieu*, I do love it when you get up on that high horse, sugar."

Jack ducked his head and kissed her, a quick hard kiss that sent her head spinning and ended much too soon, then skimmed a finger down her nose. "Why don't you go play nurse to your son while I visit with the judge."

"So, how's it feel to be back home?" Jack handed the judge one of the bottles of RC cola he'd snagged out of the refrigerator.

"I wouldn't know. Since this isn't my home," the judge reminded him.

Jack refused to apologize for having saved Beau Soleil from those mobster gamblers and the ravages of the bayou environment.

"You know what they say." The sun was beginning to set, but the heat and moisture continued to hover over the bayou like a wet blanket. Another thirty minutes and squadrons of mosquitos would begin dive-bombing anyone foolish enough to still be outside. "Home's where the heart is."

"Then I still don't have a home. Since my heart's pretty much shot."

"So you keep saying." Jack sat down on the top step of the porch, spread his legs out, and took a long swallow of cola, enjoying the cool flow down his throat. "You know, Danielle's right. From what I've seen, she's sure as hell not the same little girl who let other folks decide what was good for her. She's gotten some steel beneath that pretty cotton-candy exterior, and she's not gonna just sit by and let you die on her without a fight."

"It's not her place to tell me what to do. I'm her father."

"Then perhaps it's time you started actin' like one, you."

"Perhaps you're forgetting who you're talking to, you," the judge countered with acid sarcasm.

"Last I looked, you weren't a sitting judge anymore. So you can't sentence me back to jail." Jack tilted the neck of the bottle toward him. "Besides, DEA agents don't intimidate real easy."

"I may no longer be on the bench, but you're no DEA agent, either." He swept a critical look over Jack's long hair and earring. "Sure don't look much like one, either."

"Well, you know, I tried goin' undercover in my Brooks Brothers suit, but for some reason the cartel got suspicious. And I may no longer be on the government payroll, but I could probably find a pair of cuffs around the house somewhere. In case Danielle needs help gettin' you to the doctor."

"There's no point. I'm dying. And that's that."

"Never thought I'd see the day you'd be actin' the coward."

"I'm not a coward. I'm a realist."

Jack shook his head even as he wondered why he was bothering to have this conversation. Getting involved in the complex, tortuous relationship between Danielle and her father was like invading a nest of water moccasins. It was definitely not something a sensible man would do.

The problem was, he'd never been known for his good sense. Especially not where pretty, sweet-smelling Danielle Dupree was concerned.

"If you really are dying, what would it hurt to go through a few tests? Just to satisfy her?"

"Easy for you to say."

"Okay, maybe it'd be a real pain. Maybe you'd just as soon spend your last days on earth sitting here on this porch, scratching your butt, and watchin' the sun rise and set than putting on a paper hospital gown with no backside and having people you don' know poking and probin' at you. But the thing is, Judge, you owe her."

"How do you figure that?"

"It was you who talked her into marrying Dupree."

"Hell, I didn't have to talk all that hard. Lowell Dupree was a charming, intelligent man who knew how to treat a woman."

"Yeah, he treated his wife real well, runnin' 'round on her, then leaving her to take care of her boy all by herself. As for the charm, I always thought the guy was more slick than charmin'. Like snot on a doorknob."

"If that's any example of your descriptive powers, I find it hard to believe you're a writer."

"It's hard for me, too, most times. And it was a long and crooked path gettin' where I am."

Jack frowned as he thought about the argument he'd had with his larger-than-life father back in the seventh grade when he'd announced his decision to become a writer instead of a cop. Three days later Jake Callahan had been killed. Jack often wondered if his daddy could see the success he'd achieved. And, more important, if he was proud of him.

"But we're not talkin' about me."

He shook off the sudden and unsettling realization that there was a chance he and Danielle had something more in common than just lust. If he were writing them as two characters in one of his novels, he'd have them both sharing a subconscious need for paternal approval from fathers who couldn't—for different reasons—ever give it to them.

"We're talking about you and your daughter. About you settin' things right before you kick the bucket. About acting like a father for once in your life."

"Don't you tell me I wasn't a good father. The girl never wanted for anything."

"Except love. Hell, the only reason she chased after me that summer was because she was so damn emotionally needy she was willin' to convince herself that she was in love. That's the only way a good girl like her could allow herself to get any comfort from havin' sex."

"I don't want to talk about you having sex with my daughter."

"That makes two of us. But you know, it seems real funny to me that you'd go to prison, even though we both know you were framed—"

"You didn't tell Danielle that?"

"No." But he'd sure as hell had wanted to.

"Good. I don't want her anywhere near that crime family."

Jack hadn't been real sure about that the first time the judge had insisted he keep quiet about what he'd learned about the Maggione family wanting to get the incorruptible law-and-order judge off the bench prior to the trial of one of Papa Joe Maggione's grandsons. Having spent time with Danielle and witnessed the woman she'd become, he suspected she might actually start rocking some potentially dangerous boats.

"I'm still havin' trouble figuring out why you'd be willing to spend seven years in prison, perhaps even ruin your health, to protect your daughter from getting mixed up with mobsters."

"It wasn't just that. There was her husband's career to think of."

"There is no way in hell I'm gonna believe that you'd let yourself get convicted just to further some politician's career. Especially if you were betting on him getting elected president some day and giving you an executive pardon. Hell, you'd get better odds with Armand Trusseau."

Trusseau was bookmaker of choice for southern Louisiana gamblers, taking bets on everything from horse races to pro and college sports to whatever the market wanted. Jack had even heard stories about him making book on the cake-baking contest at the parish fair, and which high school could get its football team all the way through the season without having one of its players arrested for underage drinking. Since most of the cops, and a number of the judges, were clients, it was only when the press started getting up in arms about all the offtrack betting, that the law would put any heat on Trusseau.

And even then, all he'd throw into their net would be some middle-school kid who was being used as a runner. Since no one had the stomach to jail a little kid for trying to make a few extra bucks, the case was usually dropped.

"So you're contending that you spent seven years trying to keep Danielle from having anything to do with the Maggiones, but you won't go the extra distance and try to make up for treating your only child like a stranger all of her life? Sorry, but that just doesn't wash."

"The girl never wanted for anything." The judge's garrulous voice gained strength, sounding, for the first time, more like it had when he'd been making rulings from the bench. He did not, Jack noticed, answer the question he'd been trying to pry out of him for months. Why the hell he hadn't fought what was obviously a frame in the first place.

"Now that's where you're wrong. She didn't have the one thing she wanted. Needed. She didn't have her daddy's love."

The judge opened his mouth. Shut it. Then drilled Jack with a razor-sharp look that had gone a long way to keeping order in his courtroom.

"What's going on between you and my daughter?"

"I wish to hell I knew," Jack muttered as he polished off the cola. "But I'm not sleepin' with her, if that's what you're worried about."

"None of my business if you were." The judge took a long swallow of his own. "The hell it isn't."

His eyes were hard, his mouth a grim warning. "You take advantage of my little girl again, Callahan, and you'll have to answer to me. Even if I have to crawl off my deathbed to rip your damn heart out."

"I'll keep that in mind," Jack drawled. "And while we're on the subject of your daughter, it's past time you told her why I left thirteen years ago. Because if you don't, I will."

The judge speared him with a lethal look that would have cowered a lesser man. "You've no damn business getting between me and my child."

"I'm tired of playing your scapegoat. I wasn't lyin' when I said I don't know what's going on 'tween Danielle and me, but I do know that I want to start out with a clean slate. Which means she's gotta know the truth."

"I'll take the matter under advisement." The judge didn't appear all that surprised by Jack's ultimatum. "How much time do I have?"

Jack shrugged. "I'll let you get settled in, but if you haven't told her in a week, I'm telling Finn to quit digging around in your case files."

The judge shot him another dark, killing look from beneath beetled white brows that seven years ago had been as black as Louisiana crude. "That's blackmail."

"I prefer to think of it as an incentive." There was a tight white ring around the judge's mouth that worried Jack, just a little, but he decided that having gone this far, he wasn't about to back off.

"If I were still on the bench, I'd toss your ass in jail and throw away the key."

"Good thing you're not on the bench."

"Fuck." The judge shook his head. "All right, I'll tell her. But there's something you ought to know, Callahan."

"What's that?"

"One of the most useful things they taught us in law school was to never wade out into unknown waters; never ask a question you didn't know the answer for ahead of time. Once you open this particular can of worms, you're not going to be able to get them back in. And you might be damn surprised what crawls out."

"I think you're mixing your metaphors a bit, Judge," Jack said mildly. "But I get your meaning. And I'm willing to take my chances."

The judge shrugged. Having reluctantly accepted the ultimatum, he now seemed bored with the conversation. "Don't say I didn't warn you."

* * *

Having expected World War III, Dani had been amazed when her father had actually agreed, without being held at gunpoint, to undergo a series of medical tests. She would have been happier if he'd been willing to go to a doctor in the city, but hadn't wanted to push her luck by insisting.

The dates on the medical degrees tastefully framed on Dr. Eve Ancelet's office wall revealed her to be in her early thirties. She was a slender woman with warm eyes and a bit brisk, but friendly attitude. After shaking hands, she folded hers atop a thick manila folder. Dani was grateful when she didn't waste time with small talk but got right to the point.

"I've already discussed all this with the judge after we'd gotten the results back yesterday," she said. "He gave me permission to share the details with you."

"Which is handy, since he refuses to discuss anything about his condition with me."

"It's hard for a man accustomed to control to surrender it."

"You'd think he would have grown used to that in prison," Dani said dryly.

"He undoubtedly learned to deal with it. In his own way. But I doubt he liked it." The doctor opened the folder. "First of all, the diagnosis by the prison doctor was correct: your father does have congestive heart failure."

The word *failure* carried with it a frightening finality. Dani's heart sank.

She tried to listen carefully, but the dreadful idea of her father dying before she found a way into his heart splintered Dani's concentration and many of the words became merely a buzz in her head.

"We're not sure how he contracted it, but my educated guess is that he suffered a virus which settled in his heart muscle," Dr. Ancelet was saying when Dani dragged her mind back from wondering how emotionally harmed Matt would be if his grandfather happened to die days after he'd finally met him. "Going back through the records, and what he told me about a time shortly before his arrest, it appears he'd suffered a case of flu. It's particularly memorable since apparently it kept him off the bench for nearly two weeks and all his cases had to be reassigned."

"I remember. He was furious." At himself, Dani recalled. "In fact, it was the first time in my life I could remember him being ill, so I was going to come take care of him, but I'd just discovered I was pregnant with Matt, and he insisted I stay home rather than risk catching something that might hurt my baby."

Dani rubbed a hand against her chest, where her own heart had begun to ache. If she had insisted on returning to Blue Bayou, would her father have recovered sooner? Could she have prevented his potentially fatal heart disease?

"He was right to be cautious. The fetus is far more vulnerable in the first trimester. However," the doctor said briskly, "there's no point in wasting time on *what-ifs*. Right now we need to concentrate on managing your father's illness so he can regain a better quality of life."

"Is that possible?" Hope returned to once again flutter delicate wings in Dani's breast.

"Actually, it is. While we can't beat the disease, at least not yet, we can help people live with it. The good news is that it's reversible. Of course, any success in treatment depends on a patient's age, condition, and goals, and needless to say, a younger person is going to have different goals than someone your father's age. They'd probably want to return to work, play with their children, make love, all those physical things that are important to them. An older person tends to have less ambitious objectives. Such as being less dependent on family and friends."

"My father hates being dependent on anyone."

"That's a universal feeling," the doctor agreed. "Heart function doesn't stay static once a person gets heart failure. It's always getting worse or better. Unfortunately, for the past seven years your father has been getting worse. I'm hoping we can turn things around and buy him some valuable time with you and your son."

"What about surgery?"

"That's not currently an option in your father's case. At least not at this time while he's so weak. I'll be frank with you, Ms. Dupree—"

"Dani."

"Dani." She smiled. "And I'm Eve. As I told the judge, at this point, I'd like to try treating him with medication and a change in attitude."

Good luck getting that attitude adjustment, Dani thought, but did not say.

"Your father is very obviously depressed."

"Who wouldn't be if they'd spent seven years in prison? Most of that time in isolation?"

"Granted, imprisonment could only make things worse. But his records suggest that he may have already been clinically depressed when he arrived at Angola. From talking with him, I suspect he's suffered several depressive episodes during his life."

"I don't remember him ever being depressed."

"How about angry? Or remote?"

"Well, yes. But I always figured that was just his personality. He's always demanded perfection of everyone around him, including himself, and he's an unrelenting control freak."

"Well, whether or not he was depressed in the past, he definitely is now," Eve Ancelet said. "Which isn't surprising since depression happens to be a very common side effect of heart failure. We're just beginning to get a handle on the connection between the two."

"Could depression have kept him from fighting back when he was wrongly accused of taking that bribe?"

Eve Ancelet nodded. "It might have. As a rule, when we diagnose depression, we warn patients against making any critical decisions until their medications begin working. Choosing not to participate in your own defense could certainly qualify as a critical decision."

"Why didn't his attorney tell the court?"

"There's a good possibility he never realized what he was dealing with. After all, your father isn't the most forthcoming patient I've ever had."

"Tell me about it," Dani muttered.

"I gave him several prescriptions. One's an antidepressant. Of course, whether or not he chooses to have them filled is up to him."

"He will." If she had to sit on his chest and stuff the pills down his throat.

"Good. You've undoubtedly heard about the studies being done that link mood and physical condition of patients. Empirical evidence points to the fact, which I've witnessed myself during my practice, that optimistic, positive-minded patients feel better and tend to live longer than pessimistic, negative-minded ones.

"Perhaps it has something to do with stress being a major factor in heart disease, or perhaps the folklore about our heart being tuned to our emotions is, indeed, fact. But the sooner we can turn your father's mood around, the better off he'll be. Also we'll want to start him on an exercise regime."

"Is that safe with a weak heart?"

"Certainly. While in the past, patients were admonished not to exercise to reduce the burden on their hearts, we've since learned that such restriction on lifestyle actually produces a severe deconditioning of the heart. More recent studies have shown the beneficial effects of exercise and with that in mind, I've worked out a daily routine with your father."

Dani was still skeptical. "I'm all for physical fitness, but he could barely walk out of the prison."

"Which is why we're going to begin slowly. I've recommended he begin taking short walks, just to the corner in the morning and evening. Needless to say, after having been so severely limited in his activity these past years, any cardiac conditioning is going to take longer than it would with a younger, more active patient. Still, if he sticks to the schedule I've outlined, your father could expect some improvement within a few weeks."

While Dani was a bit more optimistic than when she'd first arrived at the office, she couldn't help still being concerned. After all, Eve Ancelet was only a family physician in a small rural town. And barely older than Dani herself was.

"I'm considering taking him to Tulane." She didn't want to insult the doctor, but also felt a responsibility to her father.

"That's not a bad idea," the doctor responded easily. "Second opinions are always helpful, and I'll be happy to recommend cardiologists with whom you might want to confer. In the meantime, the medication I'm putting the judge on can't hurt him and working to change his attitude will only make things better.

"And if it helps to ease your mind, I've shared your father's tests with cardiologists at both Tulane and Johns Hopkins. And they agree with my diagnosis."

"That's reassuring. Not that I don't trust you—"

"I understand your concern." Eve smiled. "It's difficult, but although he might not see it that way right now, your father has a great deal going for him. Plus, he has a secret weapon not all patients are fortunate to have."

"What's that?"

"His family."

As she left the office, Dani could only hope they would be enough.

17

A *week later,* while Dani was sitting at the kitchen table, helping Matt with his homework and Orèlia was in the front parlor, watching *America's Most Wanted* on television, the judge returned from his evening walk.

When he'd first started he'd barely been able to make it down the steps. Tonight he'd managed to make it all the way to the corner and back. Without his cane. And while that doctor, who seemed to know what she was doing, even if she was young and a woman, had told him that it could take at least two weeks for those antidepressants Danielle was forcing down his throat every day to kick in, this morning had been the first time in a very long while he'd actually been glad to wake up.

During his days on the bench, he'd sent hundreds—tens of hundreds—of men and women to prison and had understood, intellectually, the life to which he was sentencing them. But even while he'd been kept from the general population, and thus, reasonably safe from harm, he'd quickly realized that there was no way for anyone who hadn't experienced that inimitable sound of a cell door sliding closed to realize how hard it was to lose the simple day-to-day freedom people on the outside took for granted.

His legs were a little shaky; he sat down on the top step of the porch and relished the ability to actually look up at a sky. As the first star winked on, he thought about Jack's threat and realized that he was running out of time.

After giving it a lot of thought, he still believed that he'd been right, although with hindsight he might admit that perhaps his methodology had been a little heavy-handed. Still, if he'd ordered

Danielle to stop seeing Marie Callahan's middle son, would she have?

"Not a chance in hell," he muttered.

Running his housekeeper's son out of town was one thing. The events that followed quite another. The judge knew that he wasn't exactly beloved in Blue Bayou; however, until he'd been framed on those bribery and subjugation of perjury charges, he'd always been considered a fair magistrate. He'd also never let a personal acquaintance with a defendant influence his decisions. Which is why he couldn't overlook the fact that he'd been guilty of a crime against his daughter.

Dani seemed to have forgiven him for not having been a warm and loving parent while she'd been growing up. But he'd already been a crusty bachelor of forty-eight when he'd made what at the time had been the worst mistake of his life by marrying her gold-digging slut of a mother.

If he'd been seeing clearly at the time, he would have realized that a twenty-two-year-old court stenographer would be unlikely to fall in love with a man more than twice her age. But he'd been blinded by her dazzling blond beauty.

Even after Savannah Bodine had trapped him the old-fashioned way—by getting pregnant—his ego had enjoyed her feminine flattery. Which, unsurprisingly, had come to a screeching halt the moment she'd gotten that five-carat pear-shaped diamond ring on her finger. In fact, while he had no real proof, he'd been bedeviled by suspicions that she'd had a fling with a streaked-blond, tanned beach boy who worked the cabana at the Caribbean resort where they spent their honeymoon. And that had been just the beginning.

By their first anniversary he'd paid for breast implants and a nose job, only to have her move into her own bedroom. By the second, she'd stopped any pretense of interest in sex with him, while making him a laughingstock by spending her evenings drinking vodka gimlets and flirting down at the No Name, as well as blatantly sleeping around with seemingly every single man in the parish. And not a few married ones, as well.

He would have divorced her. Should have. But back when he'd been thinking with his seemingly born-again penis, he'd foolishly signed a prenuptial agreement—ostensibly to protect their unborn child—and refused to reward her bad behavior by handing her a substantial chunk of his estate. But he'd miscalculated yet again, when, rather than allow herself to suffer by being trapped into a marriage she no longer pretended to care about, Savannah simply continued to ignore the little fact that she had a husband and a daughter at home.

The final straw was when a shrimp boat captain's wronged wife named her as correspondent in their divorce. When it looked as if his errant wife would actually have to appear in his own courtroom—the one place he was still admired and even feared—he'd thrown in the towel.

Two weeks before the third anniversary of their marriage made in hell, she'd taken off for Los Angeles with a hefty check in hand. Having already demonstrated that she had the maternal instincts of a black widow spider, the judge wasn't all that surprised when she left behind the blond toddler she'd once told him, in a furious flare of temper before Danielle was born, wasn't even his child.

After arriving in Tinseltown, Savannah Dupree née Bodine, had parlayed the voluptuous, albeit in hindsight, common beauty and a seemingly natural-born skill for blow jobs into a career in porno films. Once, at a judicial conference in Manhattan, he'd seen her picture on a flyer in his hotel room, advertising the pay-for-view adult movies.

Assuring himself that it was only natural curiosity, he'd paid nine dollars and ninety-five cents to watch his former bride have sex in more imaginative ways than she'd ever had with him.

Her career had turned out to be a meteor, rising fast, burning brightly, only to quickly flame out. She died on what would have been their fifth anniversary, when, high on drugs and alcohol, she'd driven her car off the Pacific Coast Highway.

The judge had been surprised to learn that he was still listed on all her legal documents as her next of kin. Until he discovered that she'd burned through the money she'd gotten from him as well as whatever she'd been earning for her X-rated films and had been in debt up to her bleached-blond roots. He'd paid to have her cremated, but decided to let MasterCard, Visa, and AMEX take care of themselves.

Given her outrageous behavior, there were bound to be those in Blue Bayou who'd wondered about Danielle's parentage. But no one had ever whispered so much as a word in front of him, and he'd taken some measure of pride in the fact that he'd clothed, housed, and fed the abandoned child who looked exactly like her mother and nothing like him.

For the first few weeks after she'd been brought to Beau Soleil from the hospital, the judge had ignored the infant, turning her care over to the same black nanny he'd always felt closer to than his own parents. But then one day, when she'd been nine months old, she'd caught a summer cold that had escalated into pneumonia.

Faced with the possibility of her actually dying, he'd belatedly realized how much he'd grown accustomed to having the well-behaved baby around the house.

After clearing his court calendar, he'd spent the next five days in the pediatric intensive care wing at St. Mary's Hospital, hovering over her crib as if his presence might protect her. Her mother, who'd taken off for a supposed trip to buy clothes in Dallas, was nowhere to be found, but even if she'd been in Blue Bayou, she'd never displayed any interest in her daughter when Danielle was well, so she certainly wouldn't want anything to do with this ill, cranky, croupy baby.

When Dani turned the corner and the fever that had created hectic red flags in her satiny smooth cheeks for too many nerve-racking days subsided, she'd smiled up at him, with her pretty rosebud lips and happy eyes that hadn't yet decided whether they were going to be green or blue, and stolen his heart.

He'd been afraid during his cribside vigil. After Savannah's departure, Victor Dupree came to understand the true meaning of terror. The more he bonded with the child which, if he hadn't given life, at least had given his name to, the more he grew to fear that someday his former wife might return to Blue Bayou and decide to claim maternal rights.

Oh, she wouldn't have a chance in hell, especially in his parish, but knowing how mercurial Savannah could be, he wouldn't have put it past her to hire some thug from her seamy underworld to kidnap their daughter just for spite. Or worse yet, for ransom.

Without being aware of doing so, little by little, the judge began to protect himself—and his heart—by distancing himself from Danielle again, even after her mother had died and the threat of Savannah taking her away was no longer valid.

Never a demonstrative man, he began to build an emotional wall around himself. Not for the reasons he had during those early months, when he'd viewed Danielle as a burden he'd never asked for, but because he couldn't bear the idea of losing the one person who meant the world to him. The only problem with that behavior, he'd come to realize, was that by protecting his own heart, he'd gravely wounded Dani's over the course of her life.

Judge Victor Dupree had been brought up surrounded by the mysteries of the Roman Catholic Church. He knew he was supposed to believe in one God, the forgiveness of sins, and life everlasting. Even having witnessed the aftermath of some of the worst things man could inflict upon his fellow man, he'd never bought into the idea of heaven and hell, having come to the conclusion in law school that it was nothing more than a fanciful concept humans had created in response to an inner need for reassurance that something existed beyond the here and now.

But seven years in near solitary confinement had given Victor Dupree a lot of time for introspection. Now, approaching death, possibly facing a judicial review far more crucial than any over which he'd ever presided, he feared he might be called upon to defend the actions of a lifetime.

He'd spent years being on guard for echoes of Danielle's mother in her, signs that he was losing control of his daughter (if she even *was* his daughter) as he'd lost control of his wife. Yet he had to admit, except for that reckless Romeo and Juliet teenage love affair with Jack Callahan, she'd never given him a lick of trouble. She'd been a model child, pretty, amiable, and obedient, even when he could tell it was hard on her. Even when he'd sent her away to Atlanta to give birth to Callahan's child, assuring her that he was protecting her reputation, when he realized now that it had been his own he'd been more concerned about.

Surprisingly, without having had any maternal role model to follow, other than Marie Callahan for those few years during her teens, Danielle had turned out to be a good mother. Her son—his grandson, the judge reminded himself—was a bright, inquisitive, interesting little boy who, along with possessing much of the attributes of his mother, in some ways reminded the judge of himself when he was Matthew's age.

Hell. Victor Dupree dragged a hand down his face. He had some fences to mend. Some ties to bind. Which is why, the judge decided, he wasn't going to die. At least not just yet.

Of course, staying alive had its own problems, now that Bad Jack was back in Blue Bayou, stirring things up again. The judge had never thought of himself as a coward, but he didn't want to think what might happen if the entire truth of what had happened that past summer came out.

Jack snagged the white plastic ball that came sailing off the yellow bat. "You're gettin' better."

"I know." Matt's face could have lit up Blue Bayou for a month of Sundays with wattage left over. "Huh, Grandpa?"

"You sure are," the judge agreed robustly, unable to recall when he'd enjoyed himself more. "Keep it up and you'll be in the majors before you know it."

"I'm too young," Matt said with the literal mindedness of an eight-year-old. "I just want to be picked at recess."

"You keep working on the fundamentals, and you'll be the star of the sandlot." Jack threw a slow looping, underhand pitch, which floated under the wild swing. "That was close."

"I still missed."

"Hey, even the greatest hitters of all time strike out twice as often as they hit."

"Really?" Matt tossed the ball back with surprising accuracy for a kid who hadn't even known how to properly hold it an hour ago.

"Sure." He really was a great kid, and the fact that his father hadn't realized that was more proof of what Jack had already figured out. That the congressman had been swamp scum and the world, particularly Danielle's little corner of it, was a helluva lot better off without him. "Ever hear of anyone battin' a thousand?"

"I never thought of it that way." Matt resumed his stance, standing a lot closer to the plate than he had when they'd first begun.

"It's something to keep in mind."

Jack threw another pitch, which was clipped and went rolling across the lawn. Turnip, lying nearby, watched it, as if trying to decide whether to go chasing after it, ultimately opting to remain where she was.

"That was closer. Hard to believe you've never played before."

"Dad was too busy." This time the return throw went wild, but Jack managed to catch it before it rolled into the water. "Making up laws."

"That's real important work." Jack only gave Danielle's ex that small credit for the kid's sake.

"That's what Mom always said." He frowned. But, Jack suspected, not in concentration. "But Dad was mostly interested in politics. Which was the only reason he wanted me."

"I think you may be a bit confused, sport."

"No, I'm not. It was because of the polls. Mom said more people vote for you if you're a family man."

"Loosen your grip," Jack suggested mildly as he unclenched his own hands, which had fisted. "You've got that gorilla hold thing goin' again."

When they'd first begun, Matt had a death grip on the bat. He'd begun to loosen up. Until the conversation had shifted to his father.

"Okay." Matt flexed his fingers. Drew in a breath.

"I can't believe your mother told you that about your father," the judge said.

"She didn't say it to me." He swung, managing to connect again for a nice little squibbed bunt up the imaginary third base line that might have earned him a single if they'd been playing a real game. "I heard her say it to dad. On the phone before he died. It was the day after I had to go to the Watergate to visit them because of the lawyers and accidently ran my scooter into Robin's new car.

"She's the lady Dad was going to marry. She called me a rotten little brat, but I never told Mom about that, because I didn't want to make her cry."

"I don't think that would have made her cry." Jack could, however, imagine Danielle marching over to the Watergate and ensuring no one ever dared talk to her son that way again.

"Dad made her cry a lot. When she was talking to him on the phone, she said that the devil would be making snowballs in hell before she let me go live with him and Robin."

Jack scooped up the rolling ball and exchanged a look with the judge.

"You shouldn't be eavesdropping on your mother's phone calls," the judge scolded without heat.

"I didn't mean to. I just had to get up to go to the bathroom and I heard her say that. Then she hung up. Then she cried."

"Well, this is certainly a surprise." All three males looked up as they heard the voice of the woman in question.

"Hi, Mom," Matt greeted her. "Did you see me hit the ball?"

"I did. It was quite impressive." Her voice was calm, her eyes were not.

"I hit it harder earlier." Excited about his accomplishments, he appeared oblivious to the tension swirling around the adults. "Didn't I, Jack?"

"You sure enough did, *cher*. Slammed it nearly out of the park."

"Kid's a natural," the judge said helpfully.

"Isn't that lovely." Dani's gaze settled on Jack. "Could I talk to you inside, please?"

"Mom, me and Jack were just getting good."

"Jack and I," she corrected.

"Jack and I," he repeated obediently. "Did you know that when Barry Bonds was just a little kid, he could hit a whiffle ball hard enough to break windows?"

"Mrs. Bonds was undoubtedly thrilled by that achievement." Dani knew she should be showing more interest, but it was difficult to keep her mind on a conversation about baseball when hornets were buzzing around in her head and she was shaking from the inside out. "I'm sorry to break up the inning, but it's important."

"Sure." Jack tossed the ball to Matt, who amazed Dani by dropping the yellow plastic bat and catching it with a one-handed snag that did, indeed, appear almost natural.

"Why don't you play some catch with your grandfather," Jack suggested. "Then, after your mom and I have ourselves a little chat, we can pick up some pizzas and take 'em out to Beau Soleil for supper."

"Really?"

" 'Bout time you see where your *maman* grew up. And now that the road's finally in, we can drive there in half the time as winding through the bayou in a boat."

"That's an excellent idea," the judge said heartily. "I haven't had pizza in a coon's age."

"And you won't be having it tonight, either," Dani said. "I have your dinner in here." She lifted the white plastic bag from the Cajun Market.

"If I have to eat any more egg whites I'm going to start clucking."

Dani had to admit that she'd perhaps been overly strict since her meeting with the doctor. But she was determined to turn her father's heart disease around so he could live long enough to get to know his grandson.

"No need." Orèlia came out the kitchen door to weigh in on the discussion. "I'm cookin' my special spaghetti that I invented for my

Leon's high blood pressure. I've got a whole cookbook full of recipes so good you'll be askin' me to marry you in no time."

Dani's father narrowed his eyes. "Never realized you were such a forward woman."

"Lot you didn't realize about me, you," she retorted, her hands on her hips.

Dani left them to the bickering they'd been doing since her father's arrival at the house.

Jack took the grocery bags from her hands and carried them into the kitchen. "You're pissed at me," he diagnosed as he put them on the wooden butcher-block counter.

"You're very observant." She took an onion out of the bag.

"I like looking at you, so I don't miss much. . . . Why don't you give me these." He took the cans of salt-free tomato sauce she'd pulled from the sack away. "Jus' in case you decide to throw 'em at my handsome head."

"I should." Her hands clenched into unconscious fists at her side. "You had no right . . ." Her voice choked. She could only toss her head in the direction of the backyard. "With Matt."

"Teach him to play ball? Hell, I'm only tryin' to help the kid get along better in a new school."

"I also heard at the market that he'd been telling the other boys that you were teaching him how to brawl."

"It was boxing." He reached down, took hold of her hand, and unfolded the tightly curled fingers, one by one. "I was only showin' him how to keep his guard up."

Like she should do, Dani thought, remembering the gossip she'd overheard at the market about a long-going affair between Jack and Desiree Champagne. She'd been insisting, not just to Jack, but to herself, that she didn't want to get involved with him. But the hurt she'd felt hearing about him with another woman, especially one built like a *Penthouse* centerfold, definitely suggested that she was, on some level, already involved.

"Whatever you want to call it, the result is the same. I don't want my son viewing violence as a solution to any problem. And I'm definitely not happy the way you've been insinuating yourself into his life in order to pump him for information about my marriage."

"I'd never do such a thing." Appearing honestly shocked, Jack dropped her hand. "He volunteered the information. When he told me that the reason he didn't know how to play ball was because his daddy didn't like him."

"Hell." She let out a ragged breath, briefly closed her eyes, and shook her head. "It was never him personally. Lowell never cared about anyone—or anything—who couldn't help his career."

"Then it's true? About him wanting a kid because he thought it might win him a few votes?"

It sounded even worse hearing it from someone else, Dani considered. Seeing the dark disapproval on Jack's face. How had she been so foolish?

Because, she answered her own rhetorical question, she'd been desperate to get over this man standing so close she could smell the scent of leather balm from his baseball glove on the hand that was skimming over her shoulder.

Close enough she could feel the warmth of his sun-warmed body and catch the tang of male sweat that was strangely, in its own way, appealing.

She'd never known Lowell to perspire. Not even in the heat of a Washington summer. Not even when making love.

She could live with knowing that her husband had never loved her. But how could she have married a man who wouldn't love her son? How could she have stayed with him without realizing the damage living with such a man might do to the one person she loved most in the world?

With the twenty-twenty vision of hindsight, Dani realized that she should have cut her losses when Matthew had been born the day of Lowell's second-term election.

Steeped in her southern upbringing of putting others first, she hadn't thought to utter a single word of complaint when he'd refused to cut his final day's campaigning short to be by her side as she labored to bring their son into the world.

And despite having felt as alone and abandoned as the first time she'd given birth, the very next day, between feeding her newborn and writing out thank-you notes for the mountain of infant gifts that had arrived at the hospital, she'd dutifully telephoned the wives of each and every one of Lowell's major financial contributors, personally thanking them for their political support.

"It's not that simple." She turned away.

"Few things in life are simple." Jack came up behind her, pulled her against him, rested his chin on the top of her head. "Look at you and me."

"I try not to."

"Doesn't do much good, does it? Because whether you want to admit it or not, you keep thinkin' about me. The same way I keep thinkin' about you." He rubbed his cheek against her hair. She could feel his breath on her neck. "During the day when I'm pounding nails."

He turned her in his arms and skimmed work-roughened fingertips up the side of her face. "During the evening, when I should be workin' on my book." He circled her lips with his thumb. "At night, when I should be sleeping."

"Sleeping with Desiree Champagne?" She could have bitten off her tongue when she heard that thought escape.

"Desiree and I are friends, sure enough. And I'm not gonna lie and say that we haven't passed some good times together, since you've undoubtedly heard some gossip. But I haven't been with her since you came out to Beau Soleil."

"Why not? She's certainly a beautiful woman and isn't exactly wearing widow's weeds, mourning her dear departed late husband."

"Desiree's a survivor," Jack said mildly. "She's had to be. But as appealing as she admittedly is, I'm not interested in her that way, because I don't want to be with anyone else but you, *chère*."

His eyes held hers as he cupped the nape of her neck in his hand. "I promise I'll answer any question you have about Desiree or any other woman in my past later. Right now there's something we need to get out of the way."

18

Jack lowered his head and kissed her. There was heat, burning through every cell of her body; smoke clouded thoughts she was struggling to form in her mind. The scent of Confederate jasmine and honeysuckle floated on the soft warm air. Somewhere in the chinaberry tree, a bird warbled a sad song while sweet desire sang in Dani's blood.

His clever, wonderfully wicked mouth beguiled. Seduced. His stunningly tender hands caressed. Persuaded.

When his lips left hers, and journeyed along her jaw, up her neck, to create a blissful havoc behind her ear, Dani's breath caught in her lungs.

"I thought you were a pretty girl before," he murmured as he glided his fingers down her throat, lingering in the hollow where her blood was wildly pulsing. "But you definitely blossomed into a beauty, *mon ange*."

The skimming caress continued downward, creating sparks of heat in the triangle of skin framed by the neckline of her blouse. Dani trembled as his fingertips brushed against the aching tip of her breast, a faint rasp of calluses against ivory silk.

The male scrape of afternoon beard against her cheek as his lips trailed back to hers sent her nerves skittering. "We still fit," he murmured.

"I'm on my toes." Linking her fingers together behind his neck, she sank into the deepening kiss. Into him.

"Height don' got a thing to do with it." His hands settled at her waist, drew her closer, fitting softness to strength. "We fit together in all the ways that count."

She drew in a surprised breath when he lifted her up onto the counter, then began to move between her legs. He stopped when he got a close look at her thighs, revealed by her hitched-up skirt.

"Nice." He skimmed a light touch along the lace top of her summer sheer stocking. "You wear these for me, sugar?"

"Hardly. Since I didn't expect you to be here when I got home." She sucked in a sharp breath as he slipped a treacherous finger between the elasticized lace and her too hot flesh. "They're cooler than panty hose. And more practical."

"I can see how that'd be." The hot desire that had simmered in his eyes only a moment earlier changed to a devilish laughter that nearly was her undoing. "Nothin' more frustrating than tryin' to unwrap your woman from a pair of damn panty hose."

"I happen to be my own woman." She batted at his hand. "And stop that before someone comes in."

She'd no sooner spoken when the screen door opened with a bang. "Hey, Jack," Matt asked, "who do you think's the best shortstop? Grandpa thinks it's Nomar Garciaparra, but I say Alexander Rodriguez."

"That's a no-brainer." Jack shifted gears with an alacrity Dani, who was busily tugging down her skirt, had to admire. "A-Rod, he's second behind Cal Ripken in home runs by active shortstops and isn't just the best shortstop in the game, he's the best offensive player money can buy.

"Nomar's averages are great, but the guy's injury prone. Then you gotta factor in Jeter, who's a notch behind the other two in offense, but he's more durable over a long season."

"Grandpa called Jeter a damn Yankee."

"Well, there is that," Jack allowed.

"Watch your language," Dani gently warned her son.

"Okay. But I didn't really say it. I was only saying what Grandpa said. . . . Thanks, Jack." He was almost out the door when he glanced back over his shoulder.

"Mom?"

"Yes, dear?"

"How come you're sitting up on the counter?"

"Your mama got herself a little scrape," Jack responded before Dani could think of any valid reason. "I was just checkin' it out for her. Maybe put a little lotion on it."

"Oh. Maybe Orèlia could help. Since she's a nurse."

"Oh, that's not necessary," Dani insisted, ignoring Jack's wicked grin. "I'll be fine."

"Okay." He was out the door. "Hey, Grandpa!" he hollered with more enthusiasm than Dani had heard in months. "Jack says you're wrong and it's a no-brainer."

"Great kid," Jack murmured as the door slammed behind him. He cupped her calf in his palm. "Now where were we?"

"We were discussing why I don't want you getting too involved with my son."

"Too late. I'm already involved. With the boy and his pretty *maman*."

"That's the point." She jerked her leg away and slid off the counter back onto the floor. "I've already been married once and it didn't work out."

"You hear me proposin' *chère?*"

Heat flooded into her face. "I didn't mean . . . Goddammit, Jack—"

"Better watch your language, Danielle."

His cocky smile left her not able to decide whether to hit him or smile back. In the end she did neither. "I realize you don't take anything seriously—"

"Now, there's where you're wrong." He caught her hand as she was combing it through her hair and laced their fingers together. "There's a helluva lot I take seriously, including a certain gorgeous lady who'd obviously walk through fire for her child."

"Matt's the most important thing in the world to me."

"It shows. And you don't have to worry. I'm not gonna do anything to jeopardize that."

She shook her head. In her expressive eyes he read both temptation and a wariness she hadn't possessed when he'd last known her.

"You have to understand that my decision to return to Blue Bayou wasn't an impulsive one," she stressed. "I'd thought about it so many times, but I stayed in Virginia because I kept foolishly hoping Lowell would realize how important Matt was. And how he needed a father in his life."

"If he didn't appreciate Matt's pretty *maman*, I doubt that would have happened."

"I know." She sighed. "Then, even after he died, I still weighed my options carefully."

"Made lists."

"Yes." Her eyes narrowed. "Are you laughing at me?"

"Never." He lifted their hands, brushed his lips across her knuckles. "Lists can be a good thing. I've been known to make a few myself from time to time."

"My point is, I never expected you to be back here in Blue Bayou."

"Well, that makes us even. Because I sure as hell hadn't expected to be, either. And I definitely hadn't expected you to come home."

"I don't know where whatever this is, is going."

"Why don't we just go with the flow and see where we end up? I won't lie to you. I want to touch your curvy little body. Everywhere and often. I want to taste your sweet flesh. All over. But you want to take it slow, then that's what we'll do."

His eyes on hers, he skimmed his thumb over her lips again, then backed away, giving them both some space. "Meanwhile, I need you to help me pick out some wallpaper."

"Why don't you get yourself a decorator?"

"Because a decorator wouldn't know Beau Soleil like you do. Come on, sugar. We'll look at some samples, share a pizza, and pass a good time. Besides, don't you want Matt to see the house his *maman* grew up in?"

From the bold confidence in those bedroom eyes, Dani knew that he realized he'd found the one lure impossible for her to resist.

"You really are terrible," she complained as she threw up her hands.

"I don't like arguing with a *jolie fille*, but I'm not terrible. I'm good. Hell, better than good, I'm—"

"The best I've ever had," she repeated the claim he'd made on the way to Angola.

He laughed and put a friendly arm around her shoulder. "Now you're getting the idea, you."

They went back out to the yard, where Matt was playing fetch with Turnip, who, apparently having decided to get into the game, would scoop up the ball he'd toss her way, then run around the yard in frenzied circles before returning to drop it in front of his sneakers.

"Isn't Turnip a great dog?" Matt called out to her.

"She certainly seems to be."

"Can we get a dog, Mom?"

"We'll see," Dani said. "It'd be a bit difficult to keep a dog in the apartment." Crowded, too, she considered.

"I'd walk it every day. I promise."

"I suppose we could take a trip to the shelter. After we get settled in the apartment," she qualified. "Just to check things out."

"Really?" Dani was amazed at how such a seemingly small thing could create such a look of stunned joy on his face.

"I'm not promising anything," she warned. There were other breeds, she reminded herself. Smaller, apartment-size dogs that wouldn't take up so much room and eat as much as a horse. "But I suppose it wouldn't hurt to look."

"Thanks, Mom!"

As he threw his arms around her, Dani's eyes met Jack's over the top of her son's head. He gave her a thumbs-up, and in that brief, suspended moment Dani remembered, after a very long time, how it felt to be truly happy.

"Wow!" Matt's gaze swept over Beau Soleil's circular, pillared entry hall. "Did you really live here, Mom?"

"I certainly did." Looking at her former home through her son's eyes, Dani saw not the work still to be done, but the glory that the house once possessed. And would again, thanks to Jack. "With your grandfather. And Jack's mother."

"Wow. It's as cool as the White House." He looked up at Jack. "So you lived here, too? With my mom?"

"No. My *maman* was the judge's housekeeper. We lived in town when my dad was alive."

"Your dad died, too?"

"Yep. When I was a bit older than you."

"Did you miss him?"

"A bunch," Jack answered. "Still do, from time to time."

"Jack's father was a very special person," Dani said. "He was sheriff of Blue Bayou."

"Really? Did he have a gun?"

"Yeah," Jack answered. "But he kept the peace well enough he never had to use it." Watching him carefully, Dani saw the dark shadows move across his eyes and suspected he was remembering that day his father had died to save hers.

"Then, after he passed on, my *maman* and brothers and I moved into one of the houses here at Beau Soleil."

"Was it as nice as this?"

"Not as fancy. But we liked it well enough. Even with it bein' haunted."

"It wasn't really. Was it?" Matt's eyes grew even wider.

"Sure was. Maybe still is. The ghost's supposed to be a Confederate officer who got lost in the bayou after the battle of New Orleans and showed up here. Since a bunch of soldiers from the Union army were camped out in this house, your *maman*'s ancestor hid him in one of the little houses out back.

"She sent her own personal maid to take care of him during the day, then every night after dinner, she'd dispatch the soldiers—"

"What does that mean? Dispatch? Like she killed them?"

"Fortunately, she didn't have to go to those extremes. The way I heard the story, she was pretty liberal with the port and would get them all drunk so they'd pass out.

"Then she'd sneak out of the house and take the night shift trying to nurse that Confederate boy back to health, which was a dangerous thing to do, since harboring the enemy was a hangin' offense."

"She must've been brave."

"Must have been. But then, the women in your *maman*'s family have always been pretty special. They've always been real good about gettin' around in the dark, too." His wicked grin was designed to remind Dani of her own midnight excursions from this house.

"Unfortunately, the soldier ended up dying, and it's his ghost who supposedly haunts the place. There were stories about the lady of the house telling people that he used to come visit her at night, but since she was an old woman, people just figured she wasn't quite right in the mind."

"What do you think?"

"I wouldn't know for sure. But I guess I sorta like the idea of the two of them finding some sort of happiness together in a troubled time. They're supposed to dance in the ballroom in this house, but I've never seen them. Though sometimes," he said with a wink Dani's way, "if I listen real close, I think I can kinda hear the music."

"That's so cool. Do you think we'll hear it tonight?"

"Never know what's gonna happen. After supper I'll show you around the rest of the place, then, perhaps, if you'd like and your *maman* says it's okay, we can check out the little house before taking you back to town."

"Can we, Mom?"

"If it's not too late."

"Cool," he said again as the mural drew his attention. "This is the biggest painting I've ever seen. Bigger even than the one the teacher showed us when my class took that field trip to the National Gallery."

"It tells a story about Evangeline and Gabriel, two people who were in love, but got separated when the Acadians first came to Louisiana."

"On those ships?" He pointed at the tall-masted vessels depicted on the mural.

"That's right."

"Did they ever get back together?"

"No. I'm afraid not."

"That's too bad. Can we have the pizza now? Baseball must make a guy hungry, because I'm starving."

"Excuse me?"

Two days later, pulled from a daydream in which Jack had played a sexy starring role, Dani looked up from where she'd been doodling lopsided stars all over the list of new books she was ordering and saw the man standing in front of her desk.

"I'm sorry. I didn't notice you."

"Don't worry," he said easily. "I tend to get a lot of that."

And no wonder, Dani thought as she skimmed a quick judicial look over him. He could have been anywhere from twenty-five to forty; his body was youthfully trim, but the lines extending outward from friendly eyes that were neither blue nor gray but an indistinguishable hue in-between, suggested he'd at least hit thirty.

His medium short brown hair was neatly trimmed; he was wearing a blue chambray shirt rolled up at the sleeves, bark brown Dockers, and loafers—without the tassels, which would've been sure to get him ragged by shrimpers or oilriggers if he made the mistake of dropping into a local bar. He was neither attractive nor unattractive; merely the most ordinary man she'd ever seen. She honestly doubted he'd be noticeable in a crowd of three.

"I could use some information." His voice lacked any accent; it could have been designated Standard American.

"Well, you've come to the right place," she said with a smile.

His answering smile deepened those lines around his face, and while he didn't turn into Brad Pitt before her eyes, suddenly he wasn't quite so ordinary. "I'm seeking information on a home around here. You may have heard of it. Beau Soleil?"

Her fingers tightened on her pen. "Of course I have. It's one of the parish's last standing antebellum homes."

"So I hear." He rocked back on the heels of his cordovan loafers. "I also hear it's haunted."

Reaching into a brown billfold, he pulled out a card which read *Dr. Dallas Chapman, Parapsychologist.* Along with listing him as a consultant to the American Society for Psychological Research, there were nearly enough other letters after his name to complete an entire series of Sue Grafton alphabet mysteries.

Dani lifted a brow and tapped the edge of the card with her fingernail. "Does this mean you're a ghostbuster?"

"Oh, I don't bust them," he said quickly, with another engaging smile. "I just study them. Chronicle their environment, their behavior, examine stories of various hauntings around the country in an attempt to better understand the phenomenon.

"Although people are often disappointed to hear it, I don't spend my time blasting hotels trying to catch nasty little green ghosts, I've never worn a jumpsuit, and unfortunately, my funding doesn't come close to allowing me to build a portable nuclear-powered particle accelerator like the ones they carried in that movie. And I've never been slimed."

"I imagine that's a bit of a relief."

"Absolutely." His expression turned a bit more serious. "Certain of my colleagues disliked that film because they felt it made light of our profession. But I enjoyed it as an entertaining piece of fiction, and discovered that rather than demean my work, it actually made it easier."

"Oh?" The movie may have been fiction, but try telling that to her son, who must have seen it a dozen times and had gone through a phase, when he'd been in the first grade, of wanting to become a ghostbuster when he grew up. Dani couldn't wait to see the look on Matt's face when she took this business card home and told him she'd actually met a real live ghostbuster, right here in her library.

"Now, at least, people have some concept of what I do for a living, albeit a skewed one, and when they bring up the idea of ghostbusting, I can set them straight as to what a parapsychologist actually does. Before that film came out, despite the field being more than a hundred years old, the public simply didn't have a clue."

Dani didn't admit she wasn't all that up on the subject, either.

He shook his head with a bit of what she took to be mute frustration. "I'd introduce myself at a cocktail party or on an airplane and people would just give me sort of a blank stare. Or perhaps they'd mistake me for a psychologist. Or even a psychologist's assistant, like a paralegal. You know, *para*-psychologist," he explained at her blank look.

"Ah." Dani nodded. "I can see how that might be a problem," she agreed, fighting back a smile. He appeared to take his career very seriously, and she didn't want to risk offending him.

"Oh, it was a terrible problem. Of course you, as a librarian, undoubtedly know that the word parapsychologist refers to the study of psi, which stems from the twenty-third letter of the Greek alphabet, denoting the unknown."

"Actually, I didn't know that."

"Well then, now you do. The worst problem is when I'm confused with someone who practices witchcraft." He leaned toward her. "In fact," he said conspiratorially, "there was this one memorable time, when I was flying to London from Rome, where I'd been speaking at a joint conference of the ASPR and our European counterpart. The pilot nearly had to do an emergency landing in Milan, after I made the mistake of trying to explain the concept of life after death, or as we professionals prefer to call it, the survival of bodily death, to a little old lady who was sitting beside me.

"I no sooner mentioned the words *apparition* and *hauntings* when she started screaming bloody murder in Italian and began hitting me on top of the head with her rosary. It seems she was certain I was in league with the devil and giving her the evil eye." He sighed. "It took three flight attendants and half the bottle of a very nice Chianti I was carrying home in my carry-on from the duty-free shop to calm her down."

Dani laughed. "Well, at least it doesn't sound as if your work is boring."

"Oh, it's never boring," he agreed. "A bit wearying from time to time. Since spirits are not always the most cooperative entities, the work can often entail spending a lot of time in abandoned, unheated buildings waiting for an apparitional haunting, but it's quite satisfying.

"As a matter of fact, I met my wife at a castle on the moors in the

Scots Highlands. I was there exploring stories concerning a former laird of the castle, who'd died in the sixteen-hundreds and was allegedly slipping into women's beds at night and making mad, passionate love to them while their husbands were sleeping right beside them."

Dani wondered how it could have been all that passionate if the husbands slept through it, but didn't want to sound as if she were challenging his claim. "So your wife's a parapsychologist, too?"

"Oh, no. At least she wasn't then. She was actually there as part of a team to debunk the ghost theory."

"Who won?"

His eyes lit up. "We both did."

"That's sweet." Despite her own failed romantic relationships, Dani remained a sucker for a happy ending.

"We've been married ten years next month," he revealed. "And collaborators for eight of those years. You may be familiar with our work. We wrote a quite well-received in-depth study of the infamous Bell Witch published two years ago by the University of Tennessee Press."

"I believe I must have missed that one," Dani said mildly.

"It's another house haunting and one of our better studies, if I do say so myself. It's my hope to have the same success with the ghost or ghosts of Beau Soleil. Why, if things work out as well as I hope, that Confederate soldier could put Blue Bayou on the map."

Knowing Jack's penchant for privacy, and wanting to protect her former home from sensationalism and her hometown from hoards of tourists seeking tacky glow-in-the-dark plastic ghosts to hang from their rearview mirrors, and Lord knows what else, Dani certainly wasn't going to tell the man how to get to Beau Soleil. Of course he could get directions easily enough from the myriad local guidebooks on the shelves, but there was no point in making things easier for him.

"I imagine you know of the house," he said, his voice going up on the end of the statement, turning it into a question.

"It would be hard to live in the parish and not know of Beau Soleil," she hedged. Dani decided the fact that she'd grown up there was none of his business. Nor was she going to share any of the haunting tales that had been handed down from each succeeding generation of Duprees, or those random occasions when she'd heard weeping, or music, or some undistinguishable sound that was, undoubtedly, nothing more dramatic than an old house settling into the swamp.

Still, her library was a place of knowledge and it was her responsibility to see that patrons received the illumination they were seeking.

"I can suggest a few books." She pulled out a piece of paper, turned to her computer screen and wrote some titles down. "Not just about Beau Soleil, but other houses and supposed hauntings." She hoped she could throw him off the track.

No such luck. "Thanks. But it's Beau Soleil I'm interested in," he said, taking the paper nonetheless. "That *is* where Jack Callahan's hanging out these days, isn't it?"

The distaste of lying warred with Dani's belief that Jack deserved his privacy. Plus, she felt a twinge of something she just couldn't quite put her finger on.

He chuckled when she hesitated answering. "Don't worry about betraying a confidence. I'm pretty good at digging out information; I'll just start with these books and go from there. It's been a delight chatting with you, Ms. Dupree. Hopefully we'll be able to repeat the experience again soon." He winked. "Meanwhile, keep your spirits up.

"I'm sorry," he said with another of those friendly smiles that she decided must have helped win over his wife to his side of the ghost argument. "I can never resist saying that."

Dani watched as he took the books from the shelves over to a study table by the window. Then Mrs. Rullier came in looking for the latest true-crime murder, Sally Olivier needed help with her Internet search for wedding-cake recipes for her niece's upcoming nuptials, and Jean Babin wanted a book on fiberglassing a pirogue. The next time Dani looked up, Dallas Chapman, ghostbuster, was gone.

19

She liked it. Although he'd told himself that it shouldn't make such a difference, he'd hoped she would. Which was why Jack found himself holding his breath while Danielle waxed enthusiastic over the progress he'd made on her former bedroom since she'd last seen it, a mere week ago when they'd brought Matt out to Beau Soleil.

He'd kept two crews working nearly around the clock to complete the work; the walls were now a misty green that echoed the view outside the window, the trim was a creamy white again, the floor had been sanded and stained to a lighter finish than it had been when she'd lived here. He'd hand-sanded the rust from the lacy white bed himself, and had, with Desiree's help, located a crocheted spread at an antique store in Lafourche Crossing, which could have been the same one he remembered being on this same bed so many years ago. And while he definitely hadn't understood Desiree's contention that a woman could never have too many pillows, he'd piled a dizzying array of ruffled pillows in various shapes and sizes atop the spread.

They'd moved on to the adjoining bathroom, where he was showing off the blatantly hedonistic round whirlpool tub that was nearly large enough to swim laps in when his cell phone rang.

"I've been thinking about your ultimatum," the judge said without preamble.

"Oh?" Jack had been watching Dani run her hand up the swan's neck of the tub's faucet, indulging a hot fantasy of her stroking him with such open pleasure when her father's curt words brought him crashing back to reality.

"I've decided you're right. She deserves to know the truth."

Having admittedly been concerned about what he'd do if the judge challenged his ultimatum, Jack felt a cooling rush of relief. "I see," he said mildly, waiting to hear when, exactly, Dupree planned to admit what he'd done.

"The thing is, I'm a dying man; I don't have the strength for confrontation. If you're so hot for her to know why you left town, then you can damn well be the one to tell her."

"I understand." Jack smiled reassuringly at Dani, who'd glanced over at him, obviously curious about his curt responses.

"Well, then. That's settled." The judge hung up, ending the call as brusquely as he'd begun it.

"I suppose so," Jack murmured to dead air.

"Jack?" Dani's expression was concerned. "Is something wrong?"

He rubbed his jaw, reminding himself of the old prohibition about being careful what you wished for. Now that the old man had dumped the problem in his lap, he wasn't quite sure how to broach the subject.

"No. At least I don't think so."

How in the hell did you tell a woman that the father with whom she was struggling so hard to establish a relationship during the brief time he may have left was a common blackmailer who'd played with both their lives as if they were no more than pawns he'd moved around a chess board if for no other reason than to prove he could?

"It wasn't my father calling, was it?" A little frown drew her eyebrows together.

Jack was a world-class liar. It was a talent he'd honed to perfection, a skill that had allowed him to continue working deep undercover far longer than was safe or wise. Street junkie to Median cartel leader, it hadn't mattered, and while he'd admittedly had his detractors, everyone he'd ever worked with had proclaimed him to be the best prevaricator in the drug-enforcement business. Hands down.

But Danielle was an entirely different story. There'd always been something about her, perhaps her own unwavering sense of goodness and honesty, that made it damn near impossible to lie. Which was why he hadn't dared say goodbye to her. There would have been no way he could have looked into those soft hazel eyes and not told her the truth about why he was leaving. So, to his everlasting shame, he'd taken the coward's way out, leaving Blue Bayou, and her, without a word of explanation.

"What makes you think it was the judge?" he asked.

Her frown deepened at his slight hesitation. "I don't know. There was just something about the way you were talking. . . ." Her cheeks, which had been touched by the sun during the picnic lunch he'd picked up at Cajun Cal's for them to share in the park on her lunch hour, paled. "It's not Matt, is it? Daddy wasn't calling to say anything had happened to him?"

"*Non*. You know I'd never keep any news of your boy from you."

"Then he's all right?" Her slender hand was on his sleeve, her short, neatly buffed nails digging into his arm.

"So far as I know he's still in the kitchen makin' pralines with Orèlia, same as when we left the house."

"And my father? Nothing's happened to him?"

"Hell, Dani, I know the judge thinks he's gonna kick the bucket at any moment and since the doc thinks there's an outside chance of that happening, it makes sense you've bought into the idea, too." He couldn't quite pull off what he'd wanted to be an encouraging smile, proving yet again how difficult it was to lie to a woman who wore her heart in her eyes. "But the way I figure it, he may just outlast all of us, being how the old bastard's too tough to die."

"Everyone dies."

"Yeah, you'd think that was the case. Your mother, my *maman*, my dad, even that prick you made the mistake of marrying are all gone. But you know what the judge tol' me when he caught me vandalizing those mailboxes back when I was fifteen?"

"No."

"I made some smart-ass crack about him being an old man who wasn't always gonna be sitting up on that bench, hinting, in my less than subtle teenage juvenile delinquent wannabe fashion, that I'd outlive him and continue doing whatever I damn well pleased." Jack smiled faintly at the memory. "He pulled me out of that chair like I weighed no more than Matt and told me I shouldn't count on outlivin' him, since he was damn near invincible, and when the world finally burned itself out, the only things gonna be left were him and a bunch of cockroaches."

"Isn't that a lovely thought." She sighed, making him want to put his arms around her and reassure her that everything was going to be all right. Which was a bit difficult to do since he wasn't so sure of that himself.

Christ. He'd been working toward this moment since he'd realized that finishing what they'd begun that summer was inevitable. It was time to get things out in the open, to finally put the past behind them. Jack knew he should tell her now. But the part of him that was about to explode was arguing with equal vigor that the potentially difficult subject could be broached more easily when he wasn't so distracted by a driving need to get naked.

She went over to the window she used to climb out of to meet him and leaned her forehead against the glass. "Do you remember those balls that used to tell the future?" she asked softly.

"Sure. Nate had one." He'd also claimed it had told him he was going to lose his virginity with Misty Montgomery, which turned out to be true enough, but Jack had always put that incident down to Misty's reputation more than any psychic powers found in some dime-store black plastic ball.

"I did, too. I used to stand here, watching out the window, and ask it if you'd come to make love to me."

"That was a pretty easy one since signs definitely pointed to yes," he said.

With her back to him, he felt the smile more than saw it. "I used to ask it everything. Would I get an A on my history test, would I get elected to Homecoming Court, would I grow up to be as pretty as people say my mama was—"

"That's an easy one. You're a lot prettier."

"How would you know? Our families didn't even know each other when my mother was alive."

"Maybe not. But I saw a picture of her once." He didn't say that it'd actually been a porn flick he and Nate had rented on a clandestine trip to an adult book store across the parish line. He'd been fourteen, Nate a year younger. For the next two weeks he'd had such hot dreams that every time he'd look at Danielle, he'd see her mother in her face, and his dick, which had already begun to torture him at the slightest provocation, would get as stiff as his old hunting dog Evangeline's tail when she'd point out quail.

"She was pretty enough in a flashy sort of way," he said. Flash and trash, he realized now, deciding there was nothing to be gained by admitting that she'd also been damn hot, especially for someone's mom, for Chrissakes, in her role as the nympho nurse who'd brought a whole new meaning to bedside manner. Hell, Nate had been so impressed, he'd given up that week's idea of becoming a pro baseball player and decided to go to medical school instead.

"But yours is a deep-down beauty. The kind that lasts."

She glanced back over her shoulder, her faint smile not quite reaching her eyes. "That's nice of you to say."

"It's the truth."

"I know it sounds silly now," she murmured. "But I really believed that silly ball."

Jack shrugged, wondering where, exactly they were going with this. "Don't feel like the Lone Ranger. So did Nate."

She laughed, just a little at that. Then sobered. "Wouldn't it be nice if there really was some way to tell the future?"

"I don't know. I suppose it depends on whether it'd be possible to change the outcome of events."

If he'd known his dad was going to die the next day, he sure as hell would have gotten to the court house earlier, before that wigged-out yahoo with the gun, so he could have at least tried to prevent his father's murder. But would he have wanted to know ahead of time if he'd also known that his father's fate was inescapable? Jack didn't think so.

He came up behind her. "I won't claim to be able to read the future, *chère*, but I do know what's going to happen here for the next little while." His lips brushed her neck.

"What?" Her breath shuddered out as his teeth nipped her earlobe.

"I'm going to do things to you, Danielle." He glided his fingers over her collarbone. "With you. Wicked, impossible, exquisite things." Watching their reflections in the night-darkened glass, he skimmed a fingertip down her throat. "I'm going to take you places you've only ever dreamed of. . . .

"Then I'm going to take you." He slipped his hands beneath the hem of her blouse and cupped her breasts in his palms, embracing the warm weight of them. "And you, *mon coeur,* are going to love it."

My heart. Dani might not have spoken nearly as much French as Jack had growing up, but she definitely recognized that endearment. It had been such a very long time since a man had wanted her. Longer still since she'd wanted a man the way she wanted *this* man.

"I've been wanting to do this since that night you first came to Beau Soleil." He began to unbutton her blouse, folding back the silk with extreme care, as if he were unwrapping the most exquisite of gifts. Just the sight of his dark hands on her body created a hormonal jolt. "Pretending you were looking for carpenters."

"I *was* looking for carpenters."

"Perhaps." He bit down gently on the sensitive place where neck and shoulder joined, sending a rippling thrill of anticipation racing through her. "But your sweet little body, and your lonely heart, they wanted me to do this."

He turned her in his arms, his hand fisted in her hair, pulling her head back to allow his mouth full access to her throat while his fingers tightened on her breast. When the wanting had her trembling, Jack smiled a slow, satisfied rogue's smile.

He didn't take his eyes from her face as he slowly unfastened her bra. Then, still watching, drew the straps with infinite slowness down her arms. There was a tenderness in his gaze Dani couldn't remember ever witnessing that long-ago summer. Of course then, with the exception of their last night together, the sex had been fast and hot, like an August whirlwind. How could she have reached adulthood without ever having known this slow, glorious torment?

"Lovely," he murmured. His fingers brushed over her like whispers on silk. He lowered his head, his tongue dampening her warming flesh as it sketched concentric circles outward to her nipple.

Lowell had always preferred silence during their lovemaking, and while her former husband was the last person she wanted to be thinking about right now, old habits died hard, and Dani bit her lip to keep from whimpering.

"Don't do that." He returned his mouth to hers. "I don't want you to hold anything back. I want to know what you like." His hands tempted, his mouth seduced, his tongue as it slipped between her parted lips, promised. "I want to know what gives you pleasure."

"You do," she whispered on a ragged thread of sound.

Dani felt his smile.

He continued undressing her with agonizing slowness, treating each new bit of flesh to the same prolonged exploration.

He watched her face again as the desire rose in her, watched her innermost feelings, witnessed firsthand how weak and needy he could make her feel.

She'd been surprised to discover since returning home that she and her father actually shared something in common: They both felt a need for control. The judge had found it by wielding power while she'd chosen instead a life of tidy, predictable order.

But now, with Jack, she was discovering that there was something alluring about surrendering control, of letting a man you trusted push you to the outer limits of your sexuality. Imagined fantasies of what he might be planning flashed in her mind—erotic, vivid, demanding. Every nerve ending reached for his touch; every pore sought relief from a passion too long denied. It was frightening. And it was wonderful.

"*Bon Dieu*, you're the most responsive woman I've ever known."

Dani refused to think about the other women he'd known. They belonged in his past; she was the woman with him now.

"Only with you," she admitted on a ragged moan as he pulled her down onto the bed. Her melting, liquid thighs fell open.

"*I know.*"

His lips tugged on her other nipple while he responded to the silent, unconscious invitation of her body by pressing the heel of his hand against her mound.

"Arrogant beast," she muttered even as desire sang its clear high notes in her blood.

"It's not arrogance."

"Because it's true?" The way he was looking at her, like a man about to feast on forbidden fruit after a long fast, warmed Dani from the inside out. No man had ever looked at her like Jack did. With such vivid, focused intensity.

"No point in lyin', sugar, when we both know it's true." He continued to caress her body from her shoulders to her knees. "Because you've always had the same effect on me. Do you have any idea how many women I had to sleep with before I got over you?"

"No." Her head was spinning, making it difficult to think. To speak. Heat spread beneath her skin, across her breasts, her stomach. Moisture pooled between her lax thighs.

"I don' know, either. 'Cause I never did." His tongue made a wet hot swathe down her stomach. "We're damn good together, *chère*. You and me."

"Jack . . ." As the pressure built inside her, Dani's hips moved restlessly, wanting, needing more. "Please."

"Not yet." He lifted her hands above her head, holding them with one hand as he lowered his body onto hers, pressing her deep into the mattress.

There was something unbearably erotic about being physically restrained while his fully dressed, fully aroused body moved against her naked one. Dani felt the prick of buttons against her breasts, the sharpness of a belt buckle at her belly, the rasp of the zipper, the roughness of denim. The stony hardness of his erection.

Once again, he reminded her of a pirate. One with ravishment on his mind.

"What did you say?" he asked against her mouth.

She hadn't realized she'd spoken out loud. But imprisoned by a hunger a great deal stronger than the strong fingers which continued to hold her hands above her head, Dani could deny him nothing. So she told him the truth.

"Ever since I first saw you on the *gallerie* that night, you've reminded me of Jean Laffite."

"Was that a good thing?" He kissed her again. Deeper, this time. "Or bad?" He continued to move against her, forward, then back.

"Bad. In a good way." The friction of their bodies sparked every nerve ending in Dani's body.

"Good." His tongue slid between her lips at the same time he brought her hand down and pressed it against her mound of golden hair.

"Jack . . . no . . . I can't." This was something done in private. With the bedroom door locked and the shades pulled.

"Sure you can. I'll help you." Ignoring her halfhearted protest, he began to move their joined hands, slowly at first, increasing the pressure, escalating the tempo, until breathless, Dani came in a long, slow, rolling wave that rose, crested, then settled.

"Oh, yes." The sigh shuddered out of her. "That was wonderful." And a great deal more satisfying than doing it all by herself.

"Hell, that was just to take the edge off so we can enjoy the rest of the night." He grinned wickedly, like the pirate he could have been. Then kissed her again. Longer. Deeper.

She murmured a soft sound of protest as he left the bed. Then began to watch, enthralled as he pulled his shirt from his jeans and began unbuttoning it.

He was as she'd remembered him, but different. Heavier, but without an ounce of fat from what she could tell. His shoulders were wide, his chest broad, skin tanned to the color of walnuts stretched tight over smooth muscle and sinew.

His eyes didn't move from hers as he stripped off the shirt and tossed it onto a nearby chair. Next he unbuckled his belt, pulling it through each loop with such aching slowness, Dani had to restrain herself from leaping up and finishing the job herself.

After he'd discarded the belt onto the chair with his shirt, he opened the metal button at his waist with a quick flick of his wrist. The hiss of the metal zipper was unnaturally loud in the absolute silence broken only by the sound of their breathing.

Dressed, Jack Callahan was remarkably handsome. Nude he was magnificent. Standing naked and rampant before her, he certainly didn't look like a man who earned his living at a computer keyboard. Male power radiated from every pore as he trailed his splayed wide hand down his chest, following the arrowing of dark hair.

"You do this." His voice roughened with hunger as he curled his long fingers around his beautifully formed erection. "All I have to do is think of you and I'm hard."

If the world had been coming to an end, if meteors had begun crashing into the Earth outside the window, if the bayou was rocked with earthquakes, engulfed in flames, Dani could not have moved from this bed. Could not have dragged her gaze away from the arousing sight of that rigid flesh thrusting from a thicket of tight jet curls. A single drop of moisture shimmered on the knobbed, plum-hued tip; struck with an overwhelming urge to lick it off, she heard herself moan.

Need welled up inside her. Years of emptiness waiting to be filled. Rising to her knees, she opened her arms, held them out to him as he returned to the bed on that loose-hipped, predatory stride which never failed to thrill her. The mattress sank beneath his weight. They knelt together, face to face, soft feminine curves pressed against hard male angles.

He tunneled his hand beneath her hair, cupped the nape of her neck, and kissed her while Dani moved her hands up his back, reveling in the play of long hard muscle beneath her touch, neat short nails nipping into his skin. She closed her eyes against the sweet agony of desire and urged him even closer, wishing she could absorb him into her burning flesh.

When her mind began to shut down, Dani allowed her body—and Jack—to take over, discovering that sexual surrender to the right man could be glorious.

He explored the terrain of her body with hands and lips and teeth and tongue, discovering thrilling points of pain and pleasure she'd never known existed. He touched wherever he liked, tasted what he wanted. Murmured words against her lips, her throat, her quivering stomach, silken cords twining around her heart, binding her to him.

The more control Dani relinquished, the more pleasure she received. There was nothing Jack could have asked for that she would not have willingly given.

Her fingers curled in his hair as his lips nibbled their way up the inside of first one thigh, then the other. Her body arched and she sucked in a deep, shuddering breath when he slid first one, then two fingers into the moist giving folds of her body and began to move them in and out of her with a wet, silky, ease.

"*Mon Dieu*, you're hot," he marveled. Drawing his head back so he could watch her face, he thrust his fingers higher, stroking, caressing, adoring the very heat of her while the erotic sucking sound make her crave him all the more.

Dani gasped as the orgasm flared, but before she could recover, he'd dragged her back down to the mattress and wrapped her fingers around the white iron bed frame. She thought she heard him tell her to hang on tight, but wasn't quite sure, with the blood pounding in her ears, whether it was his voice, or her own need that had her tightening her hold.

His dark head was between her thighs, stimulating already ultrasensitive flesh by alternately nipping and licking. Her stomach tensed, her thighs tightened in expectation, she arched her pelvis against his mouth, every atom in her body concentrated on the hooded tangle of tingling nerves hidden in her slick wet lips.

White hot stars wheeled behind her closed lids. Just when Dani feared she was in danger of shattering into a million pieces, a ruthless stroke of his tongue had her pouring over his hand.

Her body went limp, but once again Jack refused to give her time to regain her senses.

"Again." His rough voice was a primal growl as he sent her up once more. Higher this time, hotter. Dani's breath was coming in short sharp pants, her eyes fluttered closed again, the better to concentrate on these exquisite, terrifying sensations. She tossed her head on the pillow while her body, desperate to feel him inside her, bowed.

"Look at me, Danielle." Jack took hold of her chin and held her gaze to his. "I want to watch your eyes when I take you."

Unable to deny him anything, Dani opened her eyes, meeting his for a thrilling, suspended moment. Then he plunged into her with a force that left them both equally stunned and breathless.

Jack recovered first. He began rocking against her, thigh to thigh, chest to chest, mouth to mouth.

He was long and thick and rock hard. Dani's body stretched, then tightened around him; her nails dug into his back and she wrapped her legs high around his hips to take him into her, deeply, fully, arching up to meet each rough stroke, hot flesh slapping against hot flesh, her soft cries muffled by his ravenous mouth, his tongue thrusting between her parted lips in rhythm with his bucking hips.

He was, as he'd promised, taking her, claiming her. Consuming her. Dani could not have been more branded if he'd burned his name into her hot slick flesh. And all the time his intense, gleaming gold eyes never left hers.

Hearts pounded, jackhammer hard, jackhammer fast. His movements quickened. Deepened. His back arched, his head was thrown back, every muscle in his body in taut relief.

This time they came together. Dani wept as a seemingly never-ending series of orgasms racked her body while Jack moaned a string of gloriously naughty sounding French words she couldn't understand against her ravaged mouth.

She had no idea how long they lay there on the tangled sheets, arms and legs entwined, but she was still shuddering from the aftershocks when he brushed a kiss against her lips and began to lever himself off her.

She made a small murmur of complaint, tightening her arms around him, holding him close. The ceiling fan was slowly spinning overhead with a faint *click, click, click* sound, the moving air cooling bare, moist flesh. "Don't go."

"I won't."

Dani wondered if Jack was talking about not leaving the bed. Or her life. But wanting to enjoy this stolen time together, she didn't ask. Instead, she cuddled against him and basked in the afterglow of passion.

"That was even better than I remembered," she said on a soft, utterly satiated sigh. Until this evening she'd always believed the G-spot was yet another myth designed to make women feel insecure about their sexuality.

"So you did think of me from time to time." He did not sound at all surprised by that revelation. In fact, she thought he sounded downright smug.

"Every once in a while," she said with exaggerated casualness. "Whenever they showed *Rebel Without a Cause* on the Movie Channel."

"I suppose bein' compared to James Dean isn't bad," he decided. "But his character in that movie was kinda a whiney wuss."

"He wasn't whiney. He was sensitive."

"*Sensitive*'s just another word for *wuss*. The guy wouldn't have lasted forty-eight hours here in the swamp."

Unfortunately, he was probably right. Bayou males had a lot of appealing traits, but sensitivity, as a rule, wasn't exactly one of them. "So, how would you describe yourself?"

"If we're talkin' fifties flicks, I guess I'd have to go with a cross between Brando in *The Wild One* and Newman in *Hud*."

It fit, Dani admitted. Brando's smolderingly dangerous force with Newman's wickedly blue-eyed, smirking sexuality that clung to him like sweat to a bottle of Dixie beer in August. "I believe *Hud* was out in the sixties. And I find it interesting that you'd choose two Neanderthal misogynists as role models."

"Hell, those guys weren't misogynists. They were men's men."

"How refreshing to find a man in the twentieth-first century whose oversize ego allows him to not even pretend to be the slightest bit politically correct," she countered dryly.

"If I wasn't in such a good mood, I might argue that misogynist label, though I will admit to having never been a real fan of political correctness. As for my oversize ego"—he skimmed a lazy finger up the inside of her thigh—"just give it a couple minutes to recuperate, and this swamp-dwelling Neanderthal will be more than happy to supersize your sweet little pussy all night long."

She couldn't help herself. She snorted. "You really are incorrigible."

He touched his lips to her temple. "I didn't hear you complainin' when you were screaming my name in my ear like a wild woman, sugar."

She flinched, just a bit, when he skimmed that treacherous fingertip over the still tingling flesh between her thighs.

"Did I hurt you?"

"It's still just a little sensitive. And I did not scream."

"Sure sounded like screaming to me. But that's okay; I didn't need that eardrum, anyway. One'll probably do me just fine." He slid down the sheets, scattering kisses down her torso. When he dipped the tip of his tongue in her navel, Dani could feel her body heating up all over again. "Jack—"

"Don't worry, darlin'," he murmured against her stomach. "I'm just gonna kiss it and make it better."

When he lifted her against his oh, so clever mouth, Dani didn't have the strength to protest. Nor did she want to as he proceeded to use his hands and lips and supersized ego to take her far beyond better all the way to sublime.

Sometime, much, much later, Dani awoke in Jack's arms, unable to remember when, exactly she'd drifted off. The soft steady breathing on the back of her neck revealed that she wasn't the only one who'd fallen asleep. She glanced over at the bedside clock.

"Oh, my God," she said, trying to extricate herself from the tangle of sheets. "It's late. I've got to get home."

He pushed himself onto his elbows and blearily eyed the fluorescent green numbers. "It's not that late."

"Easy for you to say. You're not the one who has to get an eight-year-old off to school and show up at work on time." If she left now, she just may manage to squeeze in four hours' sleep before her clock radio went off.

He snagged her wrist when she would have left the bed. "Don't go."

"I can't have Matt waking up and finding me gone."

"I'll get you back to Orèlia's before he wakes up. But before you go, we need to talk."

"Really, Jack, that's not necessary. I don't need the pretty words I did when I was seventeen. After all, I may not be the most experienced woman in the world, but I'm adult enough to know that what we did was just sex. Terrific, dynamite, world-class sex, but—"

"That's not it." He thrust a hand through his loosened hair, which earlier had felt like black silk against her breasts, stomach, her back, as he'd seemed determined to make love to every inch of her body. "There's something I need to tell you." His voice deepened with an emotion she couldn't quite decipher, rumbling like the warning of thunder on the horizon. Goose bumps rose on chilled flesh that had, just a short time ago, felt as if it was burning up.

Looking into the handsome face that appeared uncharacteristically grim, Dani suddenly realized she'd seen that expression before. Earlier, when he'd been showing off the bathroom.

"It's about that call you got earlier, isn't it?" Dani braced herself for bad news.

"In a way." He sighed heavily. "It's about that summer. About why I left Blue Bayou."

20

Dani couldn't speak as Jack related the story. Couldn't think. She could merely lie in his arms, numbed, chilled, listening in disbelief as Jack related the sordid tale.

"My father was the reason you disappeared in the middle of the night without a word?" The judge might not have been Ward Cleaver; he'd been distant and sometimes out-and-out cold. But until this moment Dani had never thought him to be viciously cruel.

"Yeah. I wanted to talk to you, to try to explain, but he refused to let me say goodbye. Said if I didn't get packed and out within the hour, *Maman* would lose her job and I'd be tossed in jail on a statutory rape charge."

His words slashed through her like a razor. "That's so hard to believe." How could her father have done such a dreadful thing?

His lips pulled into a hard tight line. "I'm not lying."

"I didn't mean it that way."

Myriad emotions bombarded Dani, so many she thought she might be crushed from the weight of them. Pushing aside her own personal pain for a moment, she lifted a trembling hand to Jack's face, felt the sensual roughness of his beard against her palm and was amazed that even as she fought against the drowning feelings of betrayal and loss, she could still feel a distant, renewed stir of desire.

"It was so horribly unfair to you. To me." To our unborn child, she thought but did not say. A sob rose in her throat, nearly choking her. "And to your mother, who kept her job, but lost one of her sons that night."

Jack hadn't deserted her. Not really. The knowledge, after believing otherwise for so many years, was staggering. Reeling, unable to remain still, Dani abandoned the warmth of the bed, the comfort of his arms, and began to pace.

"All these years." She fought against the rising pain, struggled to keep it from engulfing her. "Ever since that night, my entire life has been built on a foundation of my father's betrayal."

She'd never tried to find Jack. Never attempted to contact him. Not even after she'd learned she was pregnant. Because—oh, God—she'd believed he'd left because he'd no longer wanted her.

Memories flooded back in a torrent of painful images, the worst of them being that autumn afternoon when her father had calmly, cooly, calculatingly convinced her Jack's desertion proved he hadn't loved her, so there was no reason to believe he'd want to learn he was going to be a father.

Oh, he'd been so logical, she thought, as she whipped back and forth across the newly sanded floor, painful memories filling her head like smoke. So clear-headed when she was not, calmly ticking off all the reasons why her gilded visions of a life with Jack Callahan were merely romantic schoolgirl fantasies.

Did she have any idea the emotional costs of a shotgun wedding? he'd asked. He'd seen the results, again and again: angry, bitter men who'd take out their frustration at having been trapped into a marriage on the women they blamed for ruining their lives. Even worse, he'd seen the damage done to innocent children unfortunate to have been born into such marital war zones.

In tears Dani had argued that Jack wasn't that way. That she knew he'd never, ever lift a hand to a woman or a child. To which her father had, in the same deep, self-assured voice he'd issued edicts from the bench, asked if she could have ever suspected he'd take her virginity, use her for his own summer amusement, then abandon her.

She could not challenge that point, because it was true that she'd never, in a million years, expected such behavior from Jack. But also true was the fact that somewhere, deep down inside her, she'd known that the boy she loved was nothing like the self-indulgent portrait her father was painting.

Unfortunately, at the time, alone, afraid, pregnant at seventeen, battered by confusion and hormones, she hadn't been able to think clearly.

Oh, God. She rested her brow against the rippled glass and pressed a hand against her stomach, which heaved in her throat the same way it had that day, when, unable to hide her morning sickness any longer, she'd been forced to tell her father she was pregnant with Bad Jack Callahan's child.

"There's no denying that the judge changed both our futures that day." Lost in her own whirling thoughts, Dani hadn't heard Jack come up behind her. He wrapped his arms around her waist, leaned her back against him and rested his chin atop her pounding head. "But it didn't all turn out so bad. It's obvious you adore Matt."

"Of course I do." She felt the hot traitorous tears begin to overfill her eyes. Tears of anger and betrayal. Of regrets too numerous to calculate. "He's the most important thing to me."

Jack held her tight when she would have pulled away. "He's a beautiful, bright child, Danielle. A blessing and you've no idea how many times in the past weeks I've wished he were mine."

He turned her in his arms, and to soothe himself, as well as Dani, he brushed away the glittering moisture trailing down her face with his fingertips. Her eyes were haunted and dark with something close to desperation he couldn't quite understand. Then again, he remembered feeling as if the judge had pulled the rug out from under him. It wasn't all that surprising that Dani would feel much the same way despite the passage of time.

"As you've already pointed out, Matt wouldn't exist if you hadn't married the man you did. Which you might not have done, if your father hadn't run me out of Blue Bayou."

He watched the storm of emotions rage and knew the exact moment when she accepted that reasoning. "You're right, of course. But I think I hate how you can be so calm, when I'm not."

"I've had more time to live with it. Come to grips with it." He combed a hand through the love-tousled silk of her hair.

"Thirteen years," she murmured. She was silent for a moment. Pensive. "I thought of you. I didn't want to, but I did. I didn't want to *want* you, either. But I did. Even after what I believed you'd done."

"I thought about you." He caught her chin in his fingers, brushed his thumb over her soft, love-swollen lips. "Too much and too often. Walking away from you, was one of the few regrets of my life." Jack had never spoken truer words.

She pressed her fingers to her eyes. "I would have hated you going to jail on my account."

"Hell, that's not why I left," he said on a surge of heated resentment he'd believed he'd left behind in the past. "Whatever it was we had together back then, did together, was worth risking a jail sentence. But the decision about *Maman* was tougher.

"The only job she'd ever had in her life was being a wife and mother. She didn't have any career skills. Finn was in college, and Nate was just turning seventeen; neither one of them was in a position to take care of her.

"I didn't really believe your father would actually follow through on his threat to fire her, but I couldn't take the chance. Can you understand that?"

"Of course I can." She was steadier, her eyes clearer. "My father understood it, too. So damn well." When she bit her bottom lip, Jack could see the wheels turning in her head and sensed what was coming next. "But you could have always come back, when I was of legal age, and my father wouldn't have had any say about what I did. Or with whom. I didn't marry Lowell for another five years."

"By then I was in the navy. Working shore patrol, which was damn ironic for a kid who'd spent a good part of his teens getting busted himself. You still had another year of high school. There was no way I was going to drag you around the country to wait stateside with the other wives in military housing or even worse, some tacky little trailer while I was off on cruises. You needed to get your education and grow up a little and I needed to become a man who could offer you something worthwhile."

"I always thought *you* were worthwhile."

"Bet you didn't think that after I took off. Bet you thought I was a real SOB then."

"Perhaps," she allowed. "But after a while I realized that you reacted like a lot of eighteen-year-old boys would when a girl told him that she loved him and wanted to have his babies." Tears began swimming in her eyes again. Jack couldn't remember a time when she'd appeared more fragile.

"Babies definitely weren't in my plans back then." But, while it was surprising the hell out of him, since he'd never envisioned himself as a father, Jack was finding the mental image of Danielle ripe and round with his child more than a little appealing. Just as appealing was the idea of being a daddy to her son.

One step at a time.

"That summer was a long time ago." Wanting to get past this, so they could get on with a future the judge had denied them, Jack lifted their joined hands and touched his lips to her knuckles. "It's all water under the bridge, and as sorry as I am about having to hurt you, with all that's happened, it just doesn't seem real important in the big scheme of things. So, how about I make you a proposition? We'll just consider it kid stuff and move on."

If only it were that simple, Dani agonized. *Tell him*, a little voice of conscience urged. *You'll probably never get a better chance*.

There was so much more to say, more secrets to reveal, more truths to confess. But it was so much easier to allow herself to be lifted into his arms and carried back to bed, lovers long ago lost, but found again.

Giving herself up to the glorious feelings, to Jack, Dani tried not to think about what he'd do when she told him everything that had happened after her father had driven him out of Blue Bayou that summer.

A slow, steady anger was still simmering in Dani as she made Matt French toast for breakfast the next morning. She pretended interest as he read her last night's sports scores from the paper, forced a smile at the latest *Get Fuzzy* comic strip which usually made her laugh out loud, and managed to wave him off on the yellow bus without either bursting into tears or imploding.

Then she returned to the kitchen where her father was drinking a cup of coffee.

"You're not supposed to be drinking that," she reminded him of Dr. Ancelet's instructions.

"One cup isn't going to kill me."

"True enough. But I may."

"Ah." He glanced at her over the rim of the mug, his expression revealing not a bit of guilt that she could see. "Can I infer by that comment that you've been talking to Callahan?"

"You don't sound surprised."

"I'm not. He gave me a deadline to tell you myself, but I decided to let him handle the matter in his own way."

"Too bad you didn't use such restraint that summer. When you ran Jack out of town."

"He didn't have to leave. I gave the boy a choice," the judge said, somewhat defensively.

"Between me or his widowed mother losing her job. What the hell kind of choice is that?"

"Watch your language, Danielle. There's no reason to talk like a sailor."

"After all you've done, you're actually worried about my language?" Her voice rose up the scale; she stared at him and shoved her hair back from her face with both hands. "I'm just getting started, Father. What on earth made you think you could play God with our lives that way?"

"I had to do something to protect you after Jimbo Lott came and told me he'd found the two of you screwing out at the camp."

"The person I'd needed protection from just happened to be Lott. Did the horrid perverted man tell you that he kept his patrol car's spotlight on me the entire time I was getting dressed?"

"No." His voice stayed steady, but a muscle jerked in his cheek.

"How about the fact that he knocked Jack out with the butt of his service revolver when he tried to defend me?"

"No. But I'm not surprised at either behavior. Lott redefines slime. It's a crime he's still sheriff. And Jack always has been too impetuous for his own good."

"*He* was protecting me."

"Which wouldn't have been necessary if he hadn't taken you out there in the first place," the judge said on the same reasonable tone he'd used to convince her to give up her child. Having disliked it then, Dani hated it now.

"I was trying to protect you, too. Besides, Callahan's mother wasn't any more happy about the two of you together than I was."

That hurt. "I thought Marie liked me."

"She did. But she was concerned about her son's future. She didn't want him to pay for foolish mistakes, become a daddy at eighteen, and ruin his chances to make something of his life."

He'd *been* a father. And had never known it. Guilt settled heavily on Dani's shoulders. Guilt and a sorrow that had become so much a part of her it had seeped deep in her bones.

"Think how you'd feel if Matthew came home some day when he was still a teenager and told you he'd gotten some girl in trouble. I'll bet you won't be so sanguine then."

"I'd be concerned. Probably even upset," she allowed, saying a small mental prayer that they'd be spared that experience. "But I sure wouldn't sweep it under the rug and pretend it never happened. And I'd never, ever be ashamed of him."

As you were me. She didn't need to say the words out loud; they hovered in the still morning air between them.

Dani wanted to rant. To rave. To throw things. For the sake of her father's health—for that reason only—she forced her temper down.

"Even if you thought you were doing what was best for me, you still had no right to threaten Jack."

"I didn't have any choice. The boy wouldn't take money to leave."

She drew in a sharp breath that burned. "You offered him a bribe?" This just kept getting worse and worse.

"Not a bribe. An incentive. You were too young to know your own mind."

His gray eyes turned to steel. Despite the way his heart disease had physically weakened him, Dani had no problem envisioning him back on the bench, literally wielding the power of life and death.

"You still had a year of high school," he reminded her. "Your entire life was ahead of you, and I damn well didn't want you throwing it away on a juvenile delinquent like Jack Callahan."

"He wasn't really a delinquent. He was just angry. If his father hadn't died—"

"I would have been the one lying dead on the courthouse floor. Is that what you would have wanted?"

It was an impossible choice. Just like the one he'd given Jack. She shook her head and stared unseeingly out the window. "I don't believe you would have followed through on your threat. I cannot accept the idea that the man I've respected my entire life would have tossed the woman whose husband saved *his* life out onto the street."

"I didn't believe it would come to that." The judge shrugged. "After all, for all Callahan's faults, no one could say he didn't love his mama. Especially since even if I didn't fire her, we both knew it'd break her heart if he'd been jailed on a statutory rape charge."

"That's one of the more disgusting aspects of this." Her stomach twisted at the idea of having something as beautiful as what she and Jack had shared turned into a public disgrace. "Did Marie know what you did?"

"Not the specifics. But she must've figured I'd done something because afterward she came and thanked me for helping her boy stay on the straight and narrow. The Navy was good for him, made a man out of him.

"If he'd stayed here in Blue Bayou, he would have been just one more troublemaker, mad at the world and taking it out on everyone around him. Even those who loved him. Most especially those who loved him."

"That's not true. That boot camp you'd sent him to had changed him. It made him realize that anger never solves anything."

"So you say. But that wasn't a chance I was prepared to take."

"It wasn't *your* chance to take."

"You were underage," he reminded her. "And he sure as hell wasn't showing a lot of sense—or honor—sneaking around with you in the first place. If he'd wanted to date my daughter, he should have come to me and asked my permission like a man."

"Your permission? We weren't living in the Middle Ages, Father. And for your information, Jack wanted our relationship out in the open. I was the one who begged him to keep it a secret. Because I knew you wouldn't approve."

She shook her head, shuddered out a painful breath. "But I never, in my wildest imagination, believed you'd stoop so low."

"Don't be so fast to judge, little girl. You're a mother. The day will come when you'll understand I did what I had to do to protect you."

"No." About this, Dani was very clear. "I'll always be concerned about Matt's future. And that of any other children, if I'm fortunate enough to have them. But I would never, ever, manipulate them the way you did Jack and me."

"It never would have worked out between the two of you anyway."

"Wasn't that for me to find out? Besides, *your* choice of a husband for me wasn't exactly stellar."

"Point taken. But you did end up with a wonderful little boy."

It was the same thing Jack had said.

As emotions welled up inside her, choking her, Dani reminded herself that it was control she needed now. Cool, calming control. It would not do either of them any good if she started screeching at her ill father, no matter now much he may deserve it. No matter how badly *she* needed to do it.

"As much as I love Matt, that still doesn't excuse what you did, Father. It could never make it right."

She turned to walk away.

"I'm not the only one with secrets," he called after her. "If you're such a stickler for honesty, why don't you tell Jack where you spent your senior year of high school? And why?"

Refusing to admit that about this, at least, he had a point, Dani walked out of the room without responding.

Like many bad days, this one just got worse. Needing a chocolate boost after her confrontation with her father, Dani stopped off at the market on her way to the library, where a clutch of women were gathered around the cash register; blocking her access to the Hershey's bars.

"Did you see this, Dani, dear?" Bessie Ardoin, an eccentric, octogenarian spinster who'd claimed to have been beamed aboard a spaceship that had landed outside Blue Bayou one night back in the sixties, waved a supermarket tabloid. "It's so exciting."

"Let me guess. Elvis has been found on an ice floe with a survivor from the *Titanic*."

"It's not nice to jest about the King, dear," Edith Ardoin, Bessie's twin sister, chided. While Edith hadn't experienced her sister's alien adventure, she *had* worked as an extra in Elvis Presley's movie *King Creole* when location shooting had been done in New Orleans. The way she'd continued to talk about it for more than forty years suggested it remained the high point of her life.

"I'm sorry, Miss Ardoin," Dani said.

"That's all right, dear," Bessie answered for her sister. "No harm done. Edith knows you didn't mean any disrespect. After all, how would you have any way of knowing that Beau Soleil's ghost is now famous all over the country?"

"What?" Dani snatched the paper from Bessie's outstretched hand. "Oh, no," she groaned as she read the screaming double headline: *Things that go bump in the Bayou. Thriller writer haunted by Confederate ghosts.*

"Oh, my God," she murmured as she skimmed the outrageously exaggerated story, then looked at the byline. "I can't believe this. It's that man who came into the library looking for information about Beau Soleil." He'd lied to her, she thought furiously. Dallas Chapman was no more a parapsychologist than she was a rock star.

"Well, he certainly went to the right place," Edith said. "How nice you were able to help him with his story."

"I didn't help him. I merely pointed him to some books." To

think he'd sucked her in with that story about he and his wife falling in love at some haunted Scots castle!

"It's a lovely picture of the house," Edith said.

"And you can see the ghost," Bessie said.

"Where?" Charlotte Cassidy, the day checkout clerk, leaned over the counter and peered at the paper over the top of her glasses.

"Right here." Bessie tapped her finger against a blurry white spot that at first glance did appear to be hovering above the house.

Dani looked closer. "That's no ghost. It's only the camera's flash."

"I can understand how one could think that," Bessie said. "But it's obvious to those of us who've experienced a paranormal event that it's an apparition. That white light is an obvious energy source, and everyone knows that spirits refuse to allow themselves to be photographed."

Ever since returning from the Mothership, Bessie had alleged to have the "Sight." She'd been supplementing her Social Security checks by doing tarot card readings down at the Shear Pleasures beauty parlor every first Saturday of the month for as long as Dani could remember.

"I've heard ghosts tend to be camera shy," Charlotte allowed.

She should have checked him out, Dani thought. At least done a database search for that Tennessee witch story he'd alleged to have written with his probably fictional wife. "He said he was a parapsychologist."

"One can be a parapsychologist *and* a reporter, dear," Bessie pointed out.

"I wonder if Jack's seen this yet," Edith mused.

"Won't he be pleased?" Bessie pointed to a paragraph toward the end of the story. "Look, it even lists the titles of his books and mentions the movies."

"I bet he won't be all that happy about the suggestion that the books are being ghostwritten by a dead Confederate soldier," Charlotte offered warily.

Dani briefly closed her eyes upon hearing that ridiculous piece of tabloid journalese. Not only would Jack be less than pleased at the story that was far more fiction than fact, she feared he was going to blow sky high.

21

Are you going to marry Jack?" Matt asked later that afternoon.

Dani looked up from dropping chocolate-chip dough onto a cookie sheet. Not sure she could trust her voice, she spooned up more dough, tried to decide how to handle the question that had come from out of the blue, and decided to hedge. "Where did that come from?"

He shrugged and snitched a scoop of dough from the blue mixing bowl. "You go on dates with him."

"They're not exactly dates. I'm merely helping him decorate Beau Soleil."

"You're going to that wedding. The one you bought a new dress for."

It had been an extravagance, bought on a whim, and she couldn't really afford the expense. It was also made of silk spun as soft as a whisper that rustled when she walked, with a garden of tropical flowers blooming on the short, flirty skirt. She'd tried it on for Orèlia, who'd taken one look at it, whistled and said, "That Jack's gonna be a goner for sure, he."

The older woman had also insisted on taking her into the city where she'd located what she'd declared to be the perfect shoes to match. The bright poppy color was highly impractical, since it wouldn't go with a single other thing in Dani's closet, the heels were so high she feared getting a nosebleed, and pencil thin, which was just asking for a broken ankle, she'd complained to Orèlia while the salesman was in the back of the store, looking for her size.

They were an impossible hue, ridiculously high, and dangerously thin. But as she'd taken the strappy, glove-soft leather sandals out of the box, Dani had also known that once again Orèlia was right. They were absolutely, positively perfect.

"It's not really a date," she said, dragging her mind back to the conversation. "An old friend of Jack's is getting married, and he didn't want to go to the wedding alone, so he asked me."

"Oh." He reached for one of the cookies already cooling on a nearby rack. "I'm glad you're not getting married."

That surprised Dani, since it was obvious that her son thought Jack Callahan hung the moon. "Well then, I guess it's good I'm not."

"Yeah. Because I like Jack a lot," he said around a mouth of chocolate chips. "But if you two got married, then he'd be my dad."

"I suppose he would," she said carefully. "If we were to get married. Which I'm not planning to do with anyone anytime soon."

"Okay." He shrugged thin shoulders beneath the league baseball jersey he was so proud of. Unsurprisingly, when they'd gone to the tryouts this afternoon, he hadn't earned a spot in the starting lineup, but the coach had assured him he wouldn't be spending the summer on the bench, either. *Thanks to Jack.*

He scooped another scoop of cookie dough from the bowl with his finger. "Jack's a lot of fun, but if you got married to him, he'd become my dad, then maybe he wouldn't hang out with me or talk about baseball and stuff anymore. Or come to any of my games like he says he promised to do."

Failure rose to grab her by the throat. She'd married a man she'd come to realize she hadn't loved, in a foolish attempt to get over the one she *did*, and in doing so had set a series of events into play that ultimately had hurt her child.

"Oh, sweetie." Needing to touch him, to reassure him, Dani smoothed down his cowlick with fingers that weren't nearly as steady as she would have liked. "You don't have to worry. If Jack told you he'd come to some of your games, he will. You can count on him to keep his word."

The roar of the GTO's engine had them both looking up. "He's here!"

Practically knocking the chair over in his enthusiasm, Matt jumped down from the table and raced out of the kitchen as Jack pulled into the drive. Wiping her hands on the white chef's apron she'd donned over the T-shirt and jeans she'd worn to the tryouts today, wondering if she still had any lipstick on, and suspecting she didn't, Dani followed her son out the door.

"Hey, Jack," Matt shouted, "look!" He thrust out his chest with masculine pride, showing off the pinstriped jersey. "I made the team."

"I never had a single doubt in the world you would," Jack said, with a wink toward Dani, who was surreptitiously tucking the hair that had escaped her braid behind her ears. "Didn't I tell you that you're a natural?"

"I'm not in the starting lineup. But Coach Pitre says that it's important to be able to come off the bench, too."

"It surely is. It takes a real talent to rev up your engines on a moment's notice."

"Yeah, that's the same thing Coach Pitre said. We're the Blue Bayou Panthers. Did you know that black panthers used to live around here?"

"Seems I heard somethin' about that. Though I never saw one myself."

"That's 'cause they're all extinct now, but it's still a cool name for a team, don't you think?"

"Sounds good to me."

"Mr. Egan, who owns the barbershop, is our sponsor. We're gonna have team pictures made and everything. And we're going to go away to a special camp so we can work on fundamentals and start feeling like a real team."

"Imagine that. This calls for a celebration. Why don't you and your mom and I go out to the Cajun Café, have ourselves a nice dinner, then take in a movie down at the Emporium. I saw on the marquee that *Gone in 60 Seconds* is playin' tonight. And it's not the remake, but the original one from 'seventy-four."

"Really?" Matt turned to Dani, eyes bright and begging. "Can we, Mom?"

"I've already made spaghetti sauce." It might not be anything as mouthwatering as the Cajun fare Jack could whip up from whatever ingredients he had on hand, but it was nourishing and something Matt would eat every night of the week if she let him.

"It'll keep," Jack said. "You can serve it up tomorrow night."

"Yeah, Mom, it'll keep," Matt repeated. "We can have it tomorrow."

Excitement blazed on his face. Dani knew she'd end up feeling like the Wicked Witch of the West if she denied him this special night out.

"Isn't that the movie about stealing cars?"

"Yeah. Remember I wanted to rent it."

"I also seem to remember that it's rated PG-13, and I told you I thought it set a bad example."

"Geez, Mom. It's not like I'm gonna go out and become a car thief or anything dumb like that. It's just a make-believe story about this guy who gives up a life of crime but has to steal a bunch of cars to save his brother's life. There's this neato police chase at the end where they wreck ninety-three cars!"

"Stealing *and* wrecking cars," Dani murmured. "How encouraging."

"It's just a movie, Danielle," Jack said. "And the seventy-four version's bound to be tamer than the remake. If it'll make you feel better about things, I'll explain about the downside of drivin' cars that don't belong to you."

"You don't have to do that." Still, car theft was a serious matter. It had certainly gotten Jack in trouble. So why were her lips curving even as she fought to keep them firm?

"I suppose this *is* a special occasion." She could feel herself caving in. "After all, while I couldn't swear to it, I do believe you're the first baseball player in our family. It seems that's something to celebrate."

"Yes!" Matt pumped a small fist into the air.

"We'd better quick take her up on the offer before she changes her mind, sport," Jack suggested. "You got someone you'd like to take along?"

Matt's small brow furrowed. "You mean like a friend?"

"I mean exactly like a friend."

"There's Danny Pitre. He's the coach's son and the best player on the team. I traded him my Dodge Viper GTS for his DeTomaso Pantera at lunch recess yesterday."

"Why don't you go give him a call? I'll wait out here with your *maman*."

" 'Kay!" He ran into the house with a loud whoop, slamming the screen door behind him.

Dani shook her head as she remembered what he'd said about Jack and how he believed dads ignored their children. What a sad lesson she'd inadvertently taught her son. A lesson that was undoubtedly more harmful in the long run than a car-theft movie.

"Thank you," she said quietly. "I should have realized tonight called for more than spaghetti and meatballs."

"Nothin' wrong with spaghetti and meatballs. In fact, were you to get it into your head to invite me to a spaghetti dinner tomorrow night, I sure wouldn't turn you down."

Dani had feared that making love with Jack would have complicated their relationship. Instead, it seemed to have made it even easier. Better, richer.

She thought about him in the morning, on her way to the library, during the day, while she chatted with patrons, date-stamped books, and put others away, and in the evening, when if he didn't show up, he'd call and she'd go into the bedroom, shut the door, and was grateful that they didn't have video phones when his sexy suggestions, drawled on that deep voice that vibrated all through her, made her blush like the teenager she'd once been.

"It's a date. A deal," she corrected quickly, earning a flashed, wicked grin at her slip as they followed Matt into the house.

"Deals are what you make when you buy a car, or plea-bargain a jail term. What I'm talkin' about, Danielle, darlin', is definitely a date."

The smile he bestowed on her definitely made up for her earlier less-than-stellar day. Which brought her mind skimming back to that horrid supermarket tabloid. "Did you happen to drop by the market today?" she asked with studied casualness.

"Yeah. But it wasn't real necessary, since the phone didn't stop ringing all day. I was amazed so many people in town actually read that rag."

"I think they mostly read the headlines." She studied him cautiously. "Aren't you angry?"

"Hell, if I let every negative thing people said about me get me riled up, I'd have gotten myself an ulcer a long time ago." He shrugged. "Besides, I make a livin' tellin' lies myself."

"You write fiction. Newspapers are supposed to deal in fact."

"No halfway-intelligent person considers that thing a real newspaper." Jack looped his arms around Dani's waist, drew her to him, and sniffed. "Don' worry about it. I'm sure as hell not. 'Specially when I have my girl in my arms." He nuzzled her neck. "Damn, but you smell extra good today."

"Thank you. But I think it's the cookies."

"Cookies?" He lifted his head and glanced over at the plate. "Hot damn. Are those chocolate chip?"

"Are there any other kind?"

"I knew I should have married you way back then."

You know you're going to have to tell him, that little voice piped up again.

"We were both too young for marriage," she repeated what her father had told her then, and again just the other day when she'd confronted him about sending Jack away.

"Probably," he agreed, sobering for a moment. "I sure as hell wasn't that good a husband material back then." He flashed that devilish pirate's grin. "But I gotta tell you, *chère*, if you'd promised homemade chocolate-chip cookies every once in a while, I sure would've considered giving it the old college try."

"Now who's easy?" she murmured.

"*Mais* yeah. And along those lines, I guess this is where I tell you my other great idea."

"I'm almost afraid to ask."

"How about we let the boys go sit down in front, where they'll probably want to anyway, so they can get an up-close look at the car wrecks, while you and I hang out in the balcony and neck?"

Having had to sneak around that summer, they'd never done anything so normal as neck in a movie-theater balcony. Actually, now that she thought about it, Dani realized she'd never done that with anyone.

She laughed, feeling unreasonably young and carefree for a woman who, just a few weeks ago, had nearly been homeless with a mountain of debts. She still didn't have her own home, and while she was continuing to chip away at Lowell's debts, her life was ever so much richer than it had been before she'd returned home to Blue Bayou.

Even her relationship with her father, while still suffering from the revelation about Jack's reason for leaving the bayou, was beginning to open up. Last night, when he'd come into the kitchen while she'd been sitting at the table, balancing her checkbook, he'd told her that he was proud of how well she'd grown up. She'd been so surprised by that revelation her fingers had stumbled on the calculator keys, clearing the entire column, forcing her to begin again. But it had been worth it, just to hear those long-awaited words.

"You're right," she decided with a smile of her own. "That may be the best idea you've had yet."

"And just think," he said as he gave her a quick hot kiss that ended far too soon but still left her head spinning, "the night's still young."

"I was thinking," Dani said to Matt two days later, as they drank frosty glasses of lemonade beneath a spreading oak that took up most of Orèlia's backyard after she'd gotten home from the library, "that as soon as we get settled into the apartment, perhaps we ought to take that trip to the animal shelter."

His blue eyes widened with blazing hope. "We're really gonna get a dog?"

"Unless you'd rather have a cat."

"Nah. Cats are okay, I guess. Mark Duggan has this really weird Siamese cat who'll fetch spitballs, which is kinda neat. But mostly cats just lie around. They don't play with you like a dog does."

"Then I guess we'd better make it a dog."

"Do you really, really mean it?"

"I really, really mean it."

"Wow, thanks, Mom!" He flung his arms around her, nearly making her spill her drink. "You're the greatest mom in the whole world. The universe, even."

"You're going to have to walk him," she warned.

"That'll be fun." He paused. "You mean a real dog, don't you?"

She didn't understand. "As opposed to a make-believe dog?"

"No. I mean we oughta get a mutt. Like Turnip. Jack says they're the best. If we get us some fluffy little dog that wears pink bows and gets its toenails polished like Danny's mother's dog, all the kids'll probably make fun of me when I'm walking her and I'll have to fight again."

"You will not fight again," she said sternly. "But you don't have to worry, because I honestly cannot imagine painting a dog's toenails." Dani glanced down at her sandaled feet that were in dire need of a pedicure and couldn't remember the last time she'd managed to find time to paint her own toenails.

"Can we get him his own bowl? With his name on it?"

"I don't see why not. Of course you'll have to come up with a name."

"Yeah." He turned thoughtful. "We ought to get a boy dog. That way he can make puppies with Turnip. Wouldn't that be way cool?"

"It's certainly something to consider," Dani said, torn between being pleased such a simple idea could make her son so happy and wondering how Jack would take to having a litter of puppies running around Beau Soleil. Let him be the one to shoot the idea down, she decided.

"Boy, I can't wait for Jack to get here, so I can tell him."

They were having dinner at his house again tonight, just the two of them. Anticipation sent ribbons of desire, like streams of shimmering light, flowing through her veins.

When the GTO pulled up in front of the house, Matt went racing toward the car while Dani stayed beneath the comforting shade of the ancient oak and enjoyed the sight of Jack unfolding himself from the driver's seat.

Just as he had, that summer, he filled Dani's mind. She couldn't stop thinking about him. Her first thought in the morning was how she wished she was waking up with him beside her; her last thought at night was while her bed didn't seem at all empty when Lowell had left, now, knowing that Jack was a good six miles away, sleeping alone at Beau Soleil, made the guest bed seem as vast and arid as the Saraha. In those long hours between waking and sleeping she thought of him as well—hot, erotic, wicked, wonderful thoughts.

For the first time in years, Dani was totally aware of her body. Every nerve, every pulse, every pore was vividly, almost painfully alive.

Still, if it was merely sex, she wouldn't have been so worried. What concerned her, as they began to find time to slip away together, was that she'd come to view it as lovemaking.

Watching the way he really listened as Matt danced around him, unable to control his boyish exuberance, she thought, not for the first time, what a good father Jack would make.

Dani knew she should tell him. She'd tell herself that a dozen times a day. Then, just as often, she'd tell herself that they needed time. Time to see if these feelings were real, or merely a product of romanticized memories of a forbidden, teenage love affair.

Dani had learned the hard way that fairy tales only happened between the pages of books and in the movies; she was living proof that women who made the mistake of believing in happily-ever-after endings were more than likely to end up disappointed.

But being back here in Blue Bayou with Jack again had her remembering just how seductive happiness could be. And it terrified her. Both for herself and her son, who was, just as she'd feared, becoming so very close to Jack. Too close, perhaps. But watching him open up from an intelligent, often too-studious child into this eight-year-old ball of boyish energy, Dani didn't have the heart to limit their time together.

Besides, it was obvious that they were good for each other; the brooding, self-absorbed man she'd found that night she'd first gone out to Beau Soleil was gone, replaced by a warm, caring, generous person who laughed easily and often.

She'd tell him. Soon, Dani promised herself. She just needed a little more time.

"You're awfully quiet tonight," Jack murmured as they drove through the bayou that evening. "Rough day?"

"No. Just busy. I was just thinking."

"Now, that can get you in trouble."

She smiled as he'd meant her to. "I owe you an apology," she said.

"You don't owe me anything."

"We both know that's not true. I shouldn't have ever accused you of using Matt to get to me. You're obviously very good for him, and I appreciate you spending so much time with him."

Jack shrugged. "I like hangin' out with him. He's a great kid." He tugged on the ends of her hair. "You did good, sugar."

"I should've done better."

"Life's full of *should-haves*. If you let them, they'll just eat you up."

"I suppose you're right."

"Believe me, I'm an expert on the subject."

It had crossed Jack's mind while watching Dani's son single-handedly making a double cheeseburger, chocolate shake, French fries, and a chocolate ice-cream sundae disappear the other night, that he hadn't had any nightmares or woken up in the middle of the night in a cold sweat since Danielle had first come out to Belle Soleil and he'd cooked her supper.

In fact this morning, when he'd been drinking some chicory-flavored coffee and watching the sun rise, he had the strangest feeling that something was wrong. No, not exactly wrong, but different.

It wasn't until he'd finished his second cup that he'd realized that something was missing: the survivor guilt that had seemed to have become a part of him was no longer grinding away at his gut.

Also, except for the occasional beer, he'd just about stopped drinking, and since he didn't want to expose Danielle's son to secondhand smoke, he hadn't had a cigarette in hours.

He almost laughed at the realization that, despite the effect she was having on his hormones, Danielle Dupree was actually good for his health.

"So, you'll be movin' into the apartment soon."

"Next week. Orèlia offered to sit with Matt once school's out while I'm at work."

"Couldn't imagine you'd find anyone better."

"I know." Dani sighed. "She also suggested Daddy stay at the house with her, rather than move with us."

"Makes sense, what with her bein' a retired nurse and all. Besides, the place might look like a warehouse for the Smithsonian, but even with all the stuff she's managed to cram into it, she's still got a lot more room than you will in that apartment."

They turned a corner and Beau Soleil came into view, gleaming like a fanciful dream in the gloaming. " 'Specially now that you've promised Matt a dog."

"I suppose you're right," she said on a soft sigh as he parked in front of the house. "It's just not what I'd originally planned."

Not what she'd written down on her lists, Jack supposed as he went around the hood of the red car and opened her passenger door. "You know what they say, *chère*."

When she was standing beside him, he turned her in his arms, fitting her against him, thinking, as he had so often these past weeks, what a perfect fit they were together. "Life's what happens when you're making plans."

He slipped a hand beneath her sunset-hued top and watched desire rise in her eyes as he caressed her. "And speaking of plans . . ."

"I'm giving Michael a woman in this book," Jack announced to Nate, Alcèe, and his brother Finn, who'd returned home for the fish fry out at the Callahan camp. A more typical south Louisiana bachelor party would more likely include a trip to the city, where everyone would get drunk and work their way through the French Quarter strip clubs. But having known Alcèe for most of his life, Jack had figured the former priest would undoubtedly start trying to "save" the girls five minutes after they'd ordered their overpriced, watered-down drinks and just put a pall on any passing of a good time.

So, it had been decided that they'd hold the party out at the camp. They'd do a little fishing, Jack would cook the catch—or some shrimp he'd bring along just in case—play some cards, and rag Alcèe about being the first of the longtime friends to take the fall into matrimony.

"Big surprise." Nate snorted. He leaned back, put his boots up on the railing, and took a swallow from one of the longneck bottles of Dixie beer Jack had sitting on ice in an aluminum tub. "The guy goes through women like Tiny Dupree goes through a mess of crawfish."

Since Tiny probably weighed about three-eighty soaking wet, and was the all-time Cajun Days crawfish-eating champion, that was saying something. It was also pretty much the truth. There might be a lot of violence in his books. But Jack hadn't scrimped on the sex, either. Which, his agent had told him, was partly responsible for his large female readership.

"Not that kind of woman. You know, *the* woman."

"Son of a bitch." Nate dropped his legs down to the deck and gave Jack an incredulous look. "You're not gonna marry the guy off?"

"Well, not right away."

Jack might admittedly have romance on the mind lately, but he wasn't a fool. Part of the fictional DEA's appeal to men was his success with the ladies, while female readers seemed to have decided that he was merely soothing his broken heart while waiting for that one special woman who could make him forget his bride had been blown up in a car bombing meant for him.

Besides, since his own road to romance had been goddamn rocky, Jack saw no reason why his character should have it any easier.

"Maybe eventually," he tacked on with extreme casualness.

Jack watched the comprehension dawn in his brother's intelligent blue eyes. Nate might be the only male Callahan who hadn't become a cop, but he was no slouch at detecting, either.

Alcèe eyed Jack over the rim of a glass of iced tea. "This wouldn't have anything to do with a certain gorgeous librarian, would it?"

Jack rocked back on his heels. "It just might. I gotta tell you, bro, I haven't felt this way about another woman since Yeoman Rand." He sighed fondly at the long ago adolescent memory.

Nate's lips curved. "You fantasized about Yeoman Rand? From *Star Trek?*"

"Sure. When I was twelve, I used to imagine that the *Enterprise* was on the way to a top-secret mission on Alpha Centauri when they received a distress call from an uncharted planet."

"Which was undoubtedly a trap," Alcèe suggested.

" 'Course it was," Jack agreed. "Set up by a race of aliens who'd become so inbred they needed to leave their planet and find new blood."

"Blond blood," Nate guessed.

"Naturally. So, in my adolescent fantasy, they'd captured Yeoman Rand and were going to take her back to their actual planet, which was in a parallel universe, to use her as a sex slave."

"What did you know about sex slaves when you were twelve years old?" Alcèe challenged.

"I was a prodigy." Jack grinned at his friend, who shook his head and grinned back. "Besides, I've always had an active imagination, me."

"So," Nate continued the story, "you leaped in like Captain Kirk and rescued the lady."

"I sure as hell did." Jack nodded. "I just happened to be passing by in my snazzy two-seater star cruiser. She was, needless to say, extremely grateful."

"I can imagine." Nate shook his head. "No wonder you became a writer. To think I used to settle for sneakin' looks at Finn's *Playboy* magazines."

"The Playmates were damn sexy," Jack allowed. "But they were no Yeoman Rand. I used to spend a lot of time fantasizing about the two of us gettin' naked, but I sure never gave any thought in those days to settling down and raising us a batch of little yeomen."

"You givin' any thought to it these days?" Alcèe asked.

"I might be." For some reason, ever since the night he, Dani, and Matt had gone to the movies, Jack hadn't been able to get the image of her carrying his child out of his mind. It was nearly as appealing a fantasy as the one where he carried her over the threshold of some Caribbean resort hotel room and undressed her slowly, bit by lacy bit, teasing them both to distraction while they made love beneath a big white tropical moon.

"Son of a bitch," Nate repeated. "Well, this is unexpected."

"Think how I feel."

"I couldn't imagine. Jesus. My big brother's in love."

"Keep it to yourself. I haven't told Dani yet."

"Got any plans to do that? Or are you just gonna let her read your book when it's published and figure it out for herself?"

"I've got plans. I just haven't figured out what they are yet. . . .

"You know," he mused, "when I first bought Beau Soleil, I figured it was a nice 'in your face' gesture to the judge. The bad kid he'd run out of town coming back a success, living in the house he'd been kicked out of, romancing the daughter he'd been told to stay away from."

"That's an understandable feeling," Alcèe said. "Not exactly the most admirable, but it'd be hard not to resent the judge for what he did to you."

Since Alcèe had once been in the business of forgiving sins, Jack figured he'd have managed to turn the other cheek. And he sure as hell wouldn't have nursed a grudge as long as Jack had.

"But then things started to change. And I realized I didn't want Danielle 'cause I'd been told I couldn't have her. I wanted her for herself. Which got me to thinking that maybe we were both supposed to come back here, at this point in our lives, to be together the way we couldn't be back then."

Alcèe nodded and pulled the tab on another cola can. "The Lord moves in mysterious ways."

"Whether it's God, or fate, or destiny, I'm just damn grateful."

Jack polished off the beer and reached for another. Since they were spending the night at the camp, he didn't have to worry about drinking and driving, something he hadn't done since that summer he'd stolen Jimbo Lott's patrol car.

"I know it's gonna sound stupid, but sometimes, late at night, after I've taken Dani back to Orèlia's, I'll sit out on Beau Soleil's *gallerie*, picture the two of us laughing in the house, loving in it, and sittin' out in our rocking chairs, watching our grandkids play with Turnip's grandpups, and you know what?"

"Goin' back to DEA starts sounding real appealing?" Nate suggested.

"No. I start thinking that it's kinda a nice picture."

"Jesus, Jack, that's so damn domestic it gives me the chills."

"I'd expect nothing less from a man who believes commitment is what happens when the men in white coats show up at your door with a straitjacket and tranquilizer gun. And speaking of domesticity, how's Suzanne? I've been meaning to ask you how the skirmish over flatware turned out."

"Last I heard, she'd switched gears and ended up going with Chantilly, which wasn't even in the early running, but I won't have to worry about paying for it, since she got fed up waiting around for me to propose and got herself engaged to some old boyfriend she met during their Ole Miss graduation reunion weekend."

"Sounds like you escaped yet again."

Nate had often said that he'd just as soon go skinny-dipping with a bunch of gators than settle down for the rest of his life with one woman. Remembering how he'd once felt much the same way, Jack was looking forward to the day his brother had to eat those words.

He glanced over toward Finn, who was standing off by himself at the far end of the deck, nursing the same glass of tonic water he'd poured nearly an hour ago. He hadn't entered into the conversation. In fact, now that he thought about it, Jack doubted Finn had strung ten words together since he'd picked him up at New Orleans's Louis Armstrong Airport.

He pushed himself out of the chair and went over to join his older brother.

"Well?" he asked.

"That's a deep subject," Finn murmured, his gaze directed out over the bayou, where black clouds scudded across the deep purple sky.

"Ha ha ha. And to think people say you don't have any sense of humor."

"I hadn't realized people said anything about me."

"Christ, you can be literal." Jack shook his head, wished for a cigarette and remembered he'd thrown his last pack away after figuring that he'd cut back so far to keep from smoking in front of Matt, he may as well just quit the rest of the way. "I was speaking rhetorically. Though, thinking about it, there was a bit of a buzz around here when you got yourself a second invitation to the White House after nabbing that serial killer last month." The first had come in the prior administration when Finn had foiled an assassination attempt.

"I nailed him too damn late."

"Finn, you rescued two women from that guy's house. And I don't even want to think about how many more he could have nabbed if you hadn't stopped him."

"Try telling that to Lori Hazelton's mother."

The nineteen-year-old woman had gone missing at the San Diego county fair. Her mutilated body had later been found in Griffith Park. "You had no way of knowing ahead of time that she'd been targeted as a victim by some sadistic pervert."

"Lori was the first." Finn pressed his glass against his temple. "And, goddammit, she wasn't the last."

"No. But as tragic as those murders were, things could have ended a helluva lot worse if you hadn't tracked the monster down."

His brother's only response to that was a shrug. Of the three of them, Finn had always been the hardest on himself. Jack had taken on the role of the troublemaker, the rebel without a cause, as Dani had described him, though in reality, he'd been a helluva lot closer to a rebel without a clue.

Nate had always been the easygoing one that everyone liked, the flirtatious Callahan with the quick smile and deceptively laid-back manner. Finn had been the perfectionist whom Jack had often thought was intent on living up to their larger-than-life father's image.

An anvil-shaped cloud moved across the thin sickle slice of moon, signaling that hurricane season was just around the corner. "There's always one who haunts you," Finn said after a long pause.

"Yeah." Jack knew that only too well. He'd certainly had his share, including a once stunning Colombian woman he could still picture draped artistically across her wide white bed, her beautiful face battered nearly beyond recognition, the front of her silk ivory nightgown drenched in blood.

"You know, maybe you ought to try doin' what I did to exorcise them."

"What's that?" Finn said with a decided lack of interest which suggested he didn't believe he'd ever get rid of his personal phantoms.

"Get yourself a woman. I realized the other day that I've just about quit having nightmares since Dani came home to Blue Bayou."

Finn turned his gaze to Jack, treating him to that same deep, hard stare he'd give him back when he was fifteen, the Christmas vacation Jack came home at two in the morning with his breath reeking of beer and the rest of him smelling of pot.

"Never thought I'd hear you use *home* and *Blue Bayou* in the same sentence. . . . So, looks like you're finally putting down roots," he murmured, proving that he had been listening to the conversation, after all.

"Though there's a part of me that's still scared to death of doing somethin' to fuck it up, I guess I just might be."

"Because of Dani."

"Yeah."

Finn thought about that for a long silent moment. "Works for me," he decided.

22

The Holy Church of the Assumption was filled to standing room only for the ceremony, proof of how many lives Alcèe, in his quiet way, had somehow touched. The bride was beautiful, as all brides are supposed to be, with stars shining in her eyes; the groom, who'd looked uncharacteristically nervous while waiting at the altar, couldn't stop beaming once he'd managed to survive the double-ring ceremony.

Since weddings always made Dani a little weepy, she ducked into the rest room of the parish hall where the reception was taking place to refresh her makeup—she knew she should have forgone the mascara—when Desiree Champagne came out of one of the stalls.

The merry widow's artfully tousled cloud of black hair, which definitely hadn't been styled at the Shear Pleasures, gave her the look of having just made love amidst hot silk sheets. Her doe eyes were emphasized by a deft hand with liner, her complexion was cream, her lips red. And her body was draped in a royal blue silk wrap dress that hugged her voluptuous curves.

"Hello, Dani." The brilliant smile didn't quite reach the brunette's eyes, which skimmed over Dani's reflection from her head to the toes of her red sandals. "You're certainly looking well. Small-town life seems to agree with you." She washed her hands, then pulled a gold monogrammed compact out of a Prada bag Dani figured probably cost at least two month's worth of groceries and began powdering her nose. "I can see why Jack hasn't had time to visit his old friends lately."

"He's been very busy with the house."

Desiree's answering laugh was rich and throaty. "I suppose that's as good an excuse as any."

She laughed again, richly, her eyes dancing with that same rebellious mischief Dani had seen so often in Jack's gaze. No wonder they were drawn to each other, she thought. They were two gloriously attractive rebels.

"You're looking beautiful as always." Dani had always believed in giving credit where credit was due.

"I've always cleaned up real well." A Liz Taylor-size diamond flashed as she fluffed her hair. More diamonds blazed at her earlobes.

She took a lipstick from the bag and touched up her crimson lips. "I don't believe in beating around the bush, Dani, so I'm going to say this right out; I wish to hell you hadn't come back to town."

"I'm sorry you feel that way."

"Oh, it's okay." The dress slid off Desiree's shoulders when she shrugged, just enough to tantalize male interest. Dani wondered if it were accidental, or if she'd practiced the gesture, and decided it really didn't matter since she'd never be able to pull it off in a million years. "We've never been all that serious. I'd just gotten spoiled having him all to myself."

"Should I say I'm sorry? About cutting into Jack's time with you?"

"Don't say it if you don't mean it."

"Then I won't."

Teeth so perfect they could only be caps flashed in a dazzling smile that even Dani couldn't entirely resist. "Good for you." Desiree took a pack of cigarettes out of the bag. "This isn't exactly the most private place in town. Why don't we find ourselves a little corner and catch up?"

"I'm sorry, but I really should be getting back. Jack's going to be wondering where I am."

"Let him." She held the pack toward Dani, who shook her head. "It's good for men to realize women won't come when they snap their fingers."

"Jack's not that way."

"No. He isn't." Her expression turned serious. "Look, Dani, watching the way Jack was looking at you all during Alcèe's wedding, it's obvious that the two of you have picked up right where you left off that summer."

"You knew about that?"

"Of course. Jack and I never had any secrets from each other."

"Were you . . ." Dani pressed her fingers against her mouth, cutting off the question.

"Fucking him back then?"

She refused to react to the word she suspected Desiree had used as a test. "It doesn't matter. It was a long time ago and none of my business if you were."

"Of course it was. Because you loved him. And he loved you."

Part of Dani wanted to avoid this woman who'd experienced Jack's clever mouth and wonderfully wicked hands; who'd taken him inside her, just as Dani herself had done only hours ago after last night's rehearsal dinner. The other part of her was honestly curious about what, if anything, Desiree knew about Jack's feelings back then.

"I suppose we could talk for a few minutes in the contemplation garden," she suggested. "Catch up on old times."

This time Desiree's laugh held no humor. "Sugar, with the exception of a couple of fund-raisers you never would have invited me to if Jimmy Ray hadn't had more money than God, you and I never had any old times."

"But you and Jack did?" Dani asked as they left the building by a back door. The garden, located between the church and the rectory, had been designed for quiet contemplation and prayer. Short, leafy green hedges created private hideaways, and Dani and Desiree chose one farthest away from the reception.

"Jack's a lot like this bayou," Desiree answered obliquely as she sat down on a wrought-iron bench and lit a long slender cigarette. "Still waters and all of that. He doesn't reveal all that much, but that doesn't mean there's not a lot of depth there. . . .

"He nearly killed my stepdaddy once," she said on a stream of blue smoke.

"Oh?" That single word was all Dani could manage.

"With a bat right against the back of his head. He was coming home from baseball practice, and I think he might have killed him if my mama hadn't come by about then and started clawing at him like a wildcat." She shook her head. "Christ, that was not one of my better days."

"Why did Jack hit him?"

"Because he caught him raping me in the woodshed outside our house."

Dani gasped even as she wondered how any woman could state such a dreadful thing in such a matter-of-fact way.

"Oh, it wasn't the first time. And I sure wasn't a virgin, because

Jack and I had been screwing around for months. Lord, we were horny kids," she said on a soft laugh.

Dani didn't want to think about that. "Still, your stepfather had no right to do such an evil thing. Was he arrested?"

"No, because I didn't want to press charges. My reputation wasn't exactly polished sterling even then, so I figured no one would believe me. Jack wanted to put the bastard in jail, but he reluctantly agreed to go along with me, since he didn't have a helluva lot of faith in Jimbo Lott to arrest his second cousin, which my stepdaddy happened to be.

"So Jack cleaned me up and told me everything was going to be okay, threw some of the old man's stuff in a duffel bag, dragged him half conscious to the car, drove him to the Mississippi state line, and tossed him out alongside the road with the warning that if he ever came back to Blue Bayou again, he was a dead man."

She drew in on the cigarette. "I don't know if you've ever witnessed it, but Jack's temper is a scary thing. The madder he gets, the icier he becomes. Then he blows sky high. He's the proverbial fire-and-ice guy. Well, that day he was pretty much both, and I, for one, certainly bought the idea that he was capable of cold-blooded murder. I guess my stepdaddy figured he'd best stay out of Dodge, too, because he never came back."

"You must have been relieved," Dani murmured, wondering why Desiree was telling her such a personal story. "And grateful."

"Hell yes, I was grateful. 'Course my mama was pissed off. She didn't tell anyone he was gone, so she could keep collecting his Social Security disability check. He'd gotten himself a bad back, working construction, but that never stopped him from beating the shit out of her. She managed to pull the wool over the bureaucrats' eyes for about six months before they caught on that it wasn't him endorsing the checks and put her in jail for fraud."

Dani wrapped her arms around herself to ward off the inner chill. She'd spent her own teen years feeling sorry for herself, unhappy that she couldn't connect with her distant father, that he couldn't seem to love her. But to discover that only a few miles away, this woman had been living in hell, definitely put things in perspective.

"I'm sorry. I can't imagine how awful all that must have been for you."

"Well, of course you can't. Since you were living like a princess up at Beau Soleil. Though," she said, on afterthought, "I'll have to give you credit for not bein' one of those rich bitches who loved to gossip about me and would snicker whenever I'd walk past them in the school hallway. And you always treated me like a lady at your parties. 'Course you wouldn't have ever invited me in the first place if it hadn't been for Jimmy Ray tossing so much money in your husband's coffers, but at least you didn't snub me."

She drew in a deep, seemingly resigned breath. Blew it out on another cloud of thick blue smoke. "Since my mama died a few years ago, no one knows this story about my stepdaddy but Jack and me. And I'm only telling you so you'll understand how things are between the two of us.

"There was a time, when we were kids, that for reasons of our own, we both felt like outsiders. Which built us a bond that's held all through the years. I'll always be grateful to Jack for what he did that day and I'll always be there for him. But I'd never do anything to cause him unhappiness, which is what I'd be doing if I even tried to get between the two of you.

"My life was a little rocky for a while, but that all changed after I married my Jimmy Ray, and I don't care what his hateful, vindictive children who never paid any mind to him when he was alive believe, I loved that man dearly and took good care of him while he was dying of lung cancer. Just like he took real good care of me." Her eyes grew moist as she twisted the diamond ring. "Jimmy Ray and Jack were the only two men who ever did care about me, and I'll love them both till the day I die.

"Jack might not have told you, since, like I said, he's not all that forthcoming, but he's been through some rough times himself these past years, and they've taken their toll on him. But he's still the most standup guy I've ever met. And the most honest, which is kind of ironic when you consider he spent years working undercover."

She stubbed out the cigarette in her empty champagne glass. "He's never been one to judge anyone, which is lucky since I sure as hell haven't been a saint, but I think all those years of living a lie is probably the reason that he flat out can't abide anyone lying to him."

She stood up with a lithe, catlike grace, making Dani think yet again how much Desiree and Jack had in common. Both of them radiated sex. "Of course you don't have to worry about that, sugar. It's not that you could be keeping anything from him. Since your life these past years has pretty much been an open book, played out in all the newspapers."

Dani didn't, couldn't, respond.

"Would you think me out of line if I offered one little word of advice?"

"I suppose not."

"I'm not going to share details, because it's Jack's story to tell, but he was burned pretty badly by a woman down in Colombia. If there's anything you're keeping from him, anything at all, perhaps about that summer, you'd best tell him yourself. And soon. Before someone else does."

The ice in Dani's blood spread outward to encase her heart. "Is that a threat?"

"Of course not." Desiree's eyes flashed with irritation. "It's merely a warning. I told you I'd never do anything to cause Jack pain. But unfortunately, not everyone loves the guy as much as I do, and secrets have a real funny way of not stayin' buried."

With that she began to walk away, hips swaying in a smooth seductive way Dani couldn't have managed if she practiced for a hundred years. She was halfway to the church hall when she turned. "Did I mention that I'd worked for a while in New Orleans?"

"I believe I've heard something about that."

Desiree waved her cautious response away with a flick of her wrist. "It's not what you're thinking. I worked retail for a time, selling cosmetics in a drugstore in the Quarter. It was just an itty bitty little place on Conti Street, hardly big enough to turn around in and certainly nothin' fancy." Her gaze zeroed in like a laser on Dani's. "But you'd be surprised by how, every so often, I'd see someone from home come in there to buy something. I didn't work there long. Just a couple months in the fall. Not long after Jack took off to California."

Her words tolled like one of the buoys out in the Gulf that warned ships against going aground. It was obvious she knew something about Dani's pregnancy. Dani might have put it down as a lucky guess if she hadn't mentioned that pharmacy where she'd bought the home pregnancy test. Of course, Desiree had no way of knowing which way the test had turned out. But still, if she knew Dani's secret, someone else might, too. It was just getting too risky. Especially now that she and Jack were actually beginning to be seen together, almost like a couple.

No, she corrected, exactly like a couple.

She'd tell him, Dani promised herself. Tonight. Then all she could do was pray he'd understand that at the time she hadn't believed she'd had any other choice but to give her child—their child—up for adoption.

Which had never happened. Because even though she'd changed her mind and had decided not to let her father force her into signing those final papers, her infant girl had tragically died before she'd lived a day. And Dani, who'd yet to turn eighteen years old, had left the Atlanta maternity home for unwed mothers, forced to spend the rest of her life grieving for the daughter who'd been her only source of comfort during those long and lonely months of her pregnancy.

"Orèlia told me a little about Alcèe," Dani said as they swayed together to a slow, seductive ballad. She couldn't translate all the French, but it sounded sad. Probably a love song, she thought, remembering what Jack had said about all love affairs being tragic. "About his drinking problem. And his leaving the priesthood."

She glanced over at the tall lean man who was dancing with his bride, his expression that of a man who'd stumbled across his own platinum mine. "It's so nice things worked out for him."

"Anyone deserves happiness, it's Alcèe," Jack said. "Though there was a moment, just before Jaycee began walking down the aisle, that I was afraid he might pass out on me."

"Nervous grooms are one of those stereotypes that seem to be true."

"Seem to be," he agreed.

The music was singing in her head and her heart seemed to be beating in unison with his. Their thighs brushed as she followed his steps. He was a good dancer. Perhaps not as flashy and schooled as Lowell had been, but steady, competent, yet not entirely predictable. A woman would feel secure in his arms. In his life. But he'd still surprise her from time to time, which would, she considered, keep things from getting boring.

Dani compared herself to Desiree, who was doing a pretty good job of singing along with the band and wondered if Jack ever compared the two of them and found her boring. Which she'd be bound to be next to the glamorous widow.

"Is getting married really that stressful for a man?" she asked, genuinely curious. "Is it so hard to give up your freedom?"

"Probably no harder for a man than a woman." He pressed his hand against her lower spine and drew her closer. "And I doubt if Alcèe felt like he was giving up his freedom. My guess is that he considered today the price a guy has to pay for a piece of his own personal heaven."

His answer was definitely not what she'd been expecting, proving yet again his unpredictability. Dani never would have guessed he'd view marriage so positively.

"Then why would he be so nervous?"

He slid his leg between hers, spreading heat. "Because he's afraid of failing. Of disappointing her. Of not living up to the man she believes herself to be marrying."

"Maybe that's part of the bargain," she mused. "Disappointing your partner but loving each other enough to work it out and move on." Something that certainly hadn't happened in her own marriage.

"You may be right." His hand slid up her back; his fingers tangled in her sleek blond hair. "And speaking of moving on, what would you say to cutting out of here early?"

"Before the bride and groom leave?"

"This place is packed, they won't miss us." He touched his lips to that surprisingly sensitive little hollow behind her ear he'd discovered the first time they'd made love. "Besides, they wouldn't notice us if we were to hang around and throw rice. Not tonight."

No. It was obvious Mr. and Mrs. Bonaparte only had eyes for each other. Still, Dani had been brought up to observe protocol. And to be perfectly honest, even having decided that she could no longer keep her secret from Jack, she wasn't in any hurry to break the news that she'd cost him the chance to be a father, if only for the few too brief hours their child had lived. There would have been a time she wouldn't have believed he'd even care. She now knew she would have been wrong.

"Why don't you weigh this into your decision-making process," Jack said when she didn't immediately respond. He lowered his head. The brief public kiss was not nearly as hot and primal as others they'd shared. But still made her head swim and her knees weak.

"How fast did you say that shiny red car of yours could go?" she asked when she could speak again.

He laughed and skimmed the back of his hand down her cheek, her neck, and across her collarbone bared by the dress's neckline. "Believe me, *chère*, I'm gonna be pushing it to the red line tonight."

Driving like the hotshot drag racer he'd once been, with one hand creating havoc high on her thigh beneath her hitched-up skirt, the other on the wheel, Jack ran all three red lights through the center of town, which fortunately, was deserted with nearly everyone at the wedding reception. Even with him driving at seemingly the speed of sound the short drive out to Beau Soleil seemed to take forever.

Finally, just when Dani was about to beg him to pull over, he screeched to a stop in front of the house. When her fumbling fingers couldn't unfasten the seatbelt, he reached over and yanked it apart, then pulled her to him, capturing her avid mouth, burying his hands in her hair.

Her scent swam in Jack's head, passion pounded away at him. He wanted to feel her hot and naked beneath him, he needed to feel her perfumed flesh against his skin, wanted her hands to stroke his body as he'd caress hers until all control disintegrated.

Starved for her taste, having spent both the wedding and the reception semi-hard, Jack nipped and sucked on her succulent lips, then stabbed his tongue between them, where it tangled with hers, making her moan even as her own greedy mouth ground against his.

Her hands raced up and down his back while his kneaded her breasts; she tore at the buttons of the starched white shirt he'd worn for the occasion, he yanked down the zipper at the back of the flowered dress that was sexier than anything she'd worn since coming back to town.

Needing to touch her, to taste her, he dragged the dress down her arms, unfastened the bra—which today opened in the front, thank you, God!—and ripped it off her.

She cried out and arched against him as he took a breast into his mouth, sucking ravenously while his hand delved beneath her short skirt. She was so hot he was surprised her panties hadn't gone up in flames. Finding the damp silk a poor substitute for the dewy flesh beneath, he dragged them down her legs. As eager as he, Dani helped him pull them off.

"It's not fair," she moaned as he skimmed a finger along her slick cleft.

The windows were steaming up and it had begun to rain, the sound of the drops splattering on the metal roof and streaming down the window.

"What's not fair?"

"All you have to do is look at me and I want you. Say my name and I melt. Touch me and any self-restraint I thought I possessed is scorched away." Her sharp intake of breath and the way she arched against his seductive touch, opening for him as he exerted a gentle pressure, seconded her ragged words.

"What makes you think it's any different for me?" He managed, without ceasing his stroking caress, to free himself, then dragged her hand down to his cock, which thrust upward from the open zipper.

Dani skimmed a fingernail down the length and had him biting back a groan. When she curled her fingers around him and caressed the ridged tip with her thumb, his entire body tensed with anticipation. Then she began to stroke him, and the last ragged thread of Jack's control snapped.

He dragged her onto his lap, pushed those legs that had been driving him crazy all day apart, and surged upward into her with a strength that made her cry out.

And then she was riding him, her thighs pressed against his, leaning back against the steering wheel to achieve the deepest penetration as she ground against him. They rocked together, fevered, devouring, filling the car with breathless words and cries and the raunchy scent of uninhibited sex.

In the instant before release, when his entire body felt like a spring too tightly wound, Jack looked at her—pearly breasts shimmering in the moonlight, her dress up around her waist, the muscles of her slender thighs taut, her eyes gleaming in a way that could have gotten her burned at the stake during the days of witch hunts—and knew he'd never see a more erotic sight than Danielle Dupree at this moment.

Grasping her waist, digging his fingers into her perfumed and powdered flesh, Jack surged upward, deeper still, all the way to the back of her womb, then came in a violent, shuddering climax of his own.

23

It was the scream that woke her.

Dani and Jack had finally managed to drag themselves out of the car and into the house, where, like the insatiable teenagers they'd once been, they made love in the hedonistic Jacuzzi tub Jack had installed, before stumbling, nearly boneless, into bed. By then it had been too late, and she'd been too drained to initiate the conversation that was so long overdue. Thanks to Matt being at a five-day baseball camp, this was the first time Dani had been able to spend the entire night at Beau Soleil, which allowed her to put it off just a little bit longer.

I'll tell him in the morning, she vowed. *When we're both fresh and can think straight.*

Having made the promise to herself, Dani drifted off to sleep and dreamed of Jack. Since night in the bayou was far from silent, at first she'd thought the terrifying sound, which resembled a cry a nutria would make when being ripped apart by a hungry alligator, had somehow incorporated itself into her hot, erotic dream.

But it wasn't a nutria. Nor was it a dream. It was all too real. And it was bloodcurdling. She jerked up, nearly falling out of bed, then, breathless, her splayed hand against her bare breasts, viewed Jack, who was drenched in sweat and sitting bolt upright as well.

"Jack?" Dani could tell that he was somewhere else. Somewhere far from her; somewhere deadly and terrifying.

"Jack, wake up." She combed her fingers through the damp strands of silk jet hair, pushing it away from his forehead. "You're dreaming."

She cupped his chin in her hand, turning his head toward her. His eyes were open, but he was staring right through her, as if she had no more substance than air.

"It's a only a dream," she repeated. "A nightmare." She wrapped her arms around him, appalled that he was trembling. "It's all right."

She watched as his gaze gradually focused and was more than a little relieved when she realized he was back from that dark and dangerous place he'd ventured without her.

"It's all right." With her heart still pounding like a rabbit's she managed a faint, reassuring smile.

"Shit." He turned away so he was sitting on the edge of the bed, palms braced on his knees. Turnip, who'd been sleeping in her usual position on the floor at the foot of the bed, whined her worry and licked the back of his hand. "I'm sorry, Danielle." His voice was roughened with self-disgust. "You must have been scared to death."

"Just for a second until I realized what was happening." Her own breathing was beginning to return to normal. "I was having the most wonderful dream." She skimmed a hand down his wet back. "Yours must not have been nearly as nice."

"No. It wasn't." He squeezed his eyes shut. Tight. When he opened them again, Dani shivered at what she saw in the dark tawny depths. "I used to have the nightmares all the time. Even when I was awake. But I haven't had them since I quit drinking heavily. Not since you came out here that first night."

"I believe that may just be the nicest compliment you've ever paid me." She shifted so she was sitting beside him and touched her hand to his cheek. "Do you want to talk about it?"

"*Non*. Not really." He dragged his hand through his hair, which was loose around his moon-shadowed face, giving him the look of a fallen angel. An angel whose weary eyes were giving her a glimpse of his own private hell. "But since it appears I haven't exactly put it completely behind me, and I'm hopin' like hell you'll risk sleeping with me again, I figure you deserve the truth about what I did. What kind of man I am. Even if you may take off runnin' after you hear."

"I won't." She couldn't imagine anything he could tell her that would change how she felt about him. "And I know what kind of man you are."

"You only think you do."

"Don't insult my intelligence, Jack. I do know you. Besides," she said, looking at the huge head the dog had thrust under his hand, "Turnip obviously adores you, and you know what they say about dogs being an excellent judge of people."

Jack's expression managed to be both fond and frighteningly grave at the same time. "One could also argue that this particular dog has lousy taste. After all, she does drink out of the toilet."

"She also growled at Jimbo Lott when we ran into him outside the market the other day."

"Well, there is that." He scratched the dog behind her ear, easing her concern and causing her to turn boneless and sink to the floor in obvious dog bliss. "You know I was a DEA agent."

"Yes.

"I worked undercover. Which doesn't always involve playing by the book. I had to constantly improvise, and every so often it became a case of doing to others before they could do what they were trying to do to me."

"You were doing your job. An important job."

He shook his head at her naïveté. "Maybe you're not getting the drift. I've killed people, *chère*."

After what Desiree had told her, Dani wasn't as surprised as she once might have been. "Were they trying to kill you?"

"Hell, yes, but—"

"Well, then, you didn't have any choice."

"That's what the investigators said when I came out of surgery."

"You had surgery?"

"Yeah, after getting shot up. But I got off easy. Because of a stupid, brief fling I had in Colombia, both my best—and only—friend in the world and the woman ended up dead."

Dani vaguely wondered what he meant by brief, then decided it didn't matter. "That must have been terrible for you," she soothed.

Having been wondering how to tell her, Jack considered that this was turning out to be too easy. And he damn well hadn't trusted anything easy since he'd been thirteen.

"I'd like to hear what happened," she said quietly.

"It's not pretty."

"Newsflash, Callahan. I'm not some pampered princess who's breezed through life without pain. Without making my share of mistakes. I mean, if you want to get technical, I suppose you could consider me partly responsible for Lowell's death."

"How the hell do you figure that?"

"If I hadn't married him, he wouldn't have been elected. If he hadn't been elected, we wouldn't have gone to Washington, and he wouldn't have become so power hungry he'd do anything to further his career. If I'd been a better wife, a better lover—"

"Sugar, if you were any better lover, I would have dropped dead of a heart attack tonight out in the car."

She smiled at that. Then just as quickly sobered. "My point was, that if my husband hadn't gotten bored with me, he wouldn't have left me for another women, so he wouldn't have been moving into the Watergate that day, and been standing there on the sidewalk when her piano fell on his head."

"You realize, don't you, that's a load of crap?"

"Most days. But sometimes I wonder how much of our lives is determined by our own actions, and how much is due to fate."

"We create our own fates." It's what Jack had always believed. Until Dani had come back home and had him wondering about things like fate and destiny. "That weasel the judge married you off to locked in his fate when he was too blind and too stupid to realize how special his wife was."

"That's a very nice thing for you to say."

"It's the truth." He sighed heavily. Then picked up his sordid story, determined to get through it once and for all, so they could put it behind them and move on with the rest of their life together. "I was in Bogota, with my partner, Dave," he began slowly. "We were checking out rumors of a submarine supposedly bein' built by the Colombian drug traffickers."

"Bogota's seven thousand, five hundred feet in the Andes and at least a hundred miles from any port."

That earned a reluctant smile. "Can't fool a reference librarian. And it's two hundred miles."

"Why on earth would they build a submarine there?"

He shrugged. "Best we figured, it was easier to conceal the construction. The blueprints we found tended to suggest they'd planned to transport it on tractor-trailers in three sections to the coast.

"Dave and I spent a lot of nights staking the place out, and one night, when we'd run out of sports to talk about, we got started on women. He told me all about Trish, his wife, and I told him about you."

"Me?"

"Yeah. Oh, not everything. Just the good times. After a while we took turns—one sleeping, the other standing guard—and that conversation had gotten me feelin' a little mellow, so I remember looking up at that sky filled with whirling stars and thought about them bein' the same ones you might be looking up at, and it made me feel not quite so alone.

"Anyway, we didn't much believe it was gonna turn into anything, because, hell, even by drug-dealing standards this wacky idea was off the charts. But it turned out they'd gotten some engineers from the Russian mafia, and some ex-patriot Americans to work on it, and damned if they weren't actually building a sub capable of carrying two-hundred tons of cocaine across an ocean. The plan was to carry it down in pieces, then assemble it in the port of Cartagena.

"The operation didn't start out that big a deal. We weren't getting any kingpins but we also didn't want to take the chance that they'd actually pull the plan off. Also, we figured if we nabbed some of the middle guys, with enough pressure, we could turn one or more of them, and if we were lucky, they'd give us the names of some dealers higher up the food chain.

"Dave and I were playing L.A. dealers down there lookin' to score. We'd been hanging around the resorts for a few days, being real visible, tossing money around, acting like your typical asshole California drug hotshots."

"I wouldn't think it would be a good idea to make yourself so noticeable when you were supposedly trying to buy illegal drugs."

"Hell, sometimes it seemed as if a third of the people went down there to score drugs, another third were there to sell them, and the rest just looked the other way and tried to stay out of the gunfire. Believe me, everyone knows what's goin' on. And Dave and I got a lot better service from the hotel staff and cab drivers when they thought we were dealers than we would have gotten if they'd known we were DEA."

"Didn't it get hard?" she asked quietly. "Always living a lie?"

"*Mais* yeah. It got damn hard. But I'd been doin' it so long, I'd forgotten it wasn't the way other people—real people—lived their lives."

Dani thought guiltily about her own lie and didn't respond.

"So, things were looking pretty good. Problem was, when we showed up at this warehouse at the docks in Cartagena, neither of us had any idea that we'd already been made. Because I fucked up." It still ripped him to shreds. Even after all this time.

"Anyone can make a mistake."

"Yeah, and mine was thinkin' with my dick. I'd gotten involved a few months earlier with a woman in Barranquilla. She was a reporter who covered the cartel and worked as a part-time DEA informant."

"I didn't think reporters worked that way."

"Not in the States. But this definitely wasn't the States. So, I figured it was the best of both worlds, I could get laid regular, and every so often she'd give me some useful information about drug-trafficking. What I was too stupid to realize was that she was playing both ends against the middle, collecting money from us for information, while working for the cartel. We later learned she was the mistress of one of the traffickers and was only sleeping with me to try to learn whatever she could about our operations down there."

"I don't believe that," Dani said.

"Why not? It's the truth."

"She may have been after government secrets the first time. But after that, if she was in your bed, she was there for mind-blowing sex."

He laughed, and although he still didn't buy the idea of any outside force shaping lives, he also couldn't help wondering what he'd done to deserve a second chance with this woman. She was good for him. And he liked to think he was good for her, too.

"Well, whatever her reasons, she set us up, though she didn't get away scot-free." He figured even if he ever escaped the ghosts, he'd never entirely forget the sight of the woman he'd foolishly trusted lying dead on the bed where he'd spent so many pleasurable hours. "Her lover killed her. I suppose because he was afraid she might be as disloyal to him as she'd been to me.

"When we walked into that warehouse, all hell broke loose, and for a while it was like the shoot-out at the O.K. Corral. Then our backup blew the door, and when it looked like they were actually gonna be on the losin' end, they scattered like roaches. Well, Dave and I had a lot of time and effort invested in this, so we chased a pair of them down the waterfront, onto the beach. One of them grabbed this poor terrified tourist who just happened to be in the wrong place at the wrong time and was holding a gun to her head, so we backed off.

"That's when Dave got shot from behind. It didn't take any shooting skill, he just got ripped open with an automatic rifle. He wasn't wearing a bulletproof vest, because, just like when my dad was shot, it was too damn hot. And besides, it's a little hard to hide one of those suckers beneath the skin-tight tropical silk shirt he'd worn to fit the California image.

"I was trying to drag him off the beach when I got hit. Next thing I knew it was twelve hours later and I was waking up in the hospital."

"How badly were you hurt?"

He shrugged. "Not that bad."

"Twelve hours is a long time to be unconscious."

"Well, there was some surgery involved to dig some lead out of my chest and fix a collapsed lung, but I was out of there in time to take Dave's body home to his widow."

"I'm glad you're not doing such dangerous work anymore."

He shrugged. "I lost my stomach for it after that." He gave her a long look, relieved when he didn't find any horror on her face. "So, now you know why I quit. Why I'm back here."

"As sorry as I am about what happened, I can't be sorry that you came back to Blue Bayou." She lifted a hand to his cheek, her light touch feeling so much like a brand, Jack was amazed he couldn't hear the sizzle of burning flesh. "So we could find each other again."

She leaned forward and touched her mouth to his. Her lips softened. Parted. The soft little sound she made in her throat, half sigh, half moan, had desire pooling hot and heavy in his groin. Minds emptied. Tongues tangled. Hearts entwined. His fingers tangled in the silk of her hair. Her lips were warm, heady and unbearably sweet. Jack could have kissed her endlessly.

He dipped his tongue into the slight hollow beneath her bottom lip. When she shuddered in expectation, he pressed her back down onto the mattress and into the mists.

She didn't tell him. Oh, she had lots of excuses, after that horrible story about his lover and partner having been killed, Dani hadn't had the heart to tell Jack that he'd also lost a child he'd never known about. Then there was the fact that after their long night of lovemaking, they'd gotten up late, then made love again in the shower, putting her way off schedule, causing her to open the library late.

Since there weren't any patrons waiting, she took advantage of the peace and quiet and was preparing her monthly budget report for the parish council when Jack walked in, looking much more upbeat than he had last night when he'd shared the story of his final DEA operation.

"Come on, *chère*," he said. "I'm taking you to lunch."

"It's not even eleven o'clock."

"Brunch, then."

"I really have to get these done before Tuesday night's council meeting."

"It's a long way to Tuesday." He reached over her shoulder, pressed Save, then closed the file. "And only two blocks to the courthouse."

"We're having lunch at the courthouse?"

"Brunch," he reminded her, as he took her purse and keys from her desk drawer. "And no, we're not eating at the courthouse. I figured we'd go out for a bite afterward."

"After what?" He had his arm around her waist and was walking her to the front door.

"That's a surprise." He closed the door behind them and locked it.

"The parish council isn't paying me to sleep in late, then have lunch with you twenty minutes after I finally get to work," she argued.

"Don't worry about that. Nate knows all about me stealing you for a bit. He thinks it's a great idea."

"Are all the Callahan brothers crazy? Or is it just you?"

"I don't know about Nate and Finn," he drawled as they turned the corner. "But I'll confess I'm crazy." He tangled his hand in her hair, which she'd worn loose today, and kissed her, right out on the sidewalk in front of Espresso Express, to the obvious delight of customers sitting at the little tables outside. "Crazy about you."

"I was wrong," she muttered, even as her lips clung a moment too long for a public kiss.

" 'Bout what?" He smoothed her hair and gave her a bold grin.

"You haven't reformed. You're still Bad Jack, the devil of Blue Bayou."

"Probably," he allowed cheerfully. "Which, since you're still *ma 'tite ange*, balances things out just fine."

"Arrogant," she muttered without heat.

He skimmed a finger down her nose. "And right."

Was there any woman in the world who could resist that slow, sexy smile? Dani wondered as they cut across the park to the courthouse. And why, she wondered as she enjoyed the faintly possessive weight of his broad hand on her hip, would any woman want to?

When, without giving it any thought, she touched Captain Callahan's horse's nose, Jack caught her hand and lifted her fingers to his lips. "We already have all the luck we need, us."

His voice was low, and thick with the Cajun patois she'd discovered it always took on when his libido was heating up. It wasn't the only thing getting warm; the light touch of his mouth was setting off sparks against her fingertips. It was so easy for him, she thought. One touch, one look, and she was melting.

"You're not the only one," he murmured, proving yet again his ability to read, if not her mind, at least her expression. "You do the same thing to me." Even as she knew it was asking for trouble, Dani glanced down and viewed the proof of his statement. "Which is probably why," he said, with that wicked humor she'd come to love gleaming in his tawny eyes, "we'd better get inside before I'm tempted to take you right here on this sweet-smellin' freshly mowed lawn."

"Jimbo Lott'd love that," she muttered, her desire temporarily dampened by the thought of Blue Bayou's sheriff. "He could arrest us for indecent exposure and any other number of charges."

"He'd probably like to. But Jimbo's not gonna be in a position to be arresting anyone for a long time."

She looked up at him, surprised and puzzled.

As he held the heavy door open, Jack's broad grin was both boyish and utterly self-satisfied, reminding her of how Matt had looked when he'd caught that fly ball during baseball tryouts.

Dani was surprised to see Jack's two brothers standing in the rotunda with the sheriff and another man she didn't recognize. Nate wasn't smiling, but his expression revealed the same satisfaction she could see on Jack's face; if looks could kill, Jimbo Lott would have put all of them six feet under, while Finn's expression gave absolutely nothing away.

Dani remembered Finn Callahan as having been big for his age. That hadn't changed. He'd grown up to be a big man. But unlike the way so many former high school athletes would go to fat, he was as strong, solid, and muscular as when he'd played football for the Blue Bayou Buccaneers. His black hair was cut almost military short, he was wearing a blue suit, white shirt, and red tie, all of which were amazingly unrumpled for a steamy Louisiana summer day. His eyes were a riveting Arctic blue she suspected could chill to ice, but they warmed as she approached with Jack.

"Hey, Dani," he greeted her. "It's been a long time."

"Too long." She hadn't known Finn as well as Jack or Nate, but remembered how things around the house had always calmed down whenever he'd come home from college. Even in his teens he'd possessed a quiet strength that invited confidence. He still did.

More puzzled than she'd been when Jack had dragged her from the library, she skimmed a dismissive glance over Lott, who was inexplicably carrying a raincoat, even though the day had dawned sunny and summer steamy, then offered a polite, half smile to the man standing on the other side of the sheriff, a man nearly as large as Finn, whose face looked like ten miles of bad road. This was a man Dani would never want to meet on a dark street.

"This is Lee Thomas," Finn introduced him. "Lee, this is my brother Jack, and the prettiest lady in Louisiana, Danielle Dupree."

"It's a pleasure to meet you, Miz Dupree," Thomas said, his soft musical cadence suggesting Georgia roots.

"It's nice to meet you as well," Dani said in her best tea-party manners, even as she continued to wonder what in the world they were all doing here. "Are you with the FBI, too?"

"No ma'am, I'm with the United States Marshals Service. We're sort of the jack-of-all-trades when it comes to federal crimes and prisoners. I worked with Finn a while back when I was assigned to the Missing and Exploited Children's Task Force."

"I see," she said, not really seeing anything at all. This was getting curiouser and curiouser.

"Good to meet you, too," he said, shaking hands with Jack. "Finn's told me all about you."

"It's all lies," Jack said easily. "The Marshal's Service handles the Witness Protection Program," he told Dani.

"Well, that's certainly interesting," she said, still not having the faintest idea why Jack had dragged her to the courthouse.

"We like to think so." Lee Thomas's teeth flashed in another smile which softened the harshly carved lines of his face and made him oddly attractive. "I've been workin' on a joint effort with the Justice Department, DEA, and the FBI on this one case that's particularly interesting. It involves a New Orleans mob family."

"Really?" She felt a prickling sensation at the back of her neck.

"Yep," Finn said, looking a bit smug, Dani thought. "The Maggione family, as a matter of fact."

"There's this guy who's worked for them as a cocaine mule off and on over the years that we're currently baby-sitting until he testifies at a bunch of trials," the marshal continued the explanation. "The family businesses have pretty much been on life support since Papa Joe died, and we think, thanks to what we've learned from this informant, we'll be able to finish them off. Then Finn called me and asked me to do some digging, and damned if your daddy's name didn't come up."

"My father's name?" Light-headed from fear, Dani grasped Jack's arm. "But he's already served his sentence. He's on parole."

"Oh, yes, ma'am. I sure know that. I also know that the governor's office is working on his pardon right now."

"Pardon?" Afraid she'd heard wrong, afraid to hope, she looked up at Jack, who nodded in confirmation. "I don't understand."

"Turns out the judge was set up and framed by Lott and a former member of the state legislature, who was, until he was picked up in Baton Rouge this morning, a gambling industry lobbyist," Jack revealed.

"But why would anyone want to frame my father?"

"Papa Joe's grandson was coming to trial for grand-theft auto and attempted murder. Since there was no question about him being guilty—he'd left DNA all over the guy's car—the verdict was pretty cut and dried. Unless they could get a friendly judge to assure a mistrial. Framing your father was the easiest way, short of killing him, to get him off the bench," Finn explained. "Lucky for him, the old man was never one to advocate violence when another method would work just as well."

"According to our informant, the sheriff wasn't that wild about the idea," the marshal revealed. "Seems he wanted to pull the judge over for speeding one night, jump him, drive him a few miles out of town, shoot him, and toss him in the bayou for the gators to take care of."

Dani's gaze flew to Lott. He glowered back, his reptilian eyes seething with venom. Then her gaze moved down to his wrists, which, she noticed for the first time, were handcuffed beneath the raincoat.

"I always knew you were despicable. I just never realized how truly evil you were," Dani told the sheriff.

"That's not all," Finn said. "The fire at the library wasn't exactly an accident after all. The fire marshal found evidence of an accelerant in the crawl space above the apartment's kitchen."

Dani's blood chilled at the idea of someone purposefully setting fire to the home she and her son had planned to move into. "But the fire wasn't ruled arson."

"Not officially," Nate agreed. "Because we didn't want to tip our hand. Interestingly enough, we found some explosives in Lott's garage and a store in Lafayette that sold him the alarm clock he used as a timer. We also have two witnesses who place him at the scene the night before the fire, and a third, who'll say that he heard the sheriff suggesting doing whatever it took to make sure the judge didn't have any reason to come back here where he might start digging around."

"There's a plane waiting in Baton Rouge to take the sheriff to D.C., where he'll be formally charged with an entire laundry list of offenses, including a little drug-trafficking business he had going on the side," Lee Thomas said. "I'd say he's going to be put away for a long, long time."

Dani's eyes swam. She opened her mouth to speak. Stopped. Shook her head and tried again. "I don't know how to thank you."

"Finn and I are just doin' our job, Miz Dupree, putting the bad guys behind bars where they belong."

"It's still such a glorious surprise. Does my father know?" she asked Finn.

"We told him this morning. Although it isn't standard operating procedure, since these are special circumstances, I thought the judge might like to come along when we picked Lott up. He said he was feeling a bit peaked this morning and thought he'd pass, but the satisfaction of knowing he'd been vindicated was enough."

Even concerned as she was about her father's health, Dani's heart soared. She hugged Finn and kissed him. Then did the same to Lee Thomas.

Jack was pissed off, just a little, when the federal marshall held her just a heartbeat too long.

Christ. Who was he trying to fool? He didn't want any other man's hands on his woman for any length of time. But, since the marshal had come through for them, and put the last piece into place that cleared the judge, Jack decided he'd let him live. This time.

"Well, guess we'd better go congratulate the judge," he said, snaking his arm around Dani's waist. Mine, both the gesture and his gaze said. "You'll probably want to be there when the governor calls him."

Finn grinned at his brother's uncharacteristic possessiveness while Lee Thomas wisely backed up a step.

"So," Jack asked Dani as they walked out of the courthouse, "how come you didn't give Lott a few choice parting words?"

"I considered it. But then I decided he wasn't worth letting myself all upset."

"Good call."

She looked up at him. "You did this, didn't you?"

"I'm out of the cops-and-robbers business, remember?"

She stopped beside the horse that had definitely proven lucky today. "Jack. I want to know."

"Hell, all I did was get the ball rolling by giving Finn the name of the mule and where they could probably find him and suggesting he may be willin' to cut a deal to get himself put into the government-protection program. Finn and I knew in our guts it was Lott, but getting the proof took a bit more time. My original plan was to just have Finn shoot the bastard and save the taxpayers a lot of money, but Nate, he thought that might be overkill and counseled restraint."

"I'm glad he did. Since I'd hate to have to start visiting you in prison." Her eyes shimmered. "I owe you, Jack. More than I can ever pay back."

"Oh, I wouldn't worry about that." He grinned down at her and dropped a light kiss on the tip of her nose. "We're two intelligent people, you and me. I bet if we put our heads together, we'll think of somethin'."

24

So," *Nate asked,* the next afternoon, "you pop the question yet?"

"No." Jack shook his head as he stood on the sixteen-foot-tall ladder and trimmed in the paint along the ceiling. "I was going to the night of Alcèe's wedding, but then we sorta got sidetracked."

Nate countersunk a nail on the doorframe of the cabinet he'd built to hide the oversize television. "From the way you two were dancing, I'm not at all surprised by that."

"It wasn't sex that kept me from telling her. I'd planned to earlier, then I decided to put it off until morning. Then I ended up having one of those old nightmares and woke up in a sweat, shouting my head off."

"I can see how that might sour the mood."

"Oh, she was real good about it." Jack dipped the brush in the paint bucket and wished for a cigarette. "Said all the right things, and all, but I decided that it must have freaked her out a little, so I decided to wait till today. Soon as I get this wall done, I'm goin' over to the apartment and help her hang pictures. Matt's off at some group baseball camp that's supposed to help the boys bond as a team, so I figure I'll have the rest of today and all night to convince her."

"Sounds good to me." Nate cocked his head at a sound filtering up the stairs. "Is that the front door?"

"Yeah. I got the chimes hooked up yesterday. It's probably the FedEx guy. My agent called and said he was sending over some contracts for me to sign."

"You don't have to come down," Nate said. "If you stop trimming before you get to the corner, you'll end up with brush marks. I'll get it."

Jack had worked in some of the more dangerous places on the planet. He'd dodged death more times than he'd cared to count. But those DEA operations had been a walk in the park compared to the idea of proposing marriage. Having used visualization techniques successfully in the past to ensure a successful outcome, he was running over the words he'd so painstakingly written down, making sure he'd memorized them so as not to fuck things up when the sound of Nate clearing his throat pulled him back to the present.

"I think you'd better come downstairs, Jack."

His brother's voice was strained. His expression more grim than Jack had ever seen it. Except at their daddy's funeral. Fear struck right at his heart.

"Is it something 'bout Danielle? Is she okay?"

"Yeah." Nate dragged a hand through his shaggy, sun-tipped hair. "It's about Dani. And she's okay, so far as I know. But there's someone here I think you need to meet."

The words were directed at Jack's back as he raced down the stairs two at a time. When he hit the foyer, he came to an abrupt stop, feeling as if he'd just been gutshot. As impossible as it was, a young Dani, looking exactly the way she had back in her early teens, was standing there holding a newspaper in her hand.

"Are you Mr. Callahan?" She may be a dead ringer for a younger Danielle, but her voice revealed no trace of Louisiana.

"Yeah." He knew he was staring but couldn't help himself.

Turnip was doing her happy welcome dance all around the girl, but the dog could have been as invisible as the ghosts supposedly haunting Beau Soleil for all either one of them paid attention to her.

"I read about you. And this house." She held up the tabloid story.

"I see." Jack could not drag his eyes away from those wide blue-green hazel eyes and the sleek slide of blond hair. "Actually, I don't," he admitted.

"I'm sorry." She blushed prettily, and despite knowing absolutely nothing about adolescent girls, Jack thought she possessed a bit more poise than most. "I should have explained." She drew in a deep breath. The hand she pulled through her long hair was trembling, evidence that she wasn't as calm as she was obviously trying to appear. "My name is Holly Reese. . . . And I think . . . well, I believe you might be my father."

* * *

The apartment was finally almost looking livable. Oh, there were still boxes stashed away in the bedroom closet, there might not be as much room as there had been in Fairfax, and it certainly wasn't Beau Soliel, yet it was still home. Dani couldn't wait until Matt returned from baseball camp and saw all the team pennants she'd tacked up on his bedroom walls.

She decided to reward herself for a job well done with a long luxurious bubble bath and was lying back in the tub, her freshly washed hair wrapped in a towel, eyes closed, cooling slices of cucumber on her lids, when someone began pounding on the door.

"Danielle," Jack shouted, "open this door!"

Fear struck like a laser straight into her heart, her first thought being that something had happened to Matt. She sat up, causing the cucumber to fall into the water.

"Goddammit, Danielle," he called again. "I know you're in there."

She leaped from the velvet cling of perfumed water, leaving wet footprints on the tile floor. She'd laid her clothes out on the bed, but far more concerned about her son than how she looked, she grabbed her worn, ancient terrycloth robe from the hook, threw it on, and went racing to the door.

She flung it open, took one look at the murderous scowl on Jack's face and knew that whatever he'd come here about, it couldn't be good.

"What is it?" Her heart beat even faster. She reached out an arm which he brusquely pushed aside as he strode into the apartment. "Is it Matt? Is he hurt?"

"So far as I know Matt's fine." His eyes were hard as agate, his mouth as grim as she'd ever seen it, his words growled through clenched teeth. But relief that he'd not come here about her son had Dani relaxing marginally. Which, she discovered, was a fatal mistake.

She'd thought him dangerous when she'd first tracked him down at Beau Soleil. But a different kind of danger was emanating from him. For the first time since returning home to Blue Bayou, she was looking at the man he'd told her about. The man who'd willingly worked in the shadowy, deadly drug underworld; the man who'd killed the bad guys before they could kill him.

She swallowed, her mouth dry from fear. "Jack . . ." She held out a trembling hand. He ignored it. "What's wrong?"

"Wrong?" He spat the word at her. "How about the fact that I'm not real wild about being played for a goddamn fool?" His large hands took hold of her shoulders, his fingers dug painfully into the flesh beneath the terrycloth. She was about to tell him that he was hurting her, when his next words choked the complaint off in her throat. "Why the hell didn't you tell me we had a daughter?"

The blood drained from her reeling head in a rush. Dani swayed as her knees went weak and would have fallen if he hadn't been holding her so tightly.

"H-h-how . . ." She couldn't talk. Couldn't think. Her mind whirled. "Who told you?"

"You're going to love this." His coldly vicious smile lacked the easygoing warmth she'd come to love. Fire and ice, Dani remembered Desiree saying. "Our daughter showed up at Beau Soleil today."

White dots like the flutter of moth wings danced in front of her eyes. "That's impossible," she whispered raggedly.

"Dammit, don't try to lie your way out of this, Danielle. The timing matches up with her age and she's the spitting image of you. Hell, Nate could see it the minute he opened the door."

"It can't be." She shook her head, unable to make sense of this while her stomach was in her throat and her mind felt as if it'd been hit with a sledgehammer. "Jack." When the moths turned into a blizzard, she grabbed hold of his arms to keep from falling to the floor. "Please let me sit down." His muscles tensed beneath her fingers. "I'm going to faint."

Apparently seeing that about this, at least, she was telling the truth, he dragged her over to the couch she'd bought at an antique shop he'd taken her to in Houma, pushed her onto the cushions it had taken her two nights of sewing to cover with pretty magnolia-printed fabric, and shoved her head between her bare knees.

"Take a deep breath."

The indrawn air burned her lungs. Despite outside temperatures in the nineties, she was cold. So cold.

The towel came unwound as he pressed harder; her damp hair fell over her shoulders and face. She was shivering like a woman stumbling through an Arctic blizzard.

"Keep your head down and don't move. I'll be right back."

She couldn't have moved if she'd wanted to. As she continued to take the deep breaths that became less painful and began to clear her head, Dani heard the heels of his cowboy boots striking like hammers on the wooden floor. There was the sound of water running from the kitchen, then he was back.

"Here." He took hold of her hair, dragged her head up, and shoved a glass into her hand. "Drink this."

A little water splashed over the rim and onto her bare leg as her unsteady hand lifted the glass to her mouth. The water was cool against her throat, and helped clear out the lingering clouds of vertigo.

"Thank you," she managed.

"Don't thank me; I just don' want you passin' out on me till I get the truth." He sat down in an overstuffed chair across from her that still needed recovering and pulled a cigarette pack from his shirt pocket.

"I thought you'd quit," she said before she could stop herself.

He speared her with another of those icy looks. "And I thought I could trust you. Seems we both were wrong."

He struck the match on the sole of his boot, lit the cigarette, and inhaled. "Okay," he instructed, "start talking."

He sounded as if she were one of his prisoners he was interrogating. Dani realized on some level that while he had every right to be upset, she should be angry that after how close she'd thought they'd become, he had so little trust in her, but at the moment she was too confused to try to stand up to a man who was undoubtedly an expert at intimidation.

"I don't know where to start."

"The usual way to start a story is from the beginning. Why don't you try that?"

"All right." She drew in a ragged breath and tried to compose her thoughts. "I didn't find out I was pregnant until after you left."

"But you chose not to tell me."

Unable to bear the coldness in those eyes that had only ever looked at her with warmth, Dani looked down at her hands. "I didn't know where you were."

"You could have asked my mother."

"I didn't think you'd want to know," she said softly. Miserably.

He slammed his hand down onto the table beside the chair. "Goddammit, look at me when I'm talking to you."

She lifted her chin and returned her gaze to his. "I didn't think you'd want to know," she repeated with a bit more strength. "After all, you were certainly there when the condom tore. But instead of sticking around to make sure everything would be okay, you took off right after I'd told you that I loved you."

"You know why I left."

"Now." The part of her who'd survived being deserted by the man she loved, then given birth to a child, only to have it die, the person who'd gone on to endure a passionless marriage and not crumble when publicly humiliated in front of the entire country, rose to help her deal with this latest personal disaster. "At the time I had no way of knowing that my father had blackmailed you into leaving."

"Did *Maman* know?"

"Yes." The pain that shot into his eyes echoed within her. Dani knew that what he was obviously viewing as his mother's betrayal must hurt nearly as much—if not more—than what she'd done. "Your mother supported my father's decision that I go away, have the baby, adopt it out, then go on to college."

"What a nice, tidy little plan you all worked out," he said dryly. "Interesting that no one thought to ask my opinion."

"How could I have known what you wanted?" she asked on a flare of heat. "You never said anything about loving me, or wanting anything more than just sex. You have to understand how things were. I was seventeen, Jack, a naive and in many ways a very immature seventeen. I didn't have any legal rights, and when my father and your mother began pressuring me to give up my child—"

"Our child."

She dipped her head in acknowledgment of his gritty correction. "They convinced me that my desire to keep *our* child was a schoolgirl's romantic fantasy. That giving it up for adoption would be the right thing to do. For everyone involved, especially the baby who deserved to be raised in a loving family with a mother and a father."

"She had a mother and a father." He drew in on the cigarette, exhaled smoke on a long, frustrated breath. "Or could have, if everyone hadn't decided to keep my daughter a secret."

"I'll admit that was horribly wrong. I didn't see it then, but I do now. There was just so much pressure coming from all directions. My father found a home for unwed mothers, and Marie drove me there. There were forty of us living in the house, and while I'm sure it wasn't nearly as harsh as that camp you were in, the rules were horribly strict—we weren't allowed to ever use our last names, have phone calls or visitors, except for our parents, and we were only allowed to go outside for three hours on Saturdays, and even then we had to always be with another girl.

"We had weekly counseling sessions, which were a joke, because they all centered around how trying to raise a child would ruin our lives, that we weren't emotionally prepared to be mothers, and how there were all these wonderful, loving parents just waiting for our babies.

"I've blocked some of that time out, but I do remember lying in bed, night after night, hoping that you'd come and rescue me—"

"Which would have been a bit difficult. Since I had no idea where you were. Or why."

"I know. As I said, I was naively romantic back then. I also had these terrible dark days when I'd think that they were right, that if I was foolish enough to get pregnant, I didn't deserve to have a child. Because I wouldn't be able to take care of it, and keep it safe."

Dani pressed a hand against her stomach as old feelings of shame she'd thought she'd overcome twisted inside her. "It wasn't until I was pregnant with Matt that I realized I'd undergone some sort of brainwashing. . . .

"Really," she insisted when he arched a mocking brow. "Not one minute of our prenatal training had ever offered a single piece of information on how to take care of our babies after they were born. Because adoption was a foregone conclusion. We were nothing more than a business to them, part of a profitable, child-procurement process."

"Maybe you ought to be the one writing stories," he suggested. "You could write this one as the heroine being a pregnant Oliver Twist character."

"That isn't a very nice thing to say."

"Perhaps you haven't noticed, *chère*, but I'm not exactly in any mood to be nice." The endearment was as frosty as his gaze.

"I was honestly going to tell you, but things kept happening. . . . No," she admitted on a soft, shuddering sigh, "that's not the truth. I kept putting it off because things were going so well and I was afraid when you learned the truth, you'd hate me."

"So you thought that would be an appropriate response?"

She could see the trap. "It might have been, if you didn't understand—"

"What I understand is that you lied to me, Danielle."

"It wasn't exactly a lie. More a sin of omission."

"You lied. Hell, why should I believe you ever would have told me if it hadn't come out? If she hadn't shown up at Beau Soleil?"

This was what Dani was finding more confusing about this entire horrible event. "That's impossible," she insisted. "She couldn't be at Beau Soleil."

"Why not?"

"Because she died, dammit!" Dani leaped to her feet. "Before she was a day old. Which broke my heart and is one of the reasons I put off telling you. Because there was nothing that could ever be done to set things right, and from how you were when I first saw you, along with the nightmares, I just kept telling myself that you'd already had enough death in your life!"

Nerves had her shouting at him when what she wanted was for him to hold her, and for her to told him back, while they figured out some way to get through this pain together.

He ground the cigarette out in a little crystal dish and pushed himself out of the chair. "There's no point in keeping this farce up, Danielle. Unless you've got an identical twin out there you didn't tell me about, who got knocked up the same summer you and I were goin' at it, there's no denying the girl is yours."

"It's impossible," she repeated through lips that felt like stone. She'd seen the death certificate. And had cried her eyes out for weeks afterward. "I'd changed my mind. An hour after she was born, the lawyers arrived at the hospital with the consent forms. But I realized, after having carried her for all those months, after having brought her into the world, there was no way I could ever give her up.

"I was exhausted from nearly twenty hours of labor, confused, and more scared than I'd ever been in my life, even more than when I first realized I was pregnant and I had no idea what, exactly I was going to do. But I did know I was going to take her away with me!" She slapped a hand against his chest, angry and aching and nearly as shaken as she'd been that long ago day.

"Sure you were." She felt the spike of his heartbeat beneath her fingertips. "The same way you were going to tell me."

"I was."

Their eyes clashed. A sizzle of electrical charge zapped through her, and as she watched the black of his pupils widen, like molten obsidian flowing over topaz, she knew that Jack felt it, too.

"Goddammit, what is it about you?" His face could have been chiseled from granite. His jaw was clenched, his mouth a hard grim line. "You've kept my child from me, lied through those pretty white teeth, continue to deny the truth, even when I've confronted you with irrefutable proof, and in spite of all that, I still want you."

Dani felt another moment of dizziness. If any other man had looked at her the way he was looking at her now, with such lust-edged anger she'd be terrified. But as a familiar warmth curled through her, she didn't fear Jack. She loved him. And wanted him. Desperately.

She knew he'd seen the answering hunger on her face when his hold on her tightened, like a black velvet bond and he drew her closer, so close she could feel the heat rising off his body. His very aroused body. The short robe had loosened and the feel of denim against her bare skin was unbearably erotic.

"I want you, too," she whispered.

His curse, in French, was vicious as his mouth swooped down, crushing hers, demanding retribution, capitulation, fueling the flames that had been smoldering beneath all that ice. He splayed his hand against the back of her head, refusing to allow her to escape the plundering kiss.

Her breath was nearly knocked out of her as they fell onto the couch, his body pressing her deep into the pretty flowered cushions.

His mouth ravaged hers, his lips sped over her face, his teeth scraped the cord in her neck as she twisted beneath him. His fingertips, roughened by work, scraped against her nipples, drawing a ragged moan; her teeth nipped his bottom lip, making him curse.

Jack wanted to hate her. Needed to love her. The dual hungers burned through him as they rolled off the couch and onto a needlepoint rug blooming with soft pastel flowers. Lifting himself above her, he looked down into her flushed face. Her eyes were emerald with passion, her shallow breath was coming in quick pants, her perfumed body slick.

"Jus' so we don't have any misunderstandings about what's happening here afterward, tell me again. That you want me."

"I course I do. I always have."

If the way she arched against his roving hand was any indication, about this, anyway, she was telling the truth.

"Say it." He skimmed a hand over her, from her breasts to the soft folds of flesh that were hot to the touch. She was warm and wet and ready for him. "Say 'I want you to fuck me, Jack.' "

"Jack, please, don't make me—"

"Say it."

He could see her heart in her moist green eyes, and if he hadn't been trying so hard to hate her, the hurt he'd inflicted would have broken Jack's own heart.

"I want you, Jack."

"The rest." He pressed his hand against her, drawing forth a long, throaty moan. "Say the rest."

"I want you to fuck me."

When the words were torn from her on a stifled sob, Jack discovered that an attack of conscience didn't necessarily diminish rampant lust. Having gotten his answer, he yanked down the zipper on his jeans and surged into her.

She cried out, then wrapped her long legs around his waist as he pounded into her like a man possessed. The ripe scent of passion filled the air as mouth to mouth, hot flesh slapping against hot flesh, they moved together, driving each other to the brink of sanity. Then beyond.

She came first, with a strangled cry, the climax shuddering through her. As the inner orgasmic tremors surrounded his cock, clutched at him, a red haze shimmered in front of Jack's eyes. He gave one last deep thrust, then, clenching his teeth to keep from calling out her name, he flooded into her.

Afterward, he lay sprawled on her limp body, feeling as if the air had been sucked from his lungs. The sex, as always with Dani, had been hot, but this time, instead of leaving him feeling as if he could outrun speeding bullets and leap skyscrapers in a single bound, Jack was overcome by regrets too numerous to calculate while his body was still throbbing inside her, his mind was covered in thick dark clouds and his heart still felt as if it had been shred to ribbons.

Because he wanted to stay here with her, to gather her into his arms and try to understand what she'd been thinking and feeling back then, as well as her reasons for having deceived him this summer, he levered himself off her.

"I'll let you meet her," he said as he refastened the jeans he hadn't bothered taking off. Hell, Jack figured he'd probably had more finesse in his teens than he had just now. "Since she deserves to know her mother. And you're going to have to pretend to care. For her sake."

"I do care." She'd wept while they'd made love. No, while they'd fucked, he corrected grimly since love had had nothing to do with the hot coupling that had edged as close to violence as he'd ever want to feel with any woman. That it had happened with her only made it worse.

Her face was wet and tearstained as she sat up and tugged the short robe closed. "I still can't understand how this can be true, how she could have been alive all these years. But maybe there was a mixup at the hospital. . . ."

"Give it a break, Danielle," Jack said wearily. "The bottom line is that you gave my child away—"

"Our child," she corrected quietly as he had earlier.

"You gave her away without so much as a backward glance. Without letting her know her father. Hell, she has two uncles she's never met because of you."

Dani was on her knees now. "My God, Jack, you know how much I missed growing up without a mother, how hard it was for me never being allowed to so much as mention her name, let alone talk about her with my father. How could you believe I'd abandon my own daughter?"

It was, he allowed, a good point. And one he'd have to consider later, after the lingering shock of today's revelation had worn off, his head had cleared, and he was able to think everything through.

"How did she find you?" Dani asked on a tear-clogged voice when he didn't respond. "How did she know? Where is she now?"

Jack didn't want to talk about this anymore. Couldn't, without risking crying himself. "She's with Nate at Beau Soleil. I'll let her answer the rest of your questions when you meet."

"When? Tonight?"

"I don't know." Since it was too painful looking at that beautiful tearstained face that was both wretched and hopeful at the same time, he turned and walked away. As he shut the apartment door behind him, Jack did not look back.

If he had, he would have seen Dani slump back down to the rug she'd been so excited about finding only last week, her slender shoulders shaking as she buried her face in her hands and sobbed.

25

It didn't take Dani any time at all to figure out that it wasn't likely Jack would be so furious, or so willing to condemn her, without a very good reason. Following on that conclusion was the understanding that whatever had happened that summer, her father was behind it.

Taking a shower to wash off the scents of sex and despair, she threw on a pair of shorts, T-shirt, and sandals, and wove her wet hair into a loose braid. Not taking the time to put on any makeup, she drove straight to Orèlia's, finding the judge alone, puttering around the garden as he'd begun doing the past couple weeks since he'd begun getting a bit stronger. And, she'd thought optimistically, less negative.

Dani did not bother with pleasantries. "Father, we need to talk."

He glanced up from weeding the flowers around the brick patio, taking in her red-rimmed eyes and puffy face. "You look terrible. Are you coming down with something?"

"No. You don't have to worry. I'm not contagious." Dr. Ancelet had warned that a virus or infection another person might be able to easily throw off could be fatal for her father.

"I wasn't thinking about that." He stood up, pulling off the gloves. "Believe it or not, I was concerned for you."

"I think it's a little late for that." Her heart was pounding in her throat, her ears, her head. "Jack had a visitor out at Beau Soleil today."

He arched a brow at her formal tone. "Oh? Something about that foolish ghost story?" He poured a glass of iced tea from a pitcher on a wrought-iron patio table. "Would you like some tea?"

"No. I don't want anything but the truth. I didn't meet her, but apparently she was a child. A thirteen-year-old girl who amazingly, according to Jack, looks a great deal like I did at her age."

"Ah." He nodded.

"Is that all you have to say?"

"Did this girl happen to say who she was?"

"I didn't get her name."

How could she have let Jack leave without finding that much out? Dani agonized. What if her daughter ran away before they had a chance to meet? To talk? What if she left before Dani tried to find a way to explain something she couldn't comprehend herself?

"But she alleges that she's my daughter. Which we both know is impossible. Since my baby died."

He didn't respond. He didn't have to.

"That *is* what happened, isn't it, Father? My baby died. You did, after all, show me the death certificate." It had read Baby Jane Doe. Dani had wept that her father had not even consulted her about the baby at least being given the Dupree family name.

"There's no point in using that tone with me, Danielle. Since it's obvious that you already know the truth."

"But that's just it!" she shouted, amazed to find herself on the verge of crying again when she wouldn't have thought she'd have any tears left after this horrid afternoon. "I don't know. Oh, I thought I did. But now I realize that everyone was lying to me."

"Not everyone. Only some of the staff at the hospital, who were well paid to keep silent."

"The adoption social worker didn't know?"

"I did what I thought best on a need-to-know basis. And she didn't need to know."

"Who signed the consent forms?"

"The nursery room nurse. She agreed with me that it was the best thing for all concerned."

"What about the people who took my daughter? Did they know?"

"No. I was concerned that if they knew the truth, their consciences might overtake their good sense and desire for a child and they'd back out of the adoption."

"I see." She pressed her hand against her stomach, which was roiling. "And Marie?"

"There was no way I was going to let her know the truth. She eventually would have notified Jack, or regretted having lost the chance to be a grandmother to her first grandchild. It was a risk I couldn't take."

"There you go again!" Dani was trembling like a leaf. "Putting yourself at the center of things. Pulling the strings as if people were only puppets for you to control."

"You were my daughter. I knew what was best for you. Besides, the night before you went into labor, you told one of the nurses that you were thinking of keeping the baby."

"That's right. I was."

"Which was why," he said patiently, "I had to arrange for you to believe the child had died. So you wouldn't ruin your life. Your entire future."

"Oh, God." She dragged a hand down her face. Drew in a deep, shuddering breath. "I've tried to live up to your expectations. I've tried to be the exemplary daughter, to always do what you wanted, to somehow make us into some kind of idealized *Father Knows Best* family—"

"Your father did know best."

"No." Dani shook her head. "You didn't know anything about me. About what I wanted, what was right for me, because you never loved me enough to get to know you."

"That's not true."

"Don't lie." She felt the ice begin to flow over her heart, allowing her mind to cool. Her thoughts to calm. "I'm not leaving Blue Bayou, because I'm not going to let you chase me away from the home I've made for my child.

"My children," she said, thinking with wonder that it appeared to be true. That she did, indeed have a daughter she'd never known about, a child who'd been cruelly kept from her. And somehow, she was going to have to convince both Jack and her newly found daughter that she'd never knowingly abandoned her.

"What you did was evil and manipulative and there is no way I'm going to let either of my children anywhere near you."

"Danielle—"

"Don't." She knocked away his outstretched hand. "I don't want you to touch me. I don't want you to speak to me." She turned to leave. "And I don't want to ever see you again for the rest of my life."

He called out again, and although his weakened tone tugged familial chords and played on her conscience, Dani kept walking toward the Volvo she'd parked at the curb.

It was the sound of glass shattering that had her turning around to see that he'd dropped the tea. Then, grabbing the edge of the table with one hand, his chest with the other, as she watched in horror, the judge collapsed to the patio, pulling the glass-topped table down on top of him.

What if she'd killed him? As badly as her father had hurt her, as angry as she'd been, Dani knew she'd never be able to forgive herself.

"I knew about his heart," she said to Orèlia, who'd arrived home from grocery shopping during all the excitement. "I knew how easily he could die."

As soon as she'd seen her father collapse, Dani had rushed to him, frantically trying to remember the CPR course she'd taken at a Fairfax fire station while dialing 911 on her cell phone. She'd managed to get an aspirin down his throat and was on her knees, pressing on his chest, struggling to count out the rhythm over the screaming inside her head when the paramedics arrived after what seemed like a lifetime but had only been, she'd learned later, four minutes after her call.

They'd taken over with brisk efficiency, the man setting up a portable monitor and ripping open her father's shirt to place the defibrillator paddles while the woman snapped an oxygen mask on his face and began installing a breathing tube in his throat.

Dani's heart dived and her blood pressure spiked when she viewed her father's heartbeat wiggling all over the monitor like fluorescent green worms.

She knew that if she lived to be a hundred, she'd never forget the sight of his body jerking upward when they zapped the electrical charge into it. The paramedics established an IV, lifted him onto the rolling gurney, and rushed him into the ambulance. Dani had gone with them, while Orèlia promised to follow in her car.

He'd gone into fibrillation again as they'd careened through the streets, siren wailing, tires thudding joltingly against the cobblestones she had, until then, considered charmingly picturesque.

The moment they'd reached the ER, she'd been abruptly shut out of the process; as the double doors slammed closed, cutting her off from her father, Dani was nearly overwhelmed with guilt.

Fortunately, Orèlia, foregoing any concern about speed limits, had arrived right behind the ambulance, taking care of the admission paperwork when Dani had been too numb to answer. After promising Dani she'd be right back, she had taken off to find out what exactly was happening to the judge behind those doors.

"He's not dead, *chère,*" she said now as Dani paced the nearly deserted waiting room outside the ER.

"Not yet, maybe. But I saw his heartbeat on the monitor. It was all over the place. How can anyone survive that?"

"People have, and worse. You're not a doctor, you. So don' go jumpin' to conclusions. And sit down. You're making me nervous with all that walkin' back and forth. Besides, you look like you're gonna pass out any minute."

Dani managed a weak, humorless laugh at that diagnosis. "It appears to be the day for that," she murmured as she nevertheless sank down onto an obnoxiously orange couch. "Were you able to find out anything?"

"They've got the judge stabilized and are movin' him up to surgery."

"Surgery? I thought Dr. Ancelet said he was too weak to be a good surgical candidate."

"I'm sure they wouldn't be operating if they didn't think it was the best thing to do," the older woman assured her.

"Can't I see him, just for a minute? Talk to him?" Dani couldn't bear the thought of her father dying without her having a chance to apologize. He'd caused a great deal of emotional and personal pain, but didn't deserve to die for his actions.

"Darlin', you know I love you to pieces, but right now you'd just be in the way. Your daddy's in good hands. Seems there was a surgeon from Tulane in town to do some fishing tomorrow with the ER doctor. They called him at the Plantation Inn, where he's staying, and he came right over." She patted Dani's hand. "Isn't that lucky?"

"I'm sorry, but I'm having trouble finding anything about this day lucky."

As Dani struggled not to cry, she looked across the room and saw a little boy, running a toy truck back and forth across the green-and-white tile floor. His pregnant mother sat patiently nearby, reading a paperback romance novel. She'd told Dani she was waiting for her husband, who was in the ER getting a fish hook removed from his cheek. The pirate on the cover of the novel reminded Dani of Jack, which only increased her misery, while the sight of the boy and truck made her think of her own son.

"Do you think I should bring Matt home from baseball camp? Just in case?"

"I'd let him stay," Orèlia decided. "The camp's a big deal for the boy, and it'd take at least eight hours to get him down here. He's due home tomorrow. If the judge's gonna die, it'll probably be in the next few hours, so Matt would miss sayin' goodbye anyway even if we could get someone to drive him back to town. If he lives, there'll have been no point in disrupting his life."

"His life has been nothing but disruptions for the past two years."

"*Non*. It may have been shaken up, true enough. But you've provided a lot of stability for the child, Danielle. And it shows." She stroked Dani's hair in a soothing, reassuring way Dani had so often, during childhood, fantasized a mother doing. "Why don't I call Jack? He can come hold your hand."

"Jack wouldn't walk across the street to talk to me, let alone hold my hand."

Orange painted eyebrows flew up nearly to the birdnest hair. "*Comment sa se fait?* Did you two have yourselves a little lover's quarrel?"

"It was a lot more than a quarrel." Dani rubbed her temple with her fingertips. "It seems our daughter showed up at Beau Soleil today. Needless to say, he was surprised."

"He's not the only one." Orèlia's eyes widened and her raspberry red mouth made a little O of shock. "How could that be? Did you tell him he was mistaken?"

"At first. But I wasn't exactly standing on very firm ground having never told him I'd been pregnant in the first place."

"I can see that would be a problem," Orèlia said with a thoughtful nod. "But since the poor little *bébé* died—"

"She didn't." Dani sighed, thinking how strange it was that this should be the happiest day of her life, but was, instead, turning out to be one of her worst. "Father lied."

Orèlia exhaled a slow whistle. "Well. I wish I could say that I couldn't believe such a thing, but I suppose, knowin' the judge, it's not totally out of character. Have you met her? Your daughter? What's her name? Where is she now?"

"She's at Beau Soleil with her father and uncle, I was too shocked to ask her name, and if Jack has his way, I'll probably never meet her."

"*Non.*" Orèlia discarded that idea with a wave of her hand. "He's just angry, he. And hurt. Not to mention his male pride havin' been damaged. But Jack Callahan is a good man, Danielle. He won' try to keep your daughter from you. And it's obvious he loves you, so you'll see, all this will blow over quick enough."

Remembering Jack's face, as he'd walked out of her apartment and her life, Dani couldn't be nearly so optimistic.

She moved upstairs to another waiting room outside the CCU, which is where they told her her father would be taken after surgery and discovered the room was well named. It was as if her life had been put on hold; there was nothing to do but wait and see how this cruel trick that had been played on her was going to end. The magazines were old. Over the many months recipes and coupons had been clipped out of them, which hadn't left all that many articles intact. Not that she could have concentrated anyway.

She tried reading about the problems of the sandwich generation, stories of women tending for ill, aging parents while raising children of their own, but all that did was make her focus even more on how she could well end up discovering a daughter and losing her father all on the same day. Which she suspected, wasn't exactly the thrust of the article.

She jumped up when Eve Ancelet appeared in the door, a tall, distinguished-looking man at her side. They were both wearing green surgical scrubs.

"He's doing fine," Eve assured her.

"If he was fine, he wouldn't be here," Dani snapped. Then immediately apologized.

"Don't worry about it," the doctor brushed her apology off. "This is a stressful time, and heaven knows, hospitals aren't the most calming of places." She introduced the man as Dr. Young, who was, indeed, on the surgical staff at Tulane.

"Your father suffered an incident of arrhythmia," Eve explained. "Which is simply an irregular heartbeat. They're actually quite common and many are harmless, but given the fact that the judge is already suffering from dilated cardiomyopathy, Dr. Young and I both felt that he could benefit from an implantable defibrillator."

"I thought you said he wasn't strong enough for surgery."

"This surgery isn't all that intrusive, as surgeries go," Dr. Young said. "Earlier models were about the size of a pack of cigarettes, were implanted beneath the skin of the abdomen, and required open heart surgery to attach the electrodes to the heart. The latest model, which your father received, is much smaller, can be placed beneath the skin of the chest, and only requires a single electrode that can be routed into the heart through a vein."

"The defibrillator has a tiny computer which uses the electrode to constantly monitor the heartbeat," Eve picked up the explanation. "If it detects even a minor arrhythmia, it activates the built-in pacemaker to restabilize the heart's rhythm. If that fails, it delivers a jolt to the heart."

Dani didn't think she'd ever forget the sight of her father being violently jolted back to life by those EMTs. "Isn't that incredibly painful?"

"Not nearly as much as the muscle-contracting jolt delivered by the more traditional defibrillators you're probably thinking of," Dr. Young said.

"In fact unlike first-generation models, which could only deliver a maximum jolt several times a day, this one starts out small," Eve said. "Then, if necessary, builds, but, as Dr. Young told you, it's nothing like what you saw done to your father. In fact, patients report that the low-level charge, which often does the job, is barely noticable."

It was as if they were a medical tag team. Dani kept looking from one to the other, trying to see if there was anything they might not be telling her.

"Does this mean you expect more incidences?" she asked, thinking what a mild word that was for such a horrific event.

"There's a strong possibility," Eve allowed. "Though this has upped your father's chances for a longer life considerably, Dani. As I told you during our meeting in my office, while medication can reduce the mortality rate of ventricular tachycardia by fifteen to twenty-five percent, the implantable defibrillator cuts it down as low as two percent."

Dani asked more questions, received answers that had her feeling better than she had when she'd arrived, although she was still horribly concerned.

The doctors left. The shift changed. New nurses, their manner brisk and efficient, came on duty. Dinner trays were delivered and picked up again. More doctors arrived on the floor to put on starched white lab coats and make evening rounds. The waiting room began filling up with other patients' family members who'd come for visiting hours.

Orèlia brought Dani cups of tea and coffee and cola from the vending machine she kept forgetting to drink, food from the cafeteria she couldn't eat since it would have been impossible to swallow with a lump that felt as solid as Captain Callahan's statue stuck in her throat.

She heard a Code Blue announced and felt as if her own heart stopped as the team rushed by the waiting room door to the CCU.

"Who is it?" Dani asked the gray-haired woman manning the nurse's desk.

"Don't worry, *chère,*" the nurse assured her with a sympathetic smile. "It's not the judge."

A cooling relief rushed through Dani. A relief that was fleeting as the waiting continued.

Watching the clock, she knew that outside the hospital, night would be beginning to settle over the bayou. Inside the walls it remained constant day, the alien world lit by a complexion-draining fluorescent light. Having grown accustomed to the restful night music of bullfrogs, owls, and crickets, Dani was intensely aware of not just the loud noises, like those disembodied voices that seemed to never stop crackling over the intercom, but the softer sounds, as well. The swoosh of rubber-soled shoes, the tap of fingers on the computer keyboard, the sound of the elevator opening and closing, the click of beads and murmured prayers of a rosary being said in French from somewhere down the hallway, the occasional soft moan drifting on the antiseptic scented air, all conspired to spark at her nerves like fingernails being dragged down a chalkboard.

Gradually the visitors drifted away, leaving Dani alone in the waiting room with Orèlia. The shift changed again. And still she hadn't been allowed to see her father.

A nurse came and told Dani the judge was sleeping. "Why don't you go home and do the same thing yourself?" she suggested gently. "Get some rest so you'll be fresh for your father in the morning."

"I'll be fine," Dani said. "And I'm staying."

The nurse took one look at the determination in her eyes, exchanged a glance with Orèlia, who shrugged, then, with a resigned sigh, returned to charting meds.

Much, much later, feeling guilty that she was subjecting Orèlia, who refused to leave while Dani remained at the hospital, to the same interminable waiting, Dani arranged with the nurse for her to be able to use one of the empty rooms.

"I'll just take a short nap," the older woman promised. "So long as you promise to wake me if anything happens."

Dani promised. And her vigil continued.

She was standing at the window, staring out over the bayou, to where she could just barely make out the distant lights of the ships on the Gulf waterways, twinkling like fallen stars, when she realized she was no longer the only person in the waiting room. Steeling herself for bad news, she slowly turned toward the doorway, her knees nearly buckling when she saw Jack standing there.

26

He looked every bit as beat up as Dani felt. His hair was loose and looked as if he'd been thrusting his hands through it, his face, heavily shadowed by a midnight dark beard, was drawn and his eyes weary. But he was still the most wonderful sight she'd ever seen.

"I just heard," he said. "Actually Nate did. There was a news bulletin on the radio."

"Oh." When she hadn't been worrying about her father, Dani had been going over what she would eventually say to Jack. She'd rejected innumerable lines, but none had been as insufficient as that single word that had just come out of her mouth.

"Have you been alone all this time?"

She glanced around the waiting room as if surprised by the question. Brushed at the heavy wrinkles across the front of her shorts. "No." Determined to manage more than a stumbling monosyllable, she added, "Orèlia's been with me. I made her go take a nap."

He nodded, seeming as uncomfortable with this conversation as she was. "That's good. That she's been here. And that she's resting."

"Yes."

They were standing there across the room from each other. Exhausted and frightened and relieved that he'd come, all at the same time, Dani couldn't decide whether to weep or throw herself into his arms. So she did neither.

"I brought her," he said, breaking the silence that had stretched between them.

"You did?" Feeling as if she were having an incident of arrhythmia herself, Dani looked past him into the hallway.

"She's downstairs with Nate. I wanted a couple minutes to prepare you."

Dani opened her mouth to speak, but her throat was burning and the lump was back, blocking any words. She bit her lip, fought for composure and tried again. "Thank you."

He cursed. A rough, French word that needed no translation and seemed directed inward. Then, shaking his head, he opened his arms. *"Viens ici, mon coeur."*

Dani didn't need a second invitation. She flew into those strong outstretched arms like a sparrow winging toward safety in a hurricane. And when she felt them tighten around her, holding her close, she knew she'd come home.

"I'm so sorry," she said against the front of his shirt.

"I know." She felt his weary sigh ruffle her hair. "Me, too."

"You?" She lifted her eyes to his. "You don't have anything to apologize for."

"I didn't believe you. I was rough with you." He frowned as he took in the bruises on her upper arms.

"No." She touched her palm to his rough cheek. "You not believing me was my own fault for not having been truthful from the start. As for what happened, that was every bit as much my doing as yours." She managed a faint, wry smile. "It was also rather thrilling, while it was happening."

When she felt the deep rumbling chuckle in his chest, Dani knew that it was going to be all right. That they'd be all right.

"I know you have a lot of questions."

"They can wait." He raked a hand through his hair, then touched his palm to her cheek. "I should have been there."

And would have been, she knew now. If only she'd told him. "Of course you're right. I made a terrible decision."

"You were too young to be making any decisions under so much pressure. What I hate is the idea of you having gone through all that alone. I should have been with you when our child was born. I should have taken care of you. All the way back to Beau Soleil, I kept thinking of all the things I could have done to change things. If I'd stayed—"

"You had no choice."

"That's not true. Looking back on that day, I know that even if your father had made good his threat, my *maman* would have survived. She was a strong woman who'd overcome losing her husband. Losing her job wouldn't have been the end of the world.

"I should have stayed," he repeated with more strength. "Because I loved you. And you loved me. We may have been too young for marriage, but we would have made it work. Somehow."

Dani didn't know which surprising statement to take first. "You loved me?"

"*Mais*, yeah. Oh, I'd fought like hell against it. But that last night I realized that what we had going for us was a lot more than just sex."

"The night we made our daughter."

"Yeah." He took another deep breath, then frowned at his watch. "We need to talk. Make plans. But I figure we've got about two minutes before Nate and Holly get up here—"

"Her name's Holly?"

"Yeah." His smile lit his tawny eyes and warmed her heart. "You're gonna love her, *chère*." He brushed his lips against her temple. "And she's going to love you." Skimmed them down her cheek. "Just like I do."

They were the words she'd waited thirteen years to hear. And they were even more glorious than in her most romantic fantasies. Dani was about to tell him that she loved him, too, had always loved him, when his roving lips met hers and she was lost.

She sank into the kiss, twining her arms around his neck, going up onto her toes to kiss him back. He pulled her hard against him and held her as if he'd never let her go. As if she had any intention of going anywhere, Dani thought as her mouth clung and her heart soared.

"Hold that thought," he said, putting his hands on her shoulders as he broke off the kiss. And not a moment too soon, as Dani heard Nate clear his throat.

She braced herself as Jack ran his hands down her arms, soothing her inward tremors. Then he shifted to stand beside her and she was looking into a young face that was familiar and foreign at the same time. As she stared at this beautiful blond child poised on the brink of womanhood, a tangled blend of joy and panic clogged her throat. The years spun away and she was holding her little girl in her arms, pressing her lips against the downy fuzz atop the infant's head.

Then the doctor had snapped at the nurse who had, without thinking, broken the maternity home rules by allowing the unwed mother even that brief, fleeting moment to bond with the baby she'd carried beneath her heart for nine long months. Dani had wept after they'd snatched her daughter away and rushed her from the cold sterility of the delivery room.

She'd held firm when the grim-faced lawyers ganged up with the woman who ran the home, using every argument against her keeping her baby, even going so far as to call the judge to try to reason with her.

Then she'd screamed when, after sneaking down the hallway to the nursery before dawn the next morning, she'd been told that her baby hadn't survived the night. Refusing to believe it, she'd hysterically demanded to see her child. This child, she realized now with wonder.

They'd called a doctor, who, while two burly orderlies had held her down, injected her with something to calm her down. When she finally emerged from her drugged stupor two days later, her father had been waiting with her daughter's death certificate.

After leaving the hospital, her breasts aching from the pills they'd given her to dry up her milk, Dani would have the same dream every night. A dream that it had all been a horrible mistake, that Jack had returned home from wherever he'd gone, had been thrilled to discover he was a father, had proposed right on the spot and the three of them had all left the hospital together, their daughter dressed in a ruffled pink dress, little white socks on her pudgy feet and one of those stretchy baby headbands, to begin a new life together.

The dream had become more infrequent over the years, especially after Matt had been born, but it always returned on the anniversary of her first child's birth.

Now, wonder of wonders, it was turning out not to be a dream after all, and Dani couldn't say a word.

"Holly," Jack said, jumping into the breach to rescue her, "this is your mother. Danielle, meet Holly."

"Hi," Holly said. Beneath a poise beyond her years, Dani sensed nerves as tangled as her own.

"Oh, baby." Dani felt her eyes mist. "I want to hold you."

Holly's blue-green eyes, which were like looking into a mirror, were moist and shiny as well. "I think I'd like that," she admitted on a voice that was more child than woman.

Dani was across the room without having been aware of moving and gathered her daughter close, holding her to her breast as she'd dreamed of doing so many times.

When she'd finally accepted that what Jack had told her was true, Dani had been terrified that her child would, at worst, hate her. At best, resent her for having abandoned her. But as she felt the slender arms wrap around her waist, she allowed herself a glimmer of hope.

"Where have you been all these years? How did you know to come here to Blue Bayou? To Beau Soleil? Did you come with your"—she could not yet say the word *parents* in regard to anyone but she and Jack—"the people who adopted you?"

Holly opted to answer the last of Dani's breathless, rapid fire questions first. "My parents died when I was nearly ten. They were sailing off Depoe Bay—that's in Oregon—when their boat capsized."

Dani rubbed circles against Holly's slender back. "That must have been terrible."

"It was. I was sent to live with my uncle in Oceanside, he was in the Marines, but I'd never met him because I guess he and my dad, my adoptive dad," she corrected with a quick look Jack's way, "didn't get along real well."

"He was your dad in all the ways that counted," Jack said. "No one's going to try to take that away from you, *chère*."

Relief flittered across her face.

"Does your uncle know where you are?" Dani knew she'd be frantic if Matt just took off and left home.

"No. But he wouldn't really care."

"Of course he would," Dani said, feeling the need to stick up for this man she'd never met, if only to reassure her daughter that she was loved.

"I really don't think so, since I haven't seen him for the past couple years."

Dani exchanged a startled look with Jack, who nodded. "They got a divorce," he revealed, helping Holly out a bit with catching Dani up to date. "Apparently his wife had kids from a previous marriage and didn't feel any responsibility to her brother-in-law's child. And it was tough for him, since he's in the military and has to move around a lot."

Dani was certain there must be some sort of family hardship circumstances that would have gotten him out of the Marines, but didn't remark on this possibility since she didn't want to hurt her daughter any more than she'd already been hurt.

"So where have you been since then?" she asked, dreading the answer.

"In foster care," Holly said in a matter-of-fact way that broke Dani's heart. "Uncle Phil signed away custodial rights, so I could have been adopted out, but people don't want older kids, so that wasn't much of an option."

Dear Lord. How was she ever going to make this up to her? Dani wondered miserably.

"I told her that there're lots of people who'd love to adopt a *jolie fille* like herself," Jack revealed. "Not that she has to worry 'bout that, now that she's got us."

"Absolutely," Dani agreed, trying to read Holly's face to see what she thought about this. She desperately wanted to assure her that she had a family, a family who loved her, but still wasn't certain of how much resentment the girl might be harboring. How could she not, after all she'd been through? Dani's stomach fluttered.

"Why don't you pretty ladies sit down and have yourself a nice get-acquainted talk," Jack suggested. "While Nate and I go get you some pop from the vending machines."

Holly ordered a Diet Pepsi, as did Dani, who didn't really want anything but understood that Jack and Nate were leaving them alone to talk without an audience. She was grateful for their sensitivity until the heavy silence descended as soon as they'd left the room.

"This is harder than in my dreams," Dani murmured.

"Mine, too," Holly agreed.

Dani looked at her, surprised. "You dreamed about me? About us?"

"All the time. Sometimes I thought you were a famous opera star who traveled the world and couldn't take care of a baby. I used to watch PBS all the time, wondering if one of those ladies singing at the Lincoln Center might be my mom." She smiled a little shyly. "I know it's not cool for a kid my age, but I like opera."

"So does your grandfather Dupree. He always used to play it in his chambers. Sometimes loud enough that he could hear the music from the bench, but low enough that no one else in the courtroom other than his bailiff could."

"What's his favorite opera? Composer?"

Dani lifted her hands in a helpless gesture. "I'm afraid I don't know."

"Is he going to die tonight?"

"I hope not. The doctors seemed optimistic." She sighed at the thought of what her father had done. How many years he'd cost them all. "Let's sit down, shall we?" She took her daughter by the hand, led her over to the couch, which, rather than the obnoxious orange of the ER waiting room, was the color of a ripe lime.

They turned toward each other, knee to knee, face to face. "I'm assuming, from what you said about my father, that Jack explained some of the circumstances surrounding your birth."

Holly nodded. "Yeah, he pretty much told me all the facts. About you doing what the adults had convinced you was for the best, then you changing your mind about keeping me, and your father fixing it so you'd think I'd died."

"That's pretty much it." How strange it seemed to have the most traumatic time of her life condensed into a single concise statement.

"But what he couldn't tell me about how you were feeling, because he didn't know, you did."

"Me?"

"In your letter."

The letter! It had been the first one, and she'd spent days agonizing over what to say, finally writing the final draft the night before her daughter was born, sharing with her unborn baby the truth—that she'd been conceived in love and would always live in her mother's heart. She'd tried to explain, as best she could, why she was giving up custodial rights and how she hoped that her child would someday understand that her actions had also been born in love. Of course she'd changed her mind the next day. But it hadn't mattered, because she'd lost her child anyway.

"That's how I found you," Holly explained. "You wrote about growing up in Beau Soleil, and about how some day you'd love to introduce me to another part of my heritage, so you were going to register with that place that links up children with their adoptive parents, if they both want, when they're eighteen. You said you wouldn't try to find me, in case I didn't want my life disrupted, but that you'd always be there for me."

"That's true." Dani bit her lip to keep from bursting into tears. "I gave the letter to the social worker to give to your adoptive parents, but when I could start thinking straight again, I assumed it had been thrown away." As impossible as it seemed, Dani wondered if a part of her had continued to know, in some secret part of her heart, that her daughter was still alive. Perhaps that's why she'd felt moved to write those letters every year. Letters she couldn't wait to share with her newly found daughter.

"Well, I guess it wasn't thrown away, because I found it when I was about eight and was snooping around in a box in my parents' bedroom closet. I'd always known I was adopted, so it wasn't like it was any big surprise and I don't know why I stole it, but later I was glad I did, since it gave me something to hold on to the past two years in the foster homes. I couldn't wait to turn eighteen and could register to be matched up with you."

Dani silently blessed the social worker who, for reasons only she would ever know, had secretly gone against the judge's orders and passed on that fateful letter. "But you're not eighteen."

"I know. But once I saw the picture of Beau Soleil on the front of that newspaper, I knew where to find you, so I decided not to wait any longer."

"You ran away?"

"Yeah." Holly shrugged slender shoulders clad in a hot-pink top that looked as if it'd been created from shrink wrap. "A few days ago."

"Where were you living?"

"In San Diego County."

"That's so far away. How did you get all the way to Louisiana?"

"I hitched to Yuma, Arizona, because I was afraid to buy a bus ticket in case the police were looking for me. Then I took the bus from Yuma to here."

Even though she'd obviously survived the experience, Dani's blood turned to ice at the idea of her beautiful, young, vulnerable daughter hitchhiking. "That was horribly dangerous," she scolded in the tone she had seldom used with Matt. "I don't want you ever hitchhiking again."

Holly surprised her by laughing at that. She brushed her sleek slide of hair behind her shoulder. "Yes, Mother. . . . I still have the Pooh bear," she volunteered. "He's been restuffed twice. Mom said it was my favorite baby toy."

More memories flooded back. Dani had bought the bear at a toy store during one of her rare Saturday afternoons away from the home.

"That's so nice to hear," she managed to say on a voice clogged with emotion.

Surely it couldn't be this easy?

"I want you to know," Dani said, "that I'll understand if you resented me. Even if you still do."

"No. You did the right thing," Holly said, the bright laughter fading from her eyes as she turned serious. "Mom and Dad were wonderful and I loved them and they loved me. I'm not sure I ever would have contacted you if they hadn't died."

Dani ignored the little twinge of hurt and concentrated instead on the fact that her daughter had known at least ten years of happiness. "I understand," she said mildly.

"But I've been dreaming of this ever since they died, and I had to go live with Uncle Phil and Aunt Sara." Tears sparkled in her thick gold lashes. "But this is even better than I dreamed because I never, ever thought I'd find both my father and mother at the same time."

"It's been a strange set of circumstances," Dani murmured, thinking how all the turmoil in her life these past years had brought her back to Blue Bayou so she could find Jack again and the daughter they'd created that long-ago summer could find them.

"Yeah. Jack told me about the piano."

From the choked sound in Holly's voice, it was obvious she was trying not to laugh. But because the Steinway had been one of the stranger strings fate had pulled, Dani couldn't keep her own lips from quirking at the absurdity. "It sounds as if you and Jack had quite a conversation."

"We've been talking since I showed up. Well, except for when he came into town to tell you."

Studying her carefully, Dani was relieved not to see a hint of concern in the girl's expression. Obviously Jack had kept their personal troubles to himself.

Holly sighed. "He's so wonderful."

"You won't get any argument from me about that," Dani agreed.

"I asked him if he loved you. And he said he always had."

"That's handy, since I love him, too."

"Are you going to get married?"

Dani knew that it was more than just idle curiosity that had Holly asking the question. "He hasn't asked me yet."

"He will," Holly asserted with a childish conviction. "And if he doesn't ask you, you'll just have to propose to him."

"How old are you, anyway?" Dani asked with a faint smile, knowing the answer all too well. "Twelve going on thirty?"

"Everyone has always said I'm very mature for my age."

She would have had to have been, Dani thought sadly, to have experienced the loss of her parents, the breakup of another home, and the subsequent years in the revolving door of the foster-care system.

A nurse appeared in the doorway, accompanied by Nate and Jack, who'd returned with the cans of soda. "The judge is awake and asking for you, Ms. Dupree. Dr. Ancelet says you can visit for five minutes."

"I won't be long," she promised. She gave Holly another hug and experienced wonder that it felt so right. So natural.

"I'll be here."

Dani touched her fingertips to her daughter's smooth cheek. "I think those are the most beautiful words I've ever heard."

27

Dani's heart, which had been floating on air, took a crash dive when she walked into the CCU and saw her father looking swallowed up by the narrow hospital bed. His complexion was the color of library paste, his hands, lying limp on the sheets on either side of him, were spotted and blue-veined, and lank strands of white hair revealed a great deal of his scalp.

He'd always seemed so bold, so strong, so larger than life. Even after she learned of his heart disease, the force of his personality had kept her from realizing exactly how old he was. Oh, she knew that he'd married her mother late in his life, knew that he was now nearly seventy-eight, which didn't necessarily have to be all that ancient in these days of medical miracles such as the one humming away in his chest. Unfortunately, he looked every one of those years, and more.

She pulled a lime green vinyl chair that matched the waiting room couch up to the bed, sat down, and took one of those aged hands in both of hers.

He opened his eyes, which, amazingly, considering how the rest of him looked, were still filled with life.

"Hi, Daddy." She squeezed his fingers, which felt like chicken bones beneath her touch. "You gave us all quite a scare."

"They said you gave me CPR." His voice was raspy, but, like his eyes, not as frail as his body. "Probably saved my life."

"I think that's an exaggeration."

"Maybe it is, maybe it isn't." His eyes narrowed as he gave her one of those probing looks that had always brought witnesses and opposing counsels into line. For a long moment the only sound in the room was the beeps of the monitor and the faint hiss of the oxygen being fed into his system by a nasal tube.

"Why didn't you just let me die?"

"Don't be ridiculous. You're my father."

"Not exactly an exemplary one," he muttered.

She shrugged, refusing to hold a grudge on this day of miracles. "It's not easy being a parent. We all make mistakes."

"Have you met her?" he asked. "Your daughter?"

"Yes. And she's wonderful. Her name is Holly and she's sweet, beautiful, resourceful." Dani frowned a little when she thought about the hitchhiking. "I can't wait for you to meet her."

"Does she know what I did?"

She couldn't lie. "Yes. But she didn't seem as bitter as I might have expected. And I'm sure we can get past that, Daddy. If you want to. And we all try.

"We're going to be a family, Jack and Matt and Holly and me, and we'd like you to be part of it." Dani was not going to let the fact that Jack hadn't yet asked her to marry him get in the way of beginning the life that had been stolen from them. "I'm getting married at Beau Soleil." She figured if they all worked at it together, they could get the garden ready in no time. "And I want you to be there."

"Then you'd better not waste any time," he said. "Since I could keel over again any day."

"No, you won't, because while I've been going crazy worrying about you all day, you've been getting a brand-new shiny computer put in your chest. You're the judicial model of the six-million-dollar man and I'm not about to let you die for years and years."

"Anyone ever tell you that you can be damn bossy from time to time?" he asked without heat.

"I guess I take after my father. So you may as well get used to it." Her expression sobered. "I'm still not happy about what you did, but I love you and if there's anything the past two years has taught me, it's that life is too precious to waste."

She leaned forward, kissed his dry papery cheek, then stood up when the nurse appeared beside the bed, signaling that her time was up.

Dani squeezed her father's hand again, reassured when he squeezed back. She was almost to the door when she heard him rasp out her name.

She turned. "Yes, Daddy?"

"I'm damn proud of the woman you've become, Danielle. Your children are lucky to have you. Jack's lucky. And so am I."

Her answering smile was slow and warm and filled with all the joy she was feeling. "I know, Daddy."

Jack was alone when Dani returned to the waiting room.

"Where is everyone?" she asked.

"Nate took Holly down to the cafeteria for a midnight breakfast. I swear, for such a little thing, she's got an appetite that puts Turnip to shame."

"Lucky for Holly that her dad's a great cook."

"I'd say we're all pretty lucky. So, how's the judge doing?"

"He's certainly looked better, but I talked to the charge nurse after I left the room and she says his prognosis is very good."

"That's more good news."

She nodded. "Yes. It is. . . . He told me he was lucky to have me."

" 'Bout time." Jack stepped forward. Stopped. Never in all his years of undercover work had he been this nervous. "Remember me tellin' you how I thought about you while I was in Colombia?" he began, wondering why it was that words that could come so tripplingly off the tongues of his characters, seemed to be lodged in his throat. *Maybe you do need a ghostwriter, Callahan,* he thought with grim humor.

"Of course. It was when you were in the mountains with your partner."

"Yeah. Then, and a helluva lot of other nights as well. And I haven't stopped thinking about you—and us—since you've come back to Blue Bayou. And you know what I've decided?"

"What?" She seemed to be holding her breath. Hell, she wasn't the only one.

"Your marriage didn't really break up because your husband slept with his chief of staff and was, to the core, pretty much of a louse. I think you would have gotten divorced whoever you married."

"Well, that's certainly flattering." The soft smile took any complaint from her words.

"It's the truth. And it would've been the same way for me, if I'd ever gotten married. Neither one of us could have been happy with anyone else, because deep down inside, we would have been wanting each other."

"I can't argue with that, since the same thought has occurred to me."

"Good, because I'm willin' to wait till the judge is out of here to make an official announcement, but I want to marry you, Danielle. I want us to make ourselves a family with Matt and Holly, and maybe another baby or two, if you think that'd be a good idea, and have all our children grow up at Beau Soleil where their pretty *maman* did.

"I want to go to sleep every night with you beside me and wake up every day the same way. I make enough money to support us in pretty good style, but if you want to keep your job at the library, that'd be great, too."

"I would, absolutely, but—"

"Terrific," he said, cutting her off. Now that he'd begun, he wanted to state his case before she had a chance to think of any objections. "Fortunately, thanks to Hollywood, you'd have a rich husband who can afford all the nannies we'd ever need. Did I mention the movie folks have bought book number five?"

"I didn't think you'd finished with the fourth."

"I haven't." He raked his fingers through his hair, took another deep breath, and crossed the small space between them to stand in front of her. "But only because my hero is waitin' for the drug dealer's daughter to admit she loves him. How 'bout it, *chère?* Does she? Or doesn't she?"

"She does." Dani lifted her hand to his face. "With her entire heart."

Jack drew her into his arms with a deep sigh of relief. "Then you'll marry me? As soon as possible?"

A dazzling smile bloomed on Dani's face; her eyes were wet and brilliant, but Jack knew that this time her tears were born of happiness. "I was beginning to think you'd never ask."

POCKET BOOKS
PROUDLY PRESENTS

The second book in

The Callahan Brothers Trilogy

RIVER ROAD

JOANN ROSS

Turn the page for a preview of
River Road. . . .

Washington, D.C.

Finn Callahan hated bad guys, criminal lawyers, bureaucrats and cockroaches. At least the bad guys had provided him with a livelihood as an FBI Special Agent for the past thirteen years. Why the good Lord had created the other three remained one of those universal mysteries, like how the ancient Egyptians built the pyramids or why it always rained right after you washed your truck.

"It's not like I killed the guy," he muttered. The way Finn saw it, a broken nose, some bruises and a few broken ribs didn't begin to equal the crimes that scumbag serial killer had committed.

"Only because two agents, a Maryland state trooper and a court-appointed shrink managed to pull you off him before you could," the woman behind the wide desk said. There was enough ice in her tone to coat Jupiter. Her black suit was unadorned; her champagne blond hair, cut nearly as short as his, barely reached the collar, and her jaw thrust toward him like a spear. Put her in dress blues and she could have appeared on a U.S. Marine recruiting poster.

"I've spent the past hour on the phone with Lawson's lead attorney. Unsurprisingly, he wants to file assault and battery charges. And that's just for starters. I'm attempting to convince him to allow us to handle the matter internally."

Unpolished fingernails, trimmed short as a nun's, tapped an irritated tattoo on the gleaming desktop.

Finn had no problem with women in the Bureau; he'd worked with several and would have trusted his life to them any day. Hell, even James Bond had gotten a woman boss when Judi Dench took over as M. Finn didn't even have any problem with ice queens like Special Agent in Charge Lillian Jansen.

He did, however, have a Herculean problem with any SAC who wasn't a stand-up guy. From the day she'd arrived from the New York field office, Jansen had proven herself to be far more interested in the politics of the job than in locking up criminals.

"It's a helluva thing when an SAC takes the side of a sicko killer over one of her own men," he muttered.

"Christ, Callahan," the other man in the office warned. James Burke's ruddy cheeks were the hue of ripe cherries, suggesting that Finn's recent behavior hadn't been good for his blood pressure problem. A faint white ring around his mouth was evidence he'd been chugging Maalox directly from the bottle again.

"You're out of line, Special Agent," Jansen snapped. "Again."

Leaning back in the leather swivel chair, she dropped the sword that had been hanging over his head for the past forty-eight hours—ever since the killer it had taken Finn nearly three years to track through eight states had made the mistake of trying to escape from the hospital, just as Finn dropped by to see how the court-appointed psychiatric evaluation was going.

"I will, of course, have no choice but to turn this incident over to OPR."

The Office of Professional Responsibility was the equivalent of a police force's internal affairs bureau. Since many of its investigators possessed a guilty-until-proven-innocent attitude, a lot of agents tended to distrust the OPR right back.

The idea of being thrown to the wolves made Finn's gut churn, but unwilling to allow Jansen to know she'd gotten beneath his skin, he forced his shoulders to relax, schooled his expression to a mask, and although it wasn't easy, kept his mouth shut.

"You're scheduled to be questioned tomorrow afternoon at three o'clock. You are, of course, entitled to be represented by legal counsel."

"Now there's an idea. Maybe I can get one of those worms making up Lawson's legal dream team to represent me. Of course, the only problem with that idea is since Lawson's a gazillionaire sicko with bucks out the kazoo, I doubt any of those scumbags would want to take on the case of a middle income cop who got pissed off at their client for raping and killing coeds."

Ronald Lawson had murdered eight college women scattered across the country from California to Maryland. Finn's recurring nightmare was that there were still more missing women he hadn't yet discovered who could be linked to the guy.

"We would have had eleven victims if Callahan hadn't gotten to Lawson's house when he did and found those girls locked up in his basement." A chain-smoker, Burke's voice was as rough as a bad gravel road.

"That's part of my problem." Frustration sharpened the SAC's brisk voice. "The Georgetown girl's parents are close personal friends of the Attorney General. In fact, the AG and his wife are her godparents. They heard about Lawson's attempted escape on the nightly news and are pressuring the AG to allow Callahan's outrageous cowboy tactics to slide."

Finn shot a sideways look at Burke, whose expression told him they were thinking the same thing. That perhaps he just should have put his gun barrel into the guy's mouth and pulled the trigger in those midnight hours when they'd descended on Lawson's Pontiac mansion. Every cop in the place would have sworn on a stack of bibles that deadly force had been absolutely justified.

He'd always been a by-the-book kind of guy, the type of FBI agent Efrem Zimbalist, Jr. had played on TV, but sometimes the laws protecting the bad guys really sucked.

"How about we come up with a compromise?" Burke suggested.

"What type of compromise do you have in mind?" Jansen asked.

"Callahan takes a leave of absence until this blows over. Say, two weeks."

"That's not enough time for damage control. Four weeks suspension," she countered. "Without pay."

Finn had been staring up at the ceiling, pretending disinterest in the negotiation. When he realized Burke wasn't countering Jansen's proposal, he shot the SAC a savage look.

"Fuck that." He rubbed knuckles which had been bruised when they'd connected so satisfyingly with Lawson's jaw. *You are not*, he instructed his itchy fist, *going to screw this up worse by punching a hole through that damn trophy wall.* A wall covered with photographs of SAC Lillian Jansen with seemingly every politician in town. "I'll take my chances with OPR."

"Dammit, Finn, it's not that bad an offer." Burke plowed a hand through thinning hair the color of a rusty Brillo pad. "You haven't taken a real vacation in years. Go home, do some fishing, unwind, and when you come back all this shit will have blown over."

They both knew it'd probably take another Hurricane Andrew to blow this particular shit pile away.

"If I were you, I'd take your squad supervisor's advice." Jansen folded her arms across the front of a jacket as black as her heart.

Finn suspected that not only was she enjoying this, she was just waiting for him to squirm. *Not in this lifetime,* his expression said.

Want to bet? hers said right back. "If this goes any further, my recommendation will be to terminate you."

And she'd do it if it'd help her career. Hell, she'd probably run over her own dog if it'd get her a promotion to ADIC. Of course she didn't actually have a dog; that would take some kind of personal commitment—and from what he'd seen, the woman was only committed to her swift climb up the Bureau's political ladder.

"Two weeks." *Forget Hurricane Andrew.* Finn needed a tornado to come sweeping out of Kansas, swoop down over K Street, and drop a damn house on Lillian Jansen.

"Four." Her lips actually quirked a bit at the corners, hinting at the closest thing to a smile he'd witnessed since her heralded arrival from New York. She held out her hand, palm up. "And I'll take your weapon and shield."

Feeling Burke's gaze on him, the silent plea to make nice radiating off his squad commander like a physical presence, Finn swallowed the frustration that rose like bile in his mouth, took his .40mm Glock from his shoulder holster and resisted, just barely, the urge to throw it onto her desk.

When he failed to manage the same restraint with his shield, all three pairs of eyes watched the leather case slide off the highly polished surface onto the carpet. Finn hoped Jansen would ask him to pick it up, so he could suggest where she could plant those thin, pale lips.

"Do you know the trouble with you, Callahan?"

"No. But I have a feeling you're going to tell me."

"You've begun to believe your own press. There are those in the Bureau, including your former SAC, who may be impressed by your appearances on *Nightline* and your dinners at the White House. But as far as I'm concerned, you have a very bad attitude toward authority. You also take your work personally."

"And your point is?"

She glared at him with nearly as much contempt as he felt for her, then pressed a button on her intercom. "Please send in security to escort Special Agent Callahan out of the building."

"I'll do that," Burke offered quickly. It was obvious he wanted to get Finn out of the office before things got worse.

"It's not your job," Jansen said.

"A superior stands by his men." His tone clearly implied the SAC did not. If Jansen's eyes were frost, Burke's were flame.

Finn was willing to take the heat himself, but didn't want to cause a longtime friend any more problems. Especially since he knew Burke had put a second mortgage on his Arlington house to pay for his three kids' college tuition and couldn't afford a disciplinary suspension.

"Jim, it's okay."

"The hell it is," the older man shot back. "This whole mess stinks to high heaven." He pinned the SAC with a hard look.

Clearly unwounded, she merely shrugged in return. "You have ten minutes," she told Finn.

Finn turned on his heel with military precision, and had just opened the office door when she called his name. Glancing back over his shoulder, he imagined a black widow spider sitting in the center of her web.

"If I were you Callahan, I'd spend the next month sending out resumes. Because if and when you return, you'll be transferred to another field office, where—if I have anything to say about it, and believe me, I do—you'll be reassigned to desk duty."

Oh, she was good. Coldly efficient, deadly accurate, hitting right on target. She knew he'd rather be gut shot than spend the rest of his career stuck in some dreary outpost, shuffling papers. Finn would bet his last grade increase that, instead of playing Barbie dolls and having pretend tea parties like other little girls, SAC Jansen had spent her childhood drowning kittens.

He heard Burke clear his throat, another less-than-subtle warning. But Finn refused to justify her threat with a response.

Since his work had always been his life, he didn't have any hobbies, nor had he bothered to accumulate any superfluous stuff that might clutter up either his desk or his life. He cleaned a few personal effects from his desk and was out of the building in just under eight minutes.

And the final book in

The Callahan Brothers Trilogy

MAGNOLIA MOON

JoANN ROSS

Available in paperback from Pocket Books

Turn the page for a preview of
Magnolia Moon. . . .

New Orleans, Louisiana

"I've always adored a Libra man," the blond purred.

"Have you now?" Nate Callahan grinned and drew her closer. There were few things in life more enjoyable than making love to a beautiful woman.

"Oh, absolutely." Cuddling up against him, she fluttered her lashes in a way only a true southern belle could pull off. "Why, a Libra man can charm the birds out of the trees and flatter a girl right out of her lace panties."

"It wasn't flattery, *chère*." He refilled her crystal champagne flute. "It was the absolute truth."

Nate had always enjoyed females—he liked the way they moved, the way they smelled, their soft skin and slender ladies' hands. From the first time he'd filched one of his older brother Finn's *Playboy* magazines, he'd flat-out liked everything about women. Fortunately, they'd always liked him right back.

He toyed with a blond curl trailing down her neck. It was a little stiff and hadn't deflated much during their session of hot, steamy sex, but Nate was used to that, since most of the women he dated favored big hair. Big hair, big breasts, and, he thought with a pleasant twinge of lust, big appetites for sex.

"Your moon is in the seventh house." She trailed a glossy coral nail down his chest.

"Is that good?" He skimmed his palm down her back; she arched against the caress like a sleek, pampered cat.

Outside her bedroom, a full moon rose in a star-studded sky; inside, flames crackled cozily in the fireplace and gardenia-scented candles glowed.

"It certainly is. You're ruled by Venus, goddess of beauty."

"Seems that'd fit you better than me, sugar." He nuzzled the smooth curve of her shoulder. His accent, always more pronounced when romancing a woman, turned thick as Cajun gumbo. "Bein' how you've gotten more beautiful every year since you won that Miss Louisiana crown."

"I was only first runner-up." She pouted prettily.

"Officially," he allowed. "But everyone in the state knew the judges were obviously blind as swamp bats."

"You are so sweet." Her laugh was rich and pleased.

Nate's mind began to drift as she chattered on about the stars, which, if he were to be perfectly honest, didn't interest him. He'd never thought much about lunar signs until the afternoon he'd shown up to give the blond astrologer a bid on remodeling her bedroom.

Although he'd arrived ten minutes late at her Garden District house, he'd gotten her out of the shower; she'd shown up at the door, breathlessly apologetic for not being ready, prettily flushed, and smelling of jasmine. It was only later, when he'd remembered that her hair hadn't been wet, that Nate realized he'd been set up. Having always appreciated female wiles, he didn't mind.

She'd hung on to his every word as he'd suggested ways to open up the room—including putting a skylight over the bed—declared him brilliant, and hired him on the spot.

"You are," she'd sworn on a drawl as sweet as the sugarcane his granddaddy used to grow, "the first contractor I've interviewed who understands that a bedroom is more than just a place to sleep." She'd coyly looked up at him from beneath her lashes. "It is, after all, the most important room in the house."

When she'd touched a scarlet fingernail to the back of Nate's hand, warm and pleasant desire had ribboned through him.

"You've been so sweet. Would you do me just one teensy little favor?"

"Sure, *chère*. If I can."

Avid green eyes had swept over him in a slow, feminine perusal. "Oh, I think you're just the man for the job."

She'd untied the silk robe, revealing perfumed and powdered flesh. "I do so need to exorcise my horrid ex-husband's memory from this room." The robe dropped to the plush carpeting.

That had been six months ago. Not only had Nate done his best to exorcise her former husband's memory, he'd done a damn fine job on the remodeling, if he did say so himself. Lying on his back amid sex-tangled sheets, Nate looked up at the ghost galleon moon, decided he'd definitely been right about the skylight, and wondered why he'd never thought to put one over his own bed.

"Of course, Venus is also the goddess of love." The *L* word, slipping smoothly from her coral-tinted lips, yanked his wandering mind back to their conversation.

"She is?" he asked with a bit more caution.

"Absolutely. Make love, not war, is a phrase that could have been coined with Libras in mind. You became interested in women at a young age, you make sex a rewarding experience, and will not stop until your lover is satisfied, even if it takes all night."

"I try," he said modestly. She'd certainly seemed well satisfied when she'd been bucking beneath him earlier.

She smiled and touched her lips to his. "Oh, you not only succeed, darling, you set the standard. Libras also rule the house of partnerships."

"Now there's where your stars might be a little off, sugar." He stroked her smooth silk back, cupped her butt, and pulled her closer. " 'Cause I've always enjoyed working alone."

It wasn't that he was antisocial, far from it. But he liked being his own boss, working when he liked, and playing when he wanted.

"You weren't alone a few minutes ago, and you seemed to be enjoying yourself well enough."

"I always enjoy passin' a good time with you, angel."

"If you didn't play well with others, you wouldn't have run for mayor." She rolled over and straddled him. "Libras are not lone wolves, darling. A Libra male needs a permanent partner."

Nate's breath clogged in his lungs. "Permanent?"

Having grown up in South Louisiana, where water and land were constantly battling, with water winning most of the time, he knew that very few things were permanent. Especially relationships between men and women.

"We've been together six months," she pointed out, which exceeded any previous relationship Nate had ever had. Then again, it helped that she'd spent most of that time away, selling her astrology books at New Age festivals and talking them up on television talk shows around the country.

Doing some rapid calculation, Nate figured they'd probably been together a total of three weeks, and had spent most of that time in bed.

"I've been thinking," she murmured when he didn't respond. Her clever fingers slipped between them, encircling him. "About us."

"Us?"

"It occurred to me yesterday, when my flight was cruising at thirty thousand feet over New Mexico, that we should get married."

Married? Having not seen this coming—she'd certainly never shown one iota of domesticity—Nate didn't immediately answer.

"You don't want to." Danger sparked in her voice, like heat lightning flashing out over the Gulf. She pulled away.

Sighing, Nate hitched himself up beside her and saw any future plans for the night disappearing.

"It's nothing to do with you, *chère*." His cajoling smile encouraged one in return. "But we agreed goin' in that neither of us was the marrying kind."

"That was then." She left the bed and retrieved his shirt from where it had landed earlier. "Things change." The perfumed air swirled with temper. "The moon is also a mother sign."

"It is?" Nate caught the denim shirt she threw at him. Christ, he needed air.

"Yes." Her chin angled up. Her eyes narrowed to green slits. "Which is why Libras often repeat the same childlike behavior over and over again in their relationships."

It was a long way from charming to childish. Boyish, Nate might be willing to accept—in the right context. But he hadn't been a child since that life-altering day when he was twelve and a liquored-up, swamp-dwelling, gun-carrying idiot had blown away his father.

"If I didn't know better, I might take offense at that, darlin'." He bent to pick up his jeans from the loblolly pine floor; one of his boots came sailing toward him. "*Mon Dieu,* Charlene." He ducked the first one and snagged the second out of the air an instant before it connected with his head.

"Do you have any idea how many proposals I get every month?" She marched back across the bedroom and jabbed her finger against his bare chest.

"I'll bet a bunch." Nate reminded himself that he'd never run into a situation he couldn't smooth over.

"You damn well bet a lot!" His chest now bore little crescent gouges from her fingernail. "I've turned down two in the past six weeks—from men who make a hell of a lot more money than you—because I was fool enough to think we had a future."

"You're a wonderful woman, *chèrie*," he tried again, hopping on first one foot, then the other, as he pulled his pants up. "Smart, beautiful—"

"And getting goddamn older by the moment," she shouted.

"You don't look a day over twenty-five." Thanks to a Houston surgeon whose clever touch with a scalpel had carved a good ten years off her face and body.

When she began coming toward him again, Nate backed away and yanked on his shirt. Not pausing to button it, he scooped his keys and wallet from the bedside table and shoved them into his pocket. "Twenty-six, tops." He debated sitting down again to pull on his boots, then decided not to risk it.

"It's not going to work this time, Callahan."

A champagne glass hit the wall, then shattered. She tossed her stiff cloud of honey blond hair. "If I'd taken the time to do your full chart before hiring you, I never would have let you seduce me."

Deciding that discretion was the better part of valor, Nate wisely didn't point out that she'd been the one who'd dropped the damn robe.

"I would have realized that you're suffering from a gigantic Peter Pan complex."

Peter Pan? Nate gritted his teeth. "I'll call you, *chère*," he promised as he dodged the second flute. PMS, he decided. "Later in the month. When you're feeling a little more like yourself."

A banshee could not have screamed louder. Nate escaped the suffocating room, taking the back stairs two at a time. Something thudded against the bedroom wall; he hoped to hell she hadn't damaged the new plaster job.

Feeling blindsided, Nate drove toward his home on the peaceful bank of Blue Bayou, trying to figure out where, exactly, an evening that had begun so promising had gone offtrack.

"Peter Pan," he muttered.

Where the hell had she come up with that one?

The full moon was brighter than he'd ever seen it, surrealistically silhouetting the knobby bayou cypresses in eerie white light. Having just survived Hurricane Charlene, Nate hoped it wasn't some weird portent of yet another storm to come.